"I AM MONSTER"

"I AM MONSTER"

Life Without A Mirror

j. j. Bond

"I AM MONSTER"
LIFE WITHOUT A MIRROR

iUniverse books may be ordered through booksellers or by contacting:

iUniverse
1663 Liberty Drive
Bloomington, IN 47403
www.iuniverse.com
844-349-9409

ISBN: 978-1-6632-0994-8 (sc)
ISBN: 978-1-6632-0995-5 (e)

Print information available on the last page.

iUniverse rev. date: 09/28/2020

This Novel is dedicated to:

All those I intend to offend..
All those I didn't..
Those that need us to defend them..
And to those, whom we knew, we shouldn't..

Until Lambs Become Wolves..

Sir Robin Hood, Lord of Locksley..
Drisko Oobbew, The Viking Child

Too the brightest of futures,

May your lives be filled with creative
thoughts and visions
Naya and Arabella

In Loving memory of:

Thomas, Mildred, Kimberly, Justin, Brother Dave,
Diane and Sandra, Family, Love, GOD and TRUTH..

In God, we TRUST..

Read the last words again until you figure it out for yourselves..

To the GOOD:

May the good Lord be with you..
Now say your prayers..
Good luck and amen..

NOTE TO THE EDITOR

With a special thank you to a very talented and helpful editor..

To Jesse Mills
At: whitehatpictures@rogers.com

Based on True Events and Real Life Scenarios..

If you HATE this novel give it to a friend.. If you LOVE it, burn it, then run..

From the mind of: j. j. Bond

CONTENTS

CHAPTER ONE
More Than A Feeling

He entered the high rise tower through the double set of reflective, gold tinted glass doors.. They automatically slid open with his stride.. He stepped into the glass elevator, watching as the roof tops appeared, lifting him up in through the night sky.. The lights glistening as he stares out into the moon light, while it's dancing above the Sea of Cortez.. He enters the penthouse condo through the huge custom carved oak doors.. There she stood, beautiful, poised, yakking at him in her Mexican tongue.. Dancing, prancing, gyrating her junk like a punk, jumping, rolling, twirling with joy.. The song played, his voice sweet, strong, pounding it into the mic, note for note, *"I looked out this morning the sun was gone. I turned on some music to start my day."*, her lips moist, wet as she drooled at his sight.. He slammed the door briskly, with silence, as the air pocket muffles the sound.. He walks straight up to her, *"lost myself in a familiar song, I closed my eyes"*, knelt down to her size, looking deeply into her succulent eyes..

Her white fur coat, her dark set eyes, the way she growled at him with her wet shout, her tiny white fangs.. Her tiny tail wiggling off her ass in total fear, her bouncing off the floor on all fours.. He grabs the shiny poodle by the scruff of her neck, shaking her, *"it's more than a feeling, (more than a feeling)"*, he lifts her with ease, staring deep into her eyes.. His, ice cold steel blue, staring deep into shit filled brown trembling fear.. He takes his left index finger and drives it deep into her throat.. Through the pure fluffy white fur, then into the skin, penetrating it with precision, as it melts through, then into red.. Then deeper into the animals larynx to silence her, while her blood drips through his finger tips..

Then he broke each of her legs in order, quickly.. First the left upper, then the lower, as the animal scratched and wailed in pure agony without voice.. Silently shrieking out her blood, with pure pain.. Pulsing it through the hole, dripping it off the tips of him and onto the custom Spanish ceramic flooring.. Quickly snapping the lower right leg, then the upper, the animal was helpless.. He grabbed the parring knife from the wooden block holder there on the kitchen centre aisle.. The thin pliable, tapered stainless steel blade, double sided, serrated edge, used to pop the eyes from the tomatoes.. Shiny steel, yellow, plastic handle.. He plunges the steel into the pups left eye as he slings it from the socket.. Laying, dangling from the animals snout, shaking it as it bounced off her cheek, the lid blinking, bleeding.. He repeats the motion, now to the right, the blood dripping, the lids blinking, the balls bouncing, bouncing, in timing, to the shake, as he laughs, *"more than a feeling"*..

Okay now, hold up there cowboy, because none of this really happened.. The question though, still remains unanswered.. That is simply, how psycho can psycho get, how deep can you be driven? How far could you go.. Now that I have your attention though.. Maybe, just maybe, he really is that crazy, just maybe he is a pure bred, born and raised, psycho killer.. But what, what could have driven him that far off the edge? Look long and hard at yourself, stare deep into your mirror, lose yourself in the images it possesses, until the vision becomes a reality.. Then you'll know, then the truth will be staring, right back at you, "I Am Monster", as you ask, it will reply.. You'll question it all, in your disbelief, is this me, who I really am, or just a vision, conceived by some mad man's, psychosomatic, psychopathic serial fuckin' killer's sadistic mind? His reality, or is it all as simple as or as complex as, "Life Without A Mirror"? Well, don't we all want to know?

In 1835 a German chemist, Justus Von Liebig developed a process for depositing silver on the rear surface of a piece of glass.. The technique gained world wide acceptance.. In 1930 an aluminum vacuum deposition process was invented by a physicist and astronomer from Cal-tech, John Strong.. Today the techniques are high tech, still the result remains the same.. An exact replication of you, the purest undisturbed truth of what you are as an image.. To some people, it's how others would see us.. To most, it's simply a reflection.. Although inconspicuously impossible to change the image, it is always present.. A constant true reminder of what we look like..

To all, an object, a possession, a tool that would simply hang on a wall.. To all a possession impossible to live without.. But what good is a mirror if you can't see the truth, what purpose would it hold? Worse, what if what you saw wasn't really you? You could only imagine your horror, to awaken every day, to terror, to fear, to see the truth.. Knowing what you see is a lie.. Thinking what you see is really someone else.. A completely different person than you.. Every time you look at you, it, truly, leaving you in disbelief.. Leaving you vulnerable within it, could you imagine, "A Life Without A Mirror"?

I can't tell you in true honesty, because the truth was told to me by a liar.. But over the years, listening to all the lies, somewhere you begin to recognize the parts of the stories that are consistent.. The parts you can now recognize as the truth.. But then you stop, right there, right where you stand, you look blankly into the mirror.. You question every word they spoke to you, you question your own self image, you question what you really see.. You stare hopelessly through the glass, is this me, who I am, how I look, is this me that I see, am I, "I Am Monster"? Is this me standing here in front of this mirror, or is it a self desired, creative conception of what we think we look like? Well, is it?

The answers, frighten you, as they should.. Because of your morals and your upbringing, your own vivid imagination won't allow you to conceive the true meaning of the words.. The stories can't be true, but they are.. You know in the rambling of all this madness, somewhere, somehow the images, they have to be wrong.. So you simply stare into that trusting mirror there, in front of you and you watch, as the tears leave your eyes.. You know that within the truth, there are so many lies, but the truth is that, within thoughts lies, there is so much truth.. You question, you search hard for the answer, looking blindly into those eyes, "I Am Monster" and you question, without answers..

Nobody really knows for sure what really happened, after the reunion of the class of '82.. Nobody really knows what really made his world explode, but in the end, the young warrior left the Clan.. The Viking Child, Drisko was gone, life on the Edge had taken its toll.. The whole thing had completely changed him, forever.. Nobody can really tell you the truth but him.. He is the only one who knows what went on up there in Cripple Creek Pass.. So whether you believe it or not, this is the absolute truth, and I'm the only one he ever confessed the truth to.. He said he just couldn't take it, living up there on the Edge any longer.. Just too many memories I'd guessed.. After all of the insanity with Miller and all the stories, holy, by geez.. Watching Dooley, at the pier, on the Sea of Lost Souls, slicing and dicing Miller, Drisko just faded after that.. Sometimes revenge isn't all that sweet eh', Drisko knew it had gone way too far..

The night on the Casandra, the last night any of them lived, the night they spent with the Witch.. Seems old Bonnie was right with her prediction.. The talk in the parking lot at Boomers, the authentic Viking village with Christina.. Bonnie knowing that Drisko would never forgive her treason, he'd let her kiss the Cod and not in the good way, seems she was dead right.. Drisko in his constant battles with his own evil demons.. Then to battle the Witch, his visions of that night, his love, his life, all of it a lie.. Seeing Bonnie's naked body piled up there with the dead.. It was just more than Drisko's young mind could endure, more than any man could have, ever..

Day in and day out, passing over the bridge at the Black Water River.. Right there, that very spot, where the dirt meets the blacktop, right there where his parents perished.. Right where they took the flying leap, the full gainer, all of it now a constant reminder.. The Livery, the Black Water Emporium, the Tanger, the blue house down the dirt lane, the 68 Chevy, the Post Office, the Greystone's Petro Bar, Rose, Bonnie and uncle Bev.. The same old, same old, the repetitiousness of life in Cripple Creek Pass.. They all just figured they would all be together forever.. They were all wrong, Drisko was through with Newfoundland, the Rock and Cripple Creek Pass.. His lonely island life was over, time to move on, build the bridge, expand his resources.. His words penetrating his own soul, nobody comes to the Edge, nobody, lessen' your coming here to die, cuz it's dead here.. Him marking his own words, it was just time to go.. Then he was gone, completely off the Edge and that was that..

Drisko drove the Mustang hard like the thoroughbred she truly was.. Sliding her up, shifting her down, finding all her gears with timing.. He wasted no time finding his was out of the Gros Morne.. Galloping the Mustang, his Tanger, in through the bridge at the Black Water River, off and out of Cripple Creek Pass.. Making his way past the Black Pearl, past the Casandra, past the Sea of Lost Souls.. Floating down in through the Watch Tower Resort, twisting the turn in past Fancy's Cafe', where you can't get off the Edge, without Fancy's cookin'..

Up back through Blue Berry Hill off the back out of Misery and down the lowly tail of the Cow Head.. Down into Bights Creek following the path of the Aqua Lung, rounding the hills, heading for Hell.. He's focused, with his visions, his mind is set on silence.. The visions enhanced, he sees all, multiple images, x-raying his sight, seeing everything, through his fly eyes.. Drisko wasn't paying much mind to the beauty of the scenery surrounding him.. He'd seen it now too many times before.. Drisko was in full vision of his future, he was moving on.. His guitar, his six string Aria, his personal things, his clothes and his one good suit for the special occasions, the weddings, graduation day, the reunions and funerals, lots of funerals..

The SR75/250/15 BF Goodrich T/A steel belted radials sliced their way up and over the top of the mighty Appalachians Mountain Range.. Propelling it in and down out of the Gros Morne and into the lowlands.. Off past the Stephenville Sheriff's newly erected Police Headquarters.. Off past Chief Zuncle, out of range of the N.P.P., for good.. The two door, 1967, green, Ford Mustang with a 351 Cleveland V8, 4 speed slap stick, factory clutch, was now racing its way, as fast as Drisko could torture it, galloping her way full out.. Whipping her hard, shifting her, then re-shifting, finding her groove, groovin' to the motion, groovin' on the edge..

You're listening to 104.9 the EDGE.. Drisko cranks the volume on the Pioneer Techtronic Z1-4, AM/FM, Quadraphonic Equalizer Stereo and sparks up a doob, the leads screaming into Drisko.. The guitarist, cracking the low notes on the leads, sliding into the tune, the strings break into single notes, strong, *"I close my eyes and she slipped away, she slipped away. It's more than a feeling"*.. He slaps her again as he makes his way past the green sign, Ferry to Nova Scotia, Channel Pointe Aux Basques.. Catching the sign, he knows he'll board the Leif Ericson, the Viking ship in less than two hours, as he prepares for battle.. His little life on the Rock, his beloved Newfoundland, his Viking clan, family and friends will all be in the rear view, in no time at all.. His breath shallow, anticipating the anxiety, welcoming the thrill..

They call it the Rock, because it's over a hundred and eleven thousand kilometres of heaven floating stationary in the north of the Atlantic.. The furthest point east in Canada.. Almost sixty thousand square miles of barren terrain.. The Edge is the Gros Morne, the highest point of the Appalachian Mountain Range.. The very northern point, the highest elevation, the steepest cliffs and the most astounding and breathtaking views.. Folks not from the Edge could mistake it for the end of the world, the abyss.. Folks from the Edge, know it's where it all began.. This is it, the beginning, the place they landed, the birthplace of where it all erupted, the beginning of all Civilization in North America..

Drisko was from the far north of the island, the place they call the Gros Morne.. High in the Great Northern Mountain Range, the top of the Appalachian Mountains, up there, on Cripple Creek Pass, the Edge.. He grew up there, right where the blacktop meets the dirt.. Right at the Black Water River, at the mouth of the mighty Atlantic.. There, him and his clan, his family, friends and loved ones.. They were all car, they would tear down and build up old vehicles of all kinds right there in the Livery.. Mudders, A.T.V.'s, motorcycles, old cars and trucks, some rare, some just junk he'd keep going for friends.. They all grew up, right there in the Livery, at Cripple Creek Pass..

The bridge that divided the north and south leg is where Drisko lost his parents.. His mom Ellen and his dad Bryce, that tragic night.. The night their Mustang took a full gainer into the raging waters of the mighty Atlantic and they simply grew fins and swam away.. Drisko tried and tried to forgive and forget all of it, every tragic detail, every sick, sadistic event.. The Emporium, the Black Pearl, Boomers, the Arches, the Pissing Mare, leaving it all behind.. The thief of the Mustang, the Grave ship, the night in the Casandra, the Wizard, the Witch, the Blood Eagle at the pier there, with Miller.. All of it took its toll on Drisko and in the end, there was nothing left for the young warrior.. Nothing left for the Viking child, nothing, nothing left for him, on his sacred island..

Everything destroyed, demolished, the truth now turned completely inside out and upside down, lies, all of it.. He remembers it perfectly, he watched it distinctly, he saw it as it preformed, all of it, unwillingly coming apart.. He witnessed it, as it, uncontrollably hurtled to earth.. He knew at that very moment, at that very second in time, he recognized it as the end of his world and he knew, as they all did, it was the end.. Drisko was Viking, a warrior, he knew that with every ending, comes with it, a new.. He watched, solemnly, as the ferry slithered its way southerly across the Gulf of St. Lawrence through the open channel.. Drisko watching as the tiny

7

island evaporated into the fog, as it slowly dissolved out of his sight.. Swallowed into the deep, of the mighty blue Atlantic..

Drisko, sliding back into the bucket seat, the Mustang stalled, resting, as he watches the waves lapping in behind the ferry.. She bucks gently once from the thrust, as he switches the key onto accessory.. He hits the play button on the cassette as it regurgitates, *"So many people have come and gone. Their faces fade as the years go by."*.. Here from the parking level of the Ericson, as it slithers, he slides gently into nirvana, *"Yet I still recall as I wander on. As clear as the sun,"*, with the waves as his rhythm and the song connecting the blues..

Drisko watches, then he looks, he's bewildered.. The guitars are pulsing out the rush of the cords, *"in the summer sky. It's more than a feeling. (more than a feeling.)"*, his steel blue, ice shattering eyes, pegged, into steel blue ice shattering eyes.. The black, of his long luscious locks reflecting red to him now, somehow, reflecting.. Framing him into the view, shimmering, in the darkness of the cab.. Streaking blood red into black, streaking from the tiny lightning bolts of sunshine pulsing into him from the might of the Atlantic.. The sunlight dancing with the beat, he's mesmerized by the song, *"clear as the sun in the summer sky. It's more than a feeling,"*, hypnotized by the vision of the reflection he sees, as he drifts away.. He looks, as he stares at it, he is drawn deep into the darkness of it, into the theatre of his mind, he's changing..

Drisko now falling deeper and deeper into the whirlpool of the rhythm, the song now sucking, *"I see my Marianne walkin' away. When I'm tired and thinking cold. I hide in my music"*, sucking his soul to the bottom of the ocean floor.. He sees, transfixed, there, into the rear view, the mirror.. It, set high above the dash of the Tanger.. The Wizard, the Casandra, the Casandra, that night, his visions fired by the memories of the Witch.. The Casandra, drawing him deeper and darker into his memories.. The huge war ship, Eric's, the Grave Ship, there on Parsons Pond, there at the Arches, that night at Boomers..

8

There under the Black Pearl, there in the Sea of Lost Souls, there, torturing, slicing and dicing Miller.. Him, Miller picturesquely posed, a statue, displayed for all to witness that night, there on the pier.. Dooley prying, carving Miller as he was knelt and lashed to the post, by rope.. Preparing, designing his body, one vertebrate at a time.. Like an artist, sculpting with surgical perfection, each precise cut.. The ribs now turned outward, creating the wings of the predator.. Till finally displayed, for treason, the ritual of the King, the sacrifice, of the Blood Eagle..

Drisko, his vision, the crowd cheering, searching for blood, the giant wings of the Casandra, floating high above the crowd, the menacing look, the eyes, following, circling from the giant serpent dragons head.. Perched there above Drisko, watching in approval, as Drisko kicks the shattered and torn, bleeding, pulsing, body.. Alive, yet lifeless, a useless slab of meat, sending him completely off the Edge and deep into the mighty blue Atlantic, praising, let him kiss the Cod.. The crowd, the clan, family, friends, loved ones, all of them, each one, less none, cheering, that night, dancing, rejoicing in celebration..

The eyes tattooed into the rear view of the Mustang, the mirror above the dash.. Shadows darkening the eyes, then streaks of light dancing, bolting through the visions.. It can't be real, Drisko screaming it out, in his silent voice, it can't.. But it has to be, they all witnessed it, it has to, the mirror, lying to him, then telling him the truth.. He was there, he saw as the asteroid plummeted toward earth, he was the one screaming out the warnings as the crowd danced and gyrated to the song, as he sang, "Welcome to the jungle".. He saw it coming, ripping the island apart, crashing, killing everything in its sight.. Like the Siren of the Sea, when she attacked the tiny Viking village.. Not coming to posses, not coming to enslave, na', she is coming to devour, every, living, thing, in her path.. It came, it took, it did indeed, devour, everything.. Everything Drisko, ever held sacred, it simply annihilated, his entire life.. All of it, every single piece of his beloved Rock, was gone, all of it..

He was there, that night, on the Casandra.. The very night Boomer introduced him to the Wizard, the ugly stick, the sacred sceptre, as the Wizard poked it at Drisko's head.. He witnessed and saw the magic of the Wizard, that night on the Casandra.. The same night the Wizard introduced him to the Witch.. He watched in awe, as they all did, all that were present.. Watched in pure admiration of her beauty, her power.. Watched as her tiny body formed into blood red smoke, as they toked on her, devouring her beauty, lustfully, as she grew into this voluptuous, magical woman, impossible to resist.. The Witch without a back, only faced forward, with a multitude of faces.. Each man seeing her as he would see her, ugly, yet beautiful.. Smoking, and toking on her, and sometimes choking, all of them, drawing her in, there on the Casandra, on the Grave Ship..

The Wizard screaming, Gaelic, Gothic, ancient rhymes.. Poking the ugly stick and the secrets of the Screech, into Drisko's face, as the Witch invaded his mind.. Tell me Drisko what do you seek, ask me and I will tell you if it is true.. The Witch prompting the visions, you seek too far, beyond the reach, beyond what is required.. The truth Drisko, is always right in front of you.. The dead, the dying, the useless and used bodies, of loved ones, piled high for Drisko to see.. There the images of Millers victims, far too powerful for Drisko's young mind to contain, too powerful for any man to have survived..

The Ericson, shutters and shakes, vibrating the vibe up into the Tanger, gyrating the vessel.. It's just what it is, the currents, changing, shifting, pushing and pulling against the cold steel rudder.. It's almost frightening sometimes, but it is, just what it is.. The fear, the visions shattering, absorbing into the passengers' minds.. Helplessly feeling as if inside a Boeing 747 jet airliner, failing, falling, hopelessly, into the mighty blue Atlantic.. The Titanic, scraping, crushing, twisting and turning, sliding, impacting the tiny vessel with its ice blue iceberg spears, simply, powerfully, piercing in through it.. Sending it mercilessly into the deep darkness of a watery grave in the mighty blue Atlantic..

The Poseidon, capsizing, turning her completely upside down, slicing through, busting and breaking, pulverizing bones, falling, floating.. Visions, from each man, all, seeing her different, each man seeing her as he would, ugly, yet beautiful in its vision.. Hands trembling, clutching, eyes clenched shut, as you're floating, peacefully downward, drifting, deep, down into the bottom of your Grave Ship.. Deep, into the vision as you're devoured gently by the mighty blue Atlantic..

Drisko's eyes wrestled with the rear view, tugging, pulling, floating, drifting.. Looking without seeing, with the sight of the blind, the Wizards eyes, now white, blank.. Visions, multitudes of them, the fly's eyes.. Cascading, programmed in order, flashing in through them eyes, as if a kaleidoscope, a slide show, with timing to the song, *"thinking cold. I hide in my music, forget the day. And dream of a girl I used to know. I closed my eyes,"*, as Drisko hears, without ears.. Just the visions, the images playing in the theatre of the mind, Drisko's mind.. Drisko, floating, looking,*"slipped away."*, approaching, then stepping out, without fear, in rhythm, to the beat, to the vibe of the vessel.. Stepping forward, Drisko is, completely, off the Edge.. The song was far too powerful, the song beating him down with the back beat.. Down, deep, then deeper into the darkest depths, of the mighty blue Atlantic..

Drisko, alert, following the eyes, capturing every move, motion, every image.. Everything, reversing, the visions going back through time.. The visions, flash, the bodies, flash, the pile, flash, it's size, it's volume, it's pure evil mass ten fold, flash, flash, flash.. Piled there, in the reflection, with his beloved, piled there, with the dead.. Bonnie, partying at Boomers, smiling, sexy, suave', her image ghostly, shining through the beach burner, the party at the Pond, the night at the Arches.. Him, enthralled in her beauty, as they stood together on the shoreline, the night Drisko found the black pearl.. The stone, he tossed into the mighty Atlantic.. Flinging it with force, skipping it's perfect form, dancing it, bouncing weightlessly across the white tips of the Atlantic.. Them kissing, holding each other tight, wishing

11

upon that shooting star, hurtling toward the earth at a hundred thousand miles per hour, or thirty kilometres per second..

Bonnie and Drisko dancing at the Castle De' Marte', at their high school reunion, her swaying him, rubbing, holding him.. Her gentle reminder, "this is our song, the song you proposed to me to", reminding him to man up, git'er done, the song played for her, "Angel Eyes".. The eyes now searching, bouncing, holding, the visions, the Emporium, the fire, the assault on Bev, his uncle, the burns, the body laying lifeless, the gaze, rusty, red.. The suffering, the visions, flourishing, the eyes searching without sight.. The eyes old, white, blank, staring reflecting back into new ice blue steel..

The after party, the party in the limo, the party at the Watch Tower.. The eyes, locked into the mirror, flicking, flicking.. Drisko noticing distinctly, the white Dodge was gone from its perch, as the creeping barrage of vehicles made their way out of the castle grounds and back toward the paved flats of the Cape.. Drisko and Dooley hanging off the back of the Mudder while Rita and Bonnie sat resting on the tailgate.. Drisko, seeing himself, the vision, him standing in the night, swigging on his Black Horse Pale Ale when he catches Bonnie's eye, what you staring at lass, him asking her.. Look she said, as they sat high on the ridge overlooking the edge of the castle grounds.. From here you look north, straight up to the Cape of Port Au Choix..

The eyes flicking in the rear view, Drisko sees her pointing, while the group is following her aim.. They could see a slight gleam of brightness far to the north, hovering, above the horizon, the city lights, the eyes flashing, flashing, flashing, flicking.. But then, when you look to the south you sees perfectly up the flats across the Black Water River and up into the Edge.. So, he ask, the eyes laughing, Drisko laughing at his drunken girl's observation.. Well, all them car lights is all red eh', Bonnie blurts out, 'septin that one little light dar, the eyes tearing, staring to reach.. The group staring hard off to the south, to see what Bonnie was talking about..

There as she hollers, there, the flicking of white light, bouncing off the waters edge, seezer, coming down off da flats, out off the Edge eh', up into Cripple Creek Pass.. The eyes locked, looking into the eyes locked, black to black, wet, there aboard the Ericson.. The eyes shaking, the hair gyrating, black eyes, reflecting blood.. The tear Drisk left deposited on Bev's lip, "the I love you too uncle Bev", as he left the Emporium.. The ding ding, ding ding, of the door chimes as it rang four times.. The night he left his uncle in the old store, up there, on the Edge.. Waving through the glass as Drisk hopped into the limo, heading to the class of 1982's, ten year reunion, up on Cripple Creek Pass.. The four dings, of the elevator, in the I.C.U. as he deposited his tear and his word, only hours later..

We are of the same blood, we flow of the same river Bev, what runs through you, runs through me.. His oath, the oath of the clan, his word, as a warrior and as a Norseman.. His word that Miller, the killer, would kiss the Cod.. The eyes both tightly clenching, deeply grasping onto each other.. The salt from the ocean spray, crystallizing, obviously impairing the vision, tearing them up.. There, without mercy, in the rear view, inside the Tanger's glass walls.. The eyes clicking, flicking, the visions, the kaleidoscope, flicking, turning, turning the visions into view, tearing.. She was a goddess, her hair, striking long midnight black that cascaded over her ample breast, to lay midway across her back.. Swaying as it set against the yellowed tinge of the porch coach light, the eyes, winking, blinking.. Illuminating her god like figure, angelic, as she made her way down the stairs..

Her diamond studded silver earrings, dangled from her tiny lobes.. The silver crested necklace with diamond set pendant she selected, sparkled with every movement and bounce she made, reflecting as it danced off her shake, the eyes, reflecting, blue ice steel, bouncing.. The black gown flowing, the roped belt dangling, dancing off her hips as she sauntered, heels clicking to the burlesque tap as she took centre stage of the concrete runway.. Her body moving, slow, her breast heaving, inviting him as she stooped, slowly, into the pearl white super long stretched limousine.. The eyes locked dead on the eyes, flicking, stooping, swaying, dangling.. Bonnie, the voice silent, the eyes, searching, stretching wide open, flashing, flashing..

Drisko seeing himself at the bridge, at the Black Water River, the bees, buzzing, stinging him without feeling, as he stung Miller, pulverizing him.. Sky and her pack of hungry wolves, tearing at Millers flesh, ripping at him.. The tattoos falling from his throat, DBD, falling in tatters, colours fading into slivers of blood red.. Dooley pounding his might into Miller, blow after blow.. Leaving him alive and conscious enough to enjoy their finale.. Drisko, hearing without ears, listening as he repeats his orders, take him.. Take him to the Black Pearl, prepare him for the sacrifice of the Blood Eagle, let him kiss the Cod, in the Sea of Lost Souls.. The eyes, smiling, the pain, bringing out their joy, without being able to feel, joy.. The blues sparkling, the visions searching, the fly eyes circling, correlating, filling then refilling, searching and finding, then skillfully displaying, inside the vision, reflecting in the mirror..

The eyes, flicking in timing to the beat.. The vision of the cellophane plastic covering of his tuxedo, that night, flicking it, in the wind.. It only sounded like them screaming.. The flicking of the heater from his cigarette, splitting as it flew off the Edge.. It only looked like the distinctive box styled tail lights, flying recklessly off the Edge and beyond his tiny reach.. Deep into the rushing waters of the Black Water River.. Then out, into the deep, darkness, of the mighty blue Atlantic.. The Greystones, Irving Petro bar out on the ridge, the fire, the brutal assault on kin, the clan.. The family, left there for dead.. The eyes flicking, flicking, spinning, dancing, darting, tearing.. The attack on old man Gibbs, the postmaster, attacking him from behind, barely, escaping with his life, the fire, up on the Cliffs, the old post office..

The eyes, biting at each other, the same night, flicking, flicking, the eyes flicking.. The same night, that faithful night, up there in Cripple Creek Pass, at the Black Water River.. Right there, where the dirt meets the blacktop, straight in off the flats, straight up and off into the mighty blue Atlantic.. The animal, the Mustang, took a tragic turn for the worse, there in the darkness of the cliffs.. Flying high up and over the Edge, a perfect full gainer, then it simply grew fins and swam away.. The night Drisko's parents perished into the deep.. The pictures needed no caption, the Saint John's Tribune, simply read, "The Tire Tracks Match".. The eyes, flicking, darting, tearing, twisting, like the serpent dragons head eyes, spinning.. Like the eyes on the ugly stick, the Wizard's sceptre, following, tracking every move, white, blank, blind, but with great sight and truly incredible, creative vision..

The two eyes now black, two eyes staring back, into two eyes now black, staring back.. Spatters of white, flecking against the blackened screens.. As if an artist, cleaning his brushes, flicking the white misty paint, creatively, strategically, across the canvas.. The night sky opening into a burst of the solar system, out into the universe.. Jupiter, Mars, the Moon, now forming, the Milky Way shimmering across the black sky, filling the canvas.. The Aurora Borealis, the dancing of the Northern Lights, the brilliance of the North Star and the Devin magic, from the Eye of God, the Helix Nebula..

The black eyes crossing and flicking, staring intently into one another's black eyes.. The mirror staring back into the mirror, filling in the colours.. The visions, looking up from the cavern floor, into the bottom of the Black Pearl, reflecting the Sea of Lost Souls, picturesquely forming the universe, on the top of the cavern's sky.. The Pearl landing here, on this very spot, a thousand years ago.. A gigantic asteroid a hundred trees tall.. Landing a thousand feet above the rushing waters of the Black Water River, the Throne, they all called it, just because.. She was formed perfectly out of the asteroid's coal and when you sat in it, you were, the King of the world..

The opening high in the night, the one the old Newfie dug and fell into and went and killed himself.. The one Ragnar discovered with the old mans body, intact, from a thousand years ago, dead, but

15

looking like you and me.. The snake pit that he so bravely explored, only to discover the underworld, the sea, the Arches, the pier and the Casandra, all intact, from a thousand year ago.. The opening filling, the eyes black flicking, flashing.. The opening being blinded by the biggest asteroid he had ever witnessed, the eyes locking, twisting into one another.. The asteroid crashing through the Milky Way, shattering the Aurora Borealis, ripping through the Eye of God and eclipsing the Moon, blinding it completely.. Hurling it into a solid ball of white, misty blood.. The eyes tearing reddish, the visions, the night, all them poor little fucking Newfie's all dead, all of them.. The eyes bursting with a sun shower of streaks, then quickly darkened in the mirror, the eyes black, flashing, flashing, flashing with explosions of colour..

The Ericson shutters and shifts, lifting high out of the waves, shifting port side, travelling across her then dumping deep into the bottom of the mighty blue Atlantic.. Only to be lifted again, tossed and drop deep again into the bottom of the mighty blue Atlantic.. The passengers, bracing, the visions appearing, darting, dancing through their tiny minds.. The creatures, tearing them, shedding them, the terror, the blood, them all, each one, less none, seeing her exactly as he had seen her, beautiful, yet ugly.. Them being sucked down into the ocean floor.. Each one perfectly sculptured, beautifully designed, creatively poised, artistically displayed for all to see.. The eyes clenching, the Mustang vibrating, vibrating, lifting, shifting, laying, gently back down, the eyes locked as it shifts and settles back down on top of the wave..

The eyes strobing, flickering, turning off to on, strobing, flashing, black to white, then back to black, then white.. The mirror streaking, lights beckoning, strobing, strobing.. The tiny smoky figurine vision appears, frustratingly screaming the freakishly morbid sounds.. Taunting as the men sucked the life blood from her very soul.. Inhaling and blowing it out, up into the ribbed rafters of the Casandra.. Helpless in their attempt, as the figure is forming.. Somehow even with the full force of the Viking warriors, the clan, they could not stop the advances, of the Witch.. She grows, screaming and forming, she grows, now beyond a foot tall.. She's forming and figuring, she's naked, yet see through, translucent, as she is of smoke..

Her skin coating, turned inside out, the blood and veins protruding, visible, beating, blood red.. Her face tiny, contorting, forming the mouth of the creature, moving with arms and hands shaking.. Her legs dancing, turning, her tiny form twisting her.. She, the size of a baby, yet the physique, of a full grown voluptuous, woman.. She screams, the mimicking sounds of a thousand screeching eels, sizzling in a bath of boiling water.. Shrilling at the men, in her annoyance of their pure presence.. She grows and dances and twist and squats then screams at them.. Now she's rising, another two feet in height, then three, as they watch, without power.. Powerless to stop this demon, with no idea of how to defend against such a beautiful and torturous, sexy foe..

Her face, looking into each man, as she grew, the face different to each man, her body forming.. The men, standing, sitting, gathering around the table.. They all, saw the face as they saw the face, all, each one differently.. The Witch had no back, only front, a dead on view, precisely formed and figured, custom designed for you.. As you see her now flowering, growing, a blossom exploding, into a five foot six, busty, built and a beautiful woman.. Looking exactly like, as in without a flaw, in every way, perfection.. Every man's absolute dream girl.. Like watching a child grow into a woman, in minutes, hypnotic.. Her hair was red, long to Dooley, to Drisk she was raven black.. To some they saw her wavy, to another, she wore tied back.. To one, her hair was curly brown, shooting in every way.. Like busted springs, bouncing, as she swayed.. Another it was short and blonde, one saw her as a guy.. Then others saw her, the way they wanted, this girl, could make you cry..

The Witches eyes, were that of a gigantic, reptilian monster.. Greenish, with slight traces of cracking, yellowish highlights.. Crocodile eyes, a true marvel, they can see in different directions at the same time.. They can track, multiple targets and they're retractable, as a defence mechanism, for battles.. The cylinder shaped black slits of the sphere centred pupils, protectively circled inside the brown, fleshy coating, mesmerizing all of the men at once, with her eyes.. Her nose, the snout of a rat, thin and long, so perfectly matching the beauty of her face, similar to the ugly nose on the ugly stick..

Her lips were sensual, all four of them.. The first set, two outer sets, set across the top and the bottom, opening very wide.. Two inner sets, smaller, inside the outer set, across the top and bottom.. Behind them were the monsters fangs, the teeth of a tiger sharks, with the same force, for shredding her victims, as she desired.. Miraculously gorgeous, in her pure raw unselfish beauty, the face turned inside out, firing, blood red.. Her arms rising high above her head, the fingers twirling in the air.. Turning from fingers into curly fiery coils of lucent smoke, then back, then so on and so on.. A continuous loop, of fresh, succulent, bleeding virgin flesh.. Configuring into smoke, as they sucked and fed on her..

A masterpiece, a pure work of art.. Their hearts pounding with love for the creature, lusting for her body, desiring to kiss the lips of this most enchantingly, beautiful creature.. The most beautiful of souls, the most breathtaking woman that the world had ever seen.. Godiva, she slurred out the word, Godiva, slithering it past her mouths, the smoke raises, she whispers her name.. Her tongue long, slimy and slithery, the tongue of a giant Anaconda, massively occupying the space in her mouth.. Sliding in and out, a serpents slit, protruding out, as her tongue splits into two pokey points.. She drives it forward, deep into Drisko's open mouth, she fumes out a blast of poisonous, toxic, one hundred percent proof, the Wizards Brew.. The tongue slithering as it reforms, into the pure red smoke of Godiva, as she supercharges the toke, into Drisko's open lungs with her breath.. The eyes breathing, slow, reflecting in perfect timing into the rear view..

The ship now slowing, everything reversing, it shimmies and shutters, shaking, screaming, dancing and twirling, turning.. The Ericson, sliding, slowly, downward into the whirlpool, downward into the bottom of the mighty blue Atlantic.. The eyes screaming, searching, the red smoke evaporating into the ice blue steel, the vision, the reflection, reflecting the images.. The girls were all dressed, in their bourbons and scotch, rye whisky one's cries, I'll cry rye whisky till the day I die, she singing it out.. The others liked vodkas, sherries and schnapps.. Some wearing, their costumes, trimmed finely in cheap wines.. Some reds, whites, some blues, who really knew? Who, mostly, nobody cared, cuz any of it would do? They drank, not for flavours, aromas or taste, they drank without senses, they were already shit faced.. Some tequilas, some mixes, some spiked with some crap.. But all of them, not less, not one.. All of the kind, had kissed at least one of them horses behinds, and for all, they had felt their body shiver in cum.. All, not less, not one, had reached this place, this place all had reached, in thanks, bar none, to the secrets, of the Screech..

Some sitting, some standing, some half the way down.. The beach burners a burning, sparking out sounds.. The rhythms, the reach, the heat and the beat.. Eight maybe ten, of course, plus Bonnie and Pen.. The new nickname they gave her, a gift from a friend.. Penny on one side, Christina on the other, cuddling, asses touching together like lovers.. Sitting, half naked, in the coarse blackened beach sands of Parsons Pond, leaning, arms wrapping, hugging, touching, molesting each other.. Their backs perched, supported by the long neck of the ancient picturesque, greying, decaying, beautifully formed, black Ash drift wood log.. Authentic east coast art gifted from the sky, the Helix Nebula, the eye of God, plucked by his hand, out of the land, they call, the True North, the Rock.. The eyes smiling, the thought, twisted twirling, the eyes naked, holding, holding..

The mirror, the Shroud, the vision, what is it, it can't be true, the eyes, blue on blue, inquiring, flashing, then stead fast.. Drisko could see the Casandra coming into his view in front of the stage.. Seeing her huge dragon's serpent head and flapping wings, the head menacing, designed in magnificent detail.. The thorny brows, silver reflective eyes, the balls seemingly following them from inside its deep detailed lids.. The skin of the reptile engraved into the detailing of its scaly coat.. The wings floating with the rhythm of the sea, looking as if they were flapping in flight, in attack mode.. Drisko stopping in his tracks, Bonnie following his gaze, high into the night sky.. The black curtain now mixing with sheets of blues, yellows and reds, the gulls looking more like prehistoric predators, Pterodactyl, giant vultures, menacing, frightening..

The scene to Drisko looked like death.. Drisko realizing his déjà vu, he walked these sandy shores before, a thousand years ago, in this very scene.. He recognized the location, identical, here, on this shore.. The nails of the tides had ripped their way through the rocky shoals of the Arches of Parsons Pond.. He could feel it, see it in his mind's eye, clearly, with his own vision, as if it were now.. Him the Viking King, walking, one step in front of him, Drisko.. The visions trailing him, his mind preparing him.. Here, with her, the Casandra, with him, his King and his Bonnie, once again.. They enter the open stairway, then stepping up the three steps onto the long stretch of split log and rope lashed piers..

The huge wooden pylons securing the moorings.. Drisko could hear the familiar screams of the ropes lashing the Casandra to the dock.. He walked slowly looking up into the crafted detail as he passes under her wing.. They sauntered along the starboard side of the ship, passing the tall mount of oars, fitted, secure.. A wall of wooden armour, the massive wooden shields mounted firmly, hung over the man rail of the ship.. Then long spears, mounted, set between the oars, cast with Viking steel, pointed, sharpened to a prick.. Above him, yet below the gulls, the mast, perfectly fit, thick and tall to add to her performance and balance of this great ship..

The mast tied and the sails slung, the Casandra was alive with song and she sung.. The twisting of the beams, the rattling of the ropes and pulleys.. The clanging and banging of the parts and piece of her soul.. Drisko stops, still, staring down into the piers end, only for a moment, a vision, he thought he saw something, then something else, a bird, an Eagle.. Flashes too fast to see, vulgar, monstrous visions, blood.. He enters the ship, reaching out to Bonnie to help her aboard, she smiles at him..

A moment breaks his trance, he takes each step with caution, not of fear, but intrigue.. The feeling of his footsteps creaking across the antique planks, he inhales the texture up through his thighs, squeezing his torso, exasperating each breath and directly into his brain.. He could smell her plume, feel her sweat, he could taste her vile juices, he knew it was her, all of her, from the ancient passages, of his past.. It, walking through him, his mind shooting to him, this is, the Casandra.. This is Erica's, Eric's War Ship, ERICHIL' coma da VIK-GYK-INGK KGIKIN and it was very, very frighteningly familiar to him.. His blood, crueling inside him.. The Ericson now swaying him deeper, then deeper, the eyes flutter..

The Casandra was lavishly appointed, huge wooden beams ribbing the walls, custom cabinets filled with trinkets and souvenirs, shelving laid with books and maps, charts, some a thousand years old.. Drisko and Bonnie could feel the ancient ones here, in the Casandra, as they enter through the huge carved black Ash doors and into the Masters chamber.. The table wrapped with thirteen old wooden and silver laid chairs, hand crafted, beautifully designed, leather upholstered.. Each in its own artistically textured art.. The table, was made of sturdy huge wooden black Ash planks, perfectly round to fit exact to its size.. In the centre of the table as distinct as it could be, the Shroud.. The shield, huge in diameter to match the table, embossed with silver designs..

The shield of a great warrior, the protector of Kings.. The shield, exact in every way and portioned to sit perfectly in the centre of the huge wooden top.. Eric's shield, the exact replica in every way.. Golden stars, gems, diamonds and rubies glistering in the shield, strapped with silver designs of serpents, crisscrossing, in-laid with threads of gold.. Two swords rolling the steel blades as if they were striking each other in thunder, with laces of sparks flinging across the shield.. Circling the outer edge of the shield in front of each of the thirteen chairs, sat a raised silver cap, one inch square, one inch high and tapered to a dull point, rounded and hallowed..

In the centre of this beautiful fixture shield, painstaking, artistically mastered to perfection, na' a detail missed, the Helix Nebula, the Eye of God, exacted, replicated to the umpteenth degree by ancient hands.. Touched over one thousand years ago.. Breathtaking for Drisko to behold, he knows, his eyes filling with wet, burning in salt, the figments of his memories.. The reality, the craftsmanship, the undeniable meaning of this Shroud.. This belongs to the greatest warrior of us all, to him, this was the shield of Eric.. The exact replica of the Kings.. ERICHIL' coma da VIK-GYK-INGK KGIKIN.. The king of all kings, King to all kin, Viking da Kin.. To every Viking alive and to all who have died, here on this land, Eric is King.. His blood is true of Norseman then, so is all that flow from him.. The eyes, shattering into smile, crystal clear, ice shattering blue, Drisko's eyes, looking, smiling back at Drisko..

The eyes, closed, as he wakes into his dream, the church bells are ringing, the morning sun flooding into the room.. The crisp fresh breeze of the ocean air tainting the room, fluttering the light sheer of the curtains.. The dead fish, a big ugly four foot, five inch, three hundred and nine pound Grouper, was a hugely displayed trophy, hanging between the two open windows.. The photo of Drisko, his dad Bryce, uncle Bev and the monster fish, standing proudly displayed on the large wooden dresser top.. Pictures of family, friends and events marking the couples past, caked the walls.. The door slightly set open, as the aroma of the fresh perked coffee enters with ease..

Bonnie's got the stereo cranked, seemingly sending the signal to his senses, time to wake up.. The singer screaming up the stair well, "Hell's Bells".. The steel framed four post canopy bed, a relic, cast from iron by ancient makers of steel and pictorially enhanced with four floating cast iron bird figurines.. Drisko lays silent, deep in the colourful duvet top, submerged into the goose down pillows, staring high into the ceiling, thinking of Bev, focused on Miller the killer.. The bells still ringing in his head, the bees are busy buzzing, Drisko, feeling their sting.. The eyes, darting, dodging the ocean of tears he's battling, the mirror replying, the eyes flooding, white, blank, ancient, old, eyes..

The Ericson shutters, slowing, bouncing, heaving, heavenly, angelic, but present and powerful.. The vibe, the shimmer, the eyes shaking, shifting, switching, flicking.. The forty two by sixty four foot garage was rickety and worn from the standard of the building.. Built by Bev, Bryce and grandpa Eric, back at the turn of the century, when Eric and his wife Peg, first settled here.. They're both buried there out back in the family plot.. Along with a dozen or so extended family and of course, Drisko's dad Bryce and his mom, Ellen's marker, along with her brother, Dwayne Erickson..

Haunting, but in a comfortable memorable way.. The graves all marking the earth's rotation.. The evolution of a family, a man and the legends of the Clans.. Sacred names, with massive godlike statues, crosses, swords and insignia's of Gothic, Celtic, Gaelic and Viking, prominently adorning the head stones.. The Vikings believed, that your spirit rides for you, always attached to the next of kin, passed on to new, never singular, never alone, always with you.. Always a brave, always a warrior, always a Norseman.. The double black Ash wood slatted doors of the Livery, opened apart from each other, attached to a pulley contraption, that allow the doors to swing open in unison.. The field rock foundation set three feet high circling and wrapping the structure, primed and proven as the base.. The wooden framed studs holding high, the huge beamed rafters and the old pot belly stove, set in the corner to warm the space.. The interior plastered with relics, as was the basement of the old Black Water Emporium..

Drisko recognizing every label and logo scattered across the walls.. Stacks of tools and toys, things and contraptions all neatly displayed or stored correctly in its place.. Black Water Livery

& Blacksmith, established 1823, the old sign read, the original family business, iron smiths, steel makers.. From long before the Emporium.. The sign original, laying prominently across the back wall, high above the work bench, displayed with pride.. Bryce, Bev, Dooley, Drisko, Bonnie and Rose all grew up here, in this shop, they all had a hand on the Tanger..

Dooley wasting no time, pulls a tailor made doob from his Export "A"s cigarette pack and fires it up.. Hauling on the toxic smoke, holding it till he chokes it out, then he passes the joint to Drisko.. Wha d' dey say, coughing out the words rheumatically, the fuckin cops eh', coughing it out word for word.. They air lifted Bev to C.S.C. Memorial in St. Anthony, Drisko says, no leads on the robbery, don't know this, don't know that, don't fuckin know fuckin shit eh'.. Fuckin cops, as Drisko coughs out the words this time, fuckin cops.. Miller, Dooley says, got his mark all over it eh', everything I've heard so far points to that little piece of shit and if it's him, he goes on, as Drisko's interrupting him, not him.. Dooley stressing, what the fuck do you mean it's not him.. Drisko filling him in on the cops report, the spotting of Miller in New Brunny, the short for New Brunswick..

Miller wasn't really a killer, or at least the gang didn't know him as that, back in the days of C.C.P.H.. It was just little friendly joke, his name, worked for the rhyme, it was almost cool.. But then, he was just weird, gave off this eerie scent, dangerous.. He'd hunt cats and dogs, shoot them like prey.. Rumours of him peeping into windows at night, trying to rape young girls, molesting them, threatening them.. He'd mimic people, it was almost spooky, scary, he could act and sound like you instantly, within minutes of seeing or meeting someone, he could take on their personality.. He would be perfectly normal one moment, then a totally different person the next..

What was really, really weird though, was that Miller, through all those years of high school, like Drisko, he was just never around, he missed a lot of time.. But as time went on, the one thing the whole gang realized was, that he had never been to any of their homes, like no ones, like ever.. He was a school yard friend, showed up at the parks, games, parties, stuff like that and never has anyone that knew him, ever went to his house, it was just weird.. Almost as if he was a ghost.. He'd just appear, then disappear, that was that, he was gone.. A reputation and facade, a fear that all the women of C.C.P.H, and more likely the entire Cape.. So when Miller got arrested trying to burn down the Petro bar and the post office, the damage was done, the village shunned him.. He tattooed his body, evil stuff.. Tattooed his fingers, "DEATH TO ALL", carved across the digits, skull and mask on his neck.. DBD, on his throat, Death Before Dishonour, then finally deep across his back, big, bold, black lettering, "GOD FORGIVES" "I DON'T"..

He took it upon himself, to generate pure fear, evil, he did as he liked, he did become an outcast.. The night of the Petro bar fire, the same night as the post office, the same night Drisko's mother and father careened the Mustang off the bridge at the Black Water River.. It took months for the Sheriff to realize that there was fresh white paint on the inner beam of the wooden bridge.. They matched it to a late model Dodge pickup.. Then the Sheriff closed the case, Miller had left the Rock.. It didn't take long to make two plus two look like four, even for the class of '82..

There's only one way off the Cliff and that's in off the flats.. First though you's gotta runner high up through the Edge, down through the rugged shoal rock cliffs of Cripple Creek Pass.. Then down across the torrent of Black Water River.. Then in through the old rickety wooden bridge through the Gates of Hell, then up on into the narrows.. Right where the Mustang lost it, right there, where the dirt meets the blacktop.. Nobody comes here, nobody, unless they're coming here to die, Drisko said, in his silent voice, because its dead here.. Dooley and Drisko swore at the loss of freedom, if Miller ever made tracks up into Cripple Creek Pass, wouldn't be no cops, wouldn't be no judge or jury.. They'd throw his killer ass, straight off the Edge, let him kiss the Cod, and not in the good way, that was their vow.. They cut the palms of their hands, brother for brother and made a blood pack, brothers till we depart, word..

Bull shit, Dooley spurting at Drisko, his fuckin name's all over this, cops got shit, probably got a fuckin deer cornered down dar.. Big Fuckin Foot or sometin eh', don't fuckin know their ass from a hole in the ground, fuckin cops eh'.. Hill Billy saw him over out da howler, down by the flats, coming in off the Edge, full out eh'.. Dooley yelling it, who da fuck comes in off da flats, full fuckin out eh', if yaz not from da Edge.. Moose fuckers that who, moose fuckers, some idiot running around trying to get all fucked up by a moose that's who, other than that fucker, it's one of us.. Someone that knows the Edge, Dooley calming his roar, knows er' inside out, every fuckin inch of er', dats who..

Rita's sister Vi, saw him at the marina in fuckin Norris fuckin Point, she knows him, he was trying to fuck'er all the time, hard on her too, relentless, she was sure it was him.. Dusty Greer, you know old Captain Greer from the Galloway, ya, ya, we'll eh', he says he saw him, in the freakin Pavilion, in freakin Rocky Harbour, two fuckin nights ago, Drisk.. By george' you saw him, you just won't let yourself believe it eh', buts' you s' best believe it now brother, it's him..

Dooley looking hard, lost into the black sky, like it held the answer.. He's here, he's fuckin here on the Edge sure as sheep shit.. But I have no idea, why that fuckin brain dead piece of shit, would ever come back to the Edge.. But trust me brother, it's him eh', it's the fuckin killer.. Drisko grabs two Black Horse from the little shop fridge.. You're right brother, you're right, it's him, Drisko frowns, fuckin dumb ass fuckin cops.. Dooley fires up another doob, smoking out the words, fuckin Big Fuckin Foot eh', I tells ya eh'..

The ship shutters, he could feel the world slowly reversing, the sea grabbing, dragging him down.. The Ericson helplessly being sucked into the enormous whirlpool.. The turbines squeal, singing the songs of the Casandra.. Then gently, grasping its huge claws into the thickness of the blue.. The eyes flutter and float, floating upward into the sky.. Miller, he says looking out into the sky's, Miller, blood.. Drisko's last word was blood, standing there, with Dooley, out front of the Livery.. His eyes wide, clear but darker blue, repelling the sun, as if he closed the sky..

Storms coming he says, looking exactly like Drisko, as he checks the sky, face into the wind.. Piercing his sight into the sky off the edge, black as it appears, blood was his reply.. Big storms a comin', his voice now screeching darker, blood, dangerously the voice wails, blood storm.. They could now see the trees swaying hard behind them to the west.. The brushes shaking viciously, in, out, one way, then the next, without rhythm, without unity.. The critters all scattering in haste, deep into the forest.. The birds are flying high, then like they're being thrown, without control, deep into the shoal rocks below..

Dust, dirt and debris, weeds and russels, all being lifted and thrown abruptly with force, off the edge.. It's coming, the voice says, haunting with its words, Norseman, not him, Viking, their voices, multitudes of them, correlating.. It's coming, the voices saying, its coming and it won't be leaving no peace, the voices chilling.. Dooley grabbing Drisko, they turn, dragging him zombified, entranced, focused, to take cover in the old shop.. Drisko voicing, in his stride, it's here, there's nowhere to run, blood, you can't hide from me, screaming it, into the wind.. Then words, that none of them could understand, God like, ferocious, Gaelic, Norsemen..

The single bulb discharging the light, swaying without timing, tingling sounds all around, wind chimes grossing, bells tinging, things clanging, branches snapping, moans and groans of the wind.. The sword, falls out of the rafters of the Livery, then planting itself, readily into the dirt floor.. Bonnie squeals with fright, as Drisko and the rest turn to face her fear.. They all awe, at the wonderment staring at it, there in an amazement of total respect and fear.. Eric, Bonnie says, her voice trembling, staring into Drisko's transfixed, darkened, ice blue steel eyes, as she squawks the words out, it's He'.. Lordy be it's he, it's Eric she repeats, trembling, he's been risen mi

Lord, olie jeez-hess, mi' soul eh'.. Drisko, Dooley the Fat Man they all stare, bewildered.. He z' come free, Drisko said with his voices, it's time to be freed, to be, re-owned, as they gaze at it.. It, gazing back to them..

It's an omen, the spirits, the sign, his voices are saying.. Drisko seeing the ghost of a thousand clansmen surround him and filling the Livery, floating, flinging.. Then one, a solo, kneeling, behind the sword, one menacing figure.. It's Eric, she whispers to Drisk, heads bowed, in total silence.. His sword, she says, hiding her words, it's been hidden, in the Livery, here all this time mi Lord.. Drisko, flinging his red mane from shielding his eyes.. Now, Drisko says, now it appears, here before me.. The group staring, awing at the gleam, fearful of its power, what it represents and to whom, it was fashioned for.. For he, that would now be master to it.. The gleam from it, beaming of silvers, the shine, reflecting out, drawing them in, enthralling them all.. The grasp was of thick twisted steel, coated with silver strands.. The top thinning to a ball then forming into a ring of gold, centering the Amber stone.. The ends, where it crossed to a T, then crosses to the handle guards, also silver balls..

What does it mean, Drisko reaching, contorted, afraid.. Speaking to it, asking it, as it shines at him, lights reflecting back into his ice blue eyes.. The blade, dense steel tapered three inches thick, tapered from half inch wide and a full four feet standing straight up outta the ground.. What is it you want of me, Drisko speaking to it, asking it, as he knelt into the shops dirt floor.. His long crinkled red hair untied, dangling, dusting the ground.. The grip itself, studded with precious gems, rubies, sapphire's, blackened stones, reds, blues, greens and diamonds.. Then at the center where all the parts collide, the family crest, on the hand guard, the insignia, the Oobbew tartan.. Tilting his head now, as if he was too small, too undeserving, to be looking at, no less speaking to, the Viking King.. The eyes, flicking, flashing, staring deep into the mirror..

The Ericson shutters, vibrating to the reversing, the eyes, locked into the rear view.. The rear view, shaking, shimmering, across the top of the dashboard.. The eyes locked, solid into the centre of the mirror, floating stationary there in the middle of the mighty blue Atlantic.. The whistle blows, it shatters Drisko's senses, the announcer announcing, the ship shuttering, bouncing in the waves.. Drisko waking from his trance, staring deep into the rear view, then out of the glass wall.. The shores, unfamiliar to Drisko's Viking eyes, approaching, he hears the battle cry..

Staring deep into the rear view, blank.. Then observing ahead, the sign set high, glowing orange, flashing, flashing, neon, "Attention", the next, "Do Not Start Engines Before The Vessel Has Completely Docked".. Then the third, "All Vehicles Must Enter, CANADIAN CUSTOMS INSPECTION".. Drisko was carrying a heavy load, the eyes, the mirror.. Only reflecting the long line of cars, now sitting, waiting, patiently.. Drisko could see the shore of Port Sydney, the sign prominently displayed, "Welcome to the Jungle", he blinks, just for a moment, a second in time, the sign prominently displayed, "Welcome to Nova Scotia" "Canada's Ocean Playground"..

Drisko calculating in his own mind, holy shit, I've been sleeping this whole trip, all six hours, telling it to the mirror.. Looking through it, for approval, the truth, or the lie.. Was I sleeping, is this me I see, here in this mirror, is it me, "I Am Monster", or just the vision or, was it all just a dream.. Staring, searching without real reason, just searching for the answer.. The exact moment in time, the perfect timing, the absolute right speed, the exact spot, the Tanger, the Mustang and Drisko.. Right there, right where the dirt meets the blacktop.. His little life and everything he cherished, perished that night at the bridge, at the Black Water River, there, near the Black Pearl, there, on Cripple Creek Pass.. Nobody ever wondered about ole' Drisk, why he'd run his Tanger in through those flats so hard, on into the bridge, everyone knew, exactly why..

Drisko feels the gentle ease of the Leif Ericson, landing on its mark, like the breath of a butterfly, it flutters.. The mighty warriors vessel, comes peacefully to a halt.. They slowly lower the ramp onto its position and shackle it locked.. Lights flashing, arrows pointing, whistles blowing, Drisko's blood is crueling.. He hears the might of the ancient battle cry, he turns to the thousands of warriors following him, bravely there behind him.. He lashes for the key, the insignia, the horse, dangling below the helm.. Sirens blaring, the Ericson was singing and she sang.. Drisko orders his men without fear, today we conquer, we have no homes, nowhere to run to, no one will save you, today we fight and win or we perish.. Drisko silent, then screaming out the orders to charge..

He grabs at the key like a weapon, the blood of a thousand clansmen crueling through his veins.. He turns it with force, nailing the petrol to her with the exact amount of oxygen to octane to fire the beast up, click, click, click, dead.. Drisko frantically, confused, firing and firing the key, click, click, click.. Drisko staring deep into the mirror, ice blue eyes, staring back into ice blue eyes, he fires it once more..

The cassette player dead, the battery dead, the dead song, the song, just too powerful..

The enemy's now charging, approaching the Tanger.. Drisko lowering the window as others charge his flank.. Drisk hollering out the window.. Go Eh', gives er' a push up de ramp der' eh'.. I'll rolls er' backwards, kick start the fucka' in reverse eh'.. Drisko revs the mighty stallion, the engine obeys and charges toward the gate and up the ramp.. The song, igniting his vision, *"When I'm tired and thinking cold, I hide in my music, forget the day. And dream of a girl I used to know. I close my eyes"*, lights, flashing, flashing, green.. Drisko motors up the incline, up past the Canada Customs Inspection Station, *"and she slipped away. She slipped away"*.. Watching the Ericson disappear into the rear view, he feels the thunder pounding in his heart, the beating of the bass, beating, he feels it, as it, feels him, *"it's more than a feeling, more than a feeling"*.. Drisko is now, completely off the Edge..

CHAPTER TWO
Travelin' Man

Drisko, holding hard onto the Edge, the station barely breaking out over the static as the last notes mumble through the stereo.. He reaches to find the seek button, hitting it as the dial slides into position and locks in the sound.. The BEAT, 107.9, you're listening to the heart beat of Nova Scotia.. The heart starts beating the tempo, beating harder, then harder into the pulse, into Drisko, beating the tune out.. The song, opens into the rhythm, Drisko tapping, tapping, mouthing the words in timing as they entered the Tanger.. Spilling them out through the quadraphonic speaker system, Seger exploding on cue, mixing the notes, with the voice, *"Up with the sun, gone with the wind. She always said I was lazy. Leaving my home, leaving my friends. Running when things got too crazy"*.. Drisko, sucking the words in, gentle with feeling, breathing them out, into the wind..

    Drisko racing the Mustang high over the ridge, leaving the North Sydney Ferry Terminal in his rear view, the mirror.. Clipping the top of the hill, he throws the shifter into forth and glides down the other side, opening the views up, *"out 'neath the stars. Feeling the breeze, passin' the cars."*, clear across the horizon.. The sun slowly sinking into the west, Drisko sees it brilliant, the colours colliding into one another.. Streaking the sky, with shades of blues, greens, oranges and yellows, shivering into reds, with slashes of blacks, outlining the clouds with images of his past..

Pictures of warriors, painted, there in the sky, swords piercing into the heavens, warships cresting.. The dragons serpent head with huge wings flying stationary there in the clouds.. The Pissing Mare Falls, picturesque, flowing over the edge, dropping deep into the pond and estuaries below.. The raging torrent of the Black Water River, flowing from it, as it cascades out and over deep, into the mouth.. The Black Pearl, sitting, statistically, staring out onto the old wooden covered bridge.. The bridge, too small and too insignificant to be of much importance, barely visible.. A spec, there in the eye of the Gods, in the face of the mighty blue Atlantic, there, in the clouds, the bridge.. The sign ahead visible, big, wooden, blue, with reflective white letters.. Then the rushing of the waves, crashing, painted ocean green, circling creatively into it, as it catches Drisko's eye, Welcome to Cape Breton Island, "Your Heart Will Never Leave"..

Twenty percent of the Nova Scotia Peninsula call themselves Cape Bretoners, while the rest, well, they're all East Coasters, Bluenosers.. Drisko relaxes back, eases on the wheel to enjoy the ride, shifting, sliding, re-shifting with the wind.. The thrust of the Thrush, thrusting out the muffled sounds.. The mighty eight, obedient to his command.. Drisko's climbing, the song is singing, the wind is howling and the sky, the sky is falling.. Everywhere Drisko looks, the sun is setting gently to the west, blood sky.. He's travelling south, high in the Appalachian Mountain Range, heading south west as far as south west can go, as far away from the Rock, and the blood, as he can get..

Drisko hammers the Tanger up the Trans Canada Highway, 105 connection, up past the Main Street at junction 125 and up, *"some were so sweet, I barely got free. Others they only enraged me."*, then on to the three leaf clover, sliding the shifter high.. The green marker sign Bras d'Or, 5 kilometres, Little Bras d'Or, a little further, 6 kilometres.. Then the sign for Millville Boularderie 10 k.

"made me a wealthy soul. Travelin' man, love when I can", as he shifts up over the tiny bridge.. Then the sign for Big Bras d'Or, Drisk fumbling in his mind, the humour of it all.. Bras, little bras, big bras which one should I pick, he ask himself in his silent voice.. He pours another ounce of pure blood line octane up into the pedal, spitting enough oxygen into fuel to make the Mustang jerk her gorgeous face and obey.. The blood rushing, *"Travelin' man love when I can. Turn loose my hand, cause I'm goin','"*, pushing up into the animal as Drisk controls the thrust.. Up in through the headers, in past the custom chrome valve covers, across the top of her tiny block.. Then twisting below her tortured lungs, *"those are the memories that make me a wealthy soul."*, injecting her, hard, deep, in precision timing, pushing the venom, up into her..

Drisko steering, the venom beating up into the wild stallion, veering her left, coasting along the 105, grooving to 107, flying on past the junction of old rural route 5.. Passing the Big ole' Bras, doing about 120 and on into the sunset.. The sun still hanging in the sky, ready to dip deep behind the edge, hiding in plan sight, below the horizon.. Two hours he's thinking, two hours till the sun won't shine, and with it, comes the night, *"Travelin' man, travelin' man'."*, the drums, beating, beating into him..

Drisko cranks the tune, the music surrounds him, dragging him deep, *"Sometimes at night I see their faces, I see the traces they left on my soul"*.. The Mustang humming along the blacktop, the tune humming along behind him.. The Thrush mufflers, humming along in the rear view, *"Tell you, those are the memories that made me,"*, the lead guitar slashing out electric notes, as Drisko goes thrusting down the highway.. The sign green, clear, Antigonish 30 k., Gas, Ass or Grass nobody rides for free, next exit, he laughs.. The gas tank's empty, his belly's empty, the road is empty and bare, Drisko sparks up a doob, drifting gently off the edge..

Drisko now racing the Tanger against the sun as it is slowly setting to the west.. He revs the little Tanger high, as he approaches, *"turn loose my hand 'cause I'm goin','"*, there ahead the city limits, the sign "Welcome to Antigonish".. Drisko enjoying the views approaching, gearing down, letting the Tanger ring from the thrust as he drops her to third.. The Tanger coasting, in through the rural route into town.. Slipping past the small shops and automotive supplies stores dotting the road way, closed mostly.. The neon light, flashing ahead, Irving Petro Bar and Fundy's Diner.. The antique road side diner looked perfectly inviting.. Drisko slows the Tanger to a crawl and crawls off the highway to park in front of the painted glass windows.. The Mustangs windshield reflecting his black hair, drenched in streaks of red..

Drisko sits outside the Diner window looking in, the scene so attractive.. Looking like a scene, from a Norman Rockwell painting.. The Diner is alive with the fifties style, Drisko staring into the painting.. The waitress rushing to the tables, the cook hollering out the orders.. Drisko sees him perfectly through the huge glass window, reflecting the image, the cook, resembling uncle Bev.. The glass reflecting, the Tangers windshield reflecting, *"I'm goin' on. Travelin' man, travelin' man,"*, the rear glass windshield reflecting, as the reflections all danced in through the Tanger and into Drisko's mind.. He stares, not seeing but looking, seeing the images dance as they intertwine with the visions as they dance into Drisko's mind.. *"Sometimes at night I see their faces, I see the traces they left on my souls."*.. Drisko, the song, entwining him, devouring him, the song takes him, deep into the vision..

Drisko standing watch over his injured uncle, there in the hospital bed at C.S.C.. Him, bereaving deep in his sorrow, watching the electric gizmos flash on and off, tearing as he held his uncle in his sight.. Gently hovering his hand slightly above the rust seeping gauze bandages that wrapped eighty present of Bev's frame.. Only touching him through his energy and spirit.. I know you can feel me Bev, feel my power, feel my soul.. Feel me he demands, silently, voicing the words, his blue eyes drenched in a river of tears from within his sight.. I know you can hear me man, hear me.. The voice now trembling with fury, I am your blood, I run with you, we're kin, I run through you, we flow the same river Bev.. What is you, is me and what will always be.. Creeping now, his voice churning, drawing from his ancestral blood, his dialog rescinding, the Viking, the Norsemen, the Oobbew Clan..

Drisko leaning in close to Bev, a whisper, without a voice, a breath, flowing beyond the bandages and into the spirit of the man, into and throughout his entirety.. A kiss without motion but raptures him with feeling.. Then clothing it in some Gaelic, Gothic tongue.. A total transmutation of thoughts, Drisko propelling his commands into Bev's brain through his telepathic powers.. Soon you will awake, his voice thundering like a God, yet silent.. But he shall be never more, he, shall, kiss, the Cod, as the boy's mind pictures the power of the Gods penetrating into Bev.. I shall see it through, with my hands, my word Bev, as Drisko deposited a tear onto Bev's lips from his final motion of a kiss, it drops, my word.. Drisko wakes from the trance, revs the little Tanger as the lights of the Diner dance..

What if, what if it was all an illusion, or more so, real, but like a puppet on a string thing? What if, what if we are all controlled by some very real force, perhaps a God like creature if it needs an illusion? What if, what if we were all just pieces, pieces of a game, maybe an ancient game or maybe something more futuristic? Something, like an rubics cube, or magic dice or something more in depth, like a supersonic, mind boggling, obnoxiously impossible for us to possibly believe, but then we do? We are all controlled by an uncontrollable force, a destiny, a path.. A pre-set journey, a programmed standard input into who, what, where and when every single motion of you is.. Einstein with his theory of spacial relativity and his "man in the box", demonstration, proving light curves as mass moves.. Everything connecting, constantly creating, moving within itself, everything as a simple matter, programmed.. So why is it so hard to believe in reality? Simply, reality can make you insane..

Psychopath, as it defines a person, as suffering from a chronic mental disorder with abnormal violent behaviours.. Lack of empathy, lack of feelings for others, selfishness, lack of guilt, and a superficial charm for manipulating others.. Sociopath, a person with extreme antisocial attitudes and behaviours and a total lack of conscience.. Described as, "bottleneck attention syndrome", where they can only focus on one activity or train of thought at a time.. They lack self identity all together, they would not recognize their own responsibilities for their actions, nor of their involvement.. Schizophrenia, Narcissism, dual or multiple personality disorders, border line personality disorders, bipolar and depression.. Including the countless debilitating sub-disorders, as in, anxiety disorders, panic attacks, phobias, G.A.D., O.C.D. and P.T.S.D..

The good news about mental disorders is that, there are only about ten major disorders.. Disorders that could prompt someone to horrific acts of violence or murder.. The other good part about that news is that, they truly only represent about five percent of the world population.. Which isn't that bad as a number.. But, when you actually calculate it into ten potential mental disorders and five percent affliction level.. Well it leaves you with fifty percent of the world adult population, as potentially mentally unstable or more so, as potential, psycho killers..

So in theory, if you're sitting in a room with ten strangers, there's a fuckin good chance three of them could methodically be planning on how to kill you.. Where as studies show the other two, at any given time, more likely than not, they'll just snap on you, without warning.. To extend on that theory, calculating the probability to the umpth degree.. If you're sitting with your lover, watching Crime TV., there's a fifty fifty chance, one of you is going to be the star on the next episode, one day.. It all sounds too incredibly crazy to comprehend, truly unbelievable, simply insane.. Until you calculate into it, the factor, of time.. Then add to that, the factor of the prescription drug machines.. The billion dollar justice system and the multi billion dollar business of institutionalizing human chattel..

Most mentally impaired people don't ever get better.. In fact they get worse, pumped full of mind altering, hallucinogens, psychedelic drugs.. Compounds of AMT, MeO-DMT, ibogaine, 2C-B, 2C-1,

Carbogens, Mescaline, psilocybins, MDMA as in their street name, "Ecstasy" and "LSD".. Their purpose and primary medical function is only in altering moods and perception of the brain.. The cortex, where they activate the 5-HT2A receptors.. For most, there is no cure, but instead, guaranties a life time of reliance and addiction.. In many cases, psychiatric problems go undetected, denied or justified by friends and family.. They simply refuse to acknowledge the illness, a reflection of family values and dysfunctional behaviours within the hive.. Until they kill, then it becomes noticed by the lawmakers and families and friends, from both sides.. Then, the end, then simply the gentle rotation of the world and with it a new, a new beginning, till the end..

Drisko keys the Tanger in his trademark fashion, dangling the Mustang logo from his centre digit, his way.. Then he slowly struts up the five concrete steps, taking in the night breezes of Antigonish as it's gently blowing south east in off the Northumberland Straits, he can taste the ocean salt.. Watching as the sun sinks in beyond the horizon.. Drisko sliding in through the double doors, them reflecting back into the diner entrance.. Ding ding, ding ding the door bell chimes, jarring his memory.. The memories flashing in rhythms, a kaleidoscope of visions, the Emporium, the fire, Bev, the hospital bed, bleeding through the rusty gauze bandages, in the I.C.U.. The visions flickering through him, live and in motion.. Reflecting to him once again, as the four doors collide into each other, into perfect position, motioning the images through it, in frame by frame, in through the outer glass walls.. Moving it towards him, into his vision, all in unison, the movies flowing in through his eyes, into his own theatre, of his mind..

The rock n roll beat was breaking throughout the place as he enters into the sweet sounds of the sixties.. The old classic jukebox was rockin' out the end of Elvis, the hound dog.. Drisko could feel the buzz, the beats beating him, filling him.. Drisko losing the memories, as he takes a booth, in front of the painted glass window.. He could feel the record changing, the chug, the drop, the arm raising, the scraping and skidding of the steel as it is landing on the vinyl.. The song pouring in through him, the soulful notes, digging into his heart.. The sensational vocals of Hatfield, pitching up, for his Unchained Melody.. Drisko sitting there high above the Tanger's gleaming chrome grille, looking out as he admires her, listening, he smiles at her as he slides her a little wink.. The lyrics ignite, softly, sweetly, *"Oh, my love, my darling, I've hungered for your touch, A long, lonely time"*.. The young brunette approaches him, smiling, thank you she says, smiling straight into Drisk.. Confused Drisko replies with a hu' and a shoulder shrug..

Oh I saw you winking at me there handsome, her smiling wide, all perky, cute like, joking and flirty.. Drisko laughs, oh' my car he says, smiling.. Not to say your not worth winking at dolly, he smiles again the trademark, his lure, for when he's fishing.. Flashing her with his hook, blinking his steel, ice blue eyes in perfect harmony.. The song sings, *"I need your love, I need your love, God speed your love to me"*, she sighs.. Drisk watches her melt into the back seat of his Tanger..

Gorgeous wheels she says a tad embarrassed, but focused on Drisk and his wheels.. She could feel the song pounding in through her thighs, up to her nipples, deep into her throat and deep, deep into her heart, it twitched.. Emily, giving him her name as she drops the plastic menu and spins to hustle away.. Hold on there Emily, what's your rush? Drisko smiles out to her, grabs me a couple cold Black Horse's there would ya dolly and a, as she interrupts him, Keith's or Hounds, maybe a Black Cap, IPA, she smiles back.. Her voice ringing Gaelic and sweet, angelic, the song, singing, *"Wait for me, wait for me, I'll be coming home, wait for me"*..

Emily waltzing her way back to the booth with the rhythm of the beats, the song singing slow and soulful.. Drisko noticing her sway, her hips, thin, gentle in their movement, but timed to the beat of her heart, her sway.. Her slight of height amused him, tiny, tight, he said in his silent voice.. She leans forward to him, smiling, dropping the Keith's to the table top.. Her shirt, black, buttoned to the top, as she leans, the shirt fills him with their vision.. The sound thundering off her breast as its pounded against the black, desperately trying to escape their confinement, pushing against the tiny buttons.. Drisko's eyes filling with the motion, the spring of them, the force they welded, the mass of her, of Emily.. Him thinking, "I could help her with that", Drisko he says, throwing out his name for her, she smiles.. Know what you want Drisko, she asks, sure do, he smiles again? Then he throws a shot of ice blue into wheat field hazel, the eyes smile, trapped, she turns, trying to escape, she quickly runs away..

Drisko finishing up the last dips of the house special.. Huge slab of meatloaf, mashed potatoes smothered with homemade gravy.. Corn, peas and beans, plus the garden salad.. Two slices of Apple pie cheesed and the two Keith's Ale.. The little bit of chatter, the bantering back and forth, the jokes and laughter between them.. Drisko locked his eye on young Emily, the constant smiles, the eyes connecting, the timing, the tunes.. She approaches, swaying, Drisko's curious but tired and he knows his road is long..

He pays the bill, hesitating, her standing perfect in his view, he smiles, drops her a nice tip as he asks.. Any really good hiding spots around these parts Emily?. Somewhere I can park near the lake, little camp fire and a snooze before I head out dolly"? She grabs the napkin and scratches out the route for him.. My friends and I all hang out there, its secluded, quite and right off the edge.. Their eyes met perfectly, one last romantic truth, a lovers good bye.. Then again, as he sat in the Tanger, the eyes, a final connect, there, through the diners painted glass, she blows him a kiss..

Drisko fires up the doob, smiling, blowing the puff into the night sky.. The sky filled with black lines and red dots, dancing behind the cloud of smoke and embers as he throws another couple of logs onto the fire pit.. Drisko staring deep off into the mighty Atlantic, up beyond the magic of the Milky Way, over and into the Helix Nebula and far off the edge, deep into outer space.. He could see straight up and out, clear across the entire universe from this vantage point.. Puffing on the toxic smoke, he wanders into the vision.. The Wizard, Boomer announcing the man's presence, as if he were of royalty.. The Wizard, looking at each man one by one, staring Drisko in his eyes, bowing to Drisk without sight..

The Wizard, Boomer announcing his name again, slapping onto Drisko's lap, this is his brew.. She maybe the Witch, but only he can summon her, he is the Wizard.. Boomer speaking, as if they should be very, afraid.. Drisko, looking into the man's face, noticing, scars and cracks, he traces him to a hundred years, if not more.. Drisko simply intrigued by the man, Drisko's in awe at his presence.. Boomer again, speaking with respect, quietly, he, and he alone, holds the key to the magic of the potion.. 'Tis him and only him, who knows the secret magical ingredients to the formula.. So he and he alone, controls, the Witch..

The ole' man now speaking, in Goth, no words could be found familiar.. Drisko looking, noticing the staff, the long twisting, the bends, the inner twinning of the branch.. Drisko recognized the sacred Sceptre, from ancient tales, folklore, the stories.. The history of the Viking explorers, the parties of Leif Erickson, the colonizing, ravishing, inhabiting of the new world.. Drisko beholds the sacred staff in his vision, eyeing it, intently, searching on it, onto every detail.. Drisko recognized the root.. The staff made from a single natural twisting root of the resourceful black Ash tree..

Fraxinus Nigro, the ancient name of the sacred tree, native to Newfoundland.. This staff was snatched from the ground, during the first landing and takeover of the new world.. A tiny, injured warrior, used it to defend himself, from his vast enemies.. After killing a thousand men with it, the Clan recognized it as sacred, with mystical, magical, deadly powers.. So they deemed it a Witches staff, then deemed him the Wizard, the ruler of the Sceptre, the wheeler of all knowledge, ancient, current and beyond, even into your imagination, all seeing, all powerful..

The shaft twisting and turning a clean three feet over the stooped man's head.. The ball of it, the head, naturally formed, with tiny roots, protruding from the top, looking as if it had some evil black hair do.. The eyes, naturally set, from broken root shoots as it was ripped from the earth.. Inset, two tiny specs of natural steel balls, flowing, following you, as the shaft swayed and shimmered, in the old man's grasp.. The nose pointed, upward, like a tiny thorny horn, a Rhino's snot.. The mouth, was perfectly rounded, puckered and protruding, open to a kiss.. Detailing the final feature, forming a perfectly, ghoulish, ancient face, a voodoo thing, a human shrunken head.. A sign to all enemies of this brave warrior.. A formidable soldier, formed out of tree root, protecting and battling all and every foe, formed from the fruit of this Rock, over a thousand years ago..

The ancient man, the Wizard, cracking the wand to the wooden floor of the massive room.. Echoing the sounds in unison, one, two, three, they combine, bouncing, banging like a bass drum, the beat of the oars men, pushing the Casandra, prepping for battle.. Darting, dancing in rhythm, through the Masters Quarters, ringing back, off the darkened wooden walls.. Pinging, on and off, all that glittered, all that was silver, all the mirrors, glass and the small traces of gold, it rang.. The song filling into each ear, pounding the rhythm, squeezing the beat into them, pulsing it through into their hearts.. Deep inside their ancient blood, now, pounding, they were alert.. The old man, recklessly tossing his cape, his silver hair flinging, dangling, long to his calves, the Wizard, now swirling the staff as he's chanting, Gaelic, Gothic, dancing.. Circling the baton, high above his head, slowly, precious, like a majorette, in a parade, he swirled and twirled it, blindly, yet controlled..

Boomer leaning into Drisko, we call him the Wizard, because he's pure fucking magic.. Drisko never taking his eyes off the old man, as Boomer and him clink the Black Horses together, tail to tail.. Drisko watching as the old man chants, listening to the words, remarkably understanding.. The old man, staring, sealed into Drisko's new blue eyes and Drisko, staring into his old.. The Wizard twisting and turning the staff, shaking it, calling out words to it, then, he vibrates and giggles, screaming out a chant.. He flings the head of the shaft, straight, into Drisko's forehead, the hair barely flickering on his hair, laughing, chanting in some voodoo tongue..

Drisko's eyes filling with evil from the sticks face.. Again the old man chants into Drisko's eyes.. Drisko looking at the eyes, direct, circling, spinning, in the ugly sticks head.. The nose stretching, like a weapon, a small spear, reaching out with the point, the thorny horn, in close, up to Drisko's nose.. Then the old man thrashes the staffs puckered lips, up to touch on Drisko's lips.. With a breeze, of a kiss, he chants, Gaelic, then laughs, ghoulish..

He pulls the staff back, slowly, across the Shrouded table, drawing the face over the shield and into his own, face.. He kisses the head on the lips and screams out, harshly, hauntingly, like the Devil, evil.. The eyes, in the head of the Sceptre, now spinning.. The eye in the centre of the table still spinning.. The old man screaming, driving the Sceptre over the Eye of God, into the centre of the large, wooden table, screaming..

The Sceptre spewing, red flowing blood fluids, straight out of the wooden puckered lips, onto and into the Helix Nebula.. The eye, burning, from the potion, it smokes and screams from the fluid clogging its path, as it churns.. It whistles, the smoke thick, black, fuming.. Boomer, leaning into Drisko again, I told ya dude, pure, fucking magic.. Boomer grabs the silver cap, drawing the straw to his mouth, sucking the plume into his lungs.. Looking at Drisko, puff up dude, suck in the Witch.. The smoke bellowing, the room spinning, the music loudly filling the air, Drisko, was, a buzz.. The bee's swarming him, everything was buzzing..

Holy fuckin holy brother, by geez, what the fuck is in this stuff? The words, escaping him in slow motion, trying to form the sounds, as he exhales the toxic smoke.. I told you bro, he's magic, he's the fuckin brewmeister, the Wizard, the key to the Witch.. Stick around brother, he'll be summoning her soon, then we're all fucked.. Drisko and Boomer laughing with heart, all the men cheering, slapping and clinking their tiny silver cups.. Snapping back the shots, of pure Newfie, one hundred proof Viking Blood Screech.. Brewed by the

Meister, carried here a thousand years ago.. Throwing the shots of fire, between their burning lips.. Chasing them down with potato ale and lagers, cheering him and throwing toast, at the grandness of the Wizard..

Drisko, sitting, somewhere along the shoreline of Antigonish Harbour, seeing the embers flickering beyond him.. As he sits under the starry sky, up on the edge, there in front of the Tanger's trunk, backed into position.. Drisko sitting there, on a perfectly smoothed log, playing his six string acoustic guitar, wailing on her.. Feeling her up, rubbing her down, fucking her hard as he would, singing to her, sultry, seductively, there in front of the fire pit, as it sparks.. The light flicking, like fire flies floating off the edge.. The sound of the wounded beast screaming in his ears, over the screaming of the Aria and his beastly vocals.. He's awakened to the animals squealing, aware now, he's awaking from his self induced trance, the song, far too powerful, holding him into the visions, as he sang his own sad songs..

Aware, of the animal, wounded, blood thirsty, screaming, screaming out over the Mustang's hood, something's spooking the ole mare.. Then the shouting, clearer, closer, shouting, shouting out a name, calling to him.. Drisko, Drisko, Drisk, that you boy, the animal growling, louder and then louder.. Now the animal was on top of him, as it screams.. Drisko standing, eyes stretching, ready, he reaches into the small of his back, to the belt loop.. Gripping his Walther PPK special, the one that granddad left him, the replica, James Bond 007 side arm he carried to keep the animals at bay.. His hand wrapped around the grip, his finger poised on the trigger, the gun resting in the belt loop, ready for action, prepared for battle..

Drisko, the voice softer, echoing to Drisko as it calls, feminine, soft and sweet, young, warm, kind and a little frightened.. Drisk could see her in the dark, walking past the Tanger, slowly toward him, ghostly, calling to him, hi, hello, it's me, Emily.. Drisko smiles, releasing the grip on the PPK., hey, hello, you startled me, what are you doing here, his voice excited? Wasn't tired, bored, thought I'd see if you found your way okay, and I see you did? Ya, great spot Emily, thanks, was just enjoying the fire and the night..

Want a cold one, she ask? I stole a six pack of Hounds from the fridge, as she hands Drisko a bottle, popping the top for him, flicking it off the edge.. Careful with these Hounds doe boy, dey's got s' a bite.. Drisko soaking in her Gaelic drawl, the lingo, from the Cape.. Drisko and Em, just sitting there on the edge, staring gently into each others eyes, enjoying a couple of cold ones.. You toke Emily, oh' ya baby, why you got s' she says? Ya I got s', he smiles at her with the answer, and what I got s' is killer green, they smile bigger, brighter, the eyes igniting..

You's can call it what you will, call it Karma, intuition, transcendental meditation, wishing upon a star, or pure mind bending focus.. Call it thinking about something, imagining it, dreaming about it, making it a burning desire until it materializes.. Call it the killer green, call it the edge or the Helix Nebula.. Maybe it just is what it is, two ships passing in the night, pure coincidence, finding each other out there like a spec, in the middle of the Atlantic.. Call it fate or call it the laws of attraction.. Call it two eyes meeting two eyes, call it destiny or meant to be, call it the evolution of the world, or it's as simple as an act of God..

No mortal man breathing, no one alive really knows, what it is.. Maybe the dead know, but they've all been sworn to secrecy.. No human intelligence could ever truly say what it is for sure.. All of us however, everyone of us, each individual, every once in a while, knows it is real.. When you recognize the possible and eliminate the improbable all that can remain, in its purest form, is the truth.. Knowing it as reality and knowing, it has to come to you from some very special place, a strangely deranged, far off place.. A distinctive and completely distant place, with an impressive, illusive and unpredictable higher power.. Containing the entire secrets of the universe.. Some very real form of a cosmic energy, propelling you, completely out of your control and in some people, with mental disabilities, it is capable of sending them, spiralling, completely off the edge..

We all know it to be true, all of us, each one, less none.. Though it is incredibly hard to explain to the human mind.. Far too baffling to comprehend and even harder to truly identify.. Therefore it is simply easier to believe the lies.. Knowing the truth for us, yet believing the lies, the answer becomes simple.. A normal mind, the brain calculates, the pure depth of the issues confronting it.. Creating, reactive Neuro-transmitters, a 5-HT2A, slowing the thought patterns, organizing them into importance and then depleting them..

The brain, has highly sensitive monitors built into it.. They have triggering mechanisms controlling your reflex and awareness as a protective and defensive mechanism.. The human brain will simply divert you from such issues as it would in a feel or in-clink or that gut jerk reaction we have when we sense danger is pending.. The brain, would simply protect you.. Because the truth is, the truth could, make you completely, clinically insane.. Like the other fifty percent of the world, that do not have the proper, defensive mechanisms..

Drisko fires up the Mustang, lighting her up, as he's leading her out of the dark pasture, rolling her gently across the grass top lane.. Trotting her up the dirt path, out onto the Trans Canada Hwy 104.. Drisko looking back through the rear view, watching the edge gently drift away, catching the blacktop as he heads down the road.. The white ridges of the translucent sheets, stretching, across the horizon.. Vividly sketching out the topography of the landscape.. Highlighting the hilly terrain clear across the blackened skyline.. Night has fallen, and with it comes the daylight, a new, a new beginning, him thinking, a new adventure for Drisk, he smiles.. Drisko hammering up through the gears, putting the thoroughbred through her paces.. Climbing the rocky terrain, gliding up over the top, looking back, watching Antigonish and Cape Breton Island disappear, sinking slowly into the Atlantic..

Drisko watching as the skylight dances above the ridges, opening, page after page, mile by mile the sky is lighting up.. Catching the sign, New Glasgow 50k., Truro 115k., Moncton New

Brunswick 280k.. Then the sign to Dartmouth 90k.. Drisk was on an adventure, the stereo humming out the tune, Drisko grove n' to the rhythm, to the beat, the song filling the morning air, raging, *"Out to the road, out 'neath the stars.. Feeling the breeze, passin' the cars. Women have come, Women have gone,"..* The sign lights his eyes, his temptation rising, his blood crueling, Dartmouth, Coal Harbour, exit, Junction 102.. His temptation fires, his subconscious mind controlling him as he thinks it all out..

I got s' kin there south shores, Nova Scotia, all through them parts.. Drisk talking himself into it, talking in his silent voice, deviously.. Drisko, thinking it out, if I take the switch back around here, I's can learn the area a bit.. Then when folk is askin me where s' I's from, I's can just tell them, I'm a Bluenoser, from the east coast, Nova Scotia, his new identity, for his new life.. Drisko, swearing the blood oath, there inside the Tanger in his silent voice.. No body will ever connect me to the Rock again, as long as I live, I'm leaven her far behind, *"memories that made me a wealth soul. Travelin' man"*, forever.. Drisko looking at his long black locks hanging in the mirror, he's changed, he's complete.. He hammers the Tanger hard into second, slowing the beast, pulling the reins hard, grabbing on the bit, forcing the harness, swinging the stallions head.. Driving her left, hard and off the T.C. 104 and deep south east, on the 102, hoping to find his home..

Drisk wheels the Tanger through the main streets of Dartmouth, consciously marking his mind with details of interest.. This isn't his home, he knows that, but he needs the details for his chatter, he's relying on it, storing the knowledge, keeping the wolfs at bay.. Drisko has never left the Rock, ever, in all his 28 years.. Cripple Creek Pass has been home, his life was spent living on the edge, up by the Black Water River.. He wheels the Tanger through the city streets, catching the bypass to Halifax, cruising the main drags, noting, the Museum of Natural History, the campus of the renowned Dalhousie University and some of the other interesting tourist traps there..

Drisko fires the Tanger across the 102, to Beechville, veering left out into the back track, deep into south shores past the Halifax Exhibition Centre, down junction 333, in through Prospect Road, as he lets her go.. The Tanger flying out the backroad, connecting to the 103, taking up wind and spitting out dust as the animal gallops through the path.. Hatchet Lake, noting, noting, Brookside, Whites Lake, noting, Big Lake, East Dover and up into Peggy's Cove..

Drisk slows the stallion down, slowly approaching, the lighthouse, taking in the beauty, the serenity, the magic of the cove.. Drisk kills the engine, the song still sings as he keys the Tanger, *"I tell you those are the memories that make me a wealthy soul. Travelin' man, love when I can"*, the logo left dangling in his hand.. He enters the restaurant and heads for the ocean side patio deck.. What's can I get cha' my friend, the bubbly lady ask.. Two Hounds, he lingers, holding the words with the memories of Emily, two hounds and a menu, please, right up she smiles..

Drisko sitting there in Peggy's Cove, sucking back a Hound, waiting for his lunch order, watching the icebergs as they gently flow past him, through the sound, out in the Atlantic, the sound singing into him. *"sooner or later I'm goin' on. Travelin' man"*.. Him, soaking in the afternoon sun, soaking, warm, he slides, slowly into his memories of Emily from last night.. The thought igniting him, *"they left on my soul. Those are the memories,"*.. The kiss, stirring him, stirring his juices, he remembers her there, so easy, so open, so willing.. The kiss, the kiss that got it all started, him sitting on the smooth log, explaining to her, what the song meant to him, why he wrote it.. Singing his song as the sparks are flying out of the pit, off the burning logs.. Snapping and cracking out the back beat, sparking into the dark as he sung..

She simply couldn't resist she said, whispering as she leaned into him.. It's just too beautiful of a song, she explained, too powerful, staring into his eyes, the sparks flinging in all directions.. You wrote that for me she said, it's just so me, how.. Her lingering in front of him, hoping he would take her.. She leans, again, closer and lingers, waiting as he leans into her.. Kissing her, he blindly reaches behind him to the gun, throwing it under the car tire, exact on the mark.. Still holding the guitar, he slides it off his lap and gently leaning it onto the Tangers trunk as he holds her neck in his free hand kissing her, deep..

She lingers, standing, leaning into him, allowing him to smother her mouth with his.. He's touching her, low, hands sliding, moving, slow.. Searching, feeling the shades of each colour, finding the intricate difference from each texture, each fabric as he searches through her tiny structure.. Fondling and feeling, curving and tracing, judging the lowlands from the mountainous terrain, tracing the course, kissing her silly, into submission..

He grabs her hips, stripping her of her jeans.. She complies, holding her in his lips, sitting her, straddling her across his lap.. She thrusts and moves, finding the huge stump embedded in her crotch, he enters her.. She moans as Drisk drives the spire into place, her on him as he grinds the fuck out of her.. Holding her mouth captive in his, she can barely breathe as she thrusts, spitting out her venom onto his shaft, as she screams..

Drisko blindly finding the black cotton, the plastic feel of the buttons.. Calculating the exact location, exact latitude and longitude he was from the top of the mountains.. Blindly, he surges forward, as he felt his way through the darkness.. Her, leaning over the Tanger now, him thinking she's talking to the car.. Fuck me you animal, as Drisk enters her smoothly from behind.. Pumping her hard, her feeling his thrust, fuck me you stallion, oh fuck, she squeals out, fuck me, ya, like that, oh for fuck sake's eh', go boy.. Fuck me, pound that shifter right in through me.. Pounding through her, up into her gears, shifting with ease, ya like dat, dats it.. She pushes on him, stopping him as she frees herself.. Turning to Drisk, she jumps as he lifts her ass high onto the truck.. Her spires, dug deep into the hind of the animal.. Drisko without missing a stroke, throttling her as the Tanger bucks and the riders shake the shocks..

Drisko, grabbing Emily, dragging her down squatting her onto the soft smooth log, her face staring directly into the serpents face, and she knows, he is about to devour her.. He holds her head, gently around her chin, aiming her into perfect form.. He drives the spear forward, easing it in past her teeth, cautiously, yet curious to its depth.. He slithers it slowly over her tongue, yet without hesitation, she drives her head hard on to him quick and perfectly, devouring it and holding, the eyes locked.. Drisko looking her deep into her eyes, she's so fucking beautiful, this angle, this light, just beautiful..

He grabs her, lifting her into his arms, holding her, kissing her, carrying her, then throwing her gently onto the sleeping bag, laying there out by the fire pit, out on the edge.. He ravishes her, kissing her passionately with patience and affection.. They are lovers, making love, there by the firelight, there on the edge, there looking out over the mighty blue Atlantic.. Emily, laying there beside him, both naked, warm, spooning her.. He awakes, the fires dead, ashes, dust are all that remains..

She's gone, he looks, she's gone, her car's gone, he smiles as he looks, there on the trunk of the Tanger.. Sketched into the morning dew, a huge heart, with an arrow shot through it, with the words, Emily loves Drisko.. He laughs, then he sees in the corner, the note, "for a good time call," with her number, if you're ever back this way boy.. The waitress drops his drink, the tingle wakes him, *"Sometimes at night, I see their faces. I feel the traces they've left on my soul."*, your lunch be right up, *"those are the memories that make me a wealthy soul."*, dem flipper pies, days' be straight outta de' hole, for ya'..

CHAPTER THREE

The Immigrant Song

Drisko, fires up the 351 Cleveland, sitting idling there at Peggy's Cove.. Sitting, idling in the green, 1967 Ford Mustang coupe.. The one that him and uncle Bev re-built up in the ole Livery, up in Cripple Creek Pass.. The same one him and Bev journeyed to fetch, that cold November night, from St. John's Canadian Customs depot.. The night they dragged her home on the trailer, behind the fire engine red, 327 small block.. The 1968 mint condition, Chevy short box, the one that grandpa Eric left to Bev.. Sitting there, looking out into the mighty blue Atlantic, out past the cafe', out past the lighthouse, out past the cove and the icebergs, then deep into the blue..

He slides the crank into "R", taps the little chrome gas pedal and slides out the clutch gently, letting the animal take the lead as he hammers the "T" shifter up into first and countering the roll, as the tires lock and reverse into a forward motion, crawling.. Drisk idles her up through the dusty lane and out onto the blacktop.. Drisk hits her hard, the mighty engine roars, squealing the rubber onto the roadway.. Spraying a cloud of dust and debris up over the rear window, blinding the view of the cove as it disappears into a ghostly illusion..

Drisko heads the stallion, west northerly up the 333 to Indian Harbour on to French Village and connecting back to the 103 completing the circle and landing back just outside of Halifax.. He hangs the hard left and journeys deep into the heartbeat of Nova Scotia, you're listening to 107.9 The BEAT.. The announcer bringing his audience up to date with current events and activities going on in the area.. Then he queues his audience, with a deep seductive voice, Zeppelin, on 107.9, the song starts to sing, the guitar ringing, double picking on cue.. *"Ah-ah, ah! Ah-ah, ah! We come from the land of ice and snow. From the midnight sun where the hot springs flow. The hammer of the Gods we'll drive our ship to new lands"*. The song starts, Plant planting each note in timing..

Drisko sliding the gears up through the 103 south, deep into the heart, out past Bridgewater, out past Hunts Point, Sable River and down deep into the point, into Barrington, Drisko, noting, noting.. He takes the turn, hard, veering right, heading west, on the 3, deep into Argyle then over into Yarmouth, Nova Scotia.. Noting, noting, looking, tracking and noting, this is it, we're near it he says in his silent voice, very near, I got kin here, somewhere, Drisko noting, noting.. Drisko, cruising the town, checking it twice, looking, watching, noting..

Drisk pounds the petrol up through her pulse, she obeys and performs with precision, aiming her out over the tip and up into Beaver River, Bear Cove, over to RR# 1 and into Meteghan.. He can feel it, as he rolls along the ocean road way, making tracks to nowhere he knows, the song. *"sing and cry Valhalla, I am coming."*.. He can sees it, in his mines eye, there along the ocean.. Then it's there, the house standing in front of him, its totally familiar, he recognizes it instinctively, from old photos locked inside his mind..

The summer nights, all the cousins, relatives. visiting from all over Nova Scotia, up to the Rock, to the Edge.. All cuddling together, in the blue house, listening to the old men telling the ghostly tales of the Viking tribes up on the Edge.. Then he sees deep over the yard, out to the cliffs and out into the blue as he slows the Tanger down.. He recognizes it as familiar, except the area is different.. The photos showed nothing, nothing around the house back then, the house on the cliff was the original settlers home, the only one for miles.. Back then, back in 1856, it was the only thing here..

He stops the Tanger out front of the property, eyeing it for details, looking.. It seems vacant, empty, no one home, he parks and enjoys his view.. The large blue double story, wood sided home, the white framed fashioned windows.. Drisk could see the stained glass, hanging, a figure peering back to him.. The solid wood framed door, that opened to the porch, noting, noting.. Drisko looking, looking, watching as the waves wave, looking as the tall grasses sway in front of the sea..

The trees and bushes, strategically placed for comfort and shade, waving, friendly like.. The double car garage, set off from the house, everything about that home, seemed familiar, everything.. "I'm home", he said in his silent voice, "I've found you finally", the sign set promptly on the end of the drive, "Oobbew Estates" since 1856, "I'm home".. The song playing gently behind him, *"On we sweep with threshing oar. Our only goal will be the western shore."*..

Drisk stares out over the landscape, the visions, searching the edge, watching as the families gather, playful, watching them all there, now, at the Livery, out on the Edge, up in Cripple Creek Pass.. The friends, the people, family frolicking, the sea smiling behind them.. The picnics, the B.B.Q.'s, birthday's, weddings, anniversaries and every now and again, just a ripped up, barn burner, out there on the Edge.. Simple fun nights, hanging out with the gang, kissing the Horses ass, sucking up the Witch and smacking back the Screech.. Partying around the little camp fire, hanging off the edge.. Till someone throws a house on it, and the place takes to blazing.. Now you got yourself a party, Newfie style, he smiles, his heart felt the memories, the Livery, the Clan..

Looking, looking, he imagines the children, running, jumping, flying their kites, out off the edge.. Looking, eyeing, seeing in his vision, the owner is there now, kin, looking like him, Drisko or more so, uncle Bev.. He's riding a wild green pony or is it a deer.. He's charging it through the meadows, charging, clear across the fields with the tiny hounds trailing him.. The deer chewing, chomping. growling at everything.. Bev, sitting high in the saddle, smiling, waving, laughing it up, Drisk gently smiles.. The lady there, her summer flowered dress flowing with the breeze.. Her blonde hair shimmering in the sun as she waters the plants, out on the front stoop.. All of it trimmed nicely in white, all of it, Drisko, could feel it, noting, noting.. The scene complete, perfectly framed, autographed, as before, by Norman Rockwell, Drisko noting, noting.. *"Ah-ah, ah! Ah-ah, ah! We come from the land of ice and snow. From the midnight sun"*..

Drisko remembering, the vision, the big dark blue door of the tiny paisley house clicking closed, silently, as Bonnie raises her arms toward Drisko.. Laying bundled in the tight knitting of the Persian wool blanket, warming her.. The flames dancing lightly, lighting Bonnie's profile from the wood hearth toasting the sturdy structure.. Come here she cries out to him, her breast exposed from the sheet, the flames detailing her silhouette.. Her black hair shining, reflecting as it mirrors his movements, the light piercing his ice blue eyes, she can see his tears, com eer'..

He wallows his way through the large room, reaching her, now facing her, he breaks.. Falling to the planked wooden floor, he whimpers.. He's beneath her, crouched head first into her crotch, bent onto the floor now, weakened, defeated.. His body beaten, unable to offer support, he collapses into her and weeps.. She feels the warm moistness of his tears wet her, filling her crevasses.. He's gonna die, he cries, he wails, he tears, he's gonna die.. He's not gonna die Drisko my sweet boy.. She repels quickly, he's just in a coma, it's how they recover and they cried..

He slowly rises, kissing her neck gently, Bonnie speaking through Drisko's lifeless breaths, quietly, comforting.. It's okay baby, she repeated, it's all okay, mommy's here with you, every things gonna be okay.. Bev's made of steel Drisk baby, even Superman can't break that boy, it'll be fine, she holds him, rocking in a motion.. He roams generously around her, touching her, exploring her, holding her.. He latches onto her lip and draws it into his mouth, pinching her skillfully with his teeth.. She responds, sucking at him, wetting his mouth moist.. She tongues him, probing him, he anxiously responds, tonguing her, probing her, the tongues are wrestling.. He lashes onto the back of her neck under her black silk hair, one hand.. With his other hand guiding his thumb precisely into the jugular of her throat, controlling her head and directing it to accept his positioning, submissively..

The fireplace light flickering, erotic, glistening in the room throwing wild and frightening dark shadows of passion and fear.. He smothers her with his mouth, sucking her in.. Lashing intensely on top of her breast, her nipple naked, with his fingers, squeezing it tightly with some pain.. Now with teeth clenched, swallowing the other, pulling her in, releasing his kiss then gripping the mass and redirecting his mouth to centre it on the other, as he bites down and swallows with greed.. Cautiously, but with excruciating joy onto Bonnie's nipple and with glee he applies suction.. She screams wilfully, then she's silent, her head whipping with intensity..

He scrapes the rawness of his hand over her breast, clawing his way, dragging his nails behind it, animal like.. Pushing on the flesh, painfully, down the side of her outer thigh and up over her fine forming legs at the knee.. Drawing his hand slowly back up the inner of the thigh, spreading her legs and onto her clean crest.. Then circling her navel, three times.. Then cupping his hand and prancing, driving it rough and deep between her thighs.. Spreading her again, with a force she did not want to control..

Covering her drenched inner lips entirely, then applying pure skillful pressure, he tortures her.. Probing with manly fingers, rubbing at her briskly, massaging her to her soul, she shrills.. Her venom excruciating with agony, he probes her deeper, sensually, massaging deeper and deeper.. She lashes her tiny hand deep into his massive groin, probing, seeking, screaming, feeling.. She flings and frolics for his belt buckle twisting at it, as she ignites from his probe, howling..

The buckle simply unleashes, she jerks her locks back, black and whipping.. She grasps onto the button hook and masterfully secures its freedom.. She grasps and heaves at the zipper, cursing its existence.. She's desperate to release its cargo.. She snaps her head back, with pride, flipping her shimmering hair again, circling it into a bun and stabbing it, as she returns ready, with timing to revel her prey, waving it like a trophy.. She pushes on his chest, forcefully shoving him back into the darkened corner of the cracked and tattered old European styled, leather couch.. The fire from the hearth igniting ancient, erotic spirits, exotic, Gothic, tremendously sensual.. The naked blackened shadows dancing, pornographically, performing against the blackness of the hollows, while shimmering through the room..

The steaming of the bodies, vaporizing, clinging, sticking together, crystallizing, while truthfully reflecting the dramatization of the windows pane.. Lights dancing, colourfully into the exact rhythm and rhyme, reflecting like fairy dust.. The reflection of her feminine head in the mystic glass, slowly dancing in the shadows, skillfully, unmistakably bouncing the bun up and then down.. The other shadow, his devilish silhouette, his hair the locks jerking, flagging the mess of his mass, possessive, convulsing, devouring, un-rhythmically, hypnotic.. A parallel, to a haunting pornographic dance, from the shadows of the darkness of doom..

The visions blinding his eyes, the memories of Bonnie, entering the shop, helping herself to a Black Horse, cracking it with her hand, drawing hard to fill her thirst.. Miller she says, I fuckin know it's him, don't care what the fuckin cop have to say it's Miller eh' Drisk, as she stares at Dooley for confirmation.. The big green logoed five ton dump truck pulls up to the garage doors, half blocking the doors and the Mudder.. Cripple Creek Pass, Maintenance, "Where you only need the EDGE", creatively advertising their tranquil little piece of paradise.. Illustrated with huge seas crashing against the massive rock face, the reds, orange and yellows of the majestic sunset.. Fat Man, grab a beer baby, Dooley offers the big brother, how's it going eh'.. Big news from the Edge, Bernie announces, with privilege, from his inner circle.. Someone robbed the Blue, set the place a'blazing, old lady Fawlen was raped, tied up, beaten and left for dead, she's in a bad way eh', as he answers Dooley, Miller, he adds..

What the fuck is going on eh' up er' on da Edge, eh' wad da fuk, them understanding him but not, yet everyone got the gist.. Miller, Dooley and Bonnie replying at the same time.. You guys know Webo, Dave Webowski, the porter on the Leif Erickson, Fat Man asks.. Well he says Miller came over three nights ago, on the last run from Sydney, to Port aux Basques.. Talked right to him eh', the boys fucked up though, crazy.. What cha mean, Bonnie ask.. Well, Webo says it was like he didn't even recognize him, long scruffy blonde hair, patchy beard, like he was disguised.. Webo says it was like he wasn't even really there, talkin to the dead eh'.. He was almost scared of him, black eyes, hollow.. Dangerous, freaky eh', he couldn't quite put his finger on it, something's definitely off..

The friends sitting in silence, sipping their brew, quiet, still, thoughtful.. Webos wobble, but they don't fall down, Drisko says, slowly, as the group laughs.. That guy's always hammered eh', you can't trust a thing that drunk says, Dooley pipes up with reassurance.. The group laughs at the lighter side, smoking, drinking the brews.. Oh, Fat Man says, in a cough, hauling on the doob.. Webo says, he was driving a white beat up old shit'er of a Dodge, just a bucket eh'.. Fat Man letting out a huge bellow of laughter and smoke and choked as the rest remained silent, staring deeply, intently, into one another's eyes.. Then gazing lost off the Morne, off the edge, out into the misty Atlantic.. Blood, Drisko says, blood, let em' kiss the Cod..

Drisko's visions filling him of Sheriff Colbert there at the Livery, what the fucks going on here eh'.. Staring down the group, looking past Bernie, the Fat Man, deep into Bonnie, then across to Dooley, up and downing Drisko, then to Elvin, spill it up eh'.. Who tried to run you off the road, where and when? Elvin spilling it up, inserting every gory detail.. Then the gas damper blew eh', that's when I saw it was the Tanger, she almost caught mi tail, bitch, but I saw her clear, she was Drisko's Tanger, clear as shit Sheriff.. Drisko, not listening, eyeing intensely, Colbert.. The Sheriff, not listening but sensing, feeling the sharp, jarring, icicle blue eyes, piercing into him from Drisko, he's off the edge..

Something's off, his instinct, his training, something just didn't feel right.. His foot, now sensitive to the feel.. The ground, just slight enough, ajar enough to feel the off-ness of the texture beneath the boot.. Drisko's eyes cutting into the Sheriffs profile, the circle is closing.. Jon senses it, feeling it, cautious now something's really off.. He bends his hefty frame in a crunched, weight lifters position.. He squats, reaching downward, his hand perching, grabbing, eyeing the room for movement.. He digs and slides, he grips, then pries.. It jars, but un-budge-able, it bends, slightly, but won't rise..

Jon's realizing, he has the whole weight of both boots on the top of the object.. He steps, one foot off it.. Drisko now bent, like a raging wolf, half man, half animal, attacks Jon with his whole might.. Tackling him like a pro linebacker, sending Jon unprepared, but totally aware, into a full, back flip tumble.. He rises quickly, into a full Kung Fu stance, military trained, hand on the Sig Sauer P229 and prepared for action.. What the fuck, as Bonnie, Fat Man and Dooley surround him, he's ready for battle, but who, this is kin? Elvin now, also, missing the original show when the sword fell from the rafters, he was dumb-founded, flabbergasted, totally dumbfounded and discombobulated with no ideas in his head at all of what caused the kerfuffle.. Elvin cursing, looking, every angle, total chaos, who's who, who did what and why, this is kin, they're all blood, this is malarkey, what the fuck's going on here?

Drisko kneels, picks up the sword, raises it his full reach as voices appear from him.. Colbert, Dooley, Elvin, Bonnie, Rizer and Gleason, silent as he spoke.. Ne Go' ta tak ay das village to eye's to do god nord.. Go eh' ta seet at da table a hoy, ka noye, ta kinga tode he dies ye knod.. He says des ta da boy, day ta say eh, Go eh' spit a go se', ho lad bay to deayd dies or ay say Go eh'.. They kneel, not knowing why, they kneel, all of them, in prayer..

Uncontrollably afraid, but without fear.. Entranced, robotic as if programmed.. Hearing the voice speak in its tongue.. Recognizing every command, without knowing or understanding a single word.. Oh they've seen it, antiques and nick-knacks, family heirlooms and grave sites.. But to hear it, truly spoke, recognize it, for a new, to speak it.. The language was lost, long ago, from the ancient ones, the Kings language..

Bonnie whips the words through her throat, esey' syes mi lord, they all rise, taking places around Drisko.. Colbert barring his left, Bonnie to his right.. Then Dooley the others, all bow, Drisko's voice, again, rising in tongues.. He raises the sword, quickly releasing his might, allowing the sword to fling downward, then applying his might and flinging it upward, repeating the chant thirteen times, without ever understanding why.. His black hair blowing, ragged in the wind, again they all chant.. Releasing, this final time, the thirteenth fling, flinging it high, as it disappeared, as readily, as magical and as mystical as it originated.. Back up into the rafters and gone.. Go eh', Eh' ERICHIL' coma da VIK-GYK-INGK KGIKIN..

The wind died, the voices died, the grounds light up again.. The animals returned to the yard and the bird, all kinds of them chirping, endlessly at the warmth of this day.. The bee's, the bee's, they were all busily buzzing, again.. A silent, constant buzz, one Drisko, couldn't shake, as it stung him.. Everything was back to normal, like a group of friends hanging out on a Sunday afternoon.. Planning the day, having a BBQ, a picnic kinda day.. Drinking a couple of brewskies, puffin away on a couple of doobs.. Just having fun, except that buzzing, that constant, fucking, irritating, annoying, gnawing buzz kept stinging him..

Drisko remembering, his vision piercing through him, the news was shattering the tiny island.. The media, broadcasting the disastrous awry of violent acts perpetrated on the usually, normally, quieter than anything, island.. The smoke, rising from the fires, smoke signals bellowing out of the Morne, everywhere.. Headlights, cell phones flickering flashing out onto the coast.. Mirrored reflectors, flicking, strobing signals from up and down the edge, out to and across the blackened sea, the Edge was on fire, the Devil had come to the Rock and hell, he was on a roll..

Every man, woman and child has heard the news clear and wide.. They were broadcasting this news, via Morse Code, straight through the Port of ole' St. John's and clean on out, into the harbour, straight up da coast.. Clickety clicking, right out of the dead lighthouse, just above the walls, of the haunted fortress, of Signal Hill.. They say even the ghosts were screaming out his name, up dar, on da Hill.. Miller, they were praising him.. Everyone knew what was happening up dar in the Gros Morne, up off de Edge, up on Cripple Creek Pass.. Everyone on the tiny island had heard the terrorizing stories by now.. Everyone had reason to fear.. Everyone was in on the search, on the lookout for, the green, 67, Ford Mustang coupe, and more importantly, it's driver, Liam Miller.. The Canadian Tire stores, all the Kent Supply stores, all the big names, all the small names, all the ma and pa stores, all of them, throughout the Rock were sold out..

Everything, every arm, every weapon, all of the bows, all of the arrows and any form of gun powder and or explosive devices, including tasers and pepper spray's and mace.. Every calibre of shell, from buckshot, to salt, from 9m, to 308 and beyond.. The AK47's, Magnum 357's and every form of assault rifle, all of them, gone, sold out.. They were defenceless and in pure fright of a real life pending evil.. Their own little reality fix, a true life horror.. Here, for the first time in their small lives, a killer, a real predator, a serial killer, hiding, like a snake, somewhere on their sacred Rock.. Every single piece of stock that could be got, was got.. Small knives, Bowie knives, hunting knives, swords and machetes, all, gone, sold out.. Even the little sling shots and pellet guns were gone, nothing left to sell or be sold..

The little island was running out of protection.. Miller, the media news had now deemed him, Miller the Killer.. Miller was now and forever, a serial killer and the subject of a full-fledged man hunt, Newfoundland's most wanted.. When they find out the truth about this mad man, this psycho killer, he would be well graduated into Canada's Most Wanted.. If Colbert, Drisko, Copper, the clan or the R.C.M.P., if they don't stop him now, well, they just gotta.. His prison mug shots, a faded photo from his childhood, plastered all over the news and everywhere you looked or listened, Miller..

Drisko laughing inside, as the song plays behind the images dancing through him, watching past the blue house deep into the blue Atlantic, *"How soft your fields so green. Can whisper tales of gore.".*. The fuckin brewmeister, again, Boomer stressing his powers, fuckin brewmeister, leaning into Drisk, heads tapping heads, eye to eye, drunk.. You know the story, the powers of the Screech, well this was the original, Viking Kings Brew.. Eric, himself, handpicked the brewer, the Wizard, as he was blessed, by the King..

Eric after landing on the Rock, then returning to Norse Land, decided that the Rock, would be colonized.. He sent his trusted son, Leif to lead the landing to the new land.. With that, they sent the brewer, the secret of the brew, in trust with a young apprentice, the Molester.. A sick, sinister, depraved monster.. The most dreadful of lads.. The King originally wanted him banished, he was gonna throw him into the snake pit.. Threatened, to torture and disembowel him with the Blood Eagle, he wanted his head.. But then realizing he needed his magic..

Back in the day, in the old land, he was cursed with the tag, the Molester.. The one who touches others.. As he boarded the vessel, Leif ordered him to disguise his name, to Millouster, as there were now, women and children on board.. They would need to be assured by the King, they would not be accosted, with such a creature being sent with them to the New World.. Eric needed his brew, and his word, while months, then years of development, then a whole new generation of families grew about the island..

Then about a hundred and fifty years ago, the Country was formed, Canada.. With that came rules, regulation and census.. The government of Canada ruled, that all men, women and children, must be registered with the Queen and must have a minimum of two names.. A first, being known as, and a last, a family name a Sir name.. A thousand years of ridicule and the devils reputation.. The name holding the Millouster, translated from the Molester, the first generation of all Canadians, purebred Newfoundlanders, finally saw their chance, the chance, to change, the family name, to Miller..

The clan, all there sitting in the thirteen thrones, some standing, gathering, filling the room with all their theatrics.. The costumes, their garb, like a scene from a Hollywood blockbuster movie.. Some all-star cast production, the greatest of the great.. The party, the food, the sex, the magic of the Wizard.. The Shroud of Kings, the Helix Nebula, the Casandra, the potions, the feelings and the Witch.. The set, all, waiting, for someone to holler action, then, the movie, comes alive, becomes real..

As if it was a play, a script of some sorts, an overly zealous mind.. A rare, but ingenious mind, a brilliant creative mastermind, a chameleon.. Or was it all, just as simple as, reality.. A vision of what is real, stuck there, in some mad, sinister, monsters mind.. Is it all just an illusion to him, a premonition, a hallucination, some, psyche systematic, deranged, perverted serial killers brain.. Laying, waiting, elusively blending, a chameleon with over a hundred and sixty species, an impersonator, capable of changing into any of them in a flash, hiding in plan sight, yet invisible, inside the fish bowl..

The visions flashing, flashing, the Witch pressing her sizzling lips up to Drisko's, as she speaks to him.. Drisko can see her snake like tongue slithering around her teeth.. He can see the two, very thin, long and lanky, Razer snakes wrapping her neck like jewellery.. Their horned heads, inches from Drisko's jugular veins, on either side of his throat.. You want the truth, she says sincerely, you want to try and to understand the time that has past, slowly, slithering the words out.. You seek to far, you look beyond the distance that is required.. The truth is always close at hand Drisko, directly in front of you.. There is no seeking of, only seeing of, what is the true truth.. The truth comes from the souls of the ancient ones, the truth is always of breed, of what is bred.. Even the caterpillar, with her amazing performance of metamorphosis, must face, the solemn truth, the inevitable.. When one eliminates the probable and removes the impossible, one is left with only one ultimate answer, all that could remain, is, what is to be the truth..

From he, she screams, whom whilst cast into the snakes pit.. As they took thee, thy King, thy legend, from he, he had gave sons of three to thee.. Of one son, the disfigured one, he gave to him the lead.. Ivar, the Boneless they called him, the most despicable of the three.. Then he, had three, as the apple falls not far from the tree.. Two of man, two of he, and one, not right, not he, a female, a she.. She grew of evil, Godiva the witchy one, killing, molesting and eating the young.. Imprisoned, forgotten, a cast away slave, confused, abused and raped day by day.. A child she had, the Molester, she named it, the spit, she had carried, straight out to her crypt, here all things remain dead, here aboard, the Grave Ship..

The mixed seeds of the evil, passed through her souls for a thousand years.. The Molester, the Molester, Millouster is here.. An incestuous, brutal, rapist, a killer, a sick, sadistic, monstrous maniac, the true molester.. His seed had been planted, unwanted, yet forced.. The blood, that he shares, his blood, the blood of his coarse, Ivar.. From the gates of heaven, to bowels of hell, in one swift, easy move.. Tell me Drisko, she says to him blood spewing from her.. Speak out their names, the names of his victims, the names of your rage.. Think it out Drisko, I'll tell if you're true..

Yes she said, yes again, loudly yes, then laughing a sinister laugh, Oh' ya.. Then several times yes, yes again and again, as Drisko's mind filtered them through.. There was little left of Drisko's huge list, when the Witch finally said, that's all baby, that's it, that's all that there is.. The victims, lay lifeless in front of him now, clearly, all stacked in a row.. The truth, will live to haunt him, now that he knows.. The numbers although staggering even for Drisko's mind.. The people, the friends, family and clan, Millers violated, all of this time..

Bodies piled up to the rafters with his loves.. People so close to his heart, Rose, Vi, Rita, and so many more.. With an aching in his heart he sees her.. Finally, in-sync, his eyes sunken on her naked corpse, piled there with the others, Bonnie, his beloved.. Drisko, pulling on the straw, with the silver cap on the top.. His anger, raging beyond his ability to recognize anger.. Maybe hell fire and fury, possibly, true un-blended, cold maniac-tic, insanity.. The Witch feeds him, as the Wizard pokes the Helix Nebula with his ugly stick.. The smoke withdrawing now, from red to black, no don't go, there's more I need to know.. The Witch, draws back into tiny.. Drisko sucks one last puff, trying, staring straight into her crocodile eyes, then poof, she was gone..

Ya's' can calls her what yaz like, a fluke or an act of de God's.. No one rightly knows how it all came about that night, up der on de Edge.. All anyone really no's' is the last moment of it all.. The sun was going down, right there, where the dirt meets the blacktop, right der at the Black Water River, on the bridge up in Cripple Creek Pass.. Nobody really seen anything, witch was highly suspicious when you consider that N.A.F.T.A. reported the island was lit up like a search light..

The photo's later examined from far out in outer space, sent down to earth here by one of them der satellite tingies hummin along out dar, eh'.. Every inch of it was on fire day says, every house light, street light, candle and camp fire, every lamp and torch light was lit.. All setting their aim on Miller.. Every inch of highway and byway, every backroad and trail was lit from the beaming of car headlights.. Yet no one saw a thing eh', cept'n', Bernie and Penny.. Mark my words Sheriff, the Fat Man said, the animal must had just grown fins and simply swam out to sea..

Bernie now explaining away, the gang was simply comin home from a wild night of partyin out there at Boomers, eh', oh she be the wild time der eh' sheriff, ya ya sheriff replying as familiar.. Well that's when's we'z saw'z the car out on the edge dar eh', you's know, eh' sheriff.. We'z didn't sees the fucka buts der was no way, no way eh' no way of savin dat fucka.. I's' means, who ever the fucka was, can't tell ya what kinda car it was though.. Well it was like this sheriff, Bernie steppin up and spitting out the words no one could really quite understand, sheriff nodding along..

See me ans a Penny here, wez was just finishing up helping get the old tourist from Tennessee der, outta de hole eh', up dar eh', on Misery, das why I's in the bucket truck now eh'.. See we'z was gonna go have some dinner at Fancy's eh' sheriff, out by the Watch Tower, they's gots the bear claws on this evenings special eh', oh, an de big games on the big screen eh, Canadar' and de Rushkies eh' can't be missin dat, oh' da's' gonna be's some fista cuppin, bet cha on dat.. So we'z decided ta taker the ways' backs round, over da bridge eh'.. Bernie careful not to tell the truth of where him and Penny were heading and what his plan was, when he got there, back to the asteroid above the ridge of the Black Water River.. Back to the throne, back to where he, is, Bernardo the Great, the Viking King, back to the Black Pearl..

Well you's ainna gonna believe er' boss, but that's when I saw the car, comin in off the flats full out.. I's don't quite know what happened den, but's' we'z was in the bucket, goin straight through the centre of the bridge, when blam.. The fuckin bucket on the truck hits this huge fuckin bee's nest.. Im tellin you sheriff, the truth, she was huge, a wall of bee's, blam they's' goes flying, nest and all.. Well when the bucket hit the nest, it slugged er' like a base ball, blam, clean outta the park.. The damnedest thing you'd ever seen doe' sheriff, you's' wouldn't believes your eyes if'n' you'd seen it yourself..

Smack, crack, line driver straight off the windshield of that there car coming at me, full out, straight in off the flats.. Bernie twisting up the lie now, part truth part not.. Blam, right into the open window the cab filling it with bees and she was dat fast sheriff, blam.. Then the car lifted up and out, jumping the ridge, a full gainer, straight off the Edge.. Straight out and into the mighty Black Water River, out into the mighty Atlantic and that was that, she was gone..

The police searching endlessly, with no clue, the animal simply grew fins and swam away with the ocean current.. The photo in the St. John's Tribune showed the streak of green paint on the outer wooden beam of the covered bridge, tire tracks heading obviously up to and disappearing exhaustively, cut deep into the thinness of the air beyond Cripple Creek Pass.. The photo of the plaster casting of the tracks, matching the SR75/250/15 BF Goodrich T/A steel belted tires recently purchased for the Mustang.. The Chief of The St. John's Police, needed no caption, "The Tire Tracks Matched", the 67 Mustang, careened off the Edge.. The papers ran the story, the head lines read. Miller the Killer, Kisses the Cod..

The truth was they had no proof that it was the Mustang or Miller.. The reporter didn't even go to the scene, he just pulled the old photos and ran with it.. Was tourist season up on the Edge, so anything that would take the attention off the tiny island's mass murders and serial killer, well shit.. Anything to restore the tranquil image of their safe tiny island life.. They all just assumed it was Miller and the Mustang.. Or maybe the truth is they just turned their pretty heads, looked the other way as they do.. That was fine with Drisko and the gang and the clan.. For Drisko though, anything that kept the cops off the Edge, away from the bridge and out of the sight of the Black Pearl, was all good..

The visions swirling deep into Drisko's mind.. He wakes to the morning sun flooding into the room, the crisp fresh breeze of the ocean air tainting the room, fluttering the light sheer of the curtains.. The dead fish, a big ugly four foot, five inch, three hundred and nine pound Grouper, was a hugely displayed trophy, hanging between the two open windows.. The photo of Drisko, his dad Bryce, Bev and the monster fish, standing proudly displayed on the large wooden dresser top.. Pictures of family, friends and events marking the couples past, caked the walls..

The door slightly set open, as the aroma of the fresh perked coffee enters.. Bonnie's got the stereo cranked, seemingly sending the signal to his senses, time to wake up.. The singer screaming up the stairwell, *"Welcome to the jungle we got fun and games"*.. The steel framed four post canopy bed, a relic, cast from iron by ancient makers of steel and pictorially enhanced with four floating cast iron bird figurines.. Drisko lays silent, deep in the colourful duvet top, submerged into the goose down pillows, staring high into the ceiling, thinking of the Mustang, his Tanger, focused on Miller..

A light kiss and a pat to her rear, as he enters the kitchen.. Bonnie pouring the java into the mighty fisherman cup, white with black lettering as she dances his coffee to him.. Dancing, twirling, sexy, suave', still in her silky nightie.. Pointing her dainty finger at him, dragging it back in, beckoning him to her, rubbing at herself as she dances.. *"I wanna hear you scream. Welcome to the jungle, it gets worse here every day. You learn to live like an animal in the jungle where we play."*, as Drisk lowers the tone from it's roar once more and then kissing her again, same as the last time, I love you he says, with one slight of a hesitation.. I gotta call the gang, find out what's up eh', all done she says they'll meet us at the Pearl.. I gotta get my car, the Tanger, it's there stashed in the Livery, gotta get it out so the cops find it, back to the Black Water River, as planned, done she says again, all done, Bonnie took care of it all, all done..

No worries Drisko, go relax, have your coffee enjoy the sunshine out on the porch, I'll stir us up some brekkie, go get yourself ready, all that manly shit you do, then we'll meet up with the gang at the Pearl.. The phone rings, they stare at it for several bells, then Bonnie answers it.. This is Corporal Ron Flowers of the Royal Canadian Mounted Police force, is there a Drisko Oobbew there, Bonnie repeating the name of the officer, out loud, as he delivers it.. Drisko takes the receiver, hello, he nervously answers, this is Drisko.. Shy, like a school boy, nervous, thinking its word about Miller, they know what happened.. The officer announcing the recovery of the little green Mustang, abandoned up on the bridge of the Black Water River.. It's yours Drisk, tags match, it's your Tanger, the officer excited, full of grace for them doing such a fine job recovering the stolen property..

Drisk probing the officer, any sign of the thief, looks like Miller, his finger prints all match.. All the junk and garbage looks like it's him.. Funny though, left his wallet and things that you would had taken with you if you was on the run, but he left it all right there.. We towed the Mustang up into the Stephenville compound, you can pick her up there, later tomorrow, they're just finishing up with her.. Looks like an open and shut case though, straight up, we're figuring he just jumped.. Lost it there on the bridge, where his killing spree began.. Parked the Tanger, smoked his last Export "A", king, and took the dead mans walk..

Jumped right into the mouth of the Black Water River, straight off the old bridge to his demise.. That was that, the mighty Atlantic oceans current, just up and took him away, straight out to sea and he was gone, fish food.. More than likely that's what happened, that's our guess, officially, the case is closed, Millers dead.. Anyway, on a happier note, we're all done with the Emporium and the Tanger, they're all yours boy, enjoy, anytime you can get to it, they're yours..

Drisko drives the old Chevy slowly toward the sun slowly setting over the old rickety bridge.. Out the other side off the edge an eighth of a click out into the flats, right there, where the dirt meets the blacktop.. Dead, he says, the place is dead, as he turns the fire engine red 72 off the road to the right and down the bumpy path, he parks her.. The place is empty, a trap he's thinking his heart pounding, the cops, they know, they know everything, his mind bending from the pressure.. Drisko isn't afraid of the cops or getting caught, not by far.. He's perturbed at the fact he won't be able to complete his quest as he had planned.. Together they walk, hand and hand down the thin bushy path, squeezing in and out through the thick.. Around behind the tree line and off to the edge..

They shimmy their way down off the ledge at the foot of the Pearl.. They drop, the three feet to the edging and shimmy their way around to the incline, a thousand feet above the world, then up into and deep behind the Pearl.. The crowd awaits them as they circle the edge of the asteroid, quietly, cheering their arrival.. The land is sacred and holy it requires respect, they are welcoming, yet humble to his presence.. They are all there, hundreds of loyal warriors, gathered at the Pearl.. Sworn to the death oath, blood oath of the clans, brother to brother..

Mike was there, Bev, Penny, Jimmy, Vi, Rita and Rose.. Elvin leaning on Bernie, Pino, John and Sherlie were all there.. Brian, Christina, Hill Billy, Leo and Donna showed in her Barney Fife look and Rick, Alice.. Vagan Wolf was there with Sky and the cubs, old Dusty Greer, Dave, Zakary, Fran with her dog Fancy and the eight puppies don't forget and the three other Frans.. Charles, Ray, the Dragon, the Wizard and the chick that played the Witch from the Viking Village Performers, thank you very much, she was there.. Ted was there, Vito, Elvis, Elf, Mickey, Blaze and nurse Joy, Gary and the other cop, Vincent and Lex, and Chevaron, they came together, I think..

Didn't much matter who came with who, the fact that they were all gathered together as one clan was all that anyone cared about.. They knew each, to a man, exactly what was going to take place and exactly where they were headed, they were there as braves, as Norseman, as Vikings, as witnesses and as warriors.. Gathered there together to enter the Grave Ship and to pay homage to the thirteen kings, to carry out their rule, their Kings command..

You see, about a hundred years ago, this old timer, living out on the Edge there, all by his lonesome.. Decided one day, that there's just got to be a way around that mighty black, raging river, so he went out set, to finding it.. He thought if the river had a narrow in it's gorge somewhere, well maybe he could build himself a bridge.. So one day he went out, with his axe and his blade and his spire, like he would, as a Norseman would.. On a quest with his plan to expand his resources, looking for a better life.. He chopped and sliced his way along the high edges of the raging river, about fifty feet off the edge.. He chopped and chopped and chopped some more..

Till one day, he wailed his mighty axe and it sparked as he hit the rock.. Well, weren't really a rock, more like a bolder, well not really a bolder but something the old timer had never seen before.. Now for sure, this old timer weren't as dumb as the rock he was looking at, so he got himself this brilliant idea.. Simple, he would start digging the rock out, now this was a huge rock, like ten apartment buildings, a hundred trees tall.. But being Newfie and not a lot of other stuff occupying his mind, or time, he took to digging.. Now the boy's a Newfie, so he's like this engineering marvel, as you can imagine.. He's thinkin, if"ns' I's' digs out the outer edge, the rock will finally slid to the side and shitter' straight out off the freakin cliff.. Right off the freakin edge, freakin genius, he thinks to himself.. Then all I's gots ta do, is ta builds' da freakin bridge, straight out over her.. Using the rock as the foundation and then straight up de edge..

Stick and rope, stick and rope, stick and rope easy as shit, a freakin genius.. I'll use the fucking rock as the brace, for the foundation, Genius.. I's ties logs to her, brace them, tighten with rope, coat the fucker with goats grease, and you's gots a bridge.. So he took to digging, and he took to diggin and then he took to diggin some more, then he started diggin some more and everyday for a year the old Newfie just kepta diggin.. Rain or shine, come sleet, hail, hell or high waters, he kepta diggin..

Come sunshine or freezing over snow, the Newfie took to diggin.. Till, suddenly, one day, the ground in his hole opened clean up under him and the Newfie went and fell in.. Can ya's imagine, alls that time thens yous gos and falls ins yous own freaking hole yous was diggin, crazy eh'.. Now the funny ting was, the poor fucka died eh', ya eh', the fall went and killed him, ain't that the dangdest thing, go figure eh'.. Dar yous' are, diggin a freakin hole in da ground, then blam, you's time is up, and that was that, you's fall in a hole and you's ass is grass..

Drisko slides back the grass covered black Ash wooden doors, as they squeaked, he jerks them open, he steps one step down into the snakes pit, the evening sunlight shining across his back, lighting the hole, under the Pearl.. Crossing over each crystal hardened, solid coal stair.. Wildly circling to somewhere, very deep into the pit.. The men all bravely follow Drisko, with Bonnie behind her man.. They descend the coal stairs reflecting it's own light and with the silvers and golds, the gems on their bodies reflecting even more with every step they venture below..

Deep into the bowels of the cavern, deep into the snakes pit.. The cave twisting and turning their journey till finally all you could hear was the echoing of their awe.. It was so overwhelming, too beautiful to describe, almost angelic, supernatural in its look, they thought it was a mirage.. The refection of the vision as it opened up with every stair they descended.. Stricken with fear, self doubt and disbelief, although believing fully, completely and without question.. They all knew it to be real, everything about it was absolutely real, without a doubt..

There, laying in front of their eyes, the exact replica of the pond, behind it, there, off the shores the Arches.. Exact, compete without flaw in every, every way, every stone, every rock, every grain of sand.. The bend of the beach, the curves of the Arches, the breaking of the waves, alive, exact, as it was, above them.. The cave was alive with every aspect of the real shoreline at the Arches of Parsons Pond.. Exact in every way the stage standing there in their view.. The pier, laying, waiting, the waves rubbing up to it, the sounds of them slapping under the docks.. It was real, as real as real could get, they were there, at the pond, at the Arches, but this is from a thousand years ago..

Drisko could see the Casandra coming into view in front of him.. Seeing her huge dragons serpent head and flapping wings, the head menacing, designed in magnificent detail.. The thorny brows, silver reflective eye balls following them from inside its deep detailed lids.. The skin of the reptile engraved into the detailing of its scaly coat.. The wings floating with the rhythm of the sea, looking as if they were flapping in attack mode.. The birds floating gently, circling, more like prehistoric Pterodactyl, giant vultures, menacing, frightening.. The scene looked like death to Drisko.. Drisko realizing his déjà vu, he walked these sandy shores before, a thousand years

71

ago, in this very scene.. Sacrificing a traitor to the Blood Eagle, this very spot.. Yet today, today there she lay, the scene exact again, they were in awe at the vision, complete, original and real, but how, how did you know it was here, they ask..

Drisko hearing the words of the song, holding him in the vision, **"now you better stop. And rebuild all your ruins. For peace and trust can win the day"**, the vision holding him.. Him standing there explaining to them, about the old Newf that fell in the hole.. Well the neighbours although few, finally realized the old man was missing and went out looking for him.. They all just thought the boy was just freakin' crazy with his stories, the Black Pearl, the bridge, dang fool was all.. But as the oath of brother for brother, they searched, till one man found him.. He simply fallowed the fresh tree marks, the carving into the forest.. There he discovered the Pearl and the hole, cautiously he entered the pit.. That's where he found the old man, about a hundred feet down, on a landing.. Dead, but totally intact, as if alive, but not alive, but unspoiled, not decaying, lookin likes you and me Drisko explains with ghostly eyes..

The great warrior proceeded deeper down into the snakes pit, only to discover its miracle.. The underworld tomb of the Casandra.. The Grave Ship, here in the Sea of Lost Souls, in the Arches at Parsons Pond and this is what he discovered, this very sacred of places.. That man, the worrier that set forth to rescue his neighbour, set forth to explore, bravely, blindly into the snakes pit, only to discover the truth.. That great man was my great, great, great grandpa ten fold, Ragnar, he found the Pearl, this is his, to pass forward to all clan..

Drisko, explaining to them that the air below the surface is richer, cleaner, the water below her bow is pure clean ocean waters.. Because of that she was preserved as she was a thousand years ago.. Drisko, looks deeply down the pier into the opened deck, four men await him, the fifth, bound and gagged, feet and arms tied to the post on the pier.. Drisko knows his fate, Miller, the Killer, tonight he will be blood sacrificed.. He will die by the torture of the Blood Eagle.. Drisko, slowly walking towards the prisoner.. He recognized the location, identical, here, on this shore, the nails of the tides had ripped their way through the rocky shoals of the Arches of Parsons Pond.. He could feel it, he could taste it, see it clearly in his mind's eye, with his own vision, as if it were now.. Him the Viking King, walking one step in front of him, Drisko.. The visions trailing him, his mind preparing him.. Here, with her, the Casandra, with him, the King and his Bonnie, once again..

The mast tied and the sails slung, the Casandra was alive with song and she sung.. The twisting of the beams, the rattling of the ropes and pulleys.. The clanging and banging of the parts and piece of her soul.. Drisko could smell her plume, feel her sweat, he could taste her vile juices, he knew it was her, all of her.. This is, the Casandra, Eric's Grave Ship, Eh' ERICHIL' coma da VIK-GYK-INGK KGIKIN and it was very, very frighteningly familiar to him, his blood, curling inside him.. As he walks to the end of the pier and around Miller to his front.. Millers face is peeled back, sliced apart, ripping, dripping in blood.. His tattoos all carved off him without care, the skin still hanging from the throat.. His hair patchy, sliced from the scalp in places, mauled by the wolves.. Miller knelt and hog tied on his knee's his hands lashed to the dock with rope, bound there in front of the great King, Drisko..

Drisko, blazing into the tribe, condemning Millers life, his betrayal to the clan and his traitorous ways to the Kings rule, the blood oath of Viking and Norseman law.. Drisko passing on sentence to Miller, describing each infraction in gory detail.. The crowd of warriors cheering it all on.. Crying out Millers crimes, murderer, traitor, rapist, outcast, blood they yell, blood.. Drisko drawing the sword from its sheath, holding it under Millers chin, it shining back his bloody reflection, as he prays to it.. Drisko rising the sword twelve times, praising to it, in Gothic tones and Gaelic rhymes.. Then, Dooley steps up into Drisko's spot as the king stands back to view and woo the crowd..

Dooley takes out his blade, his hand tight on the grip, as he prepares to drive it into Millers ribs.. Drisko giving his final judgment to Miller, death, death by Blood Eagle.. He cries out, they all cheer, blood, let em' kiss the Cod.. Drisko raises the sword the thirteenth and final time, holding it up for it to shimmer into the crowd.. He's glaring straight up, eyes locking onto the Helix Nebula, the eye of God, winking down upon him, in through the opening of the cavern above.. The coal reflecting the solar system, the Milky Way and beyond.. Dancing, bouncing off the bottom of the giant asteroid sitting protective, secure up top.. Drisko gives the order of blood, Blood Eagle is given..

Dooley, simply grabs Miller by his long scraggly blonde bleeding hair and drives the blade into his side.. Far enough below the first rib of his lower left side.. He carves the meat open across the lower cage, careful not to kill Miller.. Miller breathes out words in pain, straining his voice.. Dooley leans in, smiles and screams into Millers dangling bloody ear, that's from my cousin Chevy, for raping her and leaving her for the bears.. Yanking on Millers scalp, Go eh', you traitor, then jumping his voice into the other ear.. Dooley's hair slapping across Millers face, sticking there, Go eh' as Dooley pulls away, Go eh' traitor..

Then Dooley slowly picks away at each of Millers vertebrates, slowly picking, and carving, and picking along the spine.. Meticulously as he smiles away, carving with the skills of a surgeon, carving, picking and slicing his pleasure upward.. Till finally, Miller is completely artistically sculptured, pornographically displayed.. I give you, The Blood Eagle, Drisko announces, like it was a side show creature from a circus.. The crowd cheers wildly, with lavish praise, to the Kings, to the Gods, blood, blood, blood they cry, as Miller bleeds them his blood..

Drisko's visions, shifting turning, into the mirror, sliding into and out of his visions.. Sitting out front of the little house, on the shores of Meteghan, staring deep into the blue, the song sing, *" despite of all your losing. Ooh-ooh, ooh-ooh, ooh-ooh"* the rashness of the strings, baseness, as Page pounds the rhythm into Drisko's ears. *"Ooh-ooh, ooh-ooh, ooh-ooh"*.. Fat Man, standing there on the Casandra, laughing, dumb ass cops thinkin they's gots fuckin big foot trapped down in der or some tin.. Explaining how Drisko had planned every move to a T.. The minute they left the fort the plan was in action.. Now hitting the bees nest and whacking it onto the windshield of the Tanger, well, that was from the Gods.. No one could had figured that part out, but there she were, the Bees.. Miller had slammed on the brakes right there at the mouth of the bridge.. Dooley was fast up behind him, Drisko in behind him deep on his tail..

Me facing him straight on, in the bucket truck, blocking the bridge and Elvin was racing the 650 Bonnie up behind.. In off the ridge, both guns blazing, hammering Bonnie's shifter up and down the turns.. Gleason and Rizer hanging in hard close behind.. Drisko and Bonnie in the Chevy short box.. Miller clean froze up from the bees stinging him.. Didn't no's' what was what, eh'.. Fat Man spitting it out, the pack just dove, pouncing on him, a gang of hungry wolfs, relentlessly, pounding out his flesh, the bees stinging him.. Drisko feeling their stings, welcoming them as they stung him, delivering sting after sting, beating on Miller..

Right there at the bridge, at the Black Water River, right there, where the dirt meets the blacktop.. Right there where Miller sent Drisko's mother Ellen and his father Bryce, his life, his love and his fathers original straight out of the show room Mustang, his Tanger, they beat on Miller.. Attacking him with the pack, Vagan Wolf ordering Sky and the pack of hungry wolves cubs, to fill their thirsty fangs with the glory.. Drisko slowly rising, take him, he orders Dooley quietly, calmly, as a command.. Take him to the Casandra, the Grave Ship, the Sea of Lost Souls awaits him.. We shall bury him beneath the Black Pearl, in the snake pit forever, let em kiss the Cod..

Word, Bernie said, staring mindless into the shield of the great warrior, the protector of Kings, that's exactly what happened, as Fat Man smiles at them all.. We got him, and we got the Tanger back safe and sound, and in one piece.. The shield, holding their eyes, set there in the centre of the huge wooden table top.. Eric's shield, they gazed upon it, golden stars, the gems, diamonds and rubies glistering off the shield.. Strapped with serpents from threads of gold.. Two swords rolling it, the steel blades as if striking in thunder.. Circling the outer edge of the shield, each, of the thirteen chairs, with the silver caps, all one inch square, all one inch high, on the table top..

Drisko spewing out his plans of revenge.. Feed em' to the snakes, drop his ass in the snake pit.. The brains all fast reversing, the visions, quickly playing back through time.. Back to the time of Ragnar, the true Norse King, the king of kings.. His sacrifice, his death, by deadly snake pit.. His trade of his life, to spare the life of his son, Ivar the Boneless.. The men, all knowing far too well, the absolute truth of the improbability, of that death sacrifice.. No snakes on this Rock, not a one to be found, anywhere in Newfoundland.. The Rock is, the only place in all of North America, that they all knew to be the truth, no snakes..

No man, be he of Viking blood, can spill, Viking blood, or he, will face the wrath of Viking law.. The Kings law and only with his blessings.. It calls for Viking rule, he announces, the ritual of the Blood Eagle, he must spread his wings to fly from this place, to truly perish from this land.. It is the Viking way, the torture, of the treasonous.. Drisko, Boomer, Dooley, Fat Man and the Wizard, all heads bowed in silence.. Each man, without doubt, visualized, the ritual.. The unimaginable brutality of being alive, hog tied, on your knee's.. Your arms stretched outward, lashed to the post.. Whilst, your ribs, are being separated from your spine, behind you.. The blade cursing your back with raging pain.. The ribs carved in away, then pried from their disc, individually.. Ripping the complete cage, upward, then separated, to form the wings of the Blood Eagle.. The insides of your cage is now the outside of your wings.. As you kneel there, enduring, you know you are among the un-dead, yet you are only dying.. Mostly from the pure horror, the visions, of your own imagination, of the carnage to your body.. You look as if perched, about to take flight, almost as if a beautiful piece of art.. An artistically sculptured, human statue, part Pterodactyl.. Immortalizing you for your contempt, for the realm of the Kings..

The stage was set out there on the pond.. Boomers was lite up like an asteroid from outer space.. Drisko can see it all so clearly, as if it's now.. The lights twinkling about, the strobes bouncing, reflecting, the beach burner roaring out the flames, reflecting back into the huge crowd of warriors from the caverns huge coal ceiling.. Drisko standing centre stage, the light filling him.. He looks up into it, the night.. He screams, howling into the microphone, grabbing it into his hand from its tiny stand.. He sees it, hurtling there, towards earth.. The biggest moon he had ever witnessed, and so, as he screamed, the music made song..

He stood there, gyrating like a rock star, in a suave twirl, hip pulsing, rotating back and forth movements.. The sound of a wolfs howl, in unison, louder and louder as it rises, up and then crashing down like a song, that only they knew the words too.. So he screamed, again and again lustfully, lingering it, landing it, lasting a full twenty seconds, Le Woof, howling as he did.. Then he released a potent sound, a song of words, *"Welcome to the jungle we've got fun and games. We got everything you want honey, we know the names. We are the people"*..

Vagan Wolf slamming on the leads, slashing every riff in Drisko's tone.. Zackary Bahm, Boomer footing and high sticking the life out of the drums, symbolizing every second stroke, be-dazzlingly the hooks.. Gleason, backing up the slashing and vocal thrashing, hammering on the rhythms, tough, tight, while in-casing the song around it.. Rizer, tipping and tapping out the back beat, flowing his stuff, all guns, all roses, he hits, hacks and scratches his way behind the bass.. As Drisko wails out the vocals to the crowd, *"to your shun n-n-n-n-n-n knees, knees. In the jungle, welcome to the jungle"*.. The moon now crossing over, eclipsing the Helix Nebula, blinding it in its hugeness.. Drisko thinking, shit not again, really this is really going to fuckin happen, what a fucked up place.. Him thinking, why the fuck would anyone come out to the Edge? They only come here to die, because its dead out here, him, there, singing to the dead..

The moon tortuously close now, propelling into the little island once again.. Drisko, preparing himself for impact, screaming, gyrating into the crowd, flopping his junk like a punk at them.. The words, meaningless, they just collide in perfect timing, in perfect harmony, as the asteroid strikes all dem little fuckin Newfies again.. What the hell in all tar nations going on up dar on de Edge, by gez.. Drisko laughing out the words as it impacts the song, singing it on to the bitter end, *"to the jungle, welcome to the jungle. Watch it bring you to your. It's gonna bring you down, ha!"*..

The vision is clear.. It jerks his soul, the morning sun flooding the room, the crisp fresh breeze of ocean air.. The dead fish trophy, the photo of them and the monster fish, standing, proudly displayed.. Pictures of family, friends, events hung there on the wall.. The door slightly open, the aroma of coffee.. Bonnie's got the stereo cranked, time to wake up.. The steel framed bed, Drisko lays silent, deep in the duvet, submerged in goose down pillows, staring high into the ceiling.. Thinking, this is really it, what all them city folk is looking for, life on the edge, their life in the fast lane as he laughs it off.. He russels himself, makes his way down the steep stair well.. A light kiss and a pat to her rear, as he enters the kitchen.. Bonnie pouring the java into the mighty fisherman cup, white with black lettering as she dances his coffee to him..

Dancing, twirling, sexy, suave', still in her silky nightie.. Pointing her dainty finger at him, dragging it back in, beckoning him to her, rubbing at herself as she dances.. This time Drisko grabs her hard with force, his eyes lock on her, then he twirls the little filly right round.. You like fucking eh', you like to fuck, don't ya Bonnie.. He slaps her ass as she bucks, then angrily fucks the shit outta her.. Right there on the kitchen counter, right in front of the poor little Sugar Bears.. The heavy car door slams, who the hell's that, Drisko squeals, almost finishing with Bonnie, but not? As he's slapping her ass to get her back into gallop.. The fuckin cops Bonnie offers, as he's banging her little head up against the kitchen window.. Fuck them, fuck Zuncle and fuck you bitch.. As he did, ravaging her right there..

Bonnie, the vision of herself statuesque, spread fuckin Blood Eagle, sacrificed, right there over the kitchen sink.. Her knowing he could never forgive her for her part, her treason to the King.. Drisko, his vision filled with the evil truth from the Witch.. Bonnie's lushes body naked, piled there in front of him, with the victims of Miller.. His mind unable to see past the truth.. He sees himself throwing Bonnie's body off the edge, let ya' kiss the Cod with Miller, he says to her, pounding on her.. He recalls it perfectly, his mind went blank, other than the single thought, the very moment he thought it..

He knew, in that moment, he was leaving her, leaving there, leaving the Rock.. He accepted it, the very moment, he felt it strike his blackened soul.. The moment, it beat the rhythm, into his blackened heart, pulsing it through his black veins.. Everything about him was now gone, everything, shattering his ice blue eyes into blank, black.. Blackened with pain from the Witch, from the truth, the visions.. Her secrets, Bonnie's, her treason's, let them all drown in the Sea of Lost Souls together, forever..

Drisko wakes slowly from his trance, the blue house sitting there out on the edge.. The verse now drilling it into him, beating, biting him hard, *"fight the hordes. Sing and cry, Valhalla, I am coming."*, the music driving him.. He could smell the freshness of the ocean breeze as its salting his lips, *"with thrashing oar. Our only goal will be the western shore"*, shaking his daze from the clench of the tune.. He checks the gauges, then checks the clock.. He strokes his long black locks, staring into the rear view at the view, he's changing.. The sun now faded deep to the west, off the edge, what the fuck, Drisko's thinking.. Drisk reeves the Tanger to the mat, aiming her, up past Bear Creek, pass the mile signs, feeling familiar, noting, noting.. Then he was gone, out of the twist and turns of Nova Scotia..

His path set straight in his mind, through Brunny and then on into Quebec and then deep, deep and deeper into the south, southern Ontario.. Driving the power through the pipes, thrusting the thrust, pushing the pistons into torque.. Drisko drives the pass quickly, racing her up the ocean front road.. Watching in the rear view as his home fades gently behind the hills and then off the twisting of the trails behind him.. Drisko hearing the words, attaching to his brain, *"the tides of war. We are your overlords"*, listening to the music of the guitar riff, fading, fading, fading.. Noting, noting, his vowels of secrecy, a promise to himself of leaving the Rock, the overlords and the blood, far, far behind him, forever..

CHAPTER FOUR

Fame

It wasn't long before Drisko was on the attack, the Viking child had grown into a vicious warrior, a man with a stellar reputation as a shrewd negotiator.. He landed a cool job as a specialized media rep in the big smoke, Toronto.. Working with a brand new alternative rock radio station 102.9 the EDGE and then quickly after that he was settling into his new condo and life in Burlington.. Drisko trading the ragged shoal cliffs, the brisk ocean breezes and the rushing waters of the Black Water River, of Cripple Creek Pass.. For the tranquility, of the warm sandy shoreline of Lake Ontario.. There he met a little girl named Mercedes, fell in love, married that girl and grew his family..

Soon after that, Drisko climbed the career ladder, he was brilliant and insanely creative.. Working throughout southern Ontario, growing his resources, building new bridges and working his way through all the major radio, newspaper and T.V. stations, building huge contacts.. Soon he was once again, Drisko, the King, Drisko the Viking Child.. Within leaps and bounds he had propelled himself into his own full service, marketing, promotions and advertising agency.. Drisko and the agency had captured hearts and was winning award after award.. He had found himself the Black Pearl once again and he was now sitting on top of the world.. Major international clients requesting his time, advice and skill..

His name, his reputation, his unbelievable creative input and his business suave'..

Soon Drisko was jet setting all over the world, riding the high life, life in the fast lane, as they called it, life on the edge.. The family flourished, new luxury cars, custom homes, lake houses, moving, travelling all over the globe, growing, changing.. The fast lane, the wealth, the fame, all of it.. A lifestyle Drisko never seen before or ever really wanted to.. His mind was always still out there, hanging, there at the Emporium at the Black Water River, at the Black Pearl.. No G.P.S, no cell phones, no problems, no rush and no tourist, no strangers, no desperate people, everyone knew everyone..

Right there, on the very spot, right there where the dirt meets the blacktop, out there, on the Edge.. The hustle, the bustle of the big city, the rushing, chasing, running, always late, always taking the wrong turn, detours, one ways, the wrong way, always, for Drisk.. He desperately yearned for the tranquility of the Edge, the life, the peacefulness of Cripple Creek Pass.. But there was nothing left on his sacred island, the Rock and everything about it, had been demolished by a giant hurtling asteroid from far off there in outer space.. He knew, it was the end, no life for him there and definitely no business, no reason for him to return..

The tides of time where shifting though, the winds had briskly picked up.. Drisko had pitched his sails, he could feel the gentle breezes, slowly filling them.. He knew, something was coming, he knew it was time.. He could see the trees swaying, the animals scattering into the forest, the birds flying high then being swept down deep into the rock shoals of Cripple Creek Pass.. The winds now howling the words like a god, he knew it, he could see it, the end was near.. Not clearly not just yet, but he could see, without sight, hear it as it spoke to him without ears, just his pure intuition, but he knew it was coming..

Drisko setting his sails to trim, there, in the old garage, catching the breezes, smoking his doob.. He sat and he pondered, as he pondered, he thought and as he thought, it came to him.. There, in the darkness, there at the Arches, on the Sea of Lost Soul.. There on the Casandra, the Grave Ship, Eric's warship, partying with the dead.. The answers, all came clear to him now and he knew, that it was the right answer.. He ran from the garage of the country home to the kitchen.. Finding Mercedes clearing the dishes from the washer, clinging them into the cupboard.. Drisko announcing, with pure enthusiasm his brain wave idea, it's perfect he explains..

I'll expand into B.C., open an office in Victoria, we'll live on the island and develop it with the mainland.. Mercedes, second guessing the idea, but with excitement, her thoughts of the possibilities, the romance, the adventure.. They talked and they talked and they looked at all the angles, then they decided.. Drisk hoped in his Porsche and headed to the west coast, recognizance, P.R and to establish the base camp, get everything set and ready for the big move.. Plus he was desperate to take his new toy, the midnight pearl black, Turbo 911 couple for a boot and the west coast cross Canada run, seemed like the perfect test track.. So he did, he ran it, and it was amazing, top down, sun shining through all the way..

Drisk had never seen this part of Ontario before, enjoying the views of the drive, he shifts the Porsche high into gear, sets the cruise as he makes his way up the 400 highway north.. Catching up to the junction 169 then into the split at the top of Georgian Bay and on into the great white north to Pointe au Baril, French River then on to Sudbury.. Rounding the top of the great lake Huron, the tunes busting out, *"burns your change to keep you insane (fame). Fame, (fame) what you like is in the limo. Fame, (fame)*, out past the Manitoulin Islands, north west to Sault Ste. Marie.. Than west, into Terrance Bay, Nipigon, then deep into Thunder Bay.. Turning the 17 north, heading with timing, then straight up and into the Lake of the Woods, Kenora, to the top of Ontario..

The lakes, her rivers, her twisting hills, the tree lined roadways and her lushes green forest regions.. Drisk was an outdoors man, spent his life in the wilderness, so he dragged the Porsche off the trail and into the Eagle Dogtooth, Provincial park.. Set up camp there, the place was empty that time of year, just him, Mother Nature, his Aria guitar and the mighty mystique of the quiet lake as his back drop.. His jet setting life was far to fast, he was going to slow things down for now on, enjoy the trip and discover his Canada..

Drisko sat alone, in the forest on the tiny lake.. Listening he could here the animals, the birds, the breezes shifting the trees, there in front of the beach burner.. The smoke and steam, the sparks bursting, the fire crackling in the night.. The vision of her, coming to him that night, in Nova Scotia, Emily, from the diner, the thought provoking him, his lust.. Then deeper and deeper, into Bonnie his anger for her, his life, her betrayal, her lies, her deceit.. Yet still there she was, dancing right in front of his eyes, there, vivid, at the beach burner, there at Boomers, at the Viking Village, at the Arches.. Her, dancing for him, grabbing at herself, beckoning him, dragging her tiny finger towards herself, as she massages herself..

Then Mercedes appeared, the vision of her, her love for him, him standing with her, dancing there on the edge, at the beach burner.. Them, holding each other tightly, laughing, kissing each other, embracing him, his true love.. Her sweet way of whispering in his ear, I love you Drisko.. His vision of them together there on the edge.. The children, his son, his daughter them laughing with each other and dancing, together beside them.. Then he knew, he knew why he had come this far, for them and he felt their love throughout him, it gave him strength, there with him on that shoreline.. He laughed and laughed, then shouted into the night sky, the past is the past, my word, my oath, brother for brother.. He knew without doubt, right there and then, he would go forward and conquer this big new world of his..

He rose to first light, he quickly packed up camp and high tails it out of the park and onto the highway, catching the morning sun rising up through the rear view.. He had only seen pictures, TV shows, commercials of the farmlands, the wheat fields of Manitoba or the flat lands, salt lakes and grain elevators of Saskatchewan.. The areas full of interesting and different views, flat, with enormous great lightening shows, thunder storms and amazing double rainbows.. A great place to watch your dog run away for three days.. He laughs, at his humour, then sudden realization of his words sets in, flat lands.. Watching the sun set perfectly once again, peacefully into the west, reminiscing of his picturesque sun set drives across the Great Northern Mountain Ranges of the Gros Morne, the Edge..

The loneliness of the long tedious drive now wearing hard on Drisk.. The white lines flickering in his eyes, reflecting back off the head lights from the roadway.. The black night sky now pitching back into the midnight black pearl Porsche.. The Porsche only illuminated buy the pinkish haze of the LCD lights of the jet like instrumentation panel.. The sky slowly opening up, igniting the black pearl dark interior, showering beads of light on his frozen silhouette.. While turning the sky into a glowing ball of white hazy light, stationary, with coloured lights flickering all through it..

A spaceship he thought, staring at it there, hovering above the horizon as he enters fearlessly into the blackened flats of the central prairies, just east of Regina.. Drisko feeling the edge, tired, now searching for somewhere cozy and clean to stop for the night, somewhere off the Trans Canada Highway.. Turning down the dirt lane at the welcome sign of the Moonlight Inn, sitting up on the foot hills, high above the city limits.. Drisko, sitting on the deck, pondering, puffing on a couple of doobs, kissing the horses ass, sucking back on the Screech.. Thinking about Miller, the Casandra, the asteroid, while staring down into the spaceship as it glows from the night sky, penetrating his mind with visions..

The song, Bowie, the spaceship, shining back into his eyes as he listens, deeply to the orchestrated beats.. *"Fame, (fame) what you get is no tomorrow. Fame, (fame) what you need,"*, Drisko staring off the deck into the glowing spaceship, he sees it, then he sees it there, hurtling into earth, there above the Sea of Lost Souls, there at Parsons Pond, there at the Arches.. Him standing on stage, shouting out, singing to the dead, flopping his junk like a punk, screaming out the warnings, but the words only collided into a song..

There as he watched the asteroid rocketing towards the tiny island.. Drisko could see it clearly, crashing into their sacred rock, devastating everything, demolishing his entire life.. *"Fame, bully for you, chilly for me."*, the song, tapping on him, beating it into his brain.. He sees it, *"let me get a rain check on, pain (fame)"*, the Witch, the Siren of the Sea.. She comes not to conquer nor to enslave, but to devour, every, living, thing, in her path.. Drisko saw the end, clearly, he knew, she had destroyed everything, everything he ever held sacred about his tiny rock..

Drisk watches the morning lighting up the skies with silvers and reds, shimmering across him from the east.. He fires the petro into the black pearl Porsche's engine.. He aimed the beast westerly, in front of the sun.. Following the slow grade of the inclining highway into the lowlands of Saskatchewan, passing by the spaceship town of Regina, heading deep into the foothills of Alberta.. Then quickly up into Calgary and then on into the Great Rocky Mountain Range of British Columbia..

Drisk revving her up, gearing her down, throwing the shift in and out around and around.. The Porsche obedient, finding the groove, grooving to the rhythm of the road.. The road flat, empty, the sun rising behind him, nothing, no one, anywhere, but there.. There, way ahead of him, a dot racing on the open highway.. Drisko hammers her to gain pace.. He's riding the blacktop in perfect timing of the car ahead, way ahead, a good kilometre or two, easily.. Drisk keeping pace, notices it's a cop, a cruiser, he's riding far enough behind, *"(fame), it's mine, it's mine, it's just his line."*, but keeping pace to the black car up ahead, the cruiser.. The two cars clipping along the Trans Canada Highway, cruising the 100 zone at around 120, no big deal, *"to bind your time, it drives you to crime (fame)*, just cruising along.. Drisko, puffing a doob, sunroof open, windows down, cruise control set on 120, kickin' it..

Saskatchewan is flat and empty in every direction, the highway, split, by wide large green grassy medians, with openings to allow for u-turns, all of it flat.. Drisko could see it there across the horizon, he could see it rising there, far in the distance.. He wasn't sure, but it was there.. He watched as the dot in front of him rose gently into the sky and disappear in the illusion of the heat vapour from the blacktop. *"I reject you first. Fame, fame, fame.*, from the blacktop.. Drisk cruising along the blacktop, then he sees it, *"Is it any wonder you are too cool to fool."*, there, in front of him, an illusion, a trick, but no, no trick, *"got to get a rain check on pain (fame)."*, it was real.. The highway had risen, lifting the tiny Porsche up ward, Drisk knew it was a hill.. He laughed, it's the little things in life eh', a thousand kilometres of flat lands and finally, a hill.. He puffed out the toxic smoke from his doob, mixing it into the prairie air and then killing the heater and tossing the roach to the blacktop..

He tapped the brakes, disengaging the cruise control of the black Porsche's fuel injected engine, slowing the machine as it cruises up over the knoll.. There in the grassy medium, the cruiser, facing him, the cops, staring him down, watching the Porsche 911 cruise by at around 105.. Drisko watching them, as the coppers turn the cruiser around and give chase.. Lights flashing in behind Drisk as he pulls the beast to the shoulder, searching in the rear view, *"your time, it drives you to crime (fame)."*, the cruiser sits, in the rear view, the blues, reds, whites flashing, flashing, flashing.. Drisko could see the two bodies step from the cruiser.. One short, slender approaching the passenger side.. The other, two steps behind, huge, tall, massive, the Duke..

She approached the passenger side of the black pearl Porsche as Drisk drops the volume.. Looking in at him through the sunroof down into the drives seat, the drivers face.. The sun brightening her left side, her face, her breast, her badge, glistening, as her right side laid sheltered with shadows, her gun, her holster, visible.. She was a midwestern beauty, Barnie Fyfe he thought, from the Edge, Donna, officer Macy.. Drisk recognized her beauty immediately, delivering his precious smile.. The beauty smiled back from under her Canadian sombrero, as the bustling male R.C.M.P. voice entered the drivers window.. The huge muscular head, staring deep into

Drisko's eyes, leaning into the opening, sniffing at him like a wild blood hound.. Why were you following us, he questions Drisk? Where're you coming from, licence and pink slip?

Drisk reaches into the centre console, lifting it, retrieving the documents, while smiling at the beauty, as the thug to his left, is drilling him with questions, as Drisko laughs it all off.. How did you know we were on the hill, you have a radar detector in here, drilling, drilling, then repeating the questioning, drilling.. Why were you following us? Drisko sharply answering, following you, you're the only other car on the road and you're three k in front of me.. Why'd you slow down on the hill, the officer searching, drilling, you got a radar detector in here, accusing? No I was so happy to see a hill, just lingering for the view, Drisk laughing, the beauty laughing, smiling, flirty.. Drisk, his mind, it wonders, the beauty, Donna, officer Macy, on the bridge, there at Cripple Creek Pass, there, where the dirt meets the blacktop, there at the Black Pearl..

The cops had retreated back to the cruiser to run the plates and check registration.. Drisko wonders deep into the rear view, drawing from his memories, Gleason, Rizer, sitting on the Black Pearl watching the world go by as they look aimless into the deep, blue of the Atlantic.. Staring down on the little bridge, as they deliver the play by play to Drisko.. Macy and Roscoe fucking up on the bridge.. Drisk remembering the photos, Drisk imagining the mid western beauty all served up, submissive, seductive, there on the Black Pearl, covering her face with his special sauce.. The brawny officer waking Drisk from his erotic dream.. Drisk looking for officer cutie, but no luck, she was gone with the wind.. He could see her through the rear view, still sitting in the cruiser, staring at him, their eyes holding contact..

The officer ordering Drisko to take it easy through here, have a good run to B.C.. Drisko asking in his Newfie drawl, well, wad be a good speed to cruise through here den, I gots a longs way to go eh', he added.. The officer firm, his voice in command, we take our law serious here in Saskatchewan.. The speed limits are posted, clearly,

I suggest you obey them, as the officer turns and walked away back to the beauty.. Drisko throwing the beauty a wink in the rear view, as she smiles back at him.. He fires up the black pearl Porsche 911, rattling the Thrush, cranking the tunes back up.. Slipping her back onto the blacktop, #1, the Trans Canada Highway, west, to Alberta, then on into B.C.. Squawking the tires, firing stones and kicking up a cloud, leaving the little coppers in his dust.. Drisko, the Porsche 911, gripping, grabbing, slipping through all the gears as it hums along, *"is it any wonder, you are too cool to fool (fame). Fame, bully for you, chilly for me."*, as it's humming its way along, the long, flat, long black, blacktop..

Calgary coming into his view as he makes his way onto the city limits, there in the distance, the mountains, tiny he's thinking, real tiny.. He drives the beast into town noting the space needle, the high rises, the cityscapes, the sun shining, reflecting in the glass towers.. Drisko drives deep into number 1, the road twisting, slowly climbing, heading north now, out past the Olympic Park.. Drisk recognizing the landmark, *"Fame, fame, fame. Fame, what's your name, what's your name."*, the site of the nineteen eighty eight, first Canadian Winter Olympics.. Drisko throws the Porsche some shifts, now veering her left, west bound, towards Banff, into the flatlands.. Driving, driving, shifting, gliding, full torque ahead, the sun shining..

The highway reflecting into his shades, the endless continuation of blacktop and white lines, reflecting back into the rear view mirror.. The sun shining, the song in timing, the sign approaching, Canmore, 30k., Banff 55k., the music playing.. Drisko motoring the machine into Dead Man's Flats, along the Trans Canada, the Porsche is purring, the terrain flat, mundane, then he sees it.. A trace, a track, stretching along the skyline as he motors.. There in front of him, disguising itself as clouds, pitching the colours in and out from blues and reds to browns and whites, protruding in and out of his sight.. Then he sees it, huge forming in front of him, him now feeling small, tiny, insignificant.. He can't believe his eyes, a vision from God, the Rocky Mountains.. As he races to find the top, the giant face swallows the little Porsche with ease.. The Porsche climbing, climbing, shifting, swishing, racing, racing, without power, powerless against the massive rock, the sheer, unbridled power of the rock's face..

The tiny Porsche slows, the gears gearing down, the gas releasing the pressure from the pedal and the fuel injectors take over the torque.. Drisko motoring into Kicking Horse Pass and on in through the Gates of Banff National Park marked with a huge Canadian flag, whispering in the breeze.. The castle- like structure from the early thirties stood strong and sturdy.. The field stone foundation, with massive wooden carved beams, framing it.. Trimmed nicely in wood, the entrance, the guard and Ranger station, beautifully picturesque at the foot of the Alpine Mountains.. Drisko looking up through the sunroof to where there is no sky.. Huge mountain faces, enormous white capped snow covered peaks.. Brilliant, huge cascading waterfalls, flowing into massive gorges, flowing deep beneath the blacktop, racing to the raging river, tumbling towards the Fraser and on into Hell's Gates..

Drisk wheels the Porsche 911 left and up in toward town, Banff, just to check it out.. In through the main drag, catching the shops, restaurants and the tourist.. Up over the tiny bridge, up the incline and on into Banff Rocky Mountain Ski Resort.. Beautiful drive, amazing views, breathtaking and picturesque, but it's just a pit stop.. He's in for a once around then a quick fill up, a car wash, grab a coffee and sandwich then off.. Other sights, other adventures and he has his destination in mind.. He motors the Porsche out of town onto the Trans Canada west bound..

Motoring, sun shining, music pounding, *"Fame, fame, fame, fame"*, him admiring every inch of highway.. The rock, the sheerness of its faces, the waterfalls, the trees, the trails, the moose, the mountain goats, the rivers and miles and miles of train tracks.. Tracks, cutting, carving in and out of tunnels through the mountainous terrain.. Twisting, turning, shimmering, there, in the sun set, stretching across massive wooden bridges, crisscrossing, over and over the raging of the river below..

Drisko powers the Porsche up the Rocky Mountain path, #1, Trans Canada.. West bound, into the sun, Lake Louise, 10k., the sign read, Drisko revved the mighty Porsche 911.. Hey it's all in good fun, he says to himself in his silent voice, just tourist stuff, but still important.. Drisko was on a mission, he wasn't that sure what it was all about but, a mission.. He was certain something was driving him west, to the island, to Victoria.. He was wise enough to understand the new kid on the block syndrome.. He experienced it, a lesson he learned young and remembered, moving his life to Toronto way back then, covering his tracks, knowing the areas, the terrain, the who's who.. A skill he was able to apply to his first radio gig in the big smoke with the EDGE..

He needed something that the locals could relate to him with.. He needed to see the sights and sounds of B.C., to know them first hand.. Been there done that, or not, the skill of silence, the skill of asking questions, then listening.. Allowing another to have common ground, ice breakers, questions, as in I've heard of or was wondering if you knew of.. Sales tricks, probing, open questions, smoke and mirrors and Drisk was skillful, with both, like a surgeon.. He veered the 911 towards Lake Louise and prepared himself to be astounded.. It did not disappoint him in the least..

Staring aimlessly, hypnotic, into the crystal clear reflection of the ice blue turquoise lake.. It staring back, reflecting the mountains on either side, pouring into, then onto the massive range behind it.. Funnelling, every drop of the purest glacier water into the lake.. Picture post cards, he remembers them, the colours, the photographs, vividly, sketched into his mind.. Staring out, *"Fame, fame, fame, fame"*, *"Is it any wonder,"*, he parks the Porsche at the valet entrance to Le Chateau Lake Louise.. Stopping for a lunch on the open deck and taking in this panoramic view of this remarkable, historical, touristic lake front vision..

Drisko racing against the sunset, fires the 911, slowly trolling out the gates, down the backroad lane and then on, into the Gateway to the Rookies.. Pounding the power to the pistons, deep in past Golden.. Heading high into the summit of Rogers Pass, the deep jagged gorgeous, dropping.. The river below crashing, the twisting of the rail lines, the tunnels.. Then deep he motors into Glacier National Park, he knows this is on his hit list.. He needs this one, he wants to see the wonders of his world, Banff, the pass, the Continental Divide, the glaciers, Lake Louise and the Kicking Horse Pass, all of it, all on the list.. He knows of these places, he's studied them, all of them, back in C.C.P.H, his high school geography class.. The special classes, the one he shared with Officer Macy, Donna, Barnie Fyfe, as the locals called her.. The classes designed, especially for people with P.T.S.D, exactly like Officer MacLyn and him, Drisko, the Viking Child..

He comes from a place, that's made of ice and snow.. Up there from the midnight sun, where the hot springs flow.. A place where "Valhalla I am coming", is their battle cry.. The land overflowing with massive mountain ranges, filled with explosive, crashing icebergs.. Releasing their enormous destructive power within the path of the ice floes.. Dumping them carelessly into the mighty blue Atlantic.. The Atlantic filling, rising with humongous tsunamis and tidal waves, completely capable of sinking a battleship.. He understands it's angelic power, the mystic of it all, he adores it.. He comes from the ice, he is Icelandic, his ancestors, are as him, all Norseman, all of pure Viking blood and fearless.. He wants to stand on it, on the great glacier, lay his boots on it.. Crushing it, beneath his very soul, conquer it as it flows below him.. As he approaches it, it looks nothing more than a raging river, as he closes in on it, he sees it all.. The river flowing wildly, twisting up into huge waves, monstrous whitecaps..

As he approaches, closer, closing in on it, more observant, ominous to it.. He sees it all, his fly eyes, now, showing only as an illusion, a lie, a trick.. Courtesy of the clouds, the suns brilliant reflections, glistening on it, the gentle breezes, blowing and the gift, from the heavens above, mirroring its might.. It does not flow with rage, he said, in his silent voice, at all he thought.. It is not, as it appears, wild like a beast, ferocious like a dragon that needs slaying.. It is tame, more like a kitten, docile, like a pussy cat.. Only with the slightest of vibrations, it flows smooth in constant gentle movement, while it echoes off the mountain tops.. The screams of a thousand eels, screeching in a vat of boiling hot water, a song as it sang..

The ice, was alive with sound and it sung.. Tearing, clawing at each another, as if warriors, in a battle to a slow tedious, inevitable death.. A battle of positioning, of power, to where only the strong can survive as they conquer each others territories, inching across the tundra.. Overwhelming one another, conquering, then devouring.. Like the Siren, Drisko remembers her, that moment attacking from aboard the Casandra, devouring every living thing in her path.. He feels the true power of the message as it's delivered.. His blood crueling inside him, as if he's been awakened to the meaning of what pure power truly was..

Drisko shifting gears, climbing up the inclines, coasting into the valleys deep, dark, below.. Edges thrusting hundreds of feet below, gripping, ripping on the tire tread as the Porsche simply effortlessly executes every manoeuvre.. Blasting in, up and through the mighty Rocky Mountain range, its solid rock face, the solid rock beat, **"Fame makes a man take things over. Fame lets him loose hard to swallow, Fame puts you"**, heading west bound into the solitude of the sunset.. Sinking into the solid black pearl, 911 Porsche, heading to Hell..

Drisko pours another pound of pure petrol into the tiny Porsche as he revved his way to Revelstoke, and up into Salmon Arms.. Then up past it, then north a tad and then back on westward to Hub City, as it was known, Kamloops, B.C. the desert, the driest spot in Canada.. Stopping only to refuel, checking all the fluids and coffee levels, he's off chasing the sun set, west bound, heading to Hell again.. The highway veers hard left, deeper into Kicking

Horse then south bound, right there at Cache Creek, then on south further into Spences Bridge.. Deeper now into the deep south, into North Bend, Boston Bar, along the ragged edges, the sheer rock faces.. Crossing the tiny bridges and vase craters carved into the rivers below, his mind travelling back, to the Gros Morne, to the Rock and the Black Pearl..

The black pearl, skipping, skipping, skipping along, till then, skipping till then, when he reaches, his destination, the end.. The point he must achieve, Hell's Gates, the sign read, he parked the Porsche and walks to the edge, looking down.. The sun is now setting over the mountain ridge, not fully, just hovering over the edge, glistening on the rocks below.. The rivers raging, crying out a thousand names.. Names of the lost, the souls, here, lost in this spot, it morbidly enlightened him, night is falling, he pictured himself dancing with the dead, there at the Gates of Hell..

In 1880 an explorer Simon Fraser, exploring the narrow 35 meter passage through the gorge, along the sheer rock canyon wall that would one day bear his name.. There, through where he had just travelled, he named it, Hell's Gates.. Stating that, this is a place that no human being should ever venture, for surly they will encounter the Gates of Hell.. Only decades later, with the building of the rail lines, the connecting of the continent along the way.. The Fraser River, will claim three souls for every foot of track laid.. All of them souls would pass through this spot, the spot they marked as Hell's Gates..

Then the onslaught of the automobile with the turn of the century.. The building of the Trans Canada Highway, the road along the Fraser River Pass, in through Rogers, up into Kicking Horse.. It would just give out, take the cars, trucks, buses, entire families whipped out, thrown deep into the Fraser.. Avalanches, mud slides, rock walls, failing, falling, crashing deep, deep into the Fraser.. All of it, being washed through the tiny narrows, of this very spot.. The spot they named Hell's Gates, and so appropriate, Drisk said, standing, there at the Gates of Hell, talking from the Edge, talking to the dead, there in his silent voice..

Drisko revved the tiny Porsche, slapping back the gears, slapping, shifting onward, upward, west over the mountain crest, then re-gearing, down, into the valley below.. The Porsche's fuel injectors, working, gripping the R.P.M.'s, driving the Porsche into mode.. The gouging as the throttles snapped back, gears shifting, the tunes humming the machine obeys.. Drisko running from Hell, leaving it as dust in the rear view mirror.. Hope, as he envisioned it, he could see it, the sign there ahead, shining back at him on every turn.. Hope, there through the glass, the windshield of the black 911 Porsche.. Hope he dreamt about it, as he manoeuvred the black beauty of a beast, up and down the pathways, his pathway, the pathway to Hope..

Then he sees it, it is now visible, not a dream or a mirage, but it's real.. It's huge, it's green, it's there directly in front of him, in his sights.. He sees it all, with his fly eyes, he sees it there, through the glass, it's real, the sign he's been hoping for, the sign of Hope and now it appears, Hope, 5k.. Drisko knows, he's only thirty minutes out of Harrison's Hot Springs.. He made a reservation, booked a room right on the lake.. The geothermal hot springs, right out his back door.. Some him time, he drives past leaving all Hope far behind..

Drisko sitting there on the deck of the luxurious resort, sunken deep in the valley of the Gods.. Looking out over the tiny reflective lake.. The lake views, mirroring the harshness of the reddened night sky.. The obvious ruggedness of the rigged mountain peaks, of Bear Mountain as the song plays, burning into Drisko, ***"That burns your change to keep you insane (fame)."***.. Here, as he's preparing himself to lay his beaten body into the relaxing, soothing, warmth of the aqua spas of the Harrison Hot Springs, while sliding gently into Bowie, ***"fame, fame, fame, fame."***.. Drisko listening as the cool dance beat plays, he cracks open a Kokanee beer.. Native to the area, a local favourite since 1959, brewed right here in B.C.. Drisko doing his recon, collecting his data, research and all.. But the shit did have a cool kick as he fires up a doob, relaxing on the chaise lounge..

Drisk pictures his commercial for the famous brewing company.. Highlighting the name of the brew, as he sips away on the cool refreshing lager.. The motorcycle, kicking hard down the #97, hitting it along the two thousand kilometre stretch of twisting, winding, nail biting, hairpin turns of the Kokanee highway.. The longest, continuous route in any Canadian province.. Gearing her up as the bike sings the song, kooooo, kooon, neee, beeeeerrr, as it gears it's way through the mountainous pass, screaming it out word for word.. Singing along to the words Kokanee, the announcer's deep delicious voice over, resonating above the lyrical music bed..

So cool, Drisko visualizing the bikes every movement.. The tires ripping, tapping into the edge, the road racing beneath the steel gear shifter.. The dirt, of the dirty black boot sole, hammering, then resting, on the silver chrome shifter pedal.. The sounds of the engine screeching, the thrust of the thrust, thrusting, in song.. The ripping, of the gears as they collide, echoing back as thunder, off the solid rock faces, of the ragged mountain tops.. Singing in perfect harmony, as the driver drives her, excelling the two wheeled machine dangerously close to the edge..

Holding the hard turn with a crooked smile of content.. Portraying his defiance of a man against the mountain.. Reflecting the drama in his Ray Bans, as a man against the machine.. In Drisko's case, man against himself, his demons, his living Hell, his need to conquer, to win.. Drisk opens a smile of delight, as he tokes, on the toxic potion.. Drisko picturing himself creating award winning, after award winning commercials.. Captivating the audience with his astoundingly creative points of view.. The stage is set, him, Drisko, the producer, the director, screaming out the word, action, as it all comes alive for him.. Like a scene, in a giant, blockbuster movie, the vision now becomes a reality, within his tiny reach..

Some day, he says, some day very soon, in his silent voice.. There on the deck of the Hot Springs hotel, looking, gazing into the mountains, lost in his creative thoughts.. Then deeper he starts thinking about Mercedes, her smile, her kiss, her touch, making love to her.. The kids, Mercedes beside him, with them all, here, now, enjoying the hot spring spas and the cool mountain views.. Missing all those little league games, the joy they bring, his love for them all.. He felt the pain of his sacrifice, how much he was missing them all, right now.. The family, their home, their little life there in Burlington, the song singing to him, *"Fame, fame, fame, fame. Is it any wonder you are too cool to fool. (fame)"*.. The dreams of the island, the adventure, his business and his new life, there on Vancouver Island..

Staring up at the moon, rising there above the mountain top, reflecting itself back to him, off the moonlight of the lake, beautiful he thought, just beautiful.. He readied himself, to take a walk through the paths of the huge, beautiful, historical resort.. He planned on having a peaceful dinner on the deck, overlooking the lake.. Then grabbing a relaxing dip in the hot springs pools and then he'll get ready for an early start.. The road is long, he's on a journey, he understands that.. But, he's also fully committed to and aware that he's on a timely mission, he respects that.. He lays comfortably soaking, in the warmth of the natural spas of the Harrison Springs, gazing into the mountaintops.. *"Fame, fame, fame, fame. Fame, what's your name, what's your name, what's your name, what's your name, Fame."*, listening as the nineties disco dance song, slowly fades away..

Drisko aims the 580 horsepower pearl black Porsche 911 turbo, out on to the #9, out of the resort property and up into town.. Cruising out past the Harrison camp sites, out past the little liquor and groceries store combo.. On up through the narrow road, up, out past the giant statue of the Sasquatch, a freakin Big Foot, Drisko laughs, the sight entertains his mind.. Then into Essa Junction, passing by the RCMP post, crossing the steel bridge at Harrison River and on towards Bridal Falls, then on to Chilliwack.. Then only a tad further to the connection for the Trans Canada.. Highway 1., westbound to Abbotsford, the last leg of the journey.. Then it's just a hop, skip and a jump into Horseshoe Bay, the B.C. ferry terminal and the ferry to Swartz Bay, the island, then Victoria.. The tiny Porsche catching the morning sun, blinding, behind him as it rips open the road heading west, into the deep, darkness of the mighty blue Pacific..

No idling, the huge flashing sign read, Drisko, idling the Porsche five cars back from the loading gate, lane six.. He shuts the mighty engine down, the Porsche, quiets there, at the ferry terminal in Horseshoe Bay.. Drisko watching as the great ship is unloading to the north, people, moving, cars heading in off and up the ramp, he's familiar with the ferry system, he's got a good twenty minute wait.. While he waits he fades, back to the ferry ride over to the mainland as he left his beloved Newfoundland behind, *"bully for you, chilly for me. Got to get a rain check on, pain (fame)"*, vowing then, never to return to the Rock..

But he missed the island, his tiny life there, his love, his friends and his family.. He watches as the visions unfold again.. Repeating, repeating, as always, again and again as he watched the tiny island disappear.. Swallowed, wholly, completely, there, by the mighty blue Atlantic, there as he watched it, from the deck of the Leif Ericson.. Everything he ever knew, loved, or cared about, was gone.. Everything about it, his past, his life, the island, all of it destroyed, a moment in time and poof she was gone..

The whistle alerted the passengers, the message that the Spirit of British Columbia was preparing to board.. Walk-on passengers was being broadcast through the loud speakers.. Then with it a five minute warning to return to your vehicles.. Drisko fired the Porsche's 3.8L. engine, driving juice into the 580 horses, as he waited, idling in the no idling zone.. The light flashed green as Drisko led his black beast into the cage, stopping and then fastening her down with the E' brake.. Drisko, left the animal there and headed up the steel staircase to the sixth floor dining room.. Grabbing himself a light lunch, then finding a comfortable seat right out front, as the ship set sail.. Full screen, living colour as he watched the movie unfold..

Enchanting, he thought, smooth, tranquil, soothing he noticed, beautiful.. The path was filled with twist and turns, tiny islands everywhere.. With people and cottages on them and everywhere glorious views.. Everywhere, the mountains highlighting the ocean pass, through the Straits of Juan de Fuca..

Drisko, noting, noting, nothing like the voyage across the open seas, of the Straits of St. Lawrence from the Rock to the mainland, Cape Breton Island.. Drisko laughing to himself, no wonder I watched that freakin rock sink in front of me.. This here though, she ain't the Atlantic, nor, she ain't really the Pacific.. She is what she is though, she's the Straits of Juan de Fuca, in the Salish Sea.. Drisko knows her well, it is a major migration path for the whales and Orca's from the Sea of Cortez, from the Gulf of California, in Mexico.. They travel up to Canada, through the Gulf Stream across the most northern tip of the United States and right into the Straits..

Treacherous waters there as the mouth opens into the Pacific, there between Seattle Washington and Victoria, Vancouver Island.. The opening is known as the Graveyard of the Pacific, claiming thousands of shipwrecks.. Devouring thousands upon thousands of innocent lives, sending them helplessly to the deep, floating, picturesque, like a beautiful peace of art, a sculptured statue.. Falling, floating, failing, deep, then deeper aboard your Grave Ship.. Drisko was floating safely, deep in the inlet of the sound, the Salish Seas.. Deep in the Straits of Georgia, sheltered there, surrounded by the Southern Gulf Islands.. Tucked neatly, coasting into Otter Bay, behind the beauty of Pender and Salt Spring Islands, drifting gently into the cove of Swartz Bay..

Drisko knows everything about this world, how it rotates, manoeuvres, shifts and slides.. He knows the beauty of it, he knows its secrets, he's witnessed its awesome powers and he knows it can destroy.. He knows about whales, from true whalers.. He knows about currents, tides and the oceans, from being on it, near it and around it all his life.. The great tales of the fishermen, the stories of the brave, warriors, explorers, the lost souls.. He knows latitudes and longitudes, lessons passed down from a thousand voyages, he knows the sea.. He can read the sun as it's rising and setting, tell you when it's gonna rain.. Can read the stars, the moon and the Milky Way.. He knows the migration habits of every fish, bird, animal and sea creature around the world.. He could hunt bear, trap game and skin a rattle snake alive.. He lived in the wild, lived with the wolves, lessons he had been taught from a tot.. Since he was old enough to walk, he was, a Viking Child..

They were the very first explorers, collectors of knowledge, data, creators of their own true information highway.. Now he and his mighty warriors, the hundreds of men he leads, no, thousands, had come to conquer B.C.. We have no home he says, we have no way to retreat as he watches his ships burning there in the tiny harbour off Swartz Bay.. We come to conquer or we perish he cries out, we die.. But with his cries, it seems at that very moment.. With the strangest coincident of timing.. B.C., had come to conquer him, and he at that very moment in time, had surrendered to her.. He was staying here, somehow, somewhere, he knew it at that very moment, this will be my prison, he said.. Drisko was falling in love right there and then, the beauty of the Witch, too powerful to control, too deadly of a foe.. Each man seeing her, only as he, could see her, ugly, yet beautiful..

He screamed it out, loudly, the words, word for word.. "I'm home, I'm free", this, this is my home, he screamed.. Screaming, screaming, screaming from the bows of the mighty ship, but no one took notice.. Drisk just assumed they were all really busy screaming it out too, or was it something more.. A trance, some voodoo thing, were they all just simply simultaneously and in unison, they all fell into some sort of a cult like, hypnotic trance.. Yes, that's what it is he said, that's it, the only explanation for it, a trance.. I'm in a trance he said as he smiled and screamed it all out, over the audience again, in his silent voice.. Softly this time, as to not disturb the disturbed, or to dare abruptly awaken the dead.. "I'm home", he whispered, shaking his head, gazing out through the glass, "I'm home", whispering it, home, then sipped on his coffee, gracefully..

The Porsche zooms out of the gate of the Swartz Bay ferry terminal, up along the Pat Bay Highway.. South into Sidney, out past James Island into North Saanich then along the coastal path, past Sidney Island, down into Elk Lake and up into Cardova Bay.. Drisko revving the black pearl 911 Porsche, the black Porsche is revving.. Coasting, gearing down into Saanich, linking onto the Trans Canada #1 to Victoria, gearing, shifting, re-gearing.. Straight into Douglas Street and the historic Strathcona Hotel, a Victorian landmark that dates back to the gold rush era.. Drisko could see the mountains then straight into the beautiful gardened streets of the Capital City..

Drisko picked the location for it being right down town in the heart of the city.. All the major agencies were here, all the radio, television and graphic agencies were here, this was a hub, second to Vancouver.. The waterfront, the cafe's, restaurants and bistro's all you could desire, everything was here.. The yacht club, the city harbour, the parliament buildings and the great and famous Empress Hotel.. The city was alive with commerce, retail and banking.. They say there are seven women to every man in Victoria.. No industry there, no industry mostly, on the island.. The men leave for work, the women guard the fort, the original name for Victoria, Fort Victoria..

The hotel now, well the place was rocking.. The Strathcona was beautifully appointed, the image of pure decadence lingered at every turn.. The rooms luxuriously decorated with heritage pieces and masterfully dated fixtures.. The bars and restaurants, the roof top patios, Ivy's disco, the main disco, nightclubs.. The Games Room, the Clubhouse and Big Bad John's, you need to prepare yourself to venture in there.. It's a trip back in time, pure, 1940's Hillbilly decor.. Peanuts on the floor, with thousands of dollar bills stapled and autographed on the walls, sometimes with hundreds.. Ugly women, warm beer, lousy service, some with no teeth.. Drisko parks the Porsche in the valet parking, grabs his bag from the boot, takes a good look into the sky and enters the foyer.. Easy night, check in, get ready for the morning, then tear the fuck outta this town.. Drisko unpacks his junk and grabs the cell to call Mercedes, your gonna fuckin love it here baby..

He unloads on her right off the gate, exploding with definitions of the last legs of his journey.. The beauty, the serenity, the lushness of the forest, the waterfalls, the lakes and rivers, almost beyond descriptions of his trip.. Drisko laying it on thick, the trip, the ferry ride, the tiny islands, the gorgeous passages, the treacherous waterways, the narrow passages, he, himself had narrowly survived.. His treacherous, spell binding, heroic exploration through Hell's Gates.. The mountains he'd climbed, the valleys that opened up into the most magnificent views.. The twisting and turning of a thousand miles of steel rails, that he and he alone had conquered, against all odds and totally death defying..

He went on, sharing his love for her, the kids, his family, asking for all the details.. He laid out a rough idea of his plan for her.. Telling her, swearing to the Gods that she would just love it here.. Laying out mile after mile of the places and areas, they would stop along the way, when he returns to get her.. The trip he's planned for them, the journey they would all take together.. All this before he had even hit the streets of Victoria.. He just knew, he knew he was going to conquer B.C., right there, starting with this little island he said.. Were not leaving here till I own this rock, confidently, she laughed.. Word he said strongly, I know she replied, giggling, I know..

Then as his lips moved his mouth, and he was mouthing out them exact words to her, he saw it, his dreams.. He saw them all become a reality, there as he spoke it, his vow, his oath, his word.. He then in closing, described to her, the sun as it was setting off the tip of the tiny island.. He then told her what he would be doing to her right now, under the moonlight if she were here tonight.. The sun was now sinking deep below some mountaintop, speaking to her romantically, softly.. Some unknown distant place to us, he added to her, somewhere far off to the west.. Somewhere enchanting, exotic, integrating and adventurous, he whispered to her softly, somewhere just for you and me.. Somewhere beyond the abyss, to where if you sail your ship to close to, you would surely fall off the edge.. My mother is here with me tonight sweetie, so, no worries.. She's watching over me, as she watches over you, then he laughed.. She knew how much he loved nature and what his true meaning was, she laughed.. She told him how much she truly loved him and then she kissed him goodnight, sweetly, long, then waited and then she hung up the phone..

The street lights were barely beginning to flicker to off, as Drisko's wheeling the 911 through the back streets of Victoria.. Left, then right, turning, twisting, east, then west, over through Government St., pushing in past the Parliament buildings and out past the Empress.. Taking the tight left, then on into Dallas road and to Kilometres 1, of the Trans Canada Highway, right there at the opening to Beckon Hill Park.. Drisko, twisting and turning all through the urban sprawl, finding his way then getting lost.. Lost Drisko laughing at the possibility, I'm on a freak'n island here.. Water to the left, water to the right, laughing as he torques the little Porsche's engine..

Drisko wasn't going anywhere in particular, just cruising in the Porsche, enjoying the sights.. While at the same time, checking out the neighbourhoods as he'd call it.. All part of the plan, reconnaissance, mapping out in his mind, noting, noting, the areas, the districts, the landmarks.. This was just the first phase of the plan, start inward, then work your way outward.. Second phase, would be to develop a major four part hit list, the who's who.. Checking out all the major businesses, retailers, entertainment, tourist traps, restaurants and specialty services in the area.. Categorizing them as to their priority, A's, B's and the C's, then, the lowly D's.. He was great at coming up with quick, snap, on the spot creative ideas for clients. Huge promotional, advertising, marketing and public relations campaigns.. Mind bending, award winning, creative ideas, he had already carried some fame..

Drisko took the high road, out past CFB Esquimalt and the naval base, with two huge Canadian destroyers hanging off the docks.. Twisting the left into Colwood, out past the Royal Roads Military Academy, then deep into the country side of Metchosin.. Following the roadway into Langford and then down into Sooke.. The road along the tiny cove, all twisting, all turning, then opening into magnificent breathtaking views at each and every twist, Drisko was loving the ride.. Drisk doubled the road back, quick change of plan, he then hung the left, then in through the tiny hamlet of Langford and then out the other side quickly.. The Island Highway, Trans Canada #1, bare in front of him, left to north island, Goldstream Park then up into Campbell River.. The right, would lead him back into downtown Victoria..

The sun was beaming in through the open sunroof of the Porsche.. Campbell Rivers three hours north, hour and a half in the Porsche, Drisko laughs.. The blue LCD clock in the Am. Fm. Blaupunkt stereo cassette player reads, twelve ten, high noon Drisk noted, *"let's him loose and hard to swallow. Fame puts you there where things are hollow"* as he hung the left.. Goldstream Park lays at the foot of the Malahat Highway.. Drisko hangs the right down into the enchanted forest, slowly entering the path.. The huge B.C. cedars, towering above the ground, some big enough to park the Porsche in, massive, simply unbelievable..

Drisko pulls the machine up into a hole near the stream.. The sign there is notifying him that the area is protected.. This is the main artery of the river as a Salmon spawning ground, the entrance into Goldstream Park from Mill Bay.. A passerby noticing the plate, filled Drisk in on the area.. When they're spawning there, he said, you could walk across her and not hit a drop of water, they're spread that thick, my boy.. Drisko, amazed at the sight from the vision.. Now sitting alone in the sacred park, Drisko grabs his stash, rolls himself up a couple of doobs, then points the tiny Porsche north up the Malahat..

The highway steepening, the incline rising into the mountain, trickles and traces of the cove, revealing as he climbs the hill.. He watches in fascination as the water in the bay below opens into spurts of views surrounded by mountains tops, not far in the distance.. He climbs and climbs the Porsche, floating her high onto the mountain.. There he sees it, beautiful, lookout point, a road, cut off the road, along the rocky cliffs edge, protected with steel post barriers.. He wheels the 911 into the parking area, stopping her, diagonally, along the cement walkway.. He fires up his doob and gets out of the car as he inhales the toxic potion, absorbing the invigorating views of the closed in bay and the sheltered shoreline..

Drisko pushing the tiny Porsche further north on his adventure, racing up over the Malahat, up the Island Highway, along the Tran Canada #1 north.. To the far north of the island, to, Comox, Courtney, Telegraph Cove, on to Port McNeill, then the end of the line, Port Hardy.. Drisko, just killing time, recon, he knew the end of the line was for another day, as he wheels the 911 into the town of Mill Bay.. He hangs the right at the stop light, onto Mill Bay Rd.. Driving east now into the beauty and picturesque ocean front trails into Cowichan.. Drifting, lost as he cruises the tiny bay side drive, *"fame, fame, fame."*, absorbed into the village.. Running the Porsche back north now, drifting in along the waterfront.. Then up into the park north along Cowichan Bay, veering right and into the marina for a break..

Drisko knows exactly where he is, he studied the area, well.. All the maps, all the longitudes, all the latitudes, all of it, the whole island.. Long before the journey began, he knew exactly where he was going.. Dreaming of it all, as he sits and stares out into the wonderment of Mill Bay.. Looking deep with desire and lust, out onto, into the enchantment of the Salt Spring Island.. Duncan, Chemainus, Ladysmith, Nanaimo to the north, Victoria, to the south.. Everywhere, all around him, water, the mighty blue Pacific Ocean.. He took the country road home, then back out, in through Cobble Hill..

Veering right, in toward the south end of Shawnigan Lake.. Drisko, veering tighter left along the east side of the lake, then twisting the bottom turning north up the west side of the lake, circling it.. Then further west along Renfrew's pass.. Then racing the winding backroad, south, veering left, right, left.. Then tight east, then south again, then west, west, then south, then west, south, east, then west.. Down, down, down deeper into the twisted backroads, then the twist north, then a slight west down back into Sooke, dusting through the tiny town.. Then east to Langford, Colwood, Metchosin then out up to Thetis Lake, back onto the Trans Canada Highway, south, home, for now, home to Fort Victoria..

Vancouver Island was discovered in 1778 by Captain James Cook, of the Royal British Navy.. On the thirtieth day of March.. Cook sailed his ship, the Resolution into the remote bay of Nootka Sound, on the south western tip of the island.. Fort Victoria was established in 1843 as a deport for the Hudson Bay Company, to support the northern Pacific trade.. The building standing on the spot of the Empress Hotel today.. When James Douglas discovered the area known by the Lekwungen native tribe as Comosack, the "Rush of Water".. Comosack, after it's development, was renamed Fort Victoria..

Douglas chose the spot for the abundance of water power for grain and saw mills, vast timber fields and an adequate supply of arable lands for settlers and farming.. But his primary reasoning and most importantly, it's incredible strategic defensive military positioning.. In 1958 the fort was home to a mere fifty residents, the same year they discovered gold in the Fraser River.. After that, everything about the little fort was about to change forever.. Drisko raced the black pearl 911 Porsche back to fort and parked her in front of the valet parking, at the entrance to the historic Strathcona Hotel..

Drisk knew it would take a lot of work to break into the tiny fortress, but he had a secret weapon.. He knew what was at risk, the island was secure, protected, dominated by local agents.. Smooching the clients, building lasting rapport, alliances, life long friendships..

Not an easy task for any man, but Drisko, was prepared and well experienced at this.. He'd done it all before, hell, he created it, breaking into TO., back in the day.. He'd look into the mirror as if a totally different man.. Then repeating to himself, his mantra, "successful people do what unsuccessful people will not do", "the battle is won by never surrendering"..

This was all about hard work, asking the hard questions, what Drisko would call, letting them hit the ceiling, then scraping them off, see how they land.. Drisko did his work, developing his list, extending, far beyond his tiny reach, stretching all through Ontario, back in the day.. Back when he was learning the ins and outs of radio, television, magazine and the newspaper game.. Today he was well connected, partnered, owner, with recording studios, graphic companies, signage, photography and talent.. All of it intricately connected, together, through what he called his back door.. One agency, brought together under one name, his, an award winning, full service, international agency, The Creative Factory..

The name, lingering on their lips, dancing inside their tiny brains, ringing into their virgin ears.. Their visions, eluding to this huge factory, somewhere in the wilderness.. Building, developing, creating everything huge, huge production, huge studios, scattered, throughout this huge, yet totally updated, decrepit, abandoned factory.. The name, ringing synonymous with success and hard work.. The clients saw it all, long before their King walked through the door.. Each man seeing the Witch exactly as he would see her, ugly, yet beautiful.. Talk about genius, most agencies have some fancy dancy name, Loveus and Leaveus or Dooie Screwem & Howe, bullshit names, bullshit creative, fancy boardrooms.. Fuck that, this was war, Drisko was a six pack, blue jean kinda guy..

Drisko went to work, developing his list over the next six weeks.. Travelling north through the tiny island, learning it, knowing the wheres and whats.. Figuring out the who's who of Who'sville and preparing for battle.. Drisko, noting, noting, recording and calling, stopping and poking and poking and noting.. Drisko, would just stop, out in nowhere land, pull into a small radio or newspaper, T.V. station.. He'd walk right in, just happened to be in the neighbourhood, he'd say and introduce himself in person.. Offering his services, breaking hard accounts for them, specialized promotions, designed directly to drag clients in.. They were always impressed with his ideas, concepts, always.. He worked his agency like he was in a war, keep your friends close, your enemies closer and always have a hook..

The hook, Drisko's favourite part of the process, introduce yourself, tell them what you can do for them, tell them all the gory details, then leave them with a hook.. A simple, little, if I could, would you.. Drisko was an ideas man, but smart enough not to ever give-a-way the farm, that's why he used a hook, and he kept it nice and sharp.. That's why the list, the list, the A, B, C list and most importantly the D list.. Drisko was war like, strategic in his every move, he was pro-research and recon, face to face and door crashing.. The A list was comprised of all the big names.. The A's, the ones every agent and every rep was chasing.. The hard ones, the ones with the biggest budgets..

Drisk made his A list, he shrugged at it and tossed it loosely to one side.. Then the B's and the C's, tossing them also to one side, the potentials, the less potential.. Then he created the fun list, the D's, his play list as he'd call it, the list he can play with.. The D's were easy, the D's were all about discovery, clients, no one cares about, the small company's struggling or the ones, that no one could break.. They were, of all the list, the most important to him.. Drisko looked at his gig as a battle, so he was always, preparing his attack and his defence.. The D list were his scouts, they were his informants, they were the front line of defence.. They were valiant warriors, battling for positioning, battling against the same foe.. Like the glaciers battling for positioning on top.. The C's, B's and A's, in fact, they were, D's, direct competitors, in essence their enemies.. Who doesn't like to talk about their enemies?

It kind of worked like this, say you have an A list, a Dry Cleaner you want to contact and hit with a strong idea.. First off you can't get past the secretary of an A list, little lone present an idea.. This is invitation only, VIP, who's who.. You need some ammo, big guns, explosive, something like dynamite, or even Kryptonite, something nuclear.. Secondly you don't know shit about dry cleaning, in fact you probably have trouble dressing yourself.. Well say the A guy, owns ten locations, and your D guy owns four.. The strategy was simple, ask D if he can help you out, a friendly chat, what, you'd say, help you out.. Ya', exactly, get D to help you develop the campaign for his own competition..

That's why it is a strategy, Drisko would call Mr. D, ask for a meeting.. Tell him you want to pick his brain about the dry cleaning business, casually.. If you can get them away from the office or their work location even better.. Tell him you have a phenomenal idea that you've developed.. That you're positive would create enormous residuals, for a dry cleaner in another town, far away.. You just need someone to help you fill in the blanks, while not ever divulging any real info as to A.. Now that's a hook..

D, now has to choose, one, ignore the offer to casually meet and talk about his business.. Or two, meet and find out about this phenomenal marketing idea, guaranteed to increase the profits of their major competition.. Drisko was a pro, little chance that little D, would turn him down.. Drisko knew all D had to do was to answer the phone, listen for a moment and Drisko opened the door to negotiations.. A trick, he was very proficient at.. Step two, he'd call this the last step, because if it didn't fly here, he'd drop it and follow up later.. He had his hook, it was nice and sharp, he just needed to keep the bait fresh..

N.S.Q.S., he designed it and named it, it was, as he'd call it, the Needs, Satisfaction, Questioning, Strategy.. A psychological evaluation for business, a lethal weapon and it worked, perfectly.. A simple design, most businesses have ten basic similarities and ten differences.. What makes you so different, why should I deal with your company? Then down the questions, to the most profitable thing you can do as a business, trust building questions.. Questioning D, will give Drisk the answers too, while Drisk knowing the out come to most of the answers.. While D, gets more involved with the strengths and weaknesses of his business, he becomes self absorbed.. Then to the most profitable thing you can do question.. D, now see's the potential of the media campaign and Drisko's services..

Drisk has now developed an untapped client and a new account he can build into to an A.. Worst case scenario for Drisk, D says no to the campaign.. Drisk knew, he was walking out with the complete lowdown as to the who's who of A, B and C, the good, the bad and the ugly.. Plus the ten major parts of them, how they all work, along with the most profitable thing they could do as a company and everybody leaves as friends.. Besides, there are lots of D's out there and Drisk has all the answers.. How, you would ask, simply, they're all his psychologically designed questions? Designed to create greed, through potential, develop beliefs and build trust, a true talent..

Drisko drifting back to Cripple Creek Pass, the Edge, the Rock.. The song, Bowie's singing, *"Is it any wonder I reject you first."*.. Drisk drifting into the lessons instilled into him there, by his uncle Bev, his dad Bryce and grand dad Eric, all working the farm.. Work smart kid, not hard, they'd tell him, work smart.. Life is ninety percent inspiration, ten percent perspiration, if you work smart, get a good plan, use your strategy, then execute the plan, she all comes together like that.. Drisko wasn't hitting for sales just yet, this trip was all about the plan, the strategy and when the time was right the execution of the plan.. He was ready, he knew it was time.. He knew there was enough value here on the island to sustain a small satellite office and he'd stay connected through his office in Ontario..

He parked the Porsche in the carport of the luxury house he had rented in Colwood, on a mountain top, over looking the Military Academy.. The upper deck of the home had three sides of unobstructed post card picture perfect views.. The north island, the mountain ranges, the straits, Mill Bay, Bentwood, Swartz Bay,

Juan de Fuca.. Then straight into the picturesque sunrises over the City of Victoria.. Then the beauty of the night unfolds while the lights dance and the city glistens.. The moment he saw the view, it instantly reminded him of the Black Pearl.. How when you sat upon it, you felt like the King of the World.. Drisko was going to take this island, the hard way, one bite at a time.. Drisko had taken care of his end, Mercedes took care of hers, their house and storage, all ready and organized.. He booked his flight, got packed and ready to return to his home, to Mercedes, to Ontario..

Over the next couple of weeks, Drisko and Mercedes would get the family ready, pack up the camper along with the canoe.. Ship their things ahead and then get ready for an adventure of a lifetime.. A trip, straight across Canada, with his wife and children at his side.. Enjoying the journey, together as they move west.. Taking the time out that they so desperately needed to spend together, to reunite again.. Drisko excitingly planning the six week camping trip back to Vancouver Island.. Mercedes coordinating the plan with the kids school deadlines in mind.. Drisko mapping out the route, all the great things he wanted to show them, all the things he's been obviously missing along the way, *"Fame, fame, fame, fame."*..

CHAPTER FIVE

Funeral For A Friend

The slow tempo of the church bells, quietly, then the soothing Gothic sounds from the church pipe organ, engulf him as they whirl and twirl around him, like wind.. Then the crystallizing of the piano keys, slow, warm, soothing melody.. Then colliding with the guitar notes, smooth, soothing, tempo.. Then the speed slicing of his piano, revving, revving, up and down the scales.. Then all, in unison, bringing the song together as an orchestrated concerto.. Then faster, faster, faster, combining the guitar, drums and piano.. Then the solo of the ivory keys, pounding, pounding until it explodes into song..

"The roses in the window box have tilted to one side. Everything about this house was born to grow and die. Oh, it doesn't seem a year ago to this very day. You said, sorry honey if I don't change the pace. I can't face another day.".. Drisko gearing the mighty Porsche down as he crests up over the top of the Malahat, shifting and re-shifting, catching the view into Mill Bay.. Then over the top of it all, clear into Victoria.. The city dancing there before him, clear, alive, busy.. Seeing clear around the southern point, clear across the inlet bay into the mountain range of a complete and other country, fascinated by the distant views.. The Olympic Mountains, Mount Baker and the Cascade Mountain range, all in his perfect view..

Peering straight down and into the mouth of the Straits of Juan De Fuca, somewhere near Shipwreck Bay.. Cook's landing and the opening, on into the mighty deep, blue, Pacific Ocean.. Down, down, down, deep into the Malahat, passing Goldstream Park, then hanging the right, down into the tiny hamlet of Langford.. Then a right and out through the Island Highway, screaming along the main drag, into Sooke, screaming, screaming..

The sun slowly sinking over the tiny island, Drisk watches as it sinks, darkening his pass as he motors on.. The fog lights and tungsten headlights searching, searching, clearing the way.. Something here though, he wasn't sure what it was, but at night here, on the mystic island, everything seems darker.. The island comparable to England, the fogs and misty rains, the roads, the treeline of the roads, the slick of moist dew covering the paved way, all of it darker.. Night has fallen, and with it comes the dark.. Drisko knows another secret about the island, it's haunted..

The legends being that there was a full witches colonial here, filled with ghost and goblins, spirits and potions and spells.. Conjured up by witches and warlocks, their sons and their daughters.. The soil, rich in blood from the witch hunter's massacres and the area rich in tales.. Traces of it, remain still, they're spread all through the tiny island, just ask any of the local witches.. Drisko hangs a right, steering the black pearl 911 in past the residential area at the foot of Triangle Mountain.. Turning off just north of the Royal Roads Military Academy, gearing her down, preparing for the climb to the summit..

Drisko sees it through the Porsche's windshield as he gears her into third, revving the massive engine with ease.. He sees it there as he's heading up the foot hills to the mountain top.. The music, crashing into him, pounding, pounding every beat, beating on him, beating the tune into him.. He was powerless to stop it, he was completely unaware of what laid ahead, as he climbed the twisted mountain.. *"love lies bleeding in my hand. Oh it kills me to think of you with another man. I was playing rock n' roll and you were just a fan."*, the song beating on him, he can feel it, beating, beating into him.. It, can feel him, *"But my guitar couldn't hold you so I split the band. Love lies bleeding in my hand"*..

He shifts the shifter and then there it is, as he shifts.. The moon shining in on him as he veers the black pearl Porsche through the first turn.. The moon light high above the crest of the mountain, *"Oh,oh,oh, oh."*, clear, shining.. Shining in on him, there as he turned.. He recognizes it, there looking into it, huge.. The biggest moon he had ever witnessed, or not, maybe the same as he had witnessed in his past, his life before this life.. His life sheltered on the Rock, his life shattered by that moon..

Unconsciously steering the tiny Porsche in and out of that moon, turning and twisting along every inch of the mountain pass.. Veering and steering, racing up into the top, driving with force, *"Oh, oh, oh, love lies bleeding in my hand,"*, directly up over and into the moon.. Driving, driving, up to Mercedes, driving to the kids, up to the quiet country home, up to the top of the hill.. Drisko staring into it, then instantly losing sight while rounding the turns and twist of the hilly path.. Following him, following, as it would, watching as Drisko watched it in the rear view, the mirror..

What are you doing here, he asked? Turning and twisting the tiny Porsche, running as if in fear, gearing.. Asking of it, simply, why are you here, as he stares out into it? He can't help but wonder if it was one of them there gigantic asteroid thingies out there.. From somewhere far out in the outer space there, heralding in towards him once again.. Heralding at over a thousand miles per hour, or thirty kilometres per second.. Screaming, screaming in toward the tiny planet, destined, to devour, every, living, thing, in her path..

He turned the black pearl Porsche into the driveway and under the covered carport.. Designed to complete the second story deck, delivering the panoramic views.. He parked behind the white 78 Blazer he had restored, sitting there, under the yellow glow of the porch Carriage light.. Sitting there, silently listening as the song fades out, *"bleeding in my hand. Love lies bleeding in my hand."*..

The music, the guitar, *"oh, oh, oh, oh,"*, the music, the piano, the guitars all finally fading.. Drisko looks back at the massive moon as he gets out from the Porsche..

Drisko grips the gold plated front door knob as he looks back to the black pearl.. Just for a moment, an instant, a second in time, them, screaming out to him, beyond his tiny reach.. It only looked like the distinctive box styled tail lights, of the 67 green two door, Ford Mustang coupe.. There careening up over and off the edge, a full gainer as the animal simply grew fins and swam away, out to the deep blue, mighty Atlantic.. He enters through the double sided, stained glass front door of the mountain top home, home he thought, home, safe..

Things in Ontario were going good.. Drisko had stayed in touch with every aspect of his business in the big smoke.. All the production work was on schedule, all the talent, creative people and staff were working away.. All the sales people and clients were happy and everything was cooking along like clockwork.. Drisk was busy breaking open account after account, feeding it all through his Ontario office for now.. Lightning had struck the tiny island, a bolt or two must have hit him dead on, right into his tiny skull, because the boy was on fire.. Account after account, breaking, busting, smacking out creative after creative idea, all across the tiny island.. The island was on fire, and the flames were bursting, screaming out his name Drisko Oobbew..

First a couple quick promotions for some local radio stations, a couple small name D list clients.. Then a major break with a cool little all news radio station, CFAX, ALL NEWS RADIO.. This was a coup for Drisko, the station had thousands of listener, literally a major audience.. Drisk hit them hard with a hook, if I could, would you.. They bit full bait, swallowed, hook, line and sinker.. The Back Box Promotion was born.. Drisk did all the paper work got all the licences and permits.. Then he hooked about thirty major sponsors and ten co-sponsors..

Then he did the impossible, got permission from the city, to hang a five inch by eight inch, simple black box safe, in the middle of the main intersection of Government and Douglas.. Then all you had to do was listen to win.. Find the black box's location, as the announcers give away the clues.. Then you have a chance to win a key and a major prize, by finding a hidden key at any participating sponsor's location.. Then once you have a key, the key that opens the black box wins the Grand Prize.. It blew the little cap off the Capital city and it rocketed The Creative Factory into stardom.. Drisko had made a quantum leap on his quest of conquering this tiny island, devouring it and owning it, all..

Funny thing about the island, they say if a mouse sneezes in south end, ain't long before you gonna hear about it in the north end.. As big as that tiny island was in size, it was that small in word.. Drisko recognized that fact the first day he arrived there, in fact he figured it out long before he even left to come here.. The similarities of the Rock, to that of Van Isle's.. Drisko, hammering down client after client, D list, C list, some small, some big, some, every once in a while, a B list..

He worked smart and hard.. He worked the days and the nights, no limitation, just what he needed to do, always.. His name growing as a creator of innovative promotions, all new, all existing and more so, profit generating.. Stick to the cash register he'd order his clients.. We do a major price point on a door crasher special.. We roll that through the local media as a one day only, then we rate each media as to their performance..

The cash register won't lie, it will tell you truthfully which media works best for us.. Then we fly that on a sixteen week rotation and theoretically, we sit back and watch the register ring.. Give me something we can use, a big drawing card, a door crasher special.. Then we can co-op it and get the manufacturer to pay half for you.. Then, he'd simply turn and walk away, stopping, just as he was about to leave through the doorway, he'd turn and say.. Hey, free Bic pen with every Mercedes sold today, free Mercedes with every Bic pen..

It's not the media my friend, it's the power of your message, then Drisko would politely smile, turn and simply walk out the door..

The client list growing, the miles piling up, the little brain on fire, the Thrush thrusting.. Drisk could feel the thunder pounding in his ancient heart.. He could see the tribal warriors, thrashing, in attack mode, preparing for battle, thirsting, their blood crueling.. First, a small village to the north, he could surround them and massacre everyone, take the village with ease.. He decided, this is a good day to die, he donned his chain mail armour, the small steel ring links and then he fastened his mighty ancient sword onto the leather lope of his belt and peered into the mirror, watching the battle as it would unfold..

He pulled the black pearl 911 into the underground car park of the sky rise office structure, off Dallas road, near Beacon Hill Park.. The V.I.P., section of the high security entrance sector of the head office of Canada's third largest chicken franchise and Drisko was going to ruffle some feathers, he laughs at the thought as he gives his name to the nice security officer at the secure gate.. Plucked, fucked, punked and dunked all in one smooth move.. You need a cool little character, someone folks will instantly relate to.. You need a cool caption line something we can translate into both audio and visually for print and T.V., with the radio crossover..

I got it, all right here, pre-designed and laid out for you.. This is what we do, that was it, a cool little cartoonish character looking like a white pimp.. The hat, the bell bottoms, the big boots in stride and the logo was born.. The caption for all media translation.. Those three amazingly creative words, *"GREAT OOOOGELY BOOOGELY"*, then the caption line.. *"Those Saint Sherome's Barbecued Chicken and Rib's, well they was so delicious, they nearly blew my mind."*.. The deal was done, they bit and the noise was all over the tiny island.. The warrior was on the war path, striking without warning, without mercy..

The camper company boasting as Canada's largest retailer, rental and repairs of recreational vehicles.. Drisko created an amazing ad campaign for them, directing it at their leasing factor, they had lacked.. He connected them to Canada's foremost recognized authority of financial products and investments, a true celebrity in his own right, Mr. Costello.. The professional advisor, dressed in his fine tailored suits, holding a fishing rod in front of the companies logo, on the tire cover of the R.V.. The caption line reading, get-out-a line.. Then the captivating logo line, "Selling Canada By The Mile".. Then the crossover into radio, T.V., newsprint and back cover of national magazines, the campaign was amazing and the connection was a complete success.. The recognition was instantaneous through the nation and truly effective for the client, Drisko was a star..

The mattress factory, the hardware chain, all of them now falling, without resistance to the Viking Child's command.. The restaurant chains, the fast ones, the slow ones, the chink joints, the Indian and Tia-wons, the Italian-ones, ah, wadda you say Drisko, howa bouta you, make a me, an offer I can't refuse den ah', laughing, scary like.. The fine dining, the night clubs, the bars, the cops, the crooks and ya, one lowly little crack head that he helped out once, free, met him in a bar, drew a logo up for him, right then and there, handed it to him and what the fuck eh'.. Get the fucker back on track..

He was simply unstoppable, without end, without fear of any other competitor.. The list growing in leaps and bounds then one day, he stood there bravely in front of them, his sword lifted high.. Pointing at them, then thrusting it forward, out toward the mighty blue Pacific.. Lookie there he says to them, in his ancient tongue, see what I see? There beyond your sheltered shoreline, there in Shipwreck Bay, do you see it? That is my army, my fleet, do you see them, he asked, with ice shattering, ice blue steel eyes? Do you see the fires upon the ocean once blue? See how it has now turned to red, red with the blood of my enemies and the flames of my ships?

Those, those are my ships burning there in your harbour.. Those are my thousands of fierce and deadly warriors, here upon your shores.. We have no home, we have no where to run too, we have no way to escape this Island.. I'm here today, to conquer or to perish.. Piercing each and every eye in the massive boardroom of the Kokanee Beer Company.. Drisko hits them with the hook, well baited and dangling right there in front of their greedy eyes.. Then Drisko fires up the tiny black pearl 911 Porsche and sets off into the sunset.. Up to the mountain top, then on into that moon light, recognizing it for what it was, as he enters his home..

They call it a social media, the advertising business, because it's very, very sociable.. Your out all the time, demand after demand of your time.. There are no hours to Drisko's business.. Late nights, over nights, sometimes day and night, working in the studios.. Recording commercials, jingles, creative, talent timing, all extremely demanding, splicing, dicing, video and recording tapes.. Then the early morning breakfast meetings, lunches, dinners and late night parties, all of it demanding his time.. The functions, events, promotions, nothing ever stopped, never a moment unaccounted for.. Always something, someone or had to be somewhere, all of it demanding time.. Only in the dictionary does success come before work he would say.. He knew it well, it was one of his most motivational thoughts.. Whenever he would slack off, that mantra would come back to haunt him, kick him in his ass and get him moving again..

You ever have one of those days.. Every things kind of perfect.. You're cruising along the highway of life, the sun's up, the top's down, the tunes are blaring.. You're puffin a big fatty, as you're screaming along the blacktop into the sun heading east.. Every one has had one, a day when you take a turn for the worst.. A day when you're flying high along that open coastal road east.. Staring out into the crystal blue waters of the mighty Pacific Ocean and then suddenly you realize you were supposed to be going west.. Just a perfect day, sun shining, top down, tunes a blaring.. A day when you zigged, when you should had zagged.. Or better yet, just stayed in bed.. A day when you suddenly realize, you've just taken, a turn for the worse.. A day you wish had never started..

You can't tell, there's a small clock on the control board, but other than that, you can't tell.. No one could tell, no one but the engineer working the board.. Studios are designed that way, enclosed, dark, sound proof and light proof.. No sound comes in, no light comes in, you are enclosed in glass, the fish bowl.. The simple process of the creative act, producing, directing, cutting, splicing, editing.. All of it takes you into a complete realm of focused concentration, where time, becomes timeless.. Getting it right, is the only thing, that matters..

It takes you, whether you like it or not, it, controls you.. Drisk had just completed a cool little jingle, with the ad bed added and completed for a major stereo company.. The problem was they didn't want to be known as a stereo store.. In fact they carried a large variety of highly profitable accessories and other products like cabinets and stands, and so much more.. Ya, ya Keith, that's no problem at all, I got some great ideas for you, yes, free quart of oil with every dip stick that comes in.. Drisko laughing on the outside, Keith blowing a nut.. Drisko banged his head in and out on this one, how? How do you advertise a stereo store, that doesn't want to be known as a stereo store?

Drisko's brain, frying and frying, burning inside, how, brain, brain, brain pain? *"Keith's we're not a stereo store. We're so much more"*, the song sang.. Then the ad bed, laid over the jingle.. *"Hey it's Kent calling from Keith's, are you there"*.. The spiked up voices of vintage movie stars, like John Wayne, or the other versions with Marilyn Monroe or Jimmy Stewart.. Answering back to Kent's questions, creating the conversations, in the mix.. The conversation then to interact with the commercial content, creating it as funny and very effective.. The voice overs in the back ground repeating a loop around the commercials creative music bed.. The voice overs announcing all the interesting products, *"At Keith's"*, in-laid over and as part of the jingle production..

The hours went late, deep into the darkness of the night.. They all partied in the studio, in celebration of the amazing creative production piece they had just completed.. First the green came out, then the white, then the browns and the clears, all came out, as they celebrated their efforts.. Drisko puffing on the green, while someone, no one really knows who, but someone, pulled out the white.. The lines were drawn across the dash board of the control console as it was lit like a Boeing 747..

Then the browns, one case, then another.. Then the clears, the Tequila's, Schnapps and Screeches, some Vodka's, some Gins.. Then the place took to rock'n, like someone threw a house on it and it set to blazing.. The party got a little wild, the back office, the casting couch, the hot tub, the music, the lights.. The whites, the greens and the clears, all of them just set them all a blazing.. Sitting there in the hot tub, kissing the horses ass as they called it, back on the Rock..

Clinking the bottom of the beer bottles together, making them click, ting, they congratulated one another.. You did an amazing job, I want to thank you, he said to her, sitting there beside her in the hot tub, touching the bottles together, kissing the horses ass.. My first time I've ever tried anything like this, she said.. Amazing, I'm impressed Marsha, you did a phenomenal job, thank you.. So did you Drisk, you are amazing, to take that nothing, to this, to what you created on the fly, as you go, you're just amazing to watch..

Well, thank you, some of it is planned though, I have the idea completely in my head, from start to finish.. I just see it, how it should be, how it will be, but thank you.. Make sure you leave your info with Frances my engineer, Drisk said to her, I may have some more work for you, if you're interested? There's a real career in this stuff, people travel all over the world for huge cash, just doing voices.. Cool, that's really interesting, who wouldn't love to do that, cool, she said, all girly like? Oh, and he's got my number already, she said, he's the one that told me to try out with you.. That you were a cool cat to know, he said, he did, did he? Drisko laughing.. Perfect he replied, you have talent for sure, you should pursue it..

Ya but you, you pulled it out of me.. I had no idea I could do this, you are simply amazing.. I felt almost like I was part of a grand orchestra.. I was but a single instrument, you could easily pluck.. And you, you were some magnificent conductor, leading me, forcing me, to use my voice inflection and notes.. Amazing, the feeling of being so controlled, useless, yet so useful.. The feeling of letting someone just take me, lead me and do what ever they wanted to me, force me into the unimaginable.. Allowing them to get what ever they wanted from me, what ever they asked of me, was so fucking exciting.. Drisk looking in her eyes, I have a lot of talents I like to pursue Mr. Drisko, she said, smiling.. Some I can't mention in public, looking deep into his ice blue eyes.. He laughed, I'm sure you do, he replied, sitting there, soaking in the hot tub..

He could feel her, touching ever so gently, brushing her knee up against him, every once in a while.. He could feel her, shimmying, closer and closer.. Her hip, banging off of his, ever so gently, every once in a while.. He felt her as she laughed with the others there in the tub, jiggled and giggled then she hits Drisk, like it was funny.. Or she would put her arm across his shoulders, as familiar, holding him, laughing at all the jokes.. She sat there in the hot tub, bubbling.. Her long straight black hair, tucked behind her ears, opening her face completely when she'd look at him..

Her eye lashes, long and sweeping, her eyes dark and brown.. Her nose perfectly formed, pointed and small.. Her mouth well rounded, her jaw line, her ears, the lips luscious, moist and rounded.. Drisko could see her as he glanced gently to the side.. She swims out to the centre of the tub, turns, dunks and slowly rises, totally wet, facing him.. Her long black hair soaked as she tucks it neatly behind her ears, looking into Drisko, making sure he was looking into her, she frolics.. She rises from the water line, shaking, her full formed breast, shaking them.. Them barely covered through the thin lace of her pink tiny bra, her nipples extruding.. Her thin frame, her waist, her black lace g-string panties, barley hidden by the water line, as she slides her way directly toward Drisko.. Plopping her ass down as she turns, banging him, almost sitting on him, as she falls gently into her seat, touching him.. Hand me my beer there handsome, she orders him, loosely, with a slight slur of her words as she giggles..

The day's gone he said, everyone has left, I have to get going, it's almost midnight.. Oh ya sure she said, slurring out the words again.. Just let me get my ride here, where's Frances, he drove me here.. Frances is passed out on the couch, he's gone.. Oh shit she said, I'm way the fuck out in Sooke, I'm fucked even the buses aren't running at this time.. We gotta wake Frances, he's my ride.. No, no Drisk said, no worries, Frances ain't driving anywhere tonight.. I'm up on Triangle Mountain, I'll shoot you to Sooke and then head home.. Oh Drisko that's so far out of your way.. No girl, it's all cool, half hour, twenty minutes in the Porsche, if we take the scenic route..

Drisko took the scenic route out through Beacon Hill, Mile 1.. Then up around the city onto the Trans Canada Highway 1, up the Malahat and then turning back down catching the view, racing in through Goldstream Park.. He then hung the right, cruising the black pearl Porsche up, in through Langford, then right again, back onto the Island Highway, on into Sooke.. Oh look at that moon Drisko, just look at it, it's huge, the biggest moon I've ever seen, she said.. I know a great spot along the waterfront we can go and park, smoke a couple of doobs, totally secluded, very cool.. Drisko was on his guard, he'd worked with thousands of beautiful women, nothing could sway him from Mercedes, nothing on this planet.. He was totally confident about that, and little Miss Filly here, well, all in good fun, he laughed it all off..

He pulled the Porsche left down into the waterfront road, into the trail.. Drisko cautious with the beast, she rides low, don't wanna bottom her out, not down here anyway, not with little Miss Filly here.. Carefully, slowly guiding her down to the shore, cool he says, cool spot as he's pulling in.. Perfect, sitting there on the shoreline in the black pearl 911 Porsche, perfect, he repeated it, perfect.. The island across the way, the inlet cove, the shoreline, the trees backing out from the shore, how would you ever find it, he thought.. Sitting there silently looking out.. He fires up a doob, the song plays as he loses all thought, puffing out the toxic smoke from his lungs, beautiful he said.. *"The roses in the window box. Have tilted to one side. Everything about this house."*..

The song, the view, the water, the moonlight shimmering off the water, full, round.. The green, the white or the blues, don't know what it was.. Drisko was sitting there, the song, singing, mesmerized by the lyrics and the tune, staring in the rear view.. The vision of the night in Antigonish with Emily, there on the shoreline, the drive from the Rock to Ontario.. The night he sat there on the shores with the fires burning.. He puffs on the doob and hands it off to Marsha.. The song pumping into him, the tune carrying him off into his own visions and deeper and deeper into his arousal, *"And love lies bleeding in my hand."*.. She leans in toward him, close.. She touches his face, turning it toward him, he looks at her, waiting for her to say something, he's still in his vision.. She pulls him toward her, close.. Kissing him, holding him in, sucking his lip into her open mouth, then darting him with her tongue, *"guitar couldn't hold you so I split the band. Love lies bleeding in my hand."*..

Drisko jerks quickly away from her, no, he cries, no baby you got it all wrong, no, he scolds her.. You got it all wrong, he says, I love my wife and family, girl, just hanging out having fun.. Ya Drisko, just fun she says, as she rewinds and re-approaches Drisk again.. He pushes at her, roughly this time, his no, firm, strong, *"the burning hoops of fire. That you and I pass through."*.. Drisko was knocked off the edge, the vision of sex and passion flowing, into his mind as his words, darted from his tongue, no.. I love Mercedes, my children, my family, I have no interest in this..

Drisko hasn't kissed another woman for almost seven years now.. He loved Mercedes from the moment he laid eyes on her, he loved her with all his heart and would never do anything to hurt her or his kids.. He fired up the 911, the black pearl Porsche, dropping Marsha somewhere in Sooke.. Following the Island Highway home, a right, then another right up into Triangle Mountain, up into that moon, the one he recognized.. Then up, up into his home, his life, his children and his wife, Mercedes and the family he loved so very deeply..

He entered the foyer through the double glass front doors.. The ceramic tiles, the deep wooden staircase, the warmth of the fireplace glistening back at him.. Mercedes, sitting there warmed from the hearth, sitting there reading a book.. Hello, she greets him warmly, soothing, how was the session, did you get it all done? Drisko opened to Mercedes questions, she was a great supporter and a great influence in his crazy ideas.. They talked about everything, Drisko so excited about the commercial, spilling the beans as to how well everything turned out.. Drisk laughing away, talking, talking, then he simply said the words, "then the crazy bitch kissed me", stuck her fuckin tongue straight down my throat.. Silence took the room, movement was none about.. Deafness, quiet, everything froze there in front of the fire place's warmth as it crackled, the room went cold..

Her eyes dead black, Drisko could see the fire flickering in them.. Then the water overflowing as she tried to drown the flames.. Drisko could see the fire, the flames still burning.. How could you she screamed, Mercedes, no, he replied, it was nothing, some crazy chick, just out of nowhere? I told you about it because it was nothing, meaningless.. She stops him, questioning, if it was something, would you be telling me, would you, she hollers? The fire burning in her eyes, the water insignificant enough to not retard the flames..

I love you Mercedes, you, my family nothing would ever come before that, nobody could ever sway me.. Mercedes loved Drisko, she knew Drisko loved her, but this, for the first time in her marriage, she felt it, it hurt her.. Her mind now on fire, the flames now burning up in through the roof of her tiny brain.. Like someone threw a house on it and the place just took to blazing.. All the late nights, all the phone calls, all the darting out.. All the parties, functions and conferences.. All the world travel, all the trips, the money, the cars, the fame, all of it.. She loved Drisko, she trusted him explicitly without doubt, without question ever, till now..

Drisko rose to the morning sun with the kids, preparing them all a good breakfast, hoping to patch things over with Mercedes.. She slowly descends the wooden staircase, quietly moving through the living area, entering the kitchen through the plastered archway.. Their eyes meet as Drisko offers a good morning, how you feeling? She is silent, as she reaches for the coffee brewing in the machine, she pours herself a cup.. I'll take the kids to the bus stop, he said, I'll be right back, okay.. I made some breakfast there for you, eat something.. Mercedes, silent to Drisk as she comforts each child with hugs and kisses and her cheerful goodbye..

Mercedes loved Drisko with all her heart, he was her life.. She gave up everything to follow him, uprooted her family, gave up the job she loved.. Gave up all her friends, she was alone there and always home sick.. Missing her sisters and brothers, cousins, aunts, uncle and her home.. Burlington, the town she grew up in.. Her family always close, on the phone everyday to each other, but most of all she missed her mom and dad.. Drisko returned to the kitchen, Mercedes was there waiting, leaning against the countertop in front of the sink.. Drisko tried to hold her as she angrily turns away.. Mercedes we need to talk about this.. He knows, she's hurt, real hurt, deep, he tries and tries to explain but the more he tries, the more she cries..

Drisko was a warrior, he knew nothing happened with Marsha.. He knew he would never have misplaced Mercedes' trust for him, that he could never be swayed.. But he also knew about the mirror, and the funny thing about the mirror.. That once you've broken it, it just will, never, look at you the same.. He knew that he needed to give her the time to figure it out.. He swore to her again and again nothing happened.. He swore to her, his undying love for her.. He offered her, just go home back to Ontario, go home, pull the kids out of school, go home for a visit, see your family, friends.. It's not that she said, what is it he asked, tell me what I can do.. I don't know right now she said, I just don't know, I'm too confused in my brain to think, to give it any thought.. Drisko knew she needed time, maybe even more time than he thought she needed..

The days went by, the nights went by, Drisko, cautious with every move, careful on all the turns, alert with times and places.. He was sure to be home on time every night, ignoring and rejecting any offers, or invites to functions or parties.. He became quiet, reserved and worst of all, careful, very, very careful not to upset the apple cart.. Mercedes and him went out for dinner, a play one night, a bar, the movies another and once in a while just a little cruise around the island, steering far away from Sooke..

They would just go get lost out there, have some fun, show her some romance and how much he loved her.. But, something was obviously misfiring the little Mercedes engine, the R.P.M.'s over revving her past the red line.. Drisk could feel the pressure pushing back on him every time he would apply the clutch.. The engine smoking and choking as he'd hit the little black pedal.. It didn't look good, the engine may be blown, the pistons won't fire in rotation properly.. He knew, right there and then, it could take sometime to overhaul her and maybe never, to bring her back to original..

He prayed and prayed to the Viking Gods that this, was merely a case of maintenance.. She just needed a little oil in her crank, as he'd call it, she was down a quart.. Drisko applied the oil as often as he could, keeping her well lubed, watching not to apply to much or worse, not enough.. If she goes bone dry, she could blow a main gasket.. Her tiny engine would seize, his beautiful Mercedes would be scrap and debris.. He knew she was rare and totally irreplaceable.. Drisko standing in the hallows of the darkened recording studio, staring off into the lights of the control panel..

Looking out into the voice room, looking back at himself in the reflection of the glass, as it mirrors his reflection ghostly.. He watches himself moving, staring at the image unrecognizable as if it wasn't him, ghostly.. He's laying down the music bed of the commercial tune.. Creating the noise the motorcycle would sing as it races its way down the twisted blacktop of the Kokanee Highway.. Leaning dangerously off the edge.. Death defying, tormentingly dangerous, erratically racing out of control..

He watches in the mirror as the bike goes flying high off the edge, a full gainer, deep into the mighty blue Atlantic.. It only looked like the distinctive box styled tail lights of the 67 green Ford Mustang coupe, there beyond his tiny reach at the Black Water River.. There where the dirt meets the blacktop, there on Cripple Creek Pass.. The phone rings, Frances answers in his crazy D.J. voice, "Iguana Records", "love ya like a reptile", then laughs, it's for you Drisk..

"Love lies bleeding in my hand." He looked fearful into Frances, cancel the session, cancel everything for the next couple of days, I'll call you later.. He runs to the Porsche and races it up to the mountain top, home.. Racing, racing, up the mountain top, racing against time, he sees the moon there in front of him.. He sees it hurtling, there toward the earth, at a thousand miles an hour or thirty kilometres per second.. There, heading directly toward the tiny island, once again, he watched as it hurtles.. He knew it was not coming to conquer, nor was it coming to take possessions of, nor to capture..

Na', it has but one intent, to devour, every, living, thing, in its path.. To move mountains, to stretch scarred deep crevasses into, and to turn his tiny world, once again, completely upside down.. So he watched, as he raced, up into the mountain, his face, against the moon.. Racing, praying he's made time enough to stop Mercedes from leaving.. She was gone, the house on the hill was now empty, cold and grey, *"The roses in the window box have tilted to one side. Everything about this house is gonna grow and die."*..

The days went by, the nights alone went by, the mirror, the windows, the moon.. Mercedes and Drisk talked several times over the next couple of days.. She called him the moment the plane landed at Pearson International Airport.. Why, he cried to her, why, do you know what you're doing to us, me, to our business, in his silent voice? Drisko, his blood crueling, his anger exploding inside.. Yet his exterior remained gentle, cautious and cool.. He loved Mercedes no matter what, she was his life.. Take you're time, enjoy the visit with your family, like I said earlier go have some fun, then when you're ready just come home..

I am home, she snapped at him, this is my home, all our friends, our family, they're all here.. I'm never coming back to that island.. Nothing happened Drisk explains, I would never dis you ever, you know that.. I love only you, you and my family.. Trust me, why won't you believe me, nothing happened, you know that? I know, she said to him, that I know Drisko.. I know how much you love us, I know nothing happened.. But this is my home, my family is here.. I want my children to grow up with all their family here, around them.. Not three, four thousand miles away, and you're never home, I need my family, I need my friends.. I love you Drisk, but I'm here, *"my guitar couldn't hold you so I split the band. Love lies bleeding in my hands"*..

The days dragging by, minutes seemed like hours, hours alone missing, staring deep into the mirror, looking desperately, bewildered.. The ancient images ignite him, looking almost exactly like him.. His blood crueling inside, his anger raging, pinging inside his tiny brain.. Like a bullet fired, exploding inside that black box, hanging there for everyone to see.. Pinging, pinging off every corner of the tempered steel sides, exploding on every contact.. Guessing at every clue, guessing, yet unsure where any of the clues could lead, or how any of it made sense.. Drisko, staring aimlessly into the mirror, looking for answers..

Drisko was a Viking Child, Kinga to Clan, leader of all Norseman Clan, his blood crueling.. The blood of Eric, Leif and Ivar the Boneless.. Drisko knows the mirror well, he's been staring into it for over a thousand years.. He stares, watching her appear before him, there in the image.. The Witch, there with her potions, there with her magic.. The Witch, every man seeing her as he would see her, ugly, yet beautiful.. Marsha, knelt there before him, on the pier, lashed to the post.. Drisko giving the order to Dooley of the sacrifice of the Blood Eagle..

Dooley penetrates her rib cage, carefully not to kill her, this is for your treason to the King.. There, she's strapped naked on the end of the pier.. Poised, picturesque, statuesque, alive yet dying.. Her body pulsing, there on the Sea of Lost Souls, there in the pit, at the Arches of Parsons Pond.. There, under the Black Pearl, under the giant asteroid.. He offers her up to the crowd.. Here is your blood, here, the Blood Eagle he pronounces.. Then he kicks her tattered and torn body into the might of the Atlantic.. Let her kiss the Cod, he proclaimed and they all cheered..

The days turned into weeks, the weeks somehow became months.. The months had doubled as he watched every second go by.. The rain, the fog, the dreary days of the island, it seemed to him like the sun would never shine here again.. He was alone, he missed his children, he missed her touch, her kiss, he missed the love of Mercedes.. Even with the entire force of the entire Viking Clan, all, each one, less none.. Even with the thirteen Kings, the sword, the archers and the massive fleet of warships.. Even with the power of the sacred sceptre of the Wizard, his ugly stick, nothing could defeat the Witch.. Even though she was only made of merely smoke and fire, they could not defend against her ugly evil, as they all lusted for her beauty..

Drisko was a Viking Child, a King of Clan, but even he knew, every once in a while a King, could fall, be defeated.. Nothing he could do, nothing he could think, nothing came out, motivating him, nothing creative.. He called the Kookanee Beer Company, the head office down by Dallas Road.. Just outside Mile 1, Trans Canada Highway, there near the ocean front drive, at Beacon Hill Park.. Then he hopped on a Boeing 747 jetliner, the red eye to Pearson International Airport, Terminal 1..

The house was sold, the Porsche got sold, the jeep got sold, all the furniture and junk got sold from the hilltop home or tossed away, like trash.. The office down by the wharf in Victoria got closed, with a lot of sad goodbyes.. He shipped her personal things weeks ago, to her parents home, where she was now staying.. He had rented a condo downtown Burlington, and tried to refocus his life.. They talked two, three times, then Mercedes invited Drisk over to take the kids for the day.. Then again and again she was more open to him being in their lives as often as he liked, and he liked at every opportunity..

Drisk was a strategist, a warrior, a leader of armies in battle and a King.. He knew Mercedes loved him, so he strategically made a plan and prepared for battle.. He would simply attack them at night, sneak in eliminate the entire village, steal her away, take her hostage and drag her back to his castle, easy peasy, eh'.. She answered the door, smiling all happy like to see him.. I'm leaving, he said, I'm heading back to Victoria.. I don't want to stay here without you and my family, if you don't want me in your life, I'm going on with mine.. If you can't forgive and forget this shit, then we're fucked from the start.. And truly Mercedes if you think I'd ever, have done anything to hurt you, then you don't know shit about me.. Either way I'm gone in two days, I fly out at noon.. He grabbed the kids, threw them in the pickup and headed to the park, as they waved goodbye to Mercedes..

Drisko sat alone in the dark of the high rise condo, watching Hitchcock's Psycho.. As the blade is ripping into the shower curtain scene.. The blood gushing into the tub and the dunt, dunt, dunt of the stabbing sound from the orchestra, a knock comes on the condo door, lightly, but startles him.. The building is secure, with video and intercom.. He slowly opens the door, she's standing there, in front of him, a huge fur coat draped over her.. You gonna make me stand in the hallway or you gonna invite me in, she demands? She enters the condo, the T.V., the music, still blaring as he closes the front door with a thump.. She turns without a word, smiling, then dropping the furry creature to the ground, standing in front of him.. Victoria's secret I presume, yes she replied, just for you Drisko and the rest is history..

Oh' there were some stipulations and some demands, some ups and downs and a couple of close calls, but other than that, a lot of compromise.. Too many hours, she complained, you're away too much.. I can try he promised, to downsize, not be so pushy, find more family time, and he did.. I can't give up the business he said, and it is so extremely demanding, but it's in my blood, but I do have a plan possibly.. I'll put the office in the house.. I have a chance, to go work in Corporate Canada, where I'm sure, I could keep thing going on the side.. It's all advertising, just a little different, all nine to five, shit you'll love.. It's more working on the corporate end of it, but I believe it's a great experience..

So he did, Drisk went back to the big smoke and he choked on the fumes, of the stinky old corporate machine and he did great.. Top this, top that, top over here and top some other bullshit thing.. With award after award, he just kept topping up the shit.. He needed to go, this corporate thing, a single media, all print, regimented, not deeply creative, extremely institutionalized.. After five years, of pure corporate crap, stress, deadlines and quotas, Drisko needed to break free.. He had a quick out, one step to set it up, then one move from that, to back on track.. All he needed was Mercedes to agree and one small compromise.. So he hit her with a hook..

There's a little radio station, up in this place called Barrie.. They're looking for a senior sales rep, I know it's a lateral shift, but the area is beautiful, countryside, lots of lakes and a growing community.. We always said we want to live where we would retire, this is a great compromise.. Drisk took the job at the new rock radio station, bought a country home out in Big Bay Point.. A beautiful spot on the shores of Lake Simcoe, on the point, where it meets Kempenfelt Bay, right on the very point and they flourished..

Working for a local radio station was easy for Drisk, he picked up where he left off, but focused on keeping everything low key.. Drisk was looking for the move, something that would lead to satisfying his creative skills and his promise to Mercedes, of being around more.. He knew what he wanted to do, he had a plan, it was just going to take a little skill to break in.. Just as important in this strategy was also the element of timing, the one part he couldn't predict.. So he started working his list for the local radio station and making a little list for himself.. Phone call after phone call, trying to break into and get info on and collect data and request a meeting, and turn down after turn down and so on and so on.. The message marching though his brain, pounding like a drum.. Only in the dictionary does success come before work, so he worked, smart and hard..

Till one day, the call came in, we'd like to meet with you, we think we want to do some local radio advertising, they set up an appointment.. Drisko showed up to the posh resort there in the hills of Horseshoe Valley.. He entered through the glass doors, checking his reflection, removing his glasses.. The receptionist welcomes him, I'm Drisk Oobbew, handing her his card as she shows him the way into the huge showroom office pavilion.. There's four of them introducing themselves with hefty titles and custom suits.. We're looking to do some advertising, but we don't know what to do..

We're in the midst of hiring, including a Marketing and Promotional Director.. Someone to handle all this stuff for us.. Drisko's eyes lighting on the word, Stuff, he smiles.. We're a little premature, but you we're so persistent we thought we'd meet with you.. They laid out the idea of the development of the new resort where they were trying to take it.. They showed him all the plans and pre-plans, all the layouts and costs.. Their foreseen financial target groups, demographics and the type of families they were looking for.. Then the one lad spoke up, you know my buddy, Darcy from Kookanee Beer on the island.. Yes I do Drisk replied, he said you're a freakin genius..

Well I do know Mr. Darcy personally and I can tell you, in pure confidence, that I've never known that man to lie, they all laughed and drank their brew.. The question came right there on the table, what do you think Drisko, what do you think we should do? Drisko smiled, looking at them all in one, as a group.. I saw a little park bench out front there, I'm gonna go have a sit there and give me a little time and I'll let you know what I think.. By the way, you guys got any money, he looks at them.. Oh' ya, they all agree, lots of money..

Drisk went and took a walk up the hilly side of the resort property, to the mountaintop.. Looking down into the valley green.. Looking out to the resort property, envisioning the additional structures for future development.. He stared deep into the valley green, imagining the families frolicking here.. Looking out to the centre of the property, to where they were going to put the family recreation pavilion.. The games, entertainment, conference centre, the gymnasium.. The indoor, outdoor swim-through swimming pool, complete with swim up bar.. The spas, lots of spas and hot tubs.. It looked overwhelmingly gorgeous to Drisko, he could see his exact plan of attack, see it all come alive in his vision.. Him and his thousand of warriors charging down the hill to take the tiny village.. He waltz's back through the sales centre, past the nice receptionist and into the boardroom..

Drisko enters, his sword shiny, sparkling and steel, raising it, aiming it to each one as they sat in awe at the table.. If you got the money, this is what you do.. You need to be direct, in their faces.. You need to see them in person.. Invite them to the resort to enjoy an over night, two night or three night optional stays.. We need to back up the direct, with a light ad campaign.. The direct is where we would create a display wall, showing the resort, the facilities and future developments.. We would go to all the major trade shows and events in the surrounding area, creating a mobile road show, everywhere, all the time..

We allow them to purchase, at huge discounts, during the shows, at cost.. The one, two or three night promotional offer, in return for their attendance at the resort.. By invitation only, let them see, feel and touch the lifestyle.. Let them enjoy the amenities of the resort.. Let them look at their future, see this as a real possibility.. All direct and very personal, completely qualified and interested.. Then we back that in the media as, we look forward to seeing you at the C.N.E., or boat show or car show, but we're always there, in front of them, in their faces.. The added value to that is, and a big plus, the events themselves, can co-op the campaign, pay for part of the advertising as we become a major promoter of their events.. This, this is your true target group, the people at the shows, they're already out there, doing their thing, everyday, looking for excuses, ways to spend their bags of money..

Then around all of that, Drisko announces, making sure the bait was on nice tight as he throws them the hook.. Wrapping it all nice and tight around the promotion, he hits them.. We do a five piece giveaway, the photo displayed at all events.. Sometimes, and when ever possible, the prize will be live in front of them.. A local dealer can drop the gear, prearranged, where ever we're near, cool eh', Go Eh'.. Now, believe it or not, this ain't gonna cost you squat.. We arrange five major co-sponsors, one for a fishing boat, a jet ski, snow mobile, a trip or maybe gold or an endowment, education fund.. The winner can choose any prize, but all year we're promoting the five pieces and the five major sponsors get the exposure at all the events.. How big do you wanna go, tell me, where do you want me to stop, it's huge..

All five sponsors would only split, the cost of the grand prize, in which to say, they would receive hundreds of thousands of dollars of value in direct and multi-media exposure.. For a fifth of the cost of the grand prize, of around twenty thousand dollars.. All of it backed up by the local media, geographically targeted to a three hundred kilometre radius, three hour drive of the resort.. But the best part is, now the sponsors can co-op it all through their manufacturers, who will pay half, if not all for them.. Win, win, win, win, who wouldn't submit to our demands, who? The biggest winner, is you, then he smiled, the sword, striking all of them present with one blow, an easy victory for the King, the Viking Child.. They all just stared at him, bleeding him their blood.. The four of them, their throats sliced open, their voices silenced, staring, at him, in awe, how, how could you have defeated us so easily? Then the voices chattering, in unison, gurgling out the words.. You came up with that in fifteen minutes? We've been working on this for six months.. Drisko smiled, ya, but it needs some work, well, more like a lot of work, like a lot, but ya.. That's what I see for you boys.. Then once again, Drisko, releasing that sinister smile, those ice cold steel blue eyes..

He returned home to Mercedes, telling her word for word what had taken place in the boardroom.. The crazy fuckers didn't know what happened.. They never asked if I'd ever been to the resort before.. If I've ever sat up on that hilltop, looking down into that valley green and dreamt.. Never asked if I've ever planned or plotted of how I would attack this project if I ever got my chance.. They all just figured I dreamt it all up on the spot, he laughed, they laughed and they both laughed away..

Drisko, continued on with Mercedes to say exactly, what would happen next.. He even named the time and date, they laughed.. Then he told her exactly what the budget would be that he would be able to simply demand for the project and the residuals derived from it.. This will allow us to sit back and relax.. So they did, they sat back and relaxed and on the exact date and very close to the exact time, the phone rang.. They wanna meet, looking into Mercedes eyes, they laughed, they smiled, no body ever wants to just meet with Drisko, she laughed harder.. He held her close, they kissed, he touches her body, searching her for warmth..

Drisko entered the boardroom for the second time that week.. We want you to take over the entire project.. Nobody could be better qualified than you, this is your game, your ideas.. We want you to run with it, the annual projected budget is one point four.. You'll work on a fifteen point retainer, plus an override on all guest invitations and one percent of the sales on your project.. You oversee and set up all media and promotions.. Let me tell you who we are, introducing his corporate label.. We have seven resorts in north America and three in Europe while we're developing this one here in Canada.. We want you to take the whole project and you can go to each resort and develop it worldwide..

No he said, calmly, straight out, no.. I know who you are, exactly your accomplishments.. I have done my research and I wanted this project, this opportunity.. But no, Drisko said firmly, there is much demand on the time here, get one location going properly.. Taking time away, would be a formula for failure.. This is what you need to do.. Get it going here, the start up, right now, then send their selected managers to train with us here in Ontario.. That will set the pace for total continuity, everyone trained in one system, throughout the entire corporate community.. I'll do it, but we do it my way, from here, the mother ship, right here in beautiful northern Ontario.. Drisko, no matter what the cost was keeping his promise to Mercedes, smiling at her, them laughing together.. I told you, exactly how it would happen, didn't I, they laughed, yes my Viking Kinga, yes, you did, now take me mi' Lord, they laughed again, louder..

Mercedes never really truly knew Drisko, she knew he was from a small town, out in Nova Scotia, somewhere.. A place call Meteghan, she recalled his story, the one he made to cover his past.. His mother was from somewhere near Bear Creek.. She knew his dad had some Newfie blood in him from a thousand years ago, but little else about it.. She would always just rib him as a Newfie, for a joke, when he'd do dumb things.. And when he was deep inside her, making love to her, she'd scream it to him, mi' Lord, my Viking, my Viking Kinga, Kinga she'd cry..

The winds of change were blowing, filling Drisko's sails.. Three years he had worked on this project setting it up, executing every design of it.. His name had travelled throughout the little resort community world.. He was now getting calls from around the globe, most with little interest to him.. Till one day, they called, out of the blue.. Well actually, they didn't call, they got a friend of Drisko's to call, they want to meet you, just meet.. It's all new, a completely revamped project, plus they're building, right here in Collingwood.. They just want to talk, nobody, just wants to talk to Drisko, he knew that.. He got ready for battle, preparing his speech for when he conquers the thriving four season resort town of Collingwood and with it, the tiny village of the Blue Mountains themselves..

CHAPTER SIX

The Cold November Rain

Drisko walked into the office in Collingwood, a door he would live to regret ever opening.. This is where he was about to meet the great Joey B. Rotten, a low level salesman with a big mouth, A.K.A. Joseph Always B. Rotten.. With his black skin, short stance and fat belly, he looked to Drisk, like a scruffy dressed Buddha.. He would soon gain a reputation of, "if his mouth is moving, he's lying", carried with him as a nickname, used by many and any that knew him and other names, much worse..

Years would later would put Drisk in front of another door, another company, another regret.. Right in front of Nick Gomer (Nickolas), the best of the best, a pure con artist.. Mr. I'm Not Responsible for Anything Ever, Gomer.. Never had a truer word ever been spoken about a man, by the man.. In fact, in plain truth, true words were something, seldom used by either of these two clowns.. Two men that for well over ten years would have called Drisko their friend.. Both men to whom he gave to, beyond belief, beyond any kind of friendship either would had ever known.. Both whom would take more from him, than his life..

Drisko, would lose his life, his love, his family and his wife, Mercedes.. He would also see himself behind the walls of a maximum security prison, three times.. He'd see everything in his world stripped from his life, stolen by two incredible con men friends..

He'd also see the two men responsible for it all, walking free right there in downtown Collingwood.. Wearing his clothes, his watch, his jewellery, his shoes, using his identity.. Destroying his credit and all the time conning, scheming, lying to everyone in the town, family, friends, strangers and Jacqueline..

The Collingwood O.P.P., will ignore every possible clue.. Just to make sure everyone is perfectly clear here, Drisko will be the one that will go to jail.. The two people that once loved each other, that tiered up under a cold November rain.. The two that kissed each other goodbye in front of those electronic sliding doors, of Pearson International Airport.. The lovers that wanted a life together, they would never be the same.. Both of them will soon be nothing more than victims..

When Joey stuck his head in the Presidents office, the man barked at him, with disrespect.. What are you waiting for, show him in.. Drisko had never heard the word used directly to a black man, but he read into it, what Joey's stature in the corporate hierarchy would be, as Joey laughed loudly at it all.. The years went by smoothly, there on the shores of Georgian bay, there by the tiny Blue Mountains there in Collingwood.. The main developer was building all over the 705 area waterfront property and the town was booming..

The initial meeting was to brag about the accomplishments and the need they had, customers, with money.. Bragging, bragging, laying it all on nice and thick, real juicy like, and Drisk was drooling a tad.. Bragging, over the next twenty years, over five thousand units and five major communities, we're building right here, on these shores.. Plus, three off-site presentation centres, here in Ontario.. Plus the Dominican Republic and three resorts planned for Mexico and one, possibly two in B.C., all part of our future..

It's all yours Drisko, if you want it, there is no budget, you send me the bills directly.. What ever you need or recommend, send the bills, deliver the results and it's yours.. Drisk rushed home quickly, well more like flew home or, maybe, just like a hop skip and jump and he was home, there in front of Mercedes.. It's exactly what I said it would be only bigger, he explained.. It may involve a bit of travel, but you could come with me.. How much travel she asked, well not really travel, living away, six months a year, maybe three, four locations over the next ten years..

Drisk lightening the load a bit, he didn't want his precious Mercedes blowing a gasket, not just yet.. Exotic locations, worst case, the kids learn a new language.. He could see the flames rising again, flickering there in her eyes.. Then again, maybe you guys just come for visits, Christmas, March break, we'll have some fun together.. The kids are the perfect age to experience the world, the culture and this is a perfect opportunity for that.. They'll be paying me huge, to go play in the sand somewhere, warm each winter.. Drisko's sails were pitched, filled with fresh ocean breezes.. His blood crueling inside, the voices of a thousand Viking conquerors screeching in his head, attack, take this tiny village.. Blood, blood he cries, take no prisoners.. But it's up to you of course, I wouldn't do it if you weren't behind it, one hundred percent..

Drisko went to work, the next two and a half years went by quickly.. Drisko, developing, creating, managing, day to day humdrum, until that day, the day he had been waiting for.. We're sending you to Mazatlan Mexico Drisk, we're actually sending a crew.. Drisko rushed home, preparing Mercedes and the kids, packed his bags and got ready for an adventure in the sun.. You're going with him, Joey, she asked, I thought you said he was an asshole.. He is, Drisk replied, but I have no say in who they send.. We're driving down, the three of us, me, him and his girl.. I'm going with them, we're driving all through the states.. Crossing over at El Paso, Texas and down into Durango, Mexico.. Then up through the Devils Backbone and into the Devils Breath.. Then straight on through the twisting mountains into Mazatlan, I gotta go with them, I want to see it all..

When you enter Mexico through El Paso, Texas, you're immediately stopped by the Mexican army.. You're interrogated, investigated, intimidated and warned.. "Amigo", they heartily warn you, do not try to drive through the mountain passages at night.. It is very dangerous, animals, treacherous turns, falling rocks and the Bandito's.. They're as real as it gets, they will rob you, rape you and kill you.. That's if they like you.. They will strip your car to the frame, remove every personal piece of evidence that ever existed and you will simply disappear, bones and all.. Mexico is amazingly beautiful or incredibly ugly, depending on your ability to heed the warnings and survive..

You enter into Durango, a desert barren land, up into Chihuahua.. Then through the miles of sporadic single lane dirt paths, carved through the mountains.. There since the beginning of time.. Somehow the oncoming cars and transport trucks must time their passes, in either direction.. You just stop dead, wait and pray.. There, you're hanging onto life, at the edge of three thousand foot cliffs, that disappear into the canyon below.. Then rising from the centre of its floor are massive towers of circular cylinder shaped mountains..

Drisko pulling to the edge, dangerously close to the drop, staring down, deep.. Stopping the vehicle on a grassy pad off the road, waking the two passengers.. He sees it, there, in front of him, then several of them.. Land mass formations, they're huge, sprouting upward from the centre of the earth, a miracle in itself.. He sees the tops are flattened and he stares onto the sight, with total disbelief.. Then he realizes there's a village, on the top of the one mountain.. He grabs for the camera, binoculars, squints into the vast open skies in front of him..

There, into his focus are the rope ladders, a thousand meters high and paths carved into and upward, circling this mound of life.. Drisko, staring, staring, gazing into recognition, seeing it as familiar.. The sea walls, of the Gros Morne, the Edge, distinctive, but nothing like this, no ocean here, just earth.. He just couldn't help himself, no one could.. Drisko, looking up deep into the Heavens, he ask for forgiveness for ever having one moment of doubt.. Here, is where you'll find the Gods, and they have been busy, working on this miracle..

At 30km your steering wheel turns full left, then right about every 25 seconds.. It is an incredible drive.. The roadway's nicely decorated with photos and crosses to mark the dead.. This is the passageway through the Devil's Backbone.. There's no tourist signs here, no welcome to Mexico, no warnings of the dangers impending in front and below.. The road just closes into a fine mist, first very lightly, then increasingly thickens to zero visibility, now you're in the mouth.. What the natives call, the Devil's Breath.. They say it's the end of the world, the abyss, no bottom.. Whatever it is that's down there or not, it breathes pure fine warm blinding steam.. If you go over the edge, no one will find you, no one will go get you.. No one will retrieve your body, no one has ever returned.. You're gone, completely obliterated from the face of the earth.. You get the marker, a free t-shirt and the no charge, custom inscription, "Stupid Gringos"..

Drisko was living it up in Mazatlan, it was beautiful, intriguing and a little dangerous, if you were playing on the wrong side of things.. He flew the kids and Mercedes in for the Christmas break, Christmas in Mexico.. They were completely intrigued by it all, the language, the sights, they were simply in awe, and Drisko, was ecstatic about their visit.. He missed them all so very much, when they left, he booked their flights immediately.. Then he knew, he would be seeing them again for the March break that year, in less than eight weeks.. By mid May, Drisko was home again, kicking up the summer in Big Bay Point.. That was the second time he had worked with Joey B. Rotten..

Two more years went by there on the side of that mountain, building two new resort properties.. Then they sent Drisko to Puerto Vallarta, then back home.. Then to Cancun and then back home.. Each time he'd travel, he'd fly the family down to where ever he was.. That way they could share the time in the sun with him, it was wonderful, then home.. The winds of change were blowing briskly on Drisko.. He'd seen his sail filling with the briskness of that familiar ocean breeze.. You ever have one of those days.. You're driving down the highway of life, top down, tunes blaring, your puffin' on a big fatty, flying east into the drama of the sunrise.. When you realize you was supposed to be going west.. A day when you zigged and you should have zagged.. A day when you take, a turn for the worse..

No body knows what happened, only the two of them could ever tell you what really went on, out there in the Point.. Even then, a good guess would be, they didn't even know.. But somehow it ended, it wasn't meant to end, it wasn't suppose to be over, ever.. But nobody can tell why, it just was.. The short version of the story is, Mercedes and Drisko split up.. It wasn't money or even lack of love.. In fact maybe just the opposite.. He once said, out loud, I think I loved her so much, that I didn't want to hurt her anymore..

The lifestyle, the travel, the out all the time, again.. Why, no one can answer that but them? Did it, yes it did happen, Drisko and Mercedes split up, once again.. Drisko left the point, the cottage like home and moved himself into a condo in Collingwood.. A turn for the worst, now, growing closer to Joey, hanging out and partying the shit out of that mountain.. Another property, another phase, now Drisko is about to go off the edge with a second turn.. Here he'll meet, Nicky, "Mr I'm Not Responsible For Anything Ever." Gomer, and his name said it all..

Phase four, a major development, the newest, the biggest and the brightest development, The Waterfront project.. He had been waiting for this project for years, a brand new major resort, overlooking the pristine shores of Georgian Bay and the deep water marina.. With a very elegant, high end restaurant and patio bar and the unobstructed views of Blue Mountain and it's tiny summit.. But still boasting the best down hill skiing in all of southern Ontario.. The playground of the north and a definite tourist trap, winter, summer, spring and fall.. While on the eastern side of the bay, you can catch the crystal clear views over to Wasaga Beach, the worlds longest fresh water sand beach.. Watch the sail boats, the wind surfers, wake boarders, water skiers and the bathers soaking up the sun.. The mountains and the beaches are filled to the brim, year round, with fresh, clean, cool, Big Smoke families and their money, their bags and bags of money..

The nickname came from the kids, their friends who played in the yard, in the shop, in the custom cottage like home, at Big Bay Point.. The kids' friends, they all just started one day calling him Double 0 Drisk, Drisko Bond from the video game James Bond 007.. They'd sit around as they played and eventually the challenge happened.. Come on Drisky, one said then the other.. "Just try it," JT said referring to Drisko's challenge, written all over Jessie's goalie stick.. How could he resist, the rest is history, win after win against the mini Drisko's, them impressed with his skills and high scores..

Just try it, it soon became a family motto.. Drisko wrote it on Jessie's goalie stick, "Just Try It", when he was six years old and wanted to play goal.. He had the equipment but wasn't sure if he could do it, so Drisk dressed his stick for him in a custom paint job.. Applied some graphic skills and lit the stick up like a bullseye.. It was also his initials and nick-name J.T.. Jessie Thomas, his first and middle name, after one of his great grandfathers Thomas and one of Drisko's favourite teenage rockers Jethro Tull, the Ian Anderson band.. He was easily the best goalie around his league.. Everyone wanted him on their team and all of the teams wanted him to come out for the practices.. So many times they'd play two, three practices on a Sunday morning.. They would say, the kid could stand on his head and make a save and he could..

With all that, the Bond man was born.. Then as the little guy added up his career, bouncing all over the globe, in high society, in the media biz.. It was all just too cool, it just became a quirk, a nick name, with some degree of truth, at least for the mini me's, he said.. Then only years later the kids now in their late teens, early twenties.. Drisk bought the Bond Car, the replica, as used in the movies, the 740i BMW.. It was just a fluke, no plan, just a pure Bond move.. The little freaks were freakin'.. They couldn't believe it and non-stop, asking for rides.. Driving around, stereo cranked, them all dreaming, they too, would one day too, become, the real Bond.. There's only one real bond in this world, Drisko would school them, the blood oath, brother for brother.. They'd all just laugh at him, point at him.. Ya, ya and you they'd say, Double 0 Drisk and the Bond mobile, then they'd all laugh and laugh..

Drisko met her in one of the sales centres, at the golf course.. The pavilion set just off the first tee of the first hole, of the world class P.G.A., registered golf course, there at the foot of these beautiful Blue Mountains.. She was on the sales team, Drisko was running around as usual, when she stopped him, asked for some help and advice.. It was almost strange, he noticed her keep looking at him, with this love in her eyes, admiration.. Something he hadn't seen for sometime now in a woman, a small immediate attraction.. It had been almost two year since life on the Point, his new life, here now on the mountain, by the great lake, and the tiny bay.. Jacqueline was her name, as she approached Drisk and introduced herself.. They talked several times.. Each time Drisko would enter the building, there she was, hovering around him, cheerfully, yet reserved.. Weeks later she showed up at his condo, knocked on the door, and the rest as they say, again, is history..

She was one of the sweetest girls he had ever been with.. After a twenty year marriage to Mercedes, the queen of nice, his one, real true love.. Jacqueline was a good second chance for Drisk.. They were similar in certain ways, Mercedes and Jacqueline.. Different as day and night in others, and more so, than he would have ever believed in one way, and that, he was soon going to find out.. The four years they had spent together, had brought them deeply in love with each other.. She was the last thing in his world that he wanted to lose.. He knew he wanted to be with her..

Drisko finally moved into the countryside.. The property was located at Silver Creek Drive in the peaceful little town of the affluent neighbourhood village.. Set strategically along the foot hills of the Blue Mountains of Ontario, called Collingwood, number fifteen.. The ship building, lumber industry town before the sixties, was now famous for their tourism.. The area's surrounded by the beautiful pristine waters of Georgian Bay.. By far the best downhill skiing in all of Southern Ontario with seven ski clubs.. There's a dozen golf courses in the town and a twenty minute drive would give you access to another dozen or more.. All the riches of life, pure paradise, safe, or so you'd think..

It wasn't a new home but a dream home, older, with a red brick facade.. Truthfully it could have easily used a few good upgrades.. The roof was fine, but leaked a little if you didn't keep the gutters cleaned from the snow and the leaves building up.. It needed new paint as the inside colours were drab.. The windows were old and weak, no real R-value and the furnace was nearing its last years, old and converted from oil to gas, it never did work right.. But that's what made it so absolutely interesting to Drisk.. The hook, he cut a deal with the owner of the place as soon as he saw it was for rent.. He offered to lease it with a buyout clause.. He'd simply use his own credit, his own financing, with a three year open option to purchase.. His boy's could help with the upgrades and when it was ready and he had it finished to perfection, he'd flip it.. That was his side business now and as he'd say, everybody wins..

The row of Maples that ran the centre of the property divided it equally, field and house.. Straight down off the end of the decks.. They led the way to the back workshop, garage and all the trees kept the place shaded.. The white Birch trees in front and back of the home covered it nicely protecting it from the heat of the suns rays.. On the opposite side of the home was a line of high cedars set back far enough to allow him to park his replica 007 Beemer, right at the north side of his bedroom window, guarding it.. The front of the home was set back from the road with his bedroom to the northern end of the house.. The bedroom's front window needed no curtains.. The view was obscured by an evergreen, a thirty five foot Christmas tree.. In front of the tree was a circular crushed stone driveway that lead into a very quiet street.. Maybe thirty other homes on the street end to end..

The farm at the bottom of Silver Creek, fronting onto the narrow highway sold for four million the week he moved in.. He originally figured the house and property renovated to an Epic Home, was worth somewhere around seven fifty, eight hundred thousand easy.. He cut his deal at three hundred and forty, trying to double his money.. Forty thousand down and he was in.. His new friend, his neighbour, Mr. T-Bird, as Drisk called him.. He had said, that when his property closes, Drisko could be looking at a million five maybe two, crazy but maybe three.. Drisko didn't know how many chances one would get, to make a cool mill or two on a three year flip.. But he was glad he didn't pass it up.. He was flipping, as Mr. T-Bird spoke..

The back yard on Silver Creek, held the fire pit Drisk built, carried each and every rock from the field, to its final resting place.. Flat stones, circling the ground twenty feet around, larger arm sized boulders to create its ten foot hearth, one of his landscape specialties.. The fields were wide open, no fences, perfect for snowmobiling and dirt bikes.. The boys, the men that worked for Drisk, their families, his friends, their children were all in a way, it was their home too.. They all played and worked there, on Silver Creek Drive, almost every day..

They built things in that shop, Hell, they built the shop or at least the interior, the shelving, the storage areas.. They designed things there, their products.. The antique 1950s styled Coca Cola machine along the side wall still worked perfectly, kept the garage lit at night and the beer cold for the boys.. The structure stored the tools and carried his company logo and sign.. Drisko always loved the name, so he carried the name forward to include his other interest.. Still effective, maybe even more so, The Creative Factory, Renovations * Additions * Landscape * Design.. The eight hundred custom phone number, 1-800-IDEAS-4-U in caps, prominent, underneath..

The yard was a yard and filled with white tailed deer, fox, cougars, grey squirrels, black bears and the odd and rare Le Woof, the Great Canadian Arctic Wolf, mother nature's paradise.. They played in it and partied the shit out of it.. Behind the yard was Silver Creek, a small but mighty creek bursting with trout, small bass, frogs and their beer.. Behind her twisted banks was the Georgian Trail, forty kilometres long, the original C.N., rail line.. Now it's laid with A grade stone and it's become a beautiful nature walking path..

Walk it, ride it or cross country ski it, but no motorized vehicles allowed on it by law.. So it was nice, quiet and safe.. You just had to watch out for the old folks, they'll run you down with their electric go-carts if you get in their way.. Oh ya, listen carefully here, if you walk the forty kilometres one way, guess what? Behind the trail though, was the fields of another multi-million dollar farm and behind that, the beautiful open views of the Blue Mountain range.. When you sit on the back wooden deck of the spectacular estate property at 15 Silver Creek Drive, you're about a thousand miles from nowhere and trust me, there's no place you'd rather be..

Jacqueline was the first one to see the house at Silver Creek.. Drisk brought her over to get her approval.. She liked the house right away.. As he pulled the Beemer into the circular driveway of the home, she loved it at first sight.. The parklike setting, the privacy of the grounds as they walked around the outside of the home, this is yours, she asked.. He took her in the place, through the tattered front door, into the rich but worn interior, of the entrance way.. The music quietly playing as they enter through the double glass doors that separated the main living area..

The song ringing through the long hallway off the front entrance, *"see a love restrained. But darlin' when I hold you. Don't you know I feel the same. Nothing last forever in the cold,"*.. The glass wall and doors that lead to the raised sun room.. More glass, more doors off the sun room, opening out to either side, a private deck and the million dollar views.. "Après ski" he said to her. which means, not skiing, but partying while drinking on the deck, while on a ski hill.. "We can sit in the sun room or the hot tub with our Tiki lights and Mai Tais, once I get it all set up.. We can watch the skiers, fall off the edge of the mountain, they laughed..

Drisko, leading her back through the 800 sq. ft. wooden floored living room, *"In the cold November rain."*, walking her through the glass doors.. Then they entered the pink 60's styled kitchen, old, worn, in need of a total face lift.. "My specialty" he said to her, as he explained his future plans for the house.. The clock radio playing the tune from on top of the ugly fridge, *"just trying to kill the pain, oo yeah."*.. He walked her into the dining room, describing each little personal renovation touch he'd do, in detail to her.. You could help me pick out the materials and colours, if you like..

She was deep into his life and the only place he needed her to be.. The house showed its wear and tear in the linoleum flooring, on the paint and in the wood trim.. The place was rough, no doubt, but it was beautiful too.. They walked through the wooden doors down a long hallway, into the bathroom and the dull painted pink walls.. Stained, old, pink matching porcelain sink, matching tub and toilet.. You felt the size of the room by the emptiness.. The one door missing from the sliding mirrored shower trio.. Drisk now noticing the vanity mirror, shattered completely, yet intact, in it's frame.. It was so perfect, so Drisk, so him, she said instantly, smiling, it's just so you..

He then whisked her off to the guest room, the spare room, "the dog house" he said to her, for when you're mad at me, she kissed him.. They then walked into the master, her room, in his mind, their room.. Jackie's room, for when the time was right. *"could rest my head just knowin' that you were mine, all mine."*.. The workshop, he said to her, smiling into her, holding her hand.. She knew what he meant, as she smiled.. The bed there, the dressers there, she took the lead.. She stood in front of him, he kissed her as he held her close.. Just held her there in that room.. Standing over her, behind her, holding her waist, both arms folded around her, leaning his head over her shoulder..

His face buried deep into the silkiness of her shining strands of long black hair.. Kissing her neck and cheek, he fell into a trance.. You're mine, he said in his silent voice.. I am, and you're mine, she replied, in her silent voice, *"everybody needs some time,"*.. She always smelt so good, she always felt so good, right, in his arms.. The room was huge, empty and dull, echoing.. A single light bulb hung in the centre of the ceiling it did nothing to show off the beautiful wooden floors throughout the room. *"you know you need some time all alone."*.. The strong but ugly built-in closets and drawers had the paint chipping from them..

"Crazy little concept home though eh," he said to her, lipstick and heels baby.. I'll turn this twenty dollar hooker into a million dollar call girl.. It's waiting for the designer's eye he says, as the tempo of the song catches him.. The guitars, the snares, the orchestra, the arithmetic sounds, then the voice, driving the words into him.. They walked back through the kitchen to the basement door that lead to the self-contained two bedroom apartment.. The mirrored image of the upstairs layout except the third bedroom's square footage space was divided up by a laundry room.. The furnace room and two larger storage rooms with an entrance to the yard and gardens off the main living room and directly beneath the sun room.. The apartment needed new carpeting, some kick ass lighting and paint.. Eventually he knew he'd redo it all.. The bathroom and kitchen down here to complete the epic home, but today it wasn't a priority.. The house was big, spacious, empty and cold..

"it's hard to keep an open heart, when even friends seem out to harm you. But if you could heal a broken heart. Wouldn't time be out to charm you.".. Jacqueline opened the basement door.. She took two steps down the rusty old wooden stairwell, turned back, looked at him without a smile and said "it's haunted, the house is haunted".. Someone died here, she repeated, it's haunted.. She was ghostly and she wouldn't go down the stairs..

He just held her there in the kitchen, shutting the radio off on top of the fridge.. Shutting the song off, ending it, shutting down the cold November rain, the song singing, still in his head.. He wanted her, he needed her to feel warm, safe and comfortable here.. He explained to her that there are spirits, poltergeists and phenomena of the unexplained in this world.. But believe me, there's really no such thing as ghosts, talking to her, as if he were explaining it, to a child..

People don't have fear when they understand they have options, real knowledge, logic.. Drisko lived by that rule, facts, he would always say.. Him gently holding her in his strong arms, her safe.. Lifting her lips to his lips, then kissing her softly.. Looking his love directly into her eyes, letting her see him clearly, then speaking, strongly.. The Devil doesn't come to you, with a tail and horns, he grins.. He comes cloaked, as a friend, dressed, with a smile and a story.. All man kind has the Devil in him, it's if and when he allows it out.. Life is real honey, the rest is all folklore, fireside stories, tails of ole'..

Stories, conjured up by spirit hunters and cash scammers.. If there's ghosts, how come there aren't millions of them.. Who chooses, if you're to be a ghost or you're not? Why hasn't anyone ever proven anything once, real proof? People are lemmings, followers, susceptible to fictions, con-men and their lies.. They'd rather believe in the non explainable, in fictions, than be explorers of facts of this world and the truth it holds..

Believe in yourself Jacqueline, the only thing you'll ever need to believe in.. Follow the truth, the truth is always right in front of you.. Never fear fiction, something you can't prove and just always trust your heart.. There is nothing fictitious about this world, trust me, everything here in it, is absolutely real, believe it.. Everything on this planet was created from this planet, no magic, no miracles, just real.. Everything that is contained here has a purpose and an explanation for it being here, only real.. Don't be gullible enough to believe in something that no one can explain properly or hasn't proven to be fact.. That proof being, my dear, the world is not flat.. Stories, folklore, tales of old men and haggled old witches, to conjure up fear into the naive, to gain their coppers..

Goblins, vampires, creatures from the deep, aliens from millions of miles in outer space.. They come down here to the earth, thousands of years ago.. Painted stupid pictures on all the caves, here with this infinite intelligence, incredible technology, then they just fucked off.. And somehow, I can't get a proper freakin WI-FI connection half the time.. Give it a rest girl, get real, believe in what's real only, and think for yourself.. You want to hear ghost stories, I can tell you a hundred of them, scare the shit down your leg, but all true I'll tell ya'.. Stories from before time began, stories of the Clansmen, the Norsemen, passed on to me, since I was a child.. But they, they were all real, real warriors, Vikings all, no ghost stories, just real stories.. Besides, when this place is finished, them little fuckin ghosts ain't gonna be able to afford the deposit on her.. Drisko moved into the home on Silver Creek, started getting all the renovation's going.. He hired some help as he was still busy working with the resorts, consulting..

Nicky came around one day, ya' Gomer.. He had been fired from the Brothers, the owners of another smaller property, up there at the foothills of the mountain.. Drisk knew all about him, he had worked a couple of consultations with the Brothers, they were friends.. Nick just kept getting bounced around by them, used, abused, then fired.. Drisko gave him a break, gave him some work, with his crew.. The two other guys got along with Nick fine and they all enjoyed the work and it was always fun.. It's just fuckin dirt, Drisko would shout at them when he was on a site.. Or it's fuckin drywall, nail the bitch, mud the fucker, lets go, Drisk was a warrior.. His east coast drawl, would sneak out once in a while, heavy.. The boys would look at him and say shit like, okay Newf, or hi ey' captain, all in good fun..

Nick poured it on to Drisko pretty thick and solid, only days after Drisko hired him.. The boy had gotten himself into a real dilemma.. Drisk had guessed that somehow this wasn't his first mess up in his life, no work, no home, no food, huge problemo, Senor.. He was kicked out by his wife, a week ago, separated from his little girl.. He has nowhere to actually bring her.. His wife won't allow him to see her, unless he has a proper address.. Drisk had met Nicky's wife several times over the last years.. She had also worked in the resorts, friendly, kind and sweet.. The child, without her father, the thought hurt him.. Drisko felt the hook sink deep into his heart, into his mind and his soul..

No money, no home and his wife wants alimony, of course, she needs the support.. Talk about a turn for the worse.. I need someone to work with the boys and help manage the office around here, Drisk said to him.. Drisk knew Nick had managed a call centre office for the Brothers properties.. He was aware, he had some skills around an office.. Schedule the jobs, work with the boys on the jobs.. Then make sure all's cool in the office.. Keep all their hours straight for them, all the contracts filed, and calls returned promptly.. Above all, make sure the sites are cleaned up perfectly afterward.. There's no reason for them to know we were even there when it's completed, then report to me each day..

Drisko cut Nicky a sweet deal, the sweetest deal you could imagine.. You can stay here with me in the house here, with us, here on the estate.. Drisko had already taken in one roommate, another friend.. Drisk and Nick both knew her.. She worked with you once, in one of the centres.. Melisa, Drisko said to him, cautiously staring him down, ya' Nick replied.. I know her well, she likes me, she's a pretty cool chick.. There's a spare room upstairs you can have and a smaller room off it.. We can set it up as a guest room, for your daughter, she'll have a place to come to stay with you..

I'll give you a couple free months to get yourself organized, get your money flowing again.. You can work here, help take care of the office here, schedule the jobs and keep the place clean.. Sound good, Drisk asking him, looking him in the eyes.. There's lots of food here, BBQ out back, so you can help yourself for now and make sure you're fed well.. And if you're on the job sites on time and you should be, then you're good to go, okay, they shook and smiled.. So go get your shit and you can move in tonight, Drisk said to him.. Nick replying quickly, I don't have a car, Drisko laughing, okay, lets go get your shit as they drove up the waterfront highway to Meaford, across the rigged shoals, then back down again, around, to the estate..

There were two trucks, a trailer, a skid steer there on the property.. The shop was filled to the brim with construction and landscape equipment.. Then there, beside the tree line, to the north, Drisk parked his, OO Beemer.. The Bond, 740i replica BMW, there on the property, on the foot of that mountain at Silver Creek Drive.. The year flew along easily, Drisko working in the resorts, consulting, jumping in and out of the offices, meeting the boys on the sites.. Weekends, days off and early days would find Drisk, running from the office to the sites.. Moving dirt, building walls, tearing things down, building things up.. Ditches and trenches, digging them out, filling them in.. Rock walls, paint jobs, moving walls and his specialty, creating elaborate gigantic waterfalls.. Drisk loved getting his hands dirty, filling them with rocks and dirt and the splashes of water his mother, the earth, delivers as she breathes..

The house there on Silver Creek Drive, now filled to the rafters with Drisko's personal things, his equipment, his life.. Him, Jackie, Nick and Melisa and all kinds of friends, partying there.. Enjoy the estate, the views, the hot tubs, the fire pit.. The friends, the families, there in the yard, the mountains and streams, there in front of them all, everyday.. Spring had come and gone, the summer now splitting from, hot humid days to the cooler fall nights.. So many fun filled times, him and Jackie, just enjoying their time there together..

Jackie had kept her place, there in the beach.. Spending most of her time there, at the house, with Drisko, there on Silver Creek Drive.. Or Drisko was at her place, in the little trailer park at the beach.. Then the call came in on the message machine one night with that cold November rain.. Beeping as he pushed play, we need you to go to Cabo Drisko, the voice said, next week, call me as soon as you can.. Baja, Sur California boss, San Jose' de Cabo, Mexico, you lucky fuck, call me the voice said and then hung up..

So, this is what they mean when they say, when hell freezes over.. It was cold, not snowing yet, not raining, just cold, bitter Canadian cold.. We say it twists your bones, it grabs through your nervous system up through the muscles, cracking every joint in its path.. You crunch your way through that glistening pile of frozen snow that's covering the coloured steel of what was once your warm safe car and soon maybe again, if she starts.. You adjust for every breath as you walk, painfully filling your lungs with frosty cold chilling air.. As you try to exhale, it burns.. Your finger's numb, a man's beard will frost to ice and forget about saving your balls if you got to go pee outside.. Oh ya, there's this big Canadian rule, watch out where the Huskies go and don't you eat that yellow snow..

The winds had adjusted their speed and had set their course, heading due south, south east straight through and off the ice fields of the Arctic.. Canada was bracing itself once again for another long cold one, and they ain't talking Corona buckets here.. No sir-ee Bob, winter was coming and that was Drisko's cue, it was time to go head south, hide out, stay warm.. His chosen profession permitted him to travel and work throughout the world.. This winter, he was heading for six months of fun in the sun, a great offer to work the winter of 2006/07 in Cabo, Mexico.. Lands' End, as it's translated..

There, where the Sea of Cortez meets the mighty rage of the Pacific Ocean.. There in Cabo is where they collide, its land marked with the Arch.. A hole drilled by the nails of the tides straight through the rock mass that is Lands' End.. The thought reminding him of the Edge, the Rock.. The Arches of Parsons Pond, the Casandra, Eric's Grave Ship, in the Sea of Lost Souls.. Cortez is the best place on earth to find Marlin, Orca, dolphin, sharks, seals and sea otters, barracuda, lobster, giant shrimp and sail fish.. Plus the incredibly dangerous, vicious, most ferocious man killer of the seas, the giant squid.. Cortez is the natural breeding ground of the entire world for most sea creatures.. Everybody's dream destination, Drisko's dream job..

They stood there in the cold November rain, there in the darkness of the night.. The winds reaching through her, brushing her hair briskly from one side to the other, washing itself across that beautiful face of hers.. A face he had looked into a thousand times before.. This night he needed to see it clearly, completely, see deeply into her eyes, her heart.. It was his picture of her, his last look, you know the mind shot.. The one we remember, the one that we will always keep deep inside our hearts..

He swept her long jet black hair in one clean sweep with his left hand.. Grabbing at its silkiness in his fist.. Then neatly tossing it up into a tail.. Twisting it, he held it firm between her tender dainty neck and his man size hand.. This wasn't the first time he'd had her by the tail and he reminded her of it.. He caressed her into his grip gently.. Jacqueline always moved where he moved her.. His other hand holding firmly across her black leather motorcycle jacket.. He stood there, kissing her, brushing against her, fondling her body gently..

The outer doors of the departure gates of Lester B. Pearson, Toronto's International Airport, would slide open and then closed.. Allowing the torrent of pedestrians to pass through, "Drop Off Only", the sign read.. The airport security guard rushed toward them.. Her shiny little red Chevy Sunfire had overstayed its welcome.. Then as if he was on a leash, he stopped dead in his stride, he looked at them for a long moment and then nodded at Drisko as if to say, "it's okay boy eh', takes your's times wit' er', you's ain't never gonna see's er' again".. The guard turned, looking back once, staring, then he quickly rushed away, rushing off to harass another drop-off-only violator..

He told her earlier, he would just go down first, make sure all is good and all the details finalized.. He'd take the time to look at condos for them to live in, check out the neighbourhoods.. For him, he's all good in old town Mexico.. He's at home in the hood or the quaint fishing villages.. He's from the Rock, almost the same scenario, families.. The Mexican families there are bound together from over thousands of years.. Hanging with the natives, Drisk would call it.. But her, Jacqueline, she was gringo girl, no princess, just real down to earth.. Pure Canadian Grade A Beef, sweet as maple syrup, real sugar and spice and definitely had everything nice and oh so neatly packed away.. With Jacqueline though, she never knew it, except when he'd tell her and she'd never show it, it was for him, her man, Drisko her love..

Jacqueline wasn't very well travelled, something Drisk was intending on changing in her life.. He figured he could just introduce her to his real Mexico, slowly, safely.. She'd be a lot more comfortable in gringo land, as the Mexicans call it, all whites or affluent Mexicans.. The gated compounds, armed security, all the comforts of home behind a fence.. Drisk wanted her to feel she was safe.. The place would be nice, approved to her standards, somewhere she could call home.. He told her there as he was nearing to delivering his final and most passionate kiss to her, before he missed his rocket to Margaritaville.. He couldn't escape the thought that she had asked him not to go.. To stay and work on the business here.. That was three days before he was booked to jet out.. He knew she was just scared, lover's worry, separation anxiety, something like that..

I'll see you soon, he said to her, everything will be fine.. He loved her and she loved him.. This was going to be a good move, fun for her, for all of them.. He could take care of some business there, grab some cool cash and Bob's your uncle, fun in the sun.. She didn't travel much, Jacqueline had never been anywhere other than the trip he took her on the year earlier to Florida.. She liked it, she loved it, she got the bug as he'd say, the travel bug.. She was looking forward to Mexico and sex on the beach.. He didn't know it then, but he would never hold Jacqueline like that again..

He'd never kiss her that way again, with both of them enthralled in passion.. Yes he'd see her again, even spend several nights together with her.. The whole move to Mexico, the get up and go thing.. It was all way too fast and way too much of a commitment for Jacqueline.. For her to just have stopped everything and just come to Mexico to live with him, although they had talked about it several times.. Jacqueline was planning on coming down, early January, with Drisko's daughter Ambrosia.. She was going to enjoy her winter break from her studies at University.. His son Jessie and his girlfriend

Melody, the two of them were coming to work with him for the season, stay with him.. It was a real chance to bond with his son Jessie.. They had split as a family, five years earlier.. Where could it ever be cooler to reunite, than in a world class, gold star, all-inclusive, private members only resort.. Which Drisk was going to run as part of their Executive Management Consultant team..

Jessie had seen the life many times now with Drisk.. He was going to feel it this time, from the ground up.. Jacqueline was only coming for a visit, spending New Year's Day 2007 and a couple of weeks' break from her work.. For the two of them, it was time together on the beaches of Cabo, in Mexico, on the Sea of Cortez.. Maybe she would just stay with him.. His money was always on the fact that she would.. Meanwhile, Jackie and him were going to be in each other's arms, in Cabo, in no time at all.. He kissed her goodbye, walked through those electric doors that a thousand other lovers had walked through today and boarded the plane.. He shed a tear or two, as he flew off to go work in Cabo San Lucas, Mexico..

As you step out to the debarking port, you immediately grasp the warmth of Mexico.. The sky, the dry of the desert night air, its cool breezes that interact with the heat that still remains well past the sun going down.. The November night, is now like a late July afternoon in Canada, warm, beautiful.. He crosses the tarmac where he can see the mountains rising through the night sky.. Their silhouette blinding the sky behind them, the palm trees shifting with the burst of the winds.. The sweet smell of colitis in the air.. Then there it is, the eighth wonder of the world, Millionaires Row, Cabo International Airport.. Although small, it parks more millionaires' Lear jets, than probably any other world-wide destination..

This was all old hat for Drisk now, this is five, six times he's been to Mexico.. A couple different islands and now back, to Mexico.. So he checked into the resort, in the early evening.. He chilled by the pool for a bit.. He had dinner and made ready for the next day.. The re-con, his favourite part, checking out the neighbourhood, hanging with the natives.. Drisk had spent a great day gathering info, checking out San Jose, de Cabo.. The one thing he loved was how different Mexico is in every area.. You can see it clearly in the facial features of the people like the Mayans, the Aztecs.. The difference in the music, art, even the dance, in their temples and statues of their Gods.. Every single part of it is different, every town, every tourist destination, every city.. From one coast to the other, as you live, breathe, love and learn with their culture.. You begin to even notice the subtle differences of the dialects and the accents they use..

San Jose's Central is small and easy to get around in.. The park is perfect for an afternoon rendezvous with a lover, a friend, a friend's wife or a sister in law, ah the Mexicans love, Viva Mexicano.. Small cobblestoned walkways, lush gardens, filled with trees.. Palms and Coco trees to shade and house the birds.. Vendors line the outskirts of the park, the atriums, the band shell with live music.. The Cathedrals in Central hosts a Wedding or Baptism every hour on the hour, you'd think.. And Sunday the welcome mat is out all day long.. Central is a gathering point for most festivals and major events..

The custom leather shops, café's, trinkets, booths filled with colourful Mexican T's proclaiming, No Bad Days In Cabo.. The fishing and snorkelling excursions, the jungle runs in the Hummers, Jet Skis, ATV and Scooter rentals.. Tons of fast food taco joints, plenty of fine dining and everywhere cantina's for cerveza.. Then the big kids specialty shops, like the Tequila Store selling all types, styles and tastes.. Large to small, bottles, custom designs and blown glass.. Mixtures of strawberry, cranberry and apple Tequilas, some priced over ten thousand U.S. dollars or more.. Huts filled with sunglasses and cell phones, Mexican antiques, art, furnishings and fashions.. Jewellery shops, precious gems, diamonds, turquoise, shark teeth, turtle shell and corals.. Mostly pilfered illegally from the Sea of Cortez.. Silver is a major export of Mexico.. It is one of their treasures and they are exquisite at it, 914 Mexico stamped..

Drisk made his way back along the main road and into the Hotel Zone, passing a two story sixty-foot wide Bulbed Cactus..

The thorns on it were about 3 feet long.. It was in a cactus nursery where they studied and grew cacti.. Then past the golf course and the Graveyard.. He turned the corner and headed back to the resort.. He didn't know it then, but him and Mr. Bulbed Cactus were going to see a lot of each other.. With so many interesting things and events in his day there were many things he didn't notice.. Things he would soon come to love more and more, as San Jose on that day, slowly, surely and steadily was becoming his home..

He hit the tube, he had discovered they had an American rock station via satellite.. He indulged in an array of Aerosmith and Van Halen melodies.. Then the real Slim Shady and then a crazy classic from Guns N' Roses, the Cold November Rain, reminding him of her, Jacqueline.. He quickly showered, changed into something more fitting to his beach bum image.. He poured himself a Fresca, then grabbed the novel he'd been reading.. Stealing Home, by j. j. Bond, a mind bending thriller, then headed to the deck.. The sky had pitched to black, one star shone dimly over Cortez.. He dove deep into the twist and turns of this on the edge of your seat, chilling, crime drama he had trouble putting down.. He fired up a doob, puffing without missing a word as he read.. He took a good hit on the Fresca and as the glass cleared back from his eyes he saw it.. There, out beyond the borders where the world ends, where if you took your ship too close to, you would simply fall off the edge, the abyss, Lands End..

It's 8:36pm west coast time.. In front of him and without warning, a slit appeared in the blackness of this vase.. A teeny tiny little bright slit.. He thought it was a plane, a boat's reflection, so small, like a fire fly, but no movement, no flicker.. He stared as it grew, he watched as he's mesmerized, once again by this thing, he called his God.. He watched in amazement as the moon lifted itself onto its rightful place into the Heavens.. The moon appeared before him, filling his vision, huge.. He's ten stories up, he believes he could had stepped out and walked upon it and no, Mexican ganja ain't that good.. Talk about in your face, the tourists below filled the beach, motionless, frightened.. Voices rumbling of how they were witnessing the end of the world.. Historical, they said, and he reminded himself of his thoughts of the Edge, Cripple Creek Pass, the moon and the asteroid, the Black Pearl.. The hand of God he thought, why are you here?

Drisko was tearing down mountains at work, everything was running like clockwork.. It was fun and exciting for him, a new place, new friends, all new.. The New Year was approaching, Jessie and his girl, Mel were coming to work with him this year.. Drisk had set up a couple of great jobs for them and they were going to stay with him in the condo.. They had the best job in the place, playing in the pool with the old folks.. Get them involved in the activities, you're the entertainment committee.. I'm paying you for having fun and doing activities with the guest on the Sea of Cortez, in a world class resort.. Drisko's daughter, Ambrosia was also coming down and is going to spend a couple of weeks with them.. All of them together, in Cabo.. Jacqueline was also coming, she would share the room with Drisk, and they would all have some fun in the sun..

Resorts are twenty four, seven, three sixty five, they're like the cops, they never sleep.. So, Drisk and Jessie and his girl Mel, had to work, while Ambrosia had to entertain herself in Cabo.. Drisko laid down the law, the rules, the warnings of the Mexican dogs.. He wasn't talking about the four legged critters, he warned her, but the men, they're relentless on beautiful women as he laughed.. Jacqueline didn't show up, she had some personal problems to deal with.. Drisk had planned on her and Ambrosia entertaining each other, keeping eye on each other, while Drisk worked.. I'm normally home by one, the kids a little later, but you have my cell number, enjoy, he said to her with a kiss, then the three amigo's headed off to work..

There's something about a world class resort, they are the life styles of the rich and famous.. We call them the "Awe resorts", because you people come here and walk around all day going "Awe".. With a couple of days of fun in the sun and Drisk was ready to get to work.. He knows he's brought a lot of people, friends and associates to Mexico over the years.. He would warn everyone the same, Mexico is beautiful, fun and exciting and as boring as hell, if you're not working here.. It's one thing to come on a holiday, a couple of weeks, but to live here.. Well, there's only so much sightseeing, sun tanning and shopping you can do..

Drisko was completely aware of his status and good fortune to be able to be as free as he was.. It's his own brand of lifestyle.. He affectionately called it L.B.C., Lazy Boys Club.. No, it has nothing to do with being lazy, but in truth, it means you're as good as it gets.. See L.B.C., is the ability to do your job better than, smarter than and more efficient than any other person in your field.. It's a perfect blend of beach bum, powder dog, redneck hippie freak, lumber jack, county boy, closer.. A friend, a father, family man, lover, teacher and coach.. As deadly in a boardroom, brain storming, pounding out ideas as in the poolroom, bedroom, hot tub, sauna or beach.. A chameleon, can change with the environment, mirror you, able to leap tall buildings in a single bound..

If he's playing with you, if he's on one of his little fishing expedition, his hook is sharpened and well baited.. He'll just throw you some out once in a while, then wait for you to bite.. Just waiting and watching to see.. Fishing, he'd say is all about patience.. So is business, so is God and all his miracles.. Relationships take years to build and he knows that.. Go with the flow, be willing to do the ground work, the hard stuff.. If the front end's in place properly, he liked to say, the ass end just seems to come along for the ride, easily, all on it's own..

CHAPTER SEVEN

"Psycho Killer Qu'est-ce que c'est?"

The time in Cabo went by quickly, getting the condo set up, catching up with all his friends and the non-stop partying Drisko style, beaching and touring around.. Friends had invited Drisk and the kids to a bash which he was definitely not going to miss.. The gala event, black tie, was being held in the Tower of the Crown Resort.. It was like the Needle in Seattle or the CN Tower in Toronto, only smaller, but a fantastic 360 rotating view of the Sea of Cortez, San Jose and far across to the mountains of Baja Sur California.. The whispers, from the natives, was that the resort was owned by the mob, drug money, Mexican cartel.. The local joke was calling it the gun tower.. As you'd direct people to the area, you'd say, it's right there, near or across from or just down the road two blocks past the Gun Tower..

Drisko hadn't firmed anything up with Jackie as yet, if she was going to be here in Cabo for the party or not.. His last conversation with her was that she was bogged down at work and needed to be there and would try to come down later in the year.. Drisko was cool with that, nothing he could do about it.. Jacqueline was working for the local newspaper in Drisko's home town of Collingwood.. She was on the road as an advertising rep.. A position Drisk had helped her get and backed her on it completely, not to mention she liked it.. They'd catch up all the time.. She had worked for him before, that's how he met her.. They would spend hours together just talking about advertising, promotional ideas, business concepts and how to work them to the close..

She listened to him and practised everything he'd show her, the tricks of the trade.. Even down to practising her spiel in the mirror, seeing your own facial expressions, your eyes.. Teaching her to remove the hard words from her pitch and contracts.. Words like contracts, authorization, signatures, billing.. She was having trouble getting through the doors sometimes.. She said, they would make her wait for hours.. Drisko told her to get rid of that big black brief case and purse, leave them in the car.. Just walk in carrying the presentation folder, company logo facing out front.. That way everyone in the place can see who you are.. Inside the folder, place the spec ad design, your information, rate card and their forms, filled out, ready for their approval..

See little girl, he said to her, if you're coming into my office with a truck load of shit to show me.. I can only assume you're intending on taking up my whole day and you're the last person I want to see.. On the other hand if you walk in with a folder, I need to give you a minute or two, then you're the first in line.. The lesson worked for her and she was ecstatic.. She couldn't wait to tell him how effective it had been and how well she was now doing.. She walked into the Chevy dealer all cutesy like, like his little black pearl, his black magic woman.. Her black hair, eye brows, black rimmed stylish glasses, dark Latino eyes, no make-up, no lipstick.. Jackie didn't need lipstick or pearls, she was beautiful.. The custom steel structure of her ass and those lily white perky tits, she'd stop a train if it had half a brain.. Her black leather jacket, studded, black pants and cut boots..

She walked toward the reception area she said, smiling at Drisko like a child, telling him the story.. The paper girl's here boss, the voice rang out.. Boss, looks up from his cluttered desk and sees me heading to his door, she explains, waves me in, she says to him

166

smiling.. Just your approval here and here I ordered him as she walked up beside him.. She tosses the open folder on top of the pile of shit on his desk, to lay it directly in front of him.. He said nothing, pen in hand and signed the contract.. I'll be back Wednesday, she said.. I appreciate your time and how busy you are so I'll just drop the proof with Sylvia at the front desk.. Great, he grunted, she turned and left.. He calls to her she said, with total excitement.. Just drop the proofs with me directly Jacqueline, he smiled to her, around ten, I'll make time for you.. Sure Rob, what ever you like she said to him and walked back to her car, exhaled, then lit a smoke..

There was a Scorpion at the edge of the river.. In the middle of the river swimming by, hunting, was a Water Moccasin.. The Scorpion called out to the snake, come here a moment.. He gestured to the snake to come closer, then closer.. With stealthy caution the Water Moccasin approached the river's edge.. He was faster than the Scorpion but he was wise to the deadly potent thorn prancing high on the Scorpion's back.. What would you like Scorpion, he asked? Well Mr. Moccasin, the polite bug replied.. I'd like a ride to the other side of the river on your back, if I may.. No way, said the snake, laughing.. The Scorpion replied, if you give me a ride, I'll show you the best hunting grounds you will ever see in all this land.. Filled beyond belief with the most gourmet morsels you will ever feed on..

The snake dove deep into the river in search of a morsel of food.. Returning to the rivers edge, the Scorpion says well Mr. Snake, do we have a deal.. No, again he replies to the Scorpion.. If I let you on my back you will sting me.. *"Don't be ridiculous my friend, if I sting you, we will both die"*.. With that thought the snake reluctantly agrees to the contract and gives the Scorpion a ride.. Crossing the water the Scorpion sings a peaceful song as the Moccasin swims along.. No sooner do they find the centre of the river when the snake lets out a horrifying yell.. He rears at the Scorpion in disbelief.. Why, why would you sting me, now we shall both perish? The Scorpion, his head slightly twisted and with his hideous smile, simply says, that's what I am, who I am, what I do, what I will always do, "I

Am Monster".. I am the Scorpion, didn't you recognize me, he asked.. Did you see the hook, was it well baited and sharpened nicely enough for you..

Drisko was on the last leg of his management contract, he was heading home in two month.. He'd be back in Ontario with Jacqueline, in time for the spring.. You can still come down anytime, he told her as they spoke on the phone.. I'll take care of it all, other than that, I'm going to be home by May 1st at the latest.. The calls lately not as interesting, no excitement from her, what's up Drisk asking her, probing, prying, what's going on? The house on Silver Creek, Nick's been lying to you, and Joey is living there, Drisko prying, prying.. No worries Jacky, Nick is in charge of the place and the company, it's up to him who he lets stay there, I'll call him tonight, they can't do anything.. Drisko wrote most of it off at the time, just complaints from his girlfriend, worried about Drisko's home..

Drisko went on at work, enjoying it all, having fun, hanging with the gang he worked with.. Him and Jess, inviting folks up to the condo for a swim and a beers, lots of fun.. Melody had long since left, like Drisk had told Jess, when Jessie informed him he was bringing a girl with him.. You don't bring sand to the beach, especially three month in.. The Mexican women chasing Jess down, Mel lost it, caught a quick flight out and was gone.. The winds though were shifting, there was a definite change in the breeze.. The calls from Jacky were all negative, all about the house on Silver Creek, the rumours, the parties, the sex, hookers, drugs, the Cops.. Little Jacqueline was losing it, blowing a nut.. Then the news, he's driving your Beemer, your OO Bond mobile, the windshields cracked.. What, what, what, Drisk said, Nicky, she said, he told me you gave him permission to drive it, Drisko blew a nut!!

The complaint department was wide open for business and the calls were flooding in.. Every call from Jacqueline, threats to her, lies to her from them.. The trucks are missing, your boats gone, the skid steer is nowhere to be found or the trailer.. Jacqueline, calling the cops, twenty times.. Drisko calling the house, several time, they wouldn't answer or return the calls.. That's when he called cops himself, the O.P.P., with little avail, too far away, but yes, they're investigating it.. Drisko's only three weeks from returning, if he walks out on this contract, he losses everything he set in place.. They can't do anything, he said to her, on his last call.. You can't just steal peoples things and get away with it, can you.. I trusted those two fucks, he stressed to her, we trusted them.. I have nothing but given, everything, to both of them, more than once, Drisko's blood was crueling, I know she replied, I know..

Nobody will ever believe it, no great novelist, screenwriter, playwright could had written the script.. No Lawman, Clergyman or Einstein-ish guy could ever have predicted the outcome of all this.. When Drisk returned to Ontario, the house on Silver Creek was empty.. Everything is gone, all his personal things, his guitar, his artwork, his furniture, the safe.. The wall safe, with all his history in it, his secrets, his past life.. Everything, every single thing, gone.. They had collected and kept all the rent money, all the mortgage money, defrauding the landlord, loosing all of Drisko's deposit and investment.. The shop, empty, absolutely empty, everything, all his tools, equipment, all, the coke machine, everything stolen.. Taken by two incredibly ugly con-men, friends for over ten years.. They planned it, did it, all, together.. Drisko went looking for blood, the moon staring down on him..

Drisko and Jacqueline had split up, she told him on the phone the week before he returned.. She was frightened by Nicky, his lies all the time, using her, to lie to Drisk.. Then Joey threatening her, if she came near the house, he would shove his big black cock up her ass, she was in true fear of them.. How could you have friends like these, she asked.. These people are supposed to be your good friends, her voice raising sarcastically.. This is what you hang around with, he's gonna stick his big black cock up my ass.. This is your friend, not a Jackie thing, not the way she ever spoke, ever.. They threatened you, your family, your girlfriend.. They steal from you, steal your house, lie to the owner, steal your rent money and destroy your investments..

Drisko now standing in front of Jacqueline, in the tiny trailer.. She's mad, angry, hurt, terrified, she's sounding crazy now, acting or going, Drisko was unsure.. This was everything Nick and Joey wanted.. It was their plan, their dream come true, their path to wealth and riches.. He knew she was hurting from it all, the lies, deceit, the huge losses.. He knew, he was hurting too, his huge loss, her.. What was it worth to you Drisko, she asked in anger? What was I worth to you, using his full first name? What was it worth Drisko in money, dollars and cents, Drisk had no answer? It wasn't worth anything to be losing you, he said to her, not worth a thing.. It's okay Jackie, it's okay, he said to her, buying himself some time, listening to her breath.. They did it, every single thing that was ever important to me in my life, has been destroyed, stolen, taken away..

He left the little trailer park that night, leaving Jacqueline behind.. He left the life he wanted and was building for the two of them.. He left the house on Silver Creek, the equipment, the investments, the gold.. He left the Double O Beemer, the boats, his guitar, his business and his dreams all of it, all.. It was all behind him now, left there in the double-wide, at the beach, where she lived, sometimes with him.. He walked away from it all that night.. They took it, all of it, Joey and Nick carelessly getting not only what they wanted, but what they thought they deserved..

They just took it, they took his whole life and the Collingwood Keystone cops, well, they stood there and watched it all happen.. And the bike, that went missing in 1967, well the cops are still looking for it, there, out behind Tim Horton's donut shop.. He went home to the condo alone.. He sat on the deck, he smoked a big fat dooby and thought about the ants, all of them.. Thinking, the pain she must had felt, how much the distrust and treason of the two of them.. It must had destroyed her faith completely.. They were her friends too, so she thought.. She was so hurt by all this, his fault, his error, he wasn't there to protect her and he can't save her now, she's gone..

The cleanup crew.. On the surface they looked innocent enough.. They're small as you tower over them in your God-like stature.. The ants have a life of their own.. Up top of the condo complex was a sun pad, a lookout point.. Drisko would go there sometimes with his buddies guitar, the Martin.. Looking down over San Jose, watching into the Sea of Cortez, thinking and playing.. Sometimes he'd bring a bite to eat, till one day it started that he always brought a bite to eat.. Not for him, for the ants.. Have you ever watched them, they are incredible.. It all started as an accident, a drop of bread crumb smaller than a tip of a pin.. The first ones come out, they probe and poke as they dart in and far out to safety, circling it, then the next and the next, till the circle is of hundreds.. One time Drisko brought them a fresh cockroach still moving.. Within ten minutes the carcass was moving across the deck..

The ants are strong, brave and cautious.. It takes them a long time to gather their tribe.. Around in circles almost in an uncontrolled direction, busting the big bug apart.. The wings, the claws, it's head ripped off of it.. Then the other group, now picking up the loose parts.. Moving the roach's torso thirty feet over mountains and valleys in their pin tipped size to stuff it down the hole to the nest.. Leaving behind the cleanup crew, they clean everything, every last morsel, including any juices the bug secreted.. Other times the pin ants would eventually get attacked, pushed out by the brown ants, ten, twenty times their size.. Then those ants would get overthrown by an even larger black ant, the more visible and larger of the insects.. Definite rulers, as they approach, everyone else runs for cover..

Each colony a different taste, need, purpose, place, working together, feeding off one another, sharing.. Different cultures working on a single purpose.. Then the Hermiso Rojo, the killer, the red ant, she kills, devours, consumes everything in her path, they run in huge packs.. I've seen the Red Highway, up close and personal, the river of red death, it's simply frightening and they love your flesh.. Drisko thinking, I could kill Joey this way, ant food, devour everything right down to his bones.. Wonder if he knows

171

I'm planning on feeding his big black cock to the cleanup crew.. Let mother nature take care of her own misfits..

It's a wheel.. They call it a wheel because it's made round, and it's made round, to go around and because it goes around, it always comes back.. Some people think they can beat the wheel, change it by doing something crazy, like positive thinking or meditation.. The wheel isn't controlled by us, you silly.. It's controlled by a little tiny hamster that runs on the wheel and sometimes he runs high, sometimes he runs low.. But it's a wheel, so it will always go around.. If you think of this in your life, sometimes you're up and nothing you can do, can bring you down..

Then other times you're down and nothing you do, can bring you up.. You need to know it's not you, it's the wheel, so wait.. Just wait, because it comes around.. Always be ready when the wheel is up.. Take full advantage of it, but be prepared for it when it's down.. Take full advantage of it, rest, relax, re-focus, prepare, get ready for battle, get ready for blood.. Take no prisoners, Drisko was ready for blood, the sacrifice of the Kings, he shouted, to his thousands of warriors if not more, following as he led them to the Blood Eagle..

Drisko preparing for battle, doing his recon, first the Collingwood police, they're investigating, charges pending.. Then to the insurance company, Drisk reporting the claim, nothing they could do to payout the policy until an arrest has been made.. Then to the bank, to the criminal investigation department, sitting there with the manager.. Nothing has been deposited in the account since last November, she said to him.. The rent checks, the jobs, my company, the contracts, nothing, he asked, nothing.. Nothing she replied, Drisko took the info back to the cops, nothing, they said, we're investigating it, charges pending, fraud.. Drisko's blood was crueling, the vision of the Witch, the blood sacrifice, there on the pier at the Arches, the treason to the Kings..

The winds had filled his sails, he could feel the force, lifting him up and carrying him dangerously close to the rocky shore.. Drisko, running, charging briskly, the first attack, the first charge,

Criminal Harassment, threats.. Drisko had caught up to Nicky, on the phone several times.. Drisko, tearing into him, time and time again, explaining to him, exactly how he would meet his end.. You are the Scorpion, he said to him, and your life is for one that should never be trusted.. That cost Drisko huge, a night in the lock-up and a date with a judge..

Jacqueline was running scared, frightened by all the anger and hate developed over this whole thing, it was insane for her.. Drisko trying to talk to her, get the answers, till it stopped, dead, strange, but dead.. She was acting very different, distant, the friendship that was once love was strained now, stretched out of proportion.. Drisko, now forced to second guess her, was she in on it all, was she part of the plan.. Not calling Drisk, not telling him things that went on while he was away, things she knew about, the truth.. The more he questioned her the more distant she became.. Then she struck, with her venom, don't call me anymore Drisko, I don't want to see or hear from you again, we're through..

Drisko let it go, his mind stuck on the pier, the Blood Eagle, Jacqueline, there with, Nicky and Joey, there in front of the great King Drisko, let them kiss the Cod.. It was hard for Drisk to imagine it all, that she would had been part of this treason, but the thought would not escape him.. Weeks had gone by without answers.. Drisko needed answers, so he called Jacqueline, see if they could meet.. She screamed at him, it threw him off guard, if you call again, I'll call the cops on you.. Drisko hung up the phone, she was in on it.. Strangely, as he hung up, moments later, the cops called, warning him..

Then a week later, she called him, just to chat, they did, they chatted, then she called again.. A little this a little of that, nothing big, just chat.. Then he called her one day, see if she'd like to catch dinner, she screamed at him, threatened him, she would call the cops.. Drisko was in circles with it, as the call went dead.. Strangely, as he hung up, moments later, the cops called, warning him.. Drisko, explaining to them she was calling me, so I called her back, stay away from her Drisk, she's crazy over it all..

Drisko went on, back to work, trying to forget Jacqueline, forget the nightmare, forget it all.. The fall had come, he was thinking of leaving, heading to Mexico.. October, Halloween was nearing, her favourite time of year.. Drisk drove by her home, dropped a polite note and a sweater she had left in the car.. I'm heading out in the next week, thought I'd say goodbye and wanted to return your sweater.. Tomorrow is Halloween, if you wanted to spend some time together, and he dropped the note.. Drisko was arrested, sentenced to thirty days, his second stay, this time the big house..

The prison walls of Penetang were the last place he expected to see.. One minute he's there talking to her, with her right there in his arms, alive, in love, vibrant.. Then the next he's in C-block, being strip searched and roughed up.. No two hundred dollars, no passing go, no getting outta jail free card.. This was no game senor.. Three cops in all cuffed him at the truck, outside the condo.. "Incredible" he said to the officers, "simply incredible", he scowled at the lawyers.. "She set me up", screaming to the Judge.. All her calls, the meetings, the lies from her.. How, how could this happen?

Drisko had been free for almost two months, the prison, the trailer park, the house on Silver Creek and Jacqueline all behind him now.. All but the dreams and the nightmares as he sat peacefully there, in the condo.. The bullets are flying everywhere as they riddle through the tiny house.. He dives, rolls and slides to safety, behind the black leather couch.. Still no protection, the little Golden 5 shot PP47 is no match for the onslaught of endless lead.. Lead, pouring from the barrels of the ten or twenty submachine guns and the men in black suits backing them..

Like in the movie where the bad guys come and shoot up the villa with their highly advanced techno weaponry and devour the entire building to rubble.. That was them, till they jumped into the safety, of the tunnel that Drisko dug, bare handed, just in case of this exact scenario occurring.. Jacqueline jumps in behind him.. He catches her and they escape down the secret passageway, to safety and the Bond 00 BMW.. The cave door opens as they accelerate out of the mountain wall and off into the sunset.. Then the beep, beep, beeping.. Drisko observes it, it's hopeless, there's no time, it's too late, it's ringing, ringing, ringing, it was a trap..

Jacqueline calls, the cell's ringing, it's late, 2:00am in late September.. The last days before the new moon of October.. The moon he remembered sitting under so many years, days and moments ago.. On the deck in Cabo dreaming of making love to her, above the Sea of Cortez, on the Sea of Tranquility.. Unbelievable as it may seem, he was thinking about her, right there that evening.. Wishing they had found a chance, to just talk about it.. Sitting there listening quietly to the Weather Network, watching for the reports of winter storms to come..

As most evenings he's up late, unable to sleep.. It's safe to be awake, unable to remove the life he had suffered through over the past two years, his prison.. The Farmer's Almanac reports a cold hard winter, Canada should prepare for above average snow fall and large occurrences of ice storms, freezing rain and sacrificial Blood Eagles, snake pits and hanging ropes.. Brought on by the low pressure systems and violent, destructive visions of death, continually running, through your tiny brain.. Created mostly from the greenhouse effects, the announcer said.. The greenhouse effect Drisko thought curiously, laughing as he's drawing out the details of the job he had finally secured for his little company..

Easy work the client said, as Drisko estimated the enormous task set out before him.. Take her down, stack her up, zip, zip.. Put it back up over there, zip, zip, you're done, easy job.. Easiest job you'll ever get Drisko my boy.. Zip, zip, he says, as he's hunting for the deal.. He points, out beyond his property line to the vacant lot next door, then back to the massive glass building towering beyond Drisko's peripheral vision, vertically and horizontally.. Big job, Drisk says, dangerous as all get out, lots of safety requirements..

We need safety gear, supports and lift equipment.. Just use the old tractor over there, the old farmer, again with the pointing.. I'm afraid of farm equipment, that shit's dangerous, Drisk said to him, with a smile.. Ever met a farmer with all his digits, the old guy laughs, looking at Drisko's fingers, then his own.. Drisko could see him counting them, we need safety equipment, it's all in one price.. I'll take care of it, have 'er all done by the end of October for ya.. It's thirty percent up front plus materials and rental cost..

Without his glasses that late at night, Drisko couldn't see the tiny numbers on his cell phone.. Two o'clock in the morning, he hardly noticed it ringing.. Drisko here, Drisko, the voice said, then silence.. He was stunned, frightened by the voice.. He listen to the Beatles backwards, he could hear her voices, clearly, Diablo, it's the Devil, she said.. Jacqueline, is that you, straining to see the tiny numbers on the face of the cell phone.. Still the machine wouldn't talk, are you okay.. Still silent on the line, his blood pounding hot, crueling..

I thought you were a criminal, the voice said.. Jacqueline, baby, his heart dead in his mouth.. Jackie, what are you doing? I thought you were a criminal, it spurted from the tiny box in his hand.. I thought you were somehow involved in all this, you were a criminal or undercover RCMP, a narc, she said.. I didn't know you'd go to jail.. I am a criminal he replied, now, but my only crime was loving you.. They spoke, him giving no direct thought to the court order, to not make contact with Jacqueline..

Drisk couldn't recall exactly what the conversation consisted of.. They spoke for two and a half hours about everything.. The police know you had nothing to do with it Drisko.. I didn't he said firmly, you know that Jacqueline.. They know you're a good guy, you don't have any record.. On the other hand Joey and Nick are at arm's length with their records.. This is huge Drisko, bigger than either of us ever thought.. Drisko wondering in his mind, how, how does she know this, questioning, searching?

Four thirty am., he said to her, I can't call you Jacqueline, court order.. If you need me I'm here for you, all you need to do is talk to my probation officer, then we can meet, talk, she'll set it all up.. He couldn't hang up, he knows he loves her, he knows she loves him, still.. The afternoon should warm up to highs of plus 12 cooling off in the evening to plus 8, with heavy rains expected, overnight.. He shut the TV volume down and sits there in the dark, alone, listening.. Thinking silently, in the hallows of the condo, black everywhere, black inside, black out.. What happened to us he thought, why, what does this all mean, what's she doing, what does she want?

Somehow Jacqueline wasn't that important anymore, the trust, the love, the care he had for her was truly still deep inside of him but guarded.. Guarded by a thousand miles of steel bars, red tape, secure doors, solitary confinement and strip searches.. Guarded by the murderers, con-men, wife abusers, gang brawlers, fighters, home invaders, car thieves, bank robbers, safe crackers and dope dealers.. The Choice, the Angels, the Devils, the mob, guarded by the crack dealers, the animals, the criminals and she's here on the phone again, telling him, it's all going to be okay..

What did she want, he kept thinking what is this girl up to? As he unfolded the events to himself, just let her come to you Drisko, he'd said.. It's her game, it's her ball, you're not the pitcher.. He could still feel her inside him, joined at the heart, that he knew for sure.. If she was breathing he felt her.. He had loved her, so very deeply for so long now, but he didn't know what she was doing.. The dreams no, nightmares he had in jail.. Her living in this pink house near the barking dogs, the six plex type thing, behind the gates, with decrepit people, visiting her, the lowlifes of society, sharing her, there in Mexico.. The same people that are here, with him, in his prison.. She's was there selling her body for crack, a whore, Joey's whore, there working for him and Nicky..

He drives by her, somewhere deep in Mexico, as she sees him, looking out at her, from inside, his Bond, 00 Beemer.. She stares at him, gesturing to him, swaying to the Spanish beat behind her.. She wants her hundred pesos, she doesn't know him, she never did.. She thinks she does, she feels an attraction as he slowly drives by her.. She couldn't had recognized him from Adam, then he hears the voice.. Drisko, the monkey doesn't let go of one vine, till she has her hands on another..

Now Jacqueline wanted to talk to him.. He gave it no real thought, she's was phoning him.. He loved her, still deeply, hurt and afraid, big time, but he's like de' bull, he's made of steel, water off a duck, fear no man.. Yet now afraid of a little girl.. A little girl capable of tearing his heart out, with his soul.. Out through his eyes balls, up into his nostrils and back out through his asshole with one command, while he's still smiling at her.. He was fucked, coming or going, just fucked..

Jacqueline, he said, how are you, what's up? I need to see you she said, now, it's important.. Drisko's heart stopped dead.. This is what he had been waiting for, for her.. He wanted this so desperately, for so long to be beside her again.. Her mere words, set his mind thinking of her, smelling her, the thought vivid of holding her, touching her, again.. I can't, he said, abruptly and paused, as he recalled all the laws he would break and all the nights spent, all alone, in C block, on the resort side of Georgian Bay.. I can't, he kept telling himself as the words would form, on his lips, then spit out as, where and when? As she poked and probed with the ugly stick, for a suitable place to meet, she was planning, as she spoke..

This place and that, then reasons why not to select that location.. We may get seen, she trembled.. Drisk could hear the steel doors slamming, the keys jingling in the locks.. The steel trap doors, slowly echoing one at a time, then louder and louder through the middle of the night.. The five o'clock shake ups for court call.. The six o'clock med tray and the seven o'clock revelry breakfast.. Then count dates, the minutes that took hours, the nightmare of it all, of her..

Get a hold of yourself Drisko, he said in his silent voice.. She's calling you, she's inviting you to go out.. He needed to know the truth, he needed closure.. As he looks back from here, he loved her, deeply, he wanted her, still.. He would had done it all, again, after all of it, to try and spend his life with her.. He could feel it, she was coming into his life again, into his heart, his dreams, stoking his fire, his obsessions.. Poking him with the ugly stick.. They chatted a bit more, I need to see you now Drisko, I need to talk to you.. Her voice sweet, soft, sorry, her sadness, he felt the same way.. He asked if they could meet tomorrow.. No, now, she said sternly.. Fuck it Jackie, meet me behind Timmy's he spurted out.. Fuck 'em, nobody's gonna tell me, I can't see you, if you want to see me.. They won't bother us, it's all cool, his mind recalls, the love he once had for her.. The trust he had, for her, for Joey, Nick, the house, up on Silver Creek Drive..

They can't stop us if we want to see each other, she blurted.. There he sat, thinking, how could this have happened.. How does one trust, or worse, not trust, especially someone you love.. They, being anybody else in the world.. This should really be up to you and me, she whispered to him through the speaker of the phone.. He recalls it all, as if it were yesterday, here and now, in his thoughts.. He really didn't give it much more thought than that, they made their plan.. He was going to meet Jacqueline, that was his thought, his only thought.. He was gonna see her, the girl he loved, there, that night, F.T.W.. He hung up the phone and told his roommate about the call.. Drisko left him with the impression that he would be back soon to help, to catch up for the party..

He flew into the stop at the drive through window, grabbed his coffee and then parked his black Ford F150, pick-up truck, in the open lot, out back behind the coffee shop, near the lake, at the park in Collingwood.. He backed into the spot, so she, Jacqueline, could pull in beside him.. His plan was to be courteous and gentlemanly, both of them facing window to window, driver's side to driver's side.. He waited, patiently, spying everything that went on, noticing every move, every tourist, every walking dog at the little park..

Es' cool juanito amigo, is total cool my little friend, Drisko said to himself, in his silent voice.. Then there out of the corner of his eye the little red Sunfire enters the lot.. It's her, she pulls half past the truck and backs in, go figure.. Only a part of her showing, her chin, the shoulder, covered with a black leather jacket.. It's her, he say's softly, out loud.. The window unwinds magically on its own as she leans over to fill her face into his view.. It's her, its Jacqueline, in his silent voice, he whispers..

Get in, she said, get in, he stepped from the cab of the pick-up and pushed the auto lock on the black F150 key fob and got in.. As he adjusted the belt on the passenger side seat, she pulled the little red Sunfire out and onward toward the lights and onto the highway.. Some small talk, couldn't say what it was now, but every word Drisko chose carefully, thoughtfully.. Let's go to your place, she said, the condo.. There's a party going on there, he said confused.. My roommate, his kids birthday, was she working on one cylinder he thought, is she whacked.. Still on his guard watching, waiting for the red and blue lights to come charging in, anytime from every direction..

She wheels the buggy left, down into the backroads, then down five hundred meters.. Then turning down, then deeper down into the eye, then deeper and deeper.. Into the eyesore of Collingwood, down, deep into the old grain elevators.. The landmark of the harbour entrance, of the old town for over a hundred years now.. There down behind the marina, down behind the secluded building.. Tall, white, towering, dark and desolate as the skies were falling, down behind the tiny Blue Mountains.. She searches slowly, down between her legs, she twisted the keys down, dangling from the column.. The Sunfire's engine, goes down.. The moon is hurtling down towards them, then everything goes silent, except the song.. *"Psycho Killer Qu'est-ce que c'est?"*, that's where he lost it.. There in the silence of the song, in the notes, the beat, beating.. That's where it all went down and life changes in an instant..

They sat there at the pier that night, just her and him and the little red Chevy Sunfire.. It was just a little past eight thirty, 8:36 the clock read, there under the shadow of the grain elevators.. Jacqueline watched as the sun lowered itself behind the darkness of the Blue Mountains.. As the sky fades to blackness, the song sang, *"I can't seem to face up to the facts. I'm tense and nervous and I can't relax."*, his eyes were pasted on her.. He explained the visions he saw, the dreams he'd had of her, the beach and the sunsets of Cabo.. They talked, till the sun went down, down into darkness, *"I'm a real live wire."*, down till darkness fell..

They talked about Joey and Nick.. Then they talked about themselves.. It had been two years since this mess had all started, all thanks to two brilliant con-men.. It had been two years since he held Jackie, two years in and out of jails, they laughed, they cried, they smiled and frowned.. They touched each other and held hands.. They kissed and held each other close.. He clinched her hair in his left hand, snagging it, tightly with force, *"Run, run, run, run, run away."*.. If she didn't trust him, she should have been better prepared.. She was about to be wrapped up, by a man she had just put into prison, possibly twice..

He pulled her toward him, whispering, into her ear softly, exactly, what he was going to do to her.. She sat there confident in the driver's seat patiently staring, weeping, waiting for him, the reaper.. I didn't know, she cried out to him, I honestly had no idea they would put you in jail.. He placed his thumb forcefully against her jaw, controlling her head now, completely, *"talking a lot, but not saying anything."*.. He leaned into her, kissing her, as promised, *"When I have nothing to say, my lips are sealed."*, deeply, holding the kiss.. His lips finding hers, her chin, then her neck.. He bites down on her strongly, but gentle, then finding her lips again, quickly, passionately.. He probes deep into her mouth reminding her, hypnotically.. His right hand cradling her left jaw, her cheeks and neck locked deeply into his vice..

Releasing the grip as he lowers it stealthily along her chest into the softness of her belly and belt line to find the thin of her thighs.. Three feet from the gold, he whisper to her.. She, better than anyone in his world, knows exactly what he means.. She especially knows, especially right here, right now, she knows.. He slowly moves his hand upward, below her sweater, then onto her thin skin.. The same sweater he dropped, on her BBQ that fateful night, a year ago..

He looked past her, into the darkness, looking, searching for the red and blues, the tiny lights.. Him, searching, deep into the darkness of this night.. Him feeling her breast, the nipple, the softness, their warmth, thinking they're exactly as he left them, full, perfect and round.. No wires, he recalls, his mind, no reds and no blues, searching without searching, thinking, without or trying to think, without thought.. Thinking without knowing, is this a trap, is she setting me up again..

What's going on Jackie, he abruptly, just asked her? I was under the impression you didn't like me.. Now, you're acting like you're in love with me, calling me in all these crazy hours, what's with that Jackie? Looking her deeply into her eyes, commanding her to tell him the truth.. Of course I still love you Drisko, I've always loved you.. You're my soulmate and I know you're a decent, good man.. She went on, almost reminiscing of the things they had dreamt of together.. The life they were going to share together, *"Psycho Killer, Qu'est-ce que c'est. Fa, fa, fa, fa, fa, fa, fa, fa, fa, far, better. Run, run, run,"*.. He continues kissing her, *"run, run, run, run, away."*, holding her, loving her, searching for the lights.. He sits back gathering his thoughts.. Him, sitting there, staring, out, up, looking over the harbour, beyond, up, into the Blue Mountains.. The silhouette, the silver moon, shining above them, hurtling toward them.. Remnants of a scene he left behind, on the deck, on that moon, in Cabo..

Let's go to Florida again, this spring, she said.. We can buy that place in Gulfport, as if they had never had a problem at all, like nothing had ever come between them.. Was he dreaming, was he back in prison.. Were the red and blue lights coming, what could spoil this? This is what he wanted all along, hoped for, what he believed to be true, her, Jackie.. He told everyone that would listen, the police, the judges, counsellors, his roommate, the world.. This, this was it, the spot, this very place, here, now, you could hear it.. Then everything goes silent.. That's where he lost it, in the silence.. That's where it all went down.. He wasn't crazy, she was hurt, hurt badly.. She did love him, he was right.. Life changes in an instant and Drisko knows, every ending, brings with it, a new.. A new beginning, all from the gentle rotation of the earth..

Tearing down a greenhouse is fun but dangerous work.. Removing the glass plates is for sure delicate business and dangerous, dangling high above the panes of glass.. Removing the fasteners with as little weight as possible, gently, not to shatter or worse, create a chain reaction.. The compression from one pane of glass impacting on the cement floor starting from the ground up.. The explosion of the bits could in fact, fracture.. Reacting now to every pane of glass straight up through the roof, so to speak.. Equal to the danger above is working from below.. If you're standing inside the fatal vase as it implodes, glass could remove your limbs, sever fingers, ears, eyes or throat, to the point of no repair..

Shattered glass, would penetrate every layer of skin, through the muscle shield and slice you through, to the bone.. Slicing and dicing through the arteries and ripping into the organs.. Lighter and smaller particles would embed themselves, into every inch of depth of you.. Splattering you with shrapnel, killing you painfully slow, shredding through the skin.. When you breathe, the glass dust, will now simply scour the lungs.. After dissolving the teeth and the tongue, your throat would fill with powdered glass, that you will swallow..

Once the glass comes off the frames, the steel has to be dismantled.. When the colder October, November winds start to blow.. The steel frames, will be cold, freezing in your hands.. The work won't allow the use of gloves.. The bars had to be dropped in reverse order, from their installation.. Each piece alpha coded, stock piled, then stored along with all the bits of hardware, in order, numbered and colour coded.. Drisko was working away on tearing down the greenhouse.. The crew was just putting on the finishing touches removing the final sheets of glass.. Still plenty of work to be done, removing all the steel then stacking it and storing it.. Drisko had just come home from a cold day's work, mucho frio.. This October weather bites right through your bones.. His feet are freezing off him because of the cold ground on the running shoes he's wearing to protect the glass sheets..

He hadn't heard from Jacqueline for a couple of days.. Let's go to Florida together, her words, their kiss, her touch.. The phone rings, its Jacqueline, "Hello Sunshine", she starts, how are you.. They carry on the conversation, a little bite of this, a little bite of that.. Then on to how she enjoyed being with him the other night.. More and more chat, laughing, joking, having such fun.. I spoke to the police again, she said, I spoke to constable Mike.. I went in to see him and I had a good talk with him and his partner.. You didn't tell them you were talking to me did you, Drisko quizzing her.. Yes she said, Jackie are you fuckin' crazy.. They're gonna arrest me, he's venting, shaken..

They said it was okay, she interrupted.. Don't worry you're not a suspect.. They know you're innocent, they know you had nothing to do with any of it.. I'm gonna talk to the Crown Attorney, Sunshine, try to get the charges dropped.. They know you're innocent Drisko, again she's repeating her message.. They know it was all Joey and Nick, Sunshine, her nick name for him.. Just trust me Drisko, I'm gonna fix everything, you just need to trust me, this is huge, she exclaimed.. The cops are really investigating them both, hard time.. They've got everything they need, over thirty charges pending Drisk.. They know exactly what went on, the whole thing, this is huge Drisko, it's internationally huge.. Joey's into something big Drisk, Nick's in it too.. She went on with her stories, the details, the descriptions.. His mind thinking how does she know all this, is she that in with the cops.. Either way he believed her as she spoke..

Nick had all of Drisko's keys, all the codes, he knew all of Drisko's accounts.. He found the key to the digital electronic safe, then they removed everything and ransacked his room.. The safe that held his social insurance cards, his business and bank information, passport information, licenses and owner ships, deeds and titles.. Nick did Drisko's books, he was his trusted business manager.. He had all his business accounts, he had his life and he wanted more.. He wanted Bond, he wanted Double 0 Drisk.. Drisk recalls Nick asking him once, in total bewilderment to Drisk.. Do you know who you are Drisko, as if Drisk had impressed Nick? Nick, wanted the Bond car, the replica Double O Beemer, the 740i, so he stole it.. Then lied to everyone and to Jackie about it..

He wanted the girl, his Bond girl Jacqueline.. He wanted the business, the house, the income, the rent money.. He wanted and was stealing everything in Drisko's life.. Joey, he wanted the life, the life he dreamt of, Head Pimp, gang leader and as more and more details would flow in, Drisk would soon find out the truth.. Nick's, words ringing vibrant through Drisko's mind.. Sitting there in the living room of the house on Silver Creek as he begged Drisko for his trust.. Begging to let him stay in the house, take care of it, manage the office, watch the equipment, get more contracts over the winter, sell and run the company, The Creative Factory..

It's really going to fuck me up, he said to Drisko and Jackie, if you rent the place out.. Drisko, remembering, negotiating with him, giving him an affordable great deal.. Helping him, again and again, to get his life in order, giving him the chance he asked for.. The gift Drisko gave to him, the mistake, he would live to regret, forever.. The very second he realized he had made the mistake.. That moment, the second Mercedes told him what they had said to her..

Mercedes, holding the bills in her hand, as Nick and Joey threatened her, lying to her.. Drisko left all the main bills, in connection to the house on Silver Creek, connected to the house in the Point.. So when they defaulted, the notice went to Mercedes address.. All the bills are paid up, they said, both conjuring up all their lies.. Badgering, as they tried to manipulate her, both taking turns, calling her with their lies.. Mercedes far too smart for those two con-men.. Jacqueline, earlier describing it as a feeling like she had been molested, tortured and raped.. The Devil doesn't come to you with horns and a tail, he comes dressed as a friend, clothed with a smile..

As he listened intensely to Jacqueline's cries, through the telephone line.. He realized exactly, how much damage, the Devil and his side-kick really did.. What Joey and Nick had taken from him.. Not just his life, his pride and his wealth, but his chances and plans for his life.. The life he wanted to share with this girl, now dangling by a thread, on the other end of this phone.. The girl he had loved two years ago and wanted in his life.. Instead of a life in wedlock, they were now in gridlock, they took everything.. There was nothing left in his life that belonged to him..

His things, his life, his girl, his love, his rights and soon, very soon again, his freedom, again.. I love you Drisko, still, she said, gently breathing into the line, I love you and only you.. I know you do and you know I love you, he said.. I'm hoping to just get through this mess, get done with my probation and get on with my life.. If you want to talk Jackie, to get together, all you have to do is call Ruth, my probation officer, she'll help us work it all out.. I'm going to talk to the Crown Attorney she said, both of us confused.. Anyway Drisko don't get yourself arrested, don't do anything to violate your probation.. I'm going to fix this thing for us, you just have to trust me, she said.. You're the only one calling the cops here, Drisko said to her, in his silent voice..

A Detective from the Special Investigations Unit of the O.P.P., is coming to the house to meet with me next week, the 18th she said.. You should come to the meeting, it's around two.. This is huge Drisko, a huge investigation.. They want to talk to me, they want to talk about the whole thing, her voice excited.. Are you fuckin' nuts, he asked calmly, are you whacked in the fuckin head, he said.. If I go to your house Jacqueline, they'll fuckin arrest me on the spot.. You have a restraining order against me, thinking to himself, then repeating it aloud to her..

Even now just talking to you I'm in violation of my probation.. No you're not she argues, it's me calling you.. They'd send me to jail and throw away the key if I go anywhere near your door, Drisko spurts, ignoring her comment.. Oh ya, she says chuckling, I forgot.. Even now Jacqueline, if you tell anyone we've talked, your brothers or mom, dad, I could end up in jail.. If you call the cops on me, he said, as she interrupts him, I'm not going to call the cops on you Sunshine.. He interrupts her, if you do honey, this time, I'll get two years..

I'm not going to call the cops Drisko, I promise.. If the cops or the officer call me Jackie and ask me to join you.. If they invite me to the meeting or we meet at the station, I would go, but only if it's approved first.. Jacqueline acknowledged the importance of them following the system, the danger, the privacy required between them.. I'm gonna talk to them, she said.. The cops, the Crown, to see what I need to do.. Just trust me Sunshine, just trust me one more time, I'm gonna fix this mess.. It will take a little time but I'm gonna fix it, I love you Drisko, I do want to be with you.. It's up to you, there is nothing I can do, he said sadly, nothing.. I can't call you, I can't see you and I can't be with you, it's all up to you..

He hung up the phone from Jacqueline, turning the volume back up on the Weather Network.. He sparked up a doob and thought about getting ready for bed.. Cold front moving in along the southern tip of Georgian Bay.. Rain expected in the afternoon and evening around the Bruce Peninsula.. Collingwood can expect temperatures to drop into the single digits with scattered patches of, "trust me Sunshine".. All in all it looks like it's going to be a beautiful fall day, a perfect day to die.. The plan was set, Jacqueline would talk to the cops, the Crown, get a release from the judge, take care of everything.. Then they can meet again, then they can talk again, work on their lives again..

Quickly to the shower, letting the warm water devour him, his thoughts of Jacqueline.. He cast the lights out early.. He had a big day planned.. Today we strip the steel from the greenhouse, code it, stack it and colour code and store it.. The threat of shattering glass exploding through his bones was over now, gone.. Now all he had to worry about was the sharp serrated edges, the hooks, of the twisted blue steel.. Beams of life and death, like the blades, of a power transformers spider arms.. They come crashing down, slicing their way through you, deep into the ground.. The ground that was now beginning to harden, losing its moisture, filling it with ice cold frost, from the gentle rotation of the earth..

The week went by without a hitch.. The eighteenth had come and gone and no word from Jacqueline.. The thoughts of her was in his mind, but he was going on with things.. She wasn't weighing there, only gently appearing, slipping in and out of his thoughts.. Why hadn't she called, he wondered? Why had I not heard from her. What had taken place at the meeting, the cops? What had she done about us, her and him getting back together? Had she spoken to the cops, the Crown.. It was strange to him but his mind was made up, not to try to contact her.. It was her game, she was the pitcher..

Saturday morning Drisko's off to the site early.. It has to be done today, they start the install on Monday and there's no stopping it.. Everything works in reverse, the last piece to come down is the first piece to go up.. It's dark out, 7pm, Saturday evening.. They pack up, the job's completed, everything is ready.. The greenhouse laid neatly stacked, steps away from where they will erect it Monday morning, first light.. He say's goodbye to the boys, stopping to talk with the owner, with a promise to be on site at seven am, first thing in the morning, Monday.. You should wear work boots he said.. Zip zip, the ground over there is filled with old nails and shit, it's probably dangerous without steel plated boats, zip, zip.. Plus they're warmer Drisko, he added.. Ya, ya okay I'll check 'em out Drisk replied.. He was telling Drisk, in a way of, as if asking, as he would..

Drisko headed to the condo, all the time thinking, he should just go grab some boots.. He had a good pair, before, at the house on Silver Creek.. They now belonged to Joey and Nick and knowing those two idiots, they probably both took one.. He had to break down and replace them.. Marks, he thought, the big chain store, in the Mountain Plaza, out on the highway.. He arrives there, shit, they're closed.. Walmart right next door, open late, he can't go.. It's part of his original probation order, because he met Jacqueline there once, in a violation of his probation, so it ain't gonna happen for him..

He's stuck here, he needs boots for work and if he doesn't go to Walmart, he can't get them, he can't work.. He's at odds with himself, he drives the truck around the back of the plaza through the grocery store parking lot.. Circling while he's thinking his way out of this jam.. Forget it, he says in his silent voice, he'll just go to work early Monday, get the boys set up and slip out in the morning, grab the boots then, gone, done deal..

He hit the driveway of the grocery store plaza, not stopping before he turns onto the main road, the song playing, *"I can't sleep cause my bed's on fire."*.. There she is heading to the light, Jacqueline in the little red Chevy Sunfire.. Facing him, the same direction, coming to a stop as he pulled out onto the road.. He see's her in the left lane ready to head through the light as it turns red.. He's on the same road, in the other lane, approaching her.. He slows, hoping the light will change, *"Don't touch me I'm a real live wire."*.. Forget about it Drisko, he's thinking to himself.. Fuck her, let her go, there's cars, filling in behind him, approaching his rear end.. He can't stop here, he needs to go forward to the light, it puts him in the lane beside her.. He's turning right, she's going straight.. The light's red, they're side by side at the lights, stuck together, two cars back..

He looks at her, she looks back at him.. He motions with his hand as to raise a cup to his mouth in a gesture, would you like to go for a coffee.. He's thinking about her meeting with the cops at her house in the trailer park.. She rolls down her electric power passenger side window, he rolls down his, smiling, the song singing, *"Psyco Killer, Qu'est-ce que c'est"*.. She screams at him, Drisko, if you don't stop this, I'm warning you, I mean it, leaning over, screaming out the passenger side windows, into the air..

Fuck her he's thinking, *"fa-fa-far better. Run, run, run, run, run, run, run away."*.. He turns his head from her, rolling up his window, the car in front of him finally turns right at the red light.. Drisko follows him, quickly through the light, away from this psycho bitch, the Witch.. He's had enough of this crap, he's done with this

189

bitch, done.. He drives home to the condo, showers and gets ready for bed.. Tomorrow his mother, will send her messengers, to awake him.. Only problem is, they won't find him, he'll be in Penetang, in the prison resort, at the top of beautiful Georgian Bay, once again..

What the fuck he's thinking nervously, he paces through the house, no sign of police, no call from Constable Mike? Eight o'clock rolls around, then nine, no noise.. Then the knock, it silently echo's through the house, pulsating out of the walls, shivering into the floor boards, amplifying itself into the rooms below.. Silent but deadly with authority.. Crisp and clear it exits the ceiling like a gunshot being fired into the little black box, hanging there, dangling by a thread, helpless, there on the wire.. It captivates his ears, he makes his way through the narrow hallway and up staircase of the three-story condo, he instinctively, opens the front door, it's the cops..

The officer standing there, filling the doorway, it's funny, this is it.. This is what everyone in the world had said all his life.. Everyone, everywhere as if they all knew and he didn't.. Life changes in an instant.. No mistake, no real reason for it, it just was.. One moment he was complete and filled with hope and the next the ants were carrying his sorry carcass away, down a hole.. The bitch had her puppies, Drisko remembers visiting his friend Mark, down in Mexico.. Marko, had fixed up a spot for the wild dog, Flaco, he named it, it's Mexican for skinny.. She had a brood of eight and every couple of days Mark would come home from the marina and stop by to tell Drisko about the progress of Flacos puppies.. They're all so cute, he'd say, I love them all and he did, it was just how his heart worked..

Till one day, one had died or at least was missing.. The bitch may have eaten it he guessed or some slippery fox or low-down conniving weasel found it an easy prey.. The following days brought news after news of the puppies demise.. One after another, they were dying, gone, missing.. Was she killing them, eating them, we questioned our sanity, her motives.. She knows the survival of the pups would be small, this is the jungle, they're the size of a child's fist.. They trust her, their mother, their guardian, their teacher and friend.. The animals, cats of all breads, other dogs, scavengers, packs that can sniff out prey a mile away.. The creatures, all, that live in the ocean, the turtles, crabs and snakes.. The monsters, that only a few have seen and survived to ever tell about.. Did she sense the dangers, did she weigh the risk, did she question her sanity, was she in true fear of her life..

Did she kill them for spite or for sport.. Did she know how weak, "he", really was, and more so, was she aware, he was not fully capable of properly, defending himself, against such an ugly, yet beautiful foe.. How vulnerable he was, how trusting he would have to have been.. Drisko's mind wondering from Jacqueline to Flaco.. Her, caring for her brood, "she", showing them, her love for them.. Mark found them all dead, suffocated in the sand, torn apart, eaten, only traces and pieces of their carcass, all eight of them now, he cried.. Mark had made a bed for them, providing, a good home, a good life, how? She had love, she had security, comfort, caring and she, the bitch, tore it all apart.. They died, all, each one, less none, there, face down, in the sand.. They finally realized the truth, she was burying them alive, then eating her young..

Mark had fed her and them, cared for them all, he was devastated by the loss.. The fact that any creature could have such power and control over another, over love.. To simply snuff out its life, defies the covenant of trust, of man.. To turn on this true love, to sacrifice it as only she could.. The question, still remained unanswered, how, how far can you go, how much can a simple mind take? It completely devoured both their imaginations, the horror, the thoughts, identical, her, eating her own children.. Them, both, Mark and Drisko, devouring it all in their minds.. She had done this, this was her love that she did this to, her own..

A monkey doesn't let go of one vine, till she has her hands on another, he said to Drisko.. She sounds pretty fucked up, dude.. She's going to live a very lonely and ugly old woman life, she's fucking one of them for sure brother.. The bitch set you up man, clear as shit, his R.D., tattooed covered roomy, squawking out the truth to Drisko.. Dude, face it, word, what man would ever want her, once he knows, she could eat her young? No love dude, dead inside, once a cop caller, he said to Drisko, eye to eye, straight up, always a cop caller dude, trust me, always.. Man, even if you could go back with her my friend, you do one thing to piss that bitch off and she's got you're ass right back here, control, freak.. She owns your ass mother fucker, know it dude and your balls.. His words, he would say in the calmest way, but so matter of fact, truthful as Drisko would tell him, his sad, sad tales, of his vows..

When you share a cell in range two, C-block of the prestigious lakeside resort community of Penetang, along the picturesque waterfront shoreline of beautiful Georgian Bay.. You don't really get to pick and choose your roommate and the guards, they enjoy their work a little too much sometimes.. So if you piss them off, let's just say, your new name could be Lucy.. Drisk got lucky, three roomies, over the time, all with manly names, all cool.. In for the same shit as him, stupid and in love, trusting people, caring, dip shit, jerk offs.. Drisko had finally served his time, all the shit was done, it wasn't all as easy as that though.. The time in the joint was a piece of cake, compared to the time leading up to it, after the arrest.. The court cases, the fight for the truth, job losses and loss of freedom..

As the story unfolds, he was left spellbound with all the possibilities of what the truth, really could be.. How could any of this be true, be real? His family, friends and himself, questioned every motive, every choice, all of his thoughts, the rest of his life.. Did the police cover up all their crimes.. Were they paid informants or narcs, did Jacqueline set Drisk up.. She had all the information to the crimes committed by Joey and Nick, every detail, every move.. Was she part of it all, was it all a conspiracy, a con.. She told the judge she was in fear of her life the night at the stop light.. The night, she, rolled down the electric powered window, she, leaned over into view of him.. She, screamed out the window, a warning, I'm warning you Drisko, as a lie.. Knowing, she, told him she would let him know, what the cop meeting was about, of course he would want to know, they had his life, all of it.. Is the monkey fucking a cop, are they all in it together? How do you turn on someone, devour a love, so precious? How could she kill her love, so easily, bury it alive, then eat it? The song played for him, the truth, *"Psycho Killer Qu'est-ce que c'est?"..*

CHAPTER EIGHT

No More Mr. Nice Guy

Six and a half Barracuda.. It wasn't all that bad he thought, this little thing called life.. Hitting the stereo, the song starts.. *"I got a bad reputation,"*, Alice wailing out the tune, *"and I don't know why. I brush my hair, brush my teeth, I go to church, and I'm a really nice guy, ya"*, as Drisko steadied himself in the shower, the water pouring hot from the tap.. Like rain he counted them, each droplet, at a time, in slow motion as he thought of Jacqueline, then Nick, then Joey.. Everything in frame by frame, like he had been given some magical power of deep focused thought.. *"I used to be such a sweet, sweet thing. Till they got a hold of me"*, vivid as it performed in front of him, like a stage set, filled with actors.. The stage there, at Parsons Pond, at the Arches, on the Sea of Lost Souls.. The images, colliding and connecting to one another, there in the theatre of his mind..

Again and again he replay's the skit, the show, the dance once more.. There, in front of him, he sees the truth unfolding.. How do you change the past, reverse it, when you know what's ahead of you, your future? The past which is now the future, here again as it unfolds, again, *"I open doors for little old ladies, I help the blind to see"*.. The Marina, that held the boats, the puppies, that held no chance, Flaco, her choice, her actions, her instinct.. Mark and his effort to provide and protect, it's all part of a miracle, good or bad..

It all happened to bring Drisko here, to bring him here today, to the now..

The water is warm, calm, sedate as he feels its power draw him in, draw him deep into his thoughts, the song singing behind him, into him.. Mark, is screaming at Drisko, pull up, pull up, as the line goes loose.. The graph of steel screams on its edge as Mark's fighting it, swinging the pole in and out, up and down with great arm support.. With control and marksmen techniques, he lands a sixteen inch'er.. It's distinctive silver back, glistening as he heaves it over the boat's aft, a Cuda.. He's got three in, I'm next, Drisko is thinking, between us we had five in the boat and safely released..

As Mark re-baits Drisko cast a line driver.. She's outta the park and quickly hit, a fighter, a real fighter.. She's big, Drisko can feel her dive deep and wheel upward and out as she tries to unleash the hook.. The rod bent and heaved, full crack down, then springs up as he loses her weight, it stops, still.. Is she broke, Drisko questions, no, Marko whispers? No, as he questions his own words.. She's big though, he says looking at Drisk, real big.. They watch as the line lays loose in the wake, then as it snaps back, tight again..

She's on again, she's running, he's calling, let 'er go Drisky boy, as Drisko follows his command, lets the bitch run.. Finally number six, Drisko smiles at him tied, Mr. Guide, tied.. One more pass, Mark cries out, over the whine of the engine.. Then we'll head her in, troll our way back along the banks, then we'll head back to the marina.. The beach swirled into a point right there, where the mighty Atlantic, meets the Gulf of Mexico and the opening to the lagoon.. As we round the point, the docks lay spotted just off the shore, broken and decrepit, old, ancient..

The huts although few, spotted the shore with specks of rusted corrugated steel, tarps of all colours and doors made of anything they could find.. The Mexican huts, make shifted out of anything the breeze blew in, anything that would work.. Mark cast his line deep into the reeds at the piers.. We troll past, it's haunting, exciting, ancient.. The huts line the shore, but it's reminiscent of the Gros

Morne, the Edge, home.. The Viking shacks, but built high, into the cliffs, similar, yet different from this sandy shoreline..

Mark's struck, almost that quickly, it hits him, heaves him forward, toward the edge as he grabs his footing and prepares for a battle.. Drisko seen it coming, the hit, as it burst into the boat.. He knew it was big this time, it was bigger than the big one.. Mark fought and fought, a rodeo show as if the fish had him on the hook.. She was big, the shadow razing in the wake.. She's fucking huge Drisko shouted, frightened.. Then she dives deep, yanking at Marks arm, tearing at him, the beast, that she was, a creature, from the deep..

Slack, the line goes once again, total slack.. What's up, as they catch each others eyes, at the dip, in the line, where it hits the sea? It reels with ease now, the line laying loose on the water.. Mark continues to fill the reel with line effortlessly.. It's dead, Drisko said, you fought it to death.. It pulls gently now, something's there, Mark whispers.. Drisko makes ready with the net.. The head pierces the surf, Mark drags it, lifeless, toward the boat.. It's tiny, Drisko said, what the fuck, the fish comes closer, quicker now? Mark raises his pole to allow the full weight of the Barracuda's body to dangle, hang there, lifeless, along the side of the boat.. It's puny, it's ten inches, fifteen at most, max, Drisko notices..

Then at a glance, they notice it's cut in half.. You caught half a fish Marko, mi amigo, Drisko said in his confusion, half a 'cuda.. We can't sell that one to the Mexicans, we'll have to go back and get the other half, they're gonna want a whole fish, I think, Drisk said jokingly to him.. Then they noticed the second wound on the fish, the gill was sliced, like a razor had cut it open.. Then they knew this thing was huge, this monster of the deep, protector of these sacred grounds.. Huge, to have been able to attack a forty five inch, full grown Barracuda..

After examining the victim and thoroughly investigating the scene of the murder.. Well, we, well me and my partner that is, concluded that the forty five inch Cuda, must have taken Mark's bait.. Which was the first strike Mark had felt.. Then something menacingly huge downed the Cuda, completely into its open throat, whole, one swoop.. Then the assailant accidentally caught the hook, whipping it past the boat.. That's where Drisko, the second eye witness, would had seen the line go completely slack.. But, just then snagging itself free, it chomped its prey in half, just to save the meal.. That was when Mark, must had felt the second strike and the victim, go deep.. Then the thing came back for the third strike and sliced, snapping the tiny Cuda's neck, case closed.. Life changes in an instant, the thought, came shining through.. What was this beast, this monster, a creature of the deep? They steadied the boat, let's go get this bitch, they said in unison.. Let's go get that motherfucker..

Only one other time, Mark said to Drisko.. One other time, I was out here with this guy from Toronto.. He got a half a 'cuda, now it was me, my turn, he said smiling, my turn.. How can something so defined as violent, attacking, torturous, blue death and so vividly real, become a miracle.. The same hand, that tormented the tiny 'cuda, now blessed Mark, both of the actions, both miracles.. Drisko's words coming back to him clearly, as he told Mark, I'm your witness.. This time it was you, and I was here with you, Drisko assured him.. Six and a half Barracuda, now, that's a fish story.. Drisko woke, **"I got no friends cause they read the papers, they can't be seen, with me"**, the rock song playing, then he turned the shower off and got ready to go..

Six months in prison, three month before that, three days before that.. The house on Silver Creek was dead, it was now haunted permanently, in his mind and everything in his mind, heart and soul was dead.. He was laughing on the outside, he was having fun, but he was not alive, he was dead.. Prison for some reason, destroys you.. The life you're forced into, it is just for the criminally insane and you can't escape it.. Just being in, makes you insane, it made Drisko..

The trouble with the evening is that it turns into night.. Night at one time was his favourite time, now, it brought terror to his mind.. No chance to be alone, ever.. Everything in his life, would just keep turning and turning, every move, every word, every lie, moment, trust, care, hope, dream.. Every bit would consistently go around and around in his head, a play by play, *"and I'm getting real shot down, and I'm feeling mean."*.. Even though he was in Mexico and should be just the life of the party, he was still in prison.. We all thought he was dead.. Drisko the man, Double 0 Drisk, the Bond Guy.. Drisk the father, the Viking Child, the Viking King, he was dead..

Two years had passed, since his last visit to the prison resort property at the top of Georgian Bay, his little home away from home.. The events, that had unfolded in the house on Silver Creek, Joey, Nick, Jacqueline.. The long arm of the law, the courts, the holding cells, Judges, Crowns and prison food.. All set far behind him now.. Yet, here he is once again, in his Mexico, and he's dying.. He's there, at the condo, the night has set in.. Here by the peaceful pier, the Ultramar, the dock where the ferry would pick-up and depart for Isle Mujeres, the Island of Women.. The port Mark and he would sit at to watch the beautiful Mexican women load, on and off..

He watched the moon take its place high in the sky and he did, he looked up and said to himself, remember Jacqueline, no matter where we are in this world, we're both under the same moon.. He sucked on his doob, then took a sip of his Fresca.. This time though, he said goodbye to her, wished her peace in her life and he got ready for bed.. The cool of the ocean breezes were blowing gently across his naked body as he laid restfully, on top of the sheets.. His eyes dampened from the uncontrollable thoughts, still circling in his mind.. Useless, there is no way he will sleep.. Now into his fourth, if not fifth night without sleep, delirious, dazed and confused.. His mind empty, his mind full and no way to stop the hate.. No way to think pleasant thoughts, nowhere in his mind, does he hold anything good..

This is how I will perish, he said in his silent voice.. The Witch will come and take me, he thought.. He knows now at this very moment, his life had no meaning.. He prepared himself for his final departure, tonight I will die, he said.. Simply enter the ocean, float out and never return.. The waters here are shark infested, once you clear the reef of Isla Mujeres.. Cozumel to the south, is in fact the second largest natural reef in the world, only second to the Great Barrier Reef surrounding Australia and the South Pacific..

Tiger sharks, Orca's, the Giant Man Eater Squid and the Great White, all hunt, clean, birthe and feed here and mostly they do it at night.. Just his luck, it's night, he lays hungering for answers, sobbing without control, lost.. Not the man he was at all, that man is gone.. How, where, when and then why, why did this all happen, trust? The same questions he's asked himself a thousand times now, with the same answer, none.. Joey and Nick steal everything in his life.. The cops, lawyers and Judges all ignore the crimes and now Drisko's the one, went to jail.. Jacqueline turning on him, his friend, trusted lover, lying to him, to the Judges, lawyer's, the Crown.. A girl he loved and cared about completely gone, they took everything..

Like the Witch, the Siren of the Sea, she comes not to conqueror, not to imprison, nor to enslave, na', she comes to devour, every, living, thing, in her path.. She came, she conquered and she did, destroy, everything about Drisko.. As the words, no longer able to find silence in the night, Drisko screamed.. How, how the fuck Lord, how, I've served you faithfully, my entire life, without doubt, he cried? These people that are in no way faithful to you, you serve them, you offer them, your support, your love, your protection.. How do I get my justice, how could Nick and Joey had won so easily.. How could Jacqueline have been swayed so readily, the questions, that had no answers..

There he lay, lifeless, half a man, now equal to Joey and Nick, useless.. Nothing but his word and his balls left.. The song singing through his room, he wondered aimlessly through my mind, the voices coming to him. ***"No more Mr. Nice Guy, no more Mr. Clean."***.. The Lord, would never give you more than he knows you were capable of handling.. Loud and clear as if it were hollering through the screen door, muffled in the wind, but loud.. The Lord, repeating it, stronger into his mind, clearer.. The LORD, his truth, that you have witnessed Drisko, the voices continued.. The Devil's backbone, the ride from Canada to Mexico with Joey, the first time they worked in Mazatlán.. The journey that brought you through the Devil's Breath, to the abyss, to where you could never return..

The land mass sprouting up, the little village on top, the mark, of God's hand.. Give me the answer, he screamed, loud enough to have jarred the entire barrio.. Give me the hook, he needed to insure that he, in fact all of heaven and earth would and could hear his cry.. Give me the fuckin' answer now.. The Witch now, screaming at Drisko.. How, how could you even think of this, how? Her cries vivid, staring him down.. You're a coward Drisko, the rest of us have to stay behind and suffer for you.. How, she tore at him? How could you do this to them, Jessie and Ambrosia? Finally, from the hallows of the room, the Witch appears, *"No more Mr. Nice Guy, they say he's sick, he's obscene"..*

She bitch slaps him, you're Double O Drisk, the Bond Man your a fuckin Viking Child.. Fuck dude you're brilliant, really, you're gonna lay down and let these two fucks fuck you.. She bitch slaps him again.. He starts coming to, he's startled, it hurt for real.. She comes back relentlessly with lefts, rights, uppers, lower, no holds barred.. She's gonna fuck him up, if he don't get up.. She might look like an angel, but she is the fuckin Witch and she's wheeling a fuckin' canon harpoon, full guns.. He's blocking and running, hiding and ducking.. She's faster, more ferocious than any other adversary he has faced, in his life.. He realized why, right there, he was, he was fighting for his life.. There was no way, that he was going to lay down.. She disappeared as quickly as she arrived, leaving him swinging at the air.. Determined to beat the Devil out of his thoughts, out of those two fucks, Joey and Nick..

The Witch, as he woke, he knows it wasn't a dream.. There was no way he was asleep.. A vision maybe, premonition or real, made little difference now.. He was awake and he did remember the Witch.. She had the force of a lion, ferocious, the face of Mercedes.. The woman he knew to be good and true, then her eyes and hair,

201

turning, crinkling, the face of his daughter Ambrosia, soft, flowing, trusting, as she pounded the truth into him.. The might and tenacity of Jessie, as he would have, to have fought to save his father, like Ivar, the Boneless.. Then a mix, a combination of friends and loved ones from his future and his past.. The Witch had no back could only face you, looking to each man exactly as she would look, flawless, ugly, yet beautiful..

At times the Witch seemed gigantic, almost monstrous, like the giant Godzilla of old time Japanese movies.. Other times, small, sweet, Tinker Bell fairy-like, but swift and strong as she'd fly up and down smacking him, pounding on him.. Till he'd collapse over in pain, only to strategically open him up to an upper cut, then a Gedan Barai to the cervix, to finish him off, as he collapses in pain, on to the floor.. He remembers it, he remembers it all.. So, now it was up to him and only him, the King, the Viking Child..

I have no weapons he declared, no power, no strength or wisdom, no mind.. I have nothing, he said, and yet he knew, he, could somehow defeat them, Joey and Nick.. How, how did the Witch put this power into his hand, into my mind? I have nothing, he cried, in his battle.. You have all that you need, the Lord would never ask of you more than he knew you could handle.. The truth is always right in front of you Drisko.. Just stand up man, in the biblical term, as the Witch would then, swat him back down, making him face his demons, the ugly truth.. You have everything, it screams, echoing into him, the voice of a thousand screeching eels in a vat of boiling water.. I have nothing, Drisko rebuts, weakly.. You have everything you need, again slapping him to the floor.. He cries like a beaten baby, he screams in terror..

From the days of the Pagans, with the Dogma that crucified Jesus, the Christians have risen up against all that is evil.. They rode massive black stallions, shrouded in glimmering chains and mirrored armour of silver, gems and tanned hides.. Flags waving magnetic to the wind, blood red, with white and golden emblems of the Cross.. The Serpent weaving its way through the graphics.. Blades of Glory they were named by all who would revere them, the Centurions, the Roman Christian Army and they were unforgiving.. Conform to Christ or perish..

Today nothing has changed, ten thousand years later and ten hundred million strong, most people believe in goodness.. With little left to name the houses of God, from Anglican, to Muslim, Presbyterian to Buddhist, we all pray and believe in God.. We all believe in the Divine Spirit, the almighty omnipresent, omni-powerful supreme ruler.. God knows Drisko wanted Joey and Nick to perish off the face of the earth.. My mother, had sent her army, Drisko wanted them dead.. But as his time went by, he realized, that was just too easy for them.. Lord Christopher, the Hell's Angel biker Drisko met in Cabo, had intrigued him.. His diabolical plot and the Lord knows Drisko would love to have seen them slain, but sometimes, the Lord answers with, not right now.. I have something better in mind for you, so be patient..

Drisko really didn't want them dead any longer, selfish of him.. He knew he couldn't make them dead even if he wanted too, not without paying the total price as his lawyer's words reminded him.. He wanted them to suffer, suffer for life, suffer the wrath of God.. To suffer in a way most deserving, suffer by letting the world know the truth about the Devils.. He walked the four hundred paces from the condo front door, past the neighbourhood residents, the families, that had lived there since the beginning of time.. Around the bend, along the cobblestone walkway to the corner Cantina', Le Super Marketa.. Then across the road to the Rojo Internet Café, past Rita, the young Mexican clerk, the song playing, *"No more Mr. Nice Guy, No more Mr. Clean."*.. He pounds down his twenty Pesos, priveto por favor.. He opens the internet, Facebook, if nothing else, I'll tell the story, the truth about those two fucks..

The Witch still on his mind as Drisko sat there on the deck of his new residence, back in Ontario.. A nice country property just north of Big Bay Point.. It wasn't quite what he had left behind on the Point, the cottage, the wooden framed cabin with the covered well.. It wasn't Silver Creek but real close.. It wasn't haunted, like Silver Creek was, at least like it was now, to him.. It was definitely bigger, over five acres, the creek and some bush with trails cut through.. Huge potbellied wood stove and a sun room, filled with junk, beds, tables and crappy chairs.. Perfect, he said to the landlord, it's just perfect, I'll take it, he said.. It was uncanny, a repeat of Silver Creek almost to the T, but nicer, bigger.. The only thing missing was the T, Mr. Thunderbird and his grill a gleaming..

He cut the owner a deal, just a rental deal, I love the sun room, he said.. I'll clean it up, use it for a writing room.. The man, laughing at the writer thing, but agreed to find a suitable storage place, for the junk.. He saw the five room mansion quickly fill up.. Soon there were friends in every room of the giant house and some just flopped on the couches, chairs and floors.. He chuckled at it all, just like Silver Creek, but no worries, no expenses and no big deal.. Just a simple home, a little piece of paradise..

The grounds were so private, people would approach and say, I didn't see you sitting there.. Drisko would laugh, I know, he'd reply.. The cedar rail fence sat stern with cedar trees lined behind it and the car park in front.. The patio itself was long enough to hold ten chairs and tables, although only five, six feet wide.. He'd sit out there smoking a doob, writing or playing his guitar.. He broke down and replaced the one Joey had stolen from him, when he moved into the property.. His mind focused totally on his music and a book he wanted to write.. He'd sit out there, he'd write a bit, he'd play a little, just him and the wolves.. Them and the deer, him and his Mother, there with her nature, writing, playing, hating the plot, the story..

The phone rang early one Sunday, the coffee was cooking.. The sun was already warming up the front patio deck.. The gardens around the house, Tony's wife tended to.. It had yielded a beautiful bouquet of colourful blossoms.. Near the east entrance of the circle along the other cedar rail partition starting behind the decorative torch lights, laid a row of giant sunflowers, in full display.. Behind them more cedar trees, hiding the dirt road of the Town Line..

To the east of the property lay the most interesting piece of this coincidence, the creek.. Well hidden behind high hedges, wilderness bush and patches of cedars all different in sizes unlike the manicured portion of the estate.. He grabbed his coffee as he answer the phone, its Tony.. Drisko, I have this friend, he needs a place to crash.. I told him you might be able to help him out.. Tony and him had worked out some of the details and he gave Drisk a description and a name.. The words were being pounded into the laptop's little brain.. Crap after crap flowing onto the pages, crap about this and crap about that.. Drisko needs a title, a name for all this bullshit.. How about if I just name it, "A Bunch of Crap" or How my life is full of horseshit"?

He's pounding into the keys, his hate, his anger, **"he's sick, he's obscene."**, his thoughts.. A Book of Hate, he renames it quickly.. My life and how I fucked it up, by Fuckin' Jerk, or, by A. Fool.. The stories, in spite of his mental state, when he was writing the pages were flowing, with tads of adventures.. Filling them with thoughts of lust, sex, anger, hate, love, **"my dog bite me on the leg today. My cat clawed my eyes."**, travel, deceit, corruption, Christmas, fishing, puppy dogs and God.. It was a winner, a true psycho thriller, he was enthralled by his own words, the romance, the crime.. How could I write these words, he thought? How, when I hated it all and yet it was so far behind him now? Him, loving it, every word, loving the art of it, loving the hate..

He was forced to remember it all, relive it all, putting the little words into the little box.. Pounding on it to insert them deep, to tell the story, **"I went to church incognito. When everybody rose. The reverend Smith recognized me"**, the truth to make the book, the novel, to get his revenge.. But he didn't care about revenge anymore, at least not that way.. Lord Christopher, the Centurions, the blades of glory any of it.. He didn't care about Nick, Joey or Jacqueline.. He didn't care about any of it, he was just writing a story, **"And punched me in the nose, he said. No more Mr. Nice Guy"**, he didn't even care anymore if anyone even ever read the piece of crap.. It was for him now, him, the artist, the author, the mentally impaired..

His stress, his demons, his P.T.S.D, the nightmares, the visions, the truth, the truth, the truth.. Like on the bridge, there at the Black Water River, up on the Edge.. The Mustang, the Tanger, never recovered, no one ever comes back, the words echoing through him, into him, the truth.. The gainer, the tire tracks matching, the truth, he couldn't ever stop looking for, just that little truth, with in all the lies.. The truth that he was never entitled to, never given access to.. Did they, was it them, or did they, could they have, just simply disappeared, left him behind, not caring? The two of them, Drisko and his sister, forgotten, unwanted, abandoned by their parents, no..

Him the Viking Child and her the princess, his little sister Rose, left, safely, but there, with the clan, alone.. Abandoned there, left with a man they would soon learn to call, uncle Bev.. Left there, thankfully with his love Bonnie, his trusted friend Dooley and the gang, from the Livery.. There, up on Cripple Creek Pass, up there on the Edge.. Maybe it only looked like the distinctive box styled tail lights, of the green Ford, 67 Mustang coupe, careening off the bridge there into the mighty deep dark blue Atlantic, did they?

Was his father a killer, a crazed sick serial killer, did he kill her, his one true love, their mother Ellen, up there on the Edge.. Did he bury her there, in the sand, then disappear, like a creature from the sea or a chameleon, disguising himself, blending in? Creating a whole new life, a new history, as his world gently rotates.. A new story, a greater story, to cover all his past, completely.. Was he, is he, "I Am Monster", could he had been? Drisko always looking for the exact moment, the exact speed, the exact song, everything, perfectly aligned, yet never finding that exact moment, the right time, the spot.. When you eliminate the improbable and focus on the possible, all that could remain, in it's purest form, is the simple truth.. The truth is always right in front of you Drisko, you search beyond what is required..

The Witch spewing, you seek to understand the time that has passed, you seek too far, his visions.. Every man, woman and child up on the Edge knew why.. Nobody, ever questioned why Drisko would run the flats as he did, just his crazy, his demons, everybody knew why, everybody, exactly why.. This ere's the Edge boy, folks not from the Edge, comin up ere, thinking dey's lookin' at the end of the world.. Folk from the Edge, knows it's were it all began.. This is where Drisko and his clan are from, the Edge, where it all began..

As an artist, an art director, he's always said, little Leo Da Vinci never painted no pictures for you senior, no surrey.. You might like it, you might love it, you might even wanna pay for it, own it, hang it on your wall, ya know.. But he painted it, created it, for him, only him, for his sight, as he saw.. That's art, that is an artist, that's all an artist can do, all artists.. It's about self, about self-expression, about self-love.. Not about money, not things, not selfishness, but about love, trust and truth, about the eyes.. Drisko decided a long time ago, that this is simply, just an amazing story.. More so, an amazing crime and what made it so amazing, was that the criminals, simply got away with it.. A truly unimportant crime..

He was the only one that could write it, him the artist, the victim.. The fuck of it all is, it's all true, every bit of it as he knows it, as he'd seen it from those eyes, those fly eyes of his.. Nobody could have made this up, no brilliant writer, S.K., or J.G. and gang.. No big time blockbuster movie director/writer/star.. No mad man, no Lex Luthor, no Diablo or Lucifer.. No evil, no God, none, nothing, no spirit, no person.. There could have never been a script, just a plan, their plan, their choices to destroy and to steal..

I do have to concede and I wish, I had it to share with you, I wish, I knew the truth, he once said, to me in confidence, tearing.. That's what he never had privilege to, the truth, just that, that's all, the simplest little truth.. These people with their loves and friendships for him, chose that he should only guess.. He didn't deserve them to be honest with him.. So he did as any good Christian, God-fearing, God loving servant would do, he asked God for the truth.. Well, you see Drisko, God said to him, smiling down as he would.. I always look at things this way Drisk my boy, zip zip.. When you focus on the probable and eliminate the impossible, all that could be left, would be and can only be in the simplest form, the truth..

Although only as Drisko would had known it, it is, nevertheless, the truth.. Ya thank you doe my Lord, but unfortunately, I's gots' ta' tells ya', I've heard all this shit before man, he said.. It's really gettin' a little tired, tough to swallow, if'n's you knows what I means der, Lord.. Ow's about you slidin' down one of dem dere miracle thingies dere for me right about now.. I means the Devils got me here in one of dem dere head locking thingies.. Here, I am right fuckin here, can you sees me, Lordy, lord can yas'.. Can ya's sees me, right here in front of yous, then yas knows, I's needen sumtin right now, some real fuckin help here, now, in his silent voice..

Drisk always said, I'm always right, unless I'm wrong and when I'm right, I'm never, never wrong.. A person would really have to be pretty fucked in the head, as in brain fuckin' dead or have some kind of real mental handicap to not have seen the truth.. To me though, he said. it has become a therapy.. A way to get closure, recognize my errors and mistakes, allowing me, to go on.. Give into my beliefs that I would have had to have gone through ten million people, over ten million years, to find two real true friends like Joey and Nick.. Then, when he added Jacqueline to the equation turning on him, her treason, her lies to the Judge, the truth is, she fucked him.. He only loved her, he was only ever kind to her as a person would be, when they love, he said sadly, tearing..

Drisko didn't notice the car driving in.. He was a little busy, writing Christin into the chapter.. Them getting hammered together in Slim Shady's trailer and all.. Wishing, dreaming, imagining, her, she could be his Bond Girl.. As the gravel and wheels slid in to stop directly in front of the garage, it was perfectly aligned with the walkway, leading to the front door.. He looked up at a blue car sitting there idling, the roof rack piled three layers high.. Junk, dressers, table, lamps, mattress, junk.. No one gets out, so he goes back to reading the crap he just laid down.. Again back into his lustful dreams of Christin..

He looks up as he hears the car door slam.. She's walking, bouncing in her stride, beautiful with her red hair bouncing, the tail swaying side to side as she slides her way into view and toward him.. He's invisible, undetected, he sees her old tattered sweat shirt and pants, a tad differing in colour, both grey work wear but she looks beautiful, Cinda-Fuckin-Rella he thought.. Under her tattered outerwear was a fuckin' beautiful woman.. Her face, he couldn't stop looking, directly, after her red hair, her lips, her eyes, her face, his eyes drawn like a magnet to her bounce.. Her tatter, then her bounce, and she bounced everywhere and oh, so nicely..

A woman, he hasn't seen a woman in so long now.. Not one he was enthralled with, beautiful.. She walked directly by into the house with her load.. He forgot Bond was invisible.. Bob he said, he was older as Drisk saw him standing there.. Tony had set this all up, so Drisk was just cool, letting them do their thing.. Tony's friend Bob, Drisko was thinking the beauty was his daughter or niece or just a friend.. Then she came with a flash and poof, she would be gone in a flash.. He went back to ignoring the world and writing the end of Chapter Two of his crap novel..

My Bond girl, Miss Bounce or as he'll later nick-name her, OOOSHINNY.. The room upstairs and in the back was available, great view, private terrace, was all Drisk said.. Bob knew the place, he had been here with Tony, it was all cool.. Some folks are just to themselves like me, Drisk said in his silent voice.. He gave it little thought, cleaned up, grabbed his computer and guitar and went inside.. He got a coffee ready and went to shower.. Now, he's fast in there, ten minutes, twelve max, in and out, the Bond girl was gone.. Probably for the best as all the Bond girls for some reason, keep dying off.. It's getting to be a tough business and his heart, was making it tougher..

This ain't no sex novel, he said, so what I talked dirty to my girlfriend, pulled her hair at the airport, this was crap.. As he's deep into Chapter Three, almost to the end, he feels the urge, I need to get laid, he thinks.. He's reading and rereading chapters one and two, it makes no sense.. Why, he cries into the pages, again devastated by the uselessness of this drivel? Who fuckin' cares about this shit? The book needs some balls, all you got is your word and your balls, he remembers the thought instantly.. Let them see your balls Drisko.. Write a fuckin' novel, something worth reading.. The truth always comes out, the truth will set you free..

This is an incredible story, he hears his silent voice saying, completely out loud.. Write the fuckin' story, write the truth.. These fucks stole everything from you, they took the right for you to have your life.. Take it back, write the story, find success in it, even get rich from it and fuck them.. That will get you your revenge, the voice raged.. He went back to the start, he retyped it all.. He felt the thrill of the adventure, he was Bond.. He could feel and hear the lies, between the truth, the words as they strike the page.. He saw his pain, his sex, pounding it, filling it with thrust and strokes.. Ejaculating all over it, into the stories, the story, the book, the novel, the truth, as only he knew it, as he pounds on it, hard, harder, into each stroke..

Stealing Home.. Chapter One.., he starts, *A truly unimportant story of an incredible major crime in small town Ontario..* His fictional novel, based on true events, real people, the shit that really happened, changing the names, the places, to avoid the libel, he types.. So this is what they mean when they say, "when hell freezes over".. It was cold, not snowing yet, not raining, just cold, bitter Canadian cold.. We say it twists your bones.. It grabs you through your nervous system, up through the muscles, cracking every joint in its path.. Slamming, pounding it hard, into her little box, stroking every one of her little buttons as the machine screams to climax.. Here, take this baby, he slaps her, pounding it in to her, here, take that and here, take that, the crap just oooozzing out of him, all this crap, just oooozzing as he writes the truth..

Fuck 'em good the first time, they always come back for more, the Viking oath, brother for brother, Drisko laughs.. He sat there in the light of the sun room.. The sun shining high outside, deep into this beautiful September day.. Him still swinging at his demons, the Witch in chapter three.. He notices the mornings are cooler now, as that thought brought the first words to the script, then more and more words.. He would just tell the truth, it's too fucking interesting of a story not too, he pounds on.. The Bond man now with confidence, he's writing the novel.. Canadians bracing for a long hard cold one and we ain't talking Corona buckets here folks, he hits the keys..

He finished the rewrite of chapter three and was well into four when he stopped for a break.. He sat on the big comfy couch, settled into a coffee and a sandwich, feet up, TV on.. Canada's bracing for a long cold hard one, the man on the Weather Network scolded.. Drisko losing himself in the thought of not being in Mexico and if he could find a way down.. The front door opened to awake him, could be anyone.. As he waits, the footsteps head up stairs.. He's lost in the warmth of Mexico as the thunder starts again, descending down the stairs this time, then in through the doorway, into the living area..

Miss Bounce, OOOSHINNY.. She waltzes in like a Bond girl, just plops herself down on his couch, angled to his left, but close.. She's dressed, the only problem he could see with her so far, she's cute, fluffy, stacked and in jeans, and a blab-o-matic, rattling on about Bob.. Bob, Drisko's thinking, not listening, but visualizing Bond in Technicolor with her.. Had he seen him, she asked, then this and that, some other thing, about something from outer space, then the words, message, hot stones, exercise? She's cute and a fuckin' therapist.. Yoga and Bubo mats and contortionist moves.. She's definitely a Bond girl..

He's my dad, she says, well like a dad, step-dad, we've been friends for 30 years.. He was in the boat and marina business.. OOOSHINNY was a bundle of bounce and Drisko was liking all that he saw.. She's just moved back to the area, looking for work in a spa, health club.. She saw he had been writing and asked about it.. He could have just taken her right there, right on the couch, just

211

leaned in and kissed her, you're mine baby.. Hit her with his Bond moves, he could feel it, she's receptive but he was out of touch, way out of practice and stuck on stupid.. So he was cool but she was cool too, and hot and he didn't know how to step up, papa Bob and all.. She was running out to meet someone and had to be on her way.. Drisk let her go, without a number or a name, just her Code, 00 OOOSHINNY..

After pounding away in the sun room chapter four, chapter five, the early September sky had saved the sun the bother of rising today.. Happy to hit the front deck in hope of a ray, while he fires up a smoke.. A smoke break, the voice saying as the door opens outward to the patio.. Hey Bob, how's everything, good, he replied? You're usually writing in the sun room, he said, I don't get to see you to much, we chuckled.. The girl, your daughter, what's her name, he stares me down? I have a friend, Drisk offers, he's opening a Spa in about six weeks and is looking..

Veronica, he finally replies, she's a little different, he offers, a lot of baggage, a lot of issues, strange, Drisko's thinking.. Strange thing for a father to say.. She's not really my daughter, she's my friend.. We were living together up till now.. We needed to get separate living arrangements.. Tony mentioned no girls here.. Ya it's, Drisko's mind is going nowhere, lost for words, the brakes are on.. What, Drisk is thinking, it's one of those things? Too late for Drisko to retract the offer, he's already mentioned the job, him thinking how she would had been perfect for the part, but she was gone, now? The story of my life, he thought, lost another Bond girl, it's her boyfriend, crazy..

Veronica's really busy for the next couple days, she told me to make sure I told you Drisko.. What, he asked Bob, as he walked through the front door onto the patio for a second time this week? Walking directly up to him, that job you told me about, she wants to call you, ask you about it.. Can she get your number, oh, ah, Drisko thinking in his silent voice.. The job was bullshit dude I was trying to fuck your girlfriend, OOOSHINNY, he said, *"he's sick, he's obscene."*.. Drisko gave Bob his number, then told him,

Bobby, that was a week ago.. I'm sure he's got his staff lined up, Bob oblivious to his words.. I'll give her your number, he said, *"ma's been thrown out of the social circle. And dad has to hide."*, she can do what she wants with it, he continued.. He searched for his pen and scratched the number out on a piece of paper he had ripped from the recycle trash..

Somewhere around the 8th of September Veronica called Drisk.. This is fucking un-canny, pure fuckin' coincidence.. Hello Sunshine, the voice said, only Jacqueline called him Sunshine.. It's me Veronica, Bob's friend, he gave me your number.. Do you remember me, she whines, you had mentioned about a job to Bob.. The story now getting out of hand, *"I went to church incognito, when everybody rose. The reverend Smith. He recognized me and punched me in the nose, he said."*.. Drisko needed to cut this loose, needed to tell the truth.. Veronica, sorry darling,, *"No more Mr. Nice Guy. No more Mr. Clean. No more Mr. Nice Guy."*, he cut into her, but I'm sure he's got his staff hired.. I did talk to him for you, *"He said I'm sick, I'm obscene."*, and he said, that he was very interested..

The only spa business Drisko was going to be helping poor little Veronica into was, his spa, his business, his hot tub, her and him naked.. If you want to drop off your resume to Bob, he goes on, I will pass it on for you, you never know, he offered.. Ya, sure Drisk, she stalls a moment.. But listen she said, as he waited for it, the hook.. Is there any way to catch up later tonight? Drisko laughing silently, did I tell you all, I read minds, ESP, shit like that, *"open doors for little old ladies. I help the blind to see,"*, he says in his silent voice.. There's thirty years between her and Bob.. Drisko hasn't been with a woman in a very long, long time.. She's definitely a Bond girl and she needs my Double O.. I'll bring my PP47, just in case, he thought.. Okay, I'm bad, Drisko thinking to himself, but it's Bond bad, so it's all good and you never know, she could be a double agent..

There they sat in the dim light of his favourite Chinese restaurant.. I hate Chinese food she starts.. She's fit, frisky and totally fuck-able.. You hate Chinese food really, Drisko repeats her words, how, he ask? It is the everything food, they have everything.. I'm a vegetranarian, she said, like a child, mixing her word up.. Vegetarian, Drisk repeats it, that's what I said, she fakes it, then her smile.. She's directly across from him, he's looking into her dark brown eyes, her lips are moving but it's all braille to him.. Orbs and Tinker Bells, spirits and visions, her voice tinkles, she's weird but she's deep and she's beautiful, bouncing everywhere, while sitting still in her chair..

Shall we, Drisko offers a gesture in the direction of the buffet? She rises, he walks in front of her, she crawls up beside him and grabs on to his elbow to guide her, to the food bar.. She's rubbing, bumping, burst out in laughter, excited about a shrimp, OOOSHINNY.. He could barely make it back to the table without checking her every move.. *"I got no friends cause they read the papers, they can't be seen with me.".*. Her neck, her chin, her lips, how she smiles, pouts, how she could hurt him, how she already had.. He watched her walk, the hips, flat form of her stomach, her legs, her sculpted, precision cut ass.. He's a lucky man, referring to Bob, her friend, slash, whatever, he said in his silent voice.. The voice answering him, down boy, *"No more Mr. Nice Guy,".*. Drisko following her every move, standing as she gently manoeuvres in behind the table..

She starts telling him her story.. Some shocking and more than she should be telling anyone, let alone him, a total stranger.. She carried on with more intimate tales than he'd ever heard from one person, open.. She's strong, incredibly confident and care free, spurting out her past, only stopping to stuff the hole and crunch down.. She asks about him, but has little skills in listening.. Her excitement of their first meet, sneaking around in secret, away from Bob.. He asked her, leading her, what's Bob up to tonight, probing with skills for the hunt? Oh, that Bob, I don't speak to him much, he's a blab.. Anything I tell him he blabs all over the place.. Don't tell him you seen me, in fact don't tell him anything about me.. Well wait up here, I don't understand, Drisko said? I thought you two were a couple, you lived together.!

She burst out into laughter, oh my God, she spurts, you thought me and Bob, she roars out the laughter? Oh Drisky my boy, you are so cute but you are a hoot baby.. Well what is it then, what's the deal, he asked her as she describes the living arrangements that she had tried, to let him live with her? They shared a two bedroom apartment downtown.. She was trying to help him out of some tough times, that's all.. That's it baby, that's all there is, she said, slithery.. Telling how she's known Bob since her twenties.. She just took to him as a father figure.. She's always treated him as her dad, she said.. Another man, she would grow to call, her father, but he's a pain in my ass, she said.. At the same time, she said, she loves him, he's been there for her through thick and thin.. Stopping her words, filling the hole, I hate chink, she said.. Drisko laughs at it, as she fills the hole, spurting out the words.. Who is this girl, he thinks, this girl Veronica, Veronica Bond, 00 OOOSHINNY, his new Bond girl, who the fuck is she?

The phone rings, I need you inside me now, the voice says, come and get me.. "OOOSHINNY", he interrupts, who the fuck else would it be Dick Weed, she strikes, with her venom, she's pissed off at him? It's two o'clock in the morning, he said.. I need you now, come get me and she hangs up! Shit, my father warned me about girls like this.. Fuck 'em good the first time and you keep 'em coming back.. The last two weeks with Veronica were insane, and so was she.. The girl was a wild stallion, even for Bond..

It was like all his enemies were now in one room.. Just them and him and they're all more beautiful than the last.. Built, beautiful, naked Nympho and you know they came to fuck you, up.. That was Veronica, all of them, Drisko and one very tiny room.. If she said she was turning right, she'd turn left, just to do her girl thing, then laugh.. Keep up Bond, don't be fuckin' sleeping here Dick Weed.. I ain't even started to torture your ass yet.. You would had thought Bond would had hit the ejection seat right, there and then, but nooooo, he's fuck up Bond and at this point, he's figuring out, he's fucked in every possible way..

The next weeks brought Veronica and Drisko closer.. Drisko took a small six month contract with his son Jessie in northern Ontario, out in the beautiful Kawartha Lakes.. They were going to help start up a water company, preliminary, marketing and media plans.. The office was two hours away, so Veronica would come up and stay in the cabin with them.. A little place Drisko had rented, in a private resort, they all spent the month together.. The company could not get a hold on the area and they opted out.. They all moved back home and Drisko rented a small home in the city, for him and Veronica..

Their bedroom was on the upper floor.. Right at the head of the bed was a window and the window looked down onto a busy street, but they didn't notice the noise or the street.. Above the window though was a skylight and above that was a huge Maple tree that covered the view completely.. It was theirs, it was for them, just them, the tree fort they called it.. For her and him, the Maple foliage gave it the feeling of living in a tree.. Him Tarzan, her Jane, they were together and they were falling in love.. Veronica had a good idea of Drisko's lifestyle by now, she knew what he was working on and what he did.. She knew he travelled a lot for work and she liked it.. He warned her early, I go where the work is and usually, on short notice, up and gone..

By now she knew everything, every sordid detail of prison, the cops, courts, Jacqueline, Joey, Nick, the whole story, the book, the novel.. He knew everything about her, really, from the first date.. She was beautiful, open and completely honest with him and this is a deal breaker, she'd snarl at him and place her demands on his behaviour.. "Bitch" he'd look at her, don't you know who I am, in his silent voice.. It wouldn't have mattered any, Drisko was up against it, he knew it then, as he knows it now.. He was going to fall bad, deeply, for Miss Bounce, 00 OOOSHINNY..

The call came streaming in, shoooooo, he shushes her, smoke signals coming into the tree fort, he informed her.. He answered the phone, hello, the caller said, Drisko.. Veronica was silent as he conversed with the caller.. He could see her excitement, her nipples hardening, she's squawking and clucking all over the place.. As he cut his deal and secured the contract, Veronica's bouncing, going crazy.. Veronica gets horny, when Veronica gets crazy.. The negotiations went on and on, OOOSHINNY bouncing everywhere, shaking the little tree fort from its tiny rooting.. Bouncing, bouncing with every "uhu", "okay", "uhu", "sure".. What's with her, Drisko's thinking, she's got some kinda fuckin' radar thing going on, bouncing, picking up the signals..

We're going to B.C., Parksville, he said to her, smack dab in the middle of Vancouver Island.. That made Miss Bounce, OOOSHINNY fuckin' crazy and when OOOSHINNY's fuckin' crazy, she's fuckin' crazy.. Little old Dick Weed didn't stand a chance, the phone wasn't even on the hook yet when OOOSHINNY starts kissing.. Hands clasped on his face, turning his lips into a pucker.. Kissing and squeezing all over him.. Him trying to break her grip like a mad wrestler, in some kind of quasi-psycho hold.. He latched on to her hand and twisted it gently, then the other one.. They loosen and follow him as he continue the kiss pulling and twisting her hands, till they're secure behind her back..

Then he pushes her with force, she falls back to the bed's edge, *"No more Mr. Nice Guy, No more Mr. Clean."*, bouncing, while sitting.. She looks up at him, not quite understanding his motion.. Dick Weed eh, I'm gonna show ya Dick Weed.. He pulls a doob from the tiny wooden box, laying on the night table by their bed.. He rest the joint between his lips, then with his right hand, he pulls his lighter from his pocket and fires it up.. He reaches down with his left hand, *"Mr. Clean. No more Mr. Nice Guy. He said you're sick, your obscene."*, unclasping his buckle and rips the leather from around the denim loops and unzips, Miss Bounce was bouncing..

Veronica had a classic 92 red Chevy Sunbird convertible, which he worked hard on, keeping it in mint condition.. She was a classic and a beauty and just a joy to drive.. Drisko sold the little Honda, filled Veronica's car to the rafters with their junk and headed west..

His little Bond girl has had a life.. He thought he'd seen and been through a lot, but she, she had been hurt, badly.. Men mostly, mistrust, it was probably the single most important thing about her that attracted him.. She would question him, his actions in the passages of his novel, trust.. She would ask "how could you trust those men"? When you listen to all the shit about them, how did you trust them, more important, why?

When he first met Veronica, he knew she had issues, pains, deep hidden fears.. The kind no person should have experienced, worse no child.. Especially the trust that would be given to the most important man in their lives.. Trust was something no man could earn from Veronica.. Her trust was destroyed early, in her childhood.. Drisko would sit with her, just holding her, like the child she was.. He'd often tell her, he always believed if she had a good person, someone that really loved her in her life, he would take that pain away.. But how could she learn to trust, let anyone in? Drisko was determined, to let her feel, she could trust him, with her life.. Determined to be the one she trusted, even if she couldn't be, ever, but that road would be long and so would be the journey..

Drifting, sails filled through the low lands of the prairies, unsure, uncaring as to the path.. Winding their way through the great Canadian Rockies.. You need to believe in God, you need to trust, you need to allow love in, he told her.. If you want love, you need to lay it down, to pick it up.. Then he'd answer the question, the same answer as he would to anyone that would ask, how do you not trust? They were my friends, he said.. They asked for help, I helped them, he said.. Trust, a question OOOSHINNY will never have an answer to, nor will he, nor will Veronica, nor would anyone.. It makes us all unique, all of us, all of those, that their lives, Joey's, Nick's, Jacqueline's, touched.. We all have been damaged by them, all, each one, less none..

He watched her doze, laid back in the seat of the little red Sunbird, drooling like a baby, still bouncing, while sitting still in her seat.. He sees how beautiful she really is, how childlike, how easy he could love her.. Veronica was a book in herself, an incredible story of love, trust and deception.. Her young life, ripped from her very soul, the destruction of trust, from the one person, you should be able to trust the most.. See the author's tears, as she writes this lowly story, see the hate, the hurt and the fears.. Drisko listening to every word of her sad, sad story, his blood crueling, "A Life Without a Mirror", by OOOSHINNY..

Remembering Jacqueline's words, of course I still love you, you're my soulmate.. Remembering OOOSHINNY's words, how could you trust them? Driving, thoughtfully blind, auto pilot, thinking deeply, how do you trust? Wishing the top was down, wishing that it wasn't minus 20 with the wind chill factor, according to the announcer on Z-ROC 99.2 the Wolf.. He cruises, wishing he was heading south, find Veronica a little patch of beach.. Cabo's only six thousand miles away, while the ghost, of the house on Silver Creek are dancing in the rear view mirror.. The past, far enough behind him now or so he thinks..

Chapters Ten, Eleven, Twelve and Thirteen, now he's stuck, how does he go on? It's all caving in on Drisko, it's all over, it's the end, this time for real.. Bonds world, Drisko's world, Veronicas world, his family, his friends, their friends, all.. Every family, every person in the whole fucking world is about to come to a complete and uncontrollable realization of our money and our economy.. Things were happening all over the world that was beyond his explanation, even angelic.. The world economy was dying.. The U.S., Europe, Mexico, Italy and Canada were facing Chapter Eleven.. Our world was changing and his business, everywhere was dying.. Tourism was gone, no one was travelling, no one was buying anything.. California, New York, Toronto and Vancouver were collapsing and the areas that weren't collapsing, were waiting patiently, to die, scared to death..

He saw it coming, they were only in the new resort for five minutes.. The client base had dwindled to a trickle.. The resort had an impressive property, square between Victoria and Campbell

River B.C., smack in the heart of cottage country, breath taking and incredible.. Veronica and Drisk set up house finally, renting a place in Qualicum Beach, fifteen minutes from the resort.. The failure was in no way the responsibilities of middle management, Drisk advised them.. Sales, marketing or promotions his report would read and strongly recommend exactly, what they didn't want to hear..

The onus is on the Director of Sales and Marketing, i.e. VP Operations.. The company had raped the neighbourhood, treating the local residents poorly.. So now that the time had come, that they needed the support of the community, in this economical crises.. Well the community simply refused to support them.. He continues with his education of good business ethics, *"No more, Mr. Nice Guy, No more Mr. Clean."*.. When he was told, that the meeting would be postponed.. The VP was skiing this week, *"the Reverend Smith, recognized me and punched me in the nose, he said. No more Mr. Nice Guy,"*, in Whistler and hasn't been around for three months.. Meanwhile, the company was entering into Chapter Eleven and has now applied for Bankruptcy protection against their shareholders, well, too little, too late..

CHAPTER NINE

"Dirty Deeds"

Ten weeks after his report to the executive team and his personal meeting with the V.P., their shareholders pulled the plug.. They closed them down, and were now in the process of legal action, for fraud and possible embezzlement charges.. You need to lay it down to pick it up, Drisk ended his report.. Got his final payout and went home to Veronica.. Let's take a drive baby, we'll head to the mountains.. He kissed her and told her how much he loved her, then they went out and fired up the little red Sunbird..

They wound the Sunbird up the mountain pass over the Alberni Highway, up the centre of the Island from Parksville to Tofino.. Only one way in, only one way out, through the most picturesque winding mountain roads.. He planned the day with Veronica.. They were going to climb Upper Qualicum Falls, the pathway takes you all through the lookout point.. It winds in and out, over and through the river as it then falls deep, into the thundering gorges.. Then snaking it's way throughout the park, spectacular, but so was most of this island..

They hiked the complete circle, kissing their way through the trails, holding hands and hugging in and out, stopping, looking, holding, laughing.. It's early, they make their way up the highway.. Drifting along, top down, sun shining in on them, the music playing.. Deeper and deeper up into the mountaintop and down into the mist, of Cathedral Grove.. The song singing, *"Dirty Deeds, done dirt cheap, Dirty Deeds.",* as they enter into the ancient forest..

Thousands of them, huge cedars, reaching beyond their sight.. They walk deeper into the forest.. Poor little Veronica, so unsuspecting, so enthralled in the views, holding, kissing, touching him, trusting him.. He slowly manoeuvres them off the beaten trail, past the sign that read "out of bounds, danger, gorges ahead".. Veronica didn't notice the signs, she, still in awe of the pure size of the statues, bursting from the ground.. Her being splattered by the fairy dust as it's sprinkled on her by the flickering sunlight.. She says, fairies are here, almost child like..

They roam, hearing the thunder of the gorge, moving slowly towards it, just holding, kissing, admiring the array of wild protected flowers in the park.. The wild Orchids and the rare, beautiful and protected Trillium, stopping at the fenced area of the gorge.. Let's sit, he offers her, holding her hand guiding her as she sits on the smooth fallen log.. He fires up a doob as they watch the water falling.. She's so beautiful in this natural setting, the fairy dust on her face.. She's so happy being here and having fun out here in the nature of his mother.. He kisses her, she returns it slowly, warm.. The outdoors, the towering cedars, the ancient forests, the fairy dust.. The Gorge, the cascading waters, whatever it was in that forest, it was angelic.. Spiritual, and making his little Miss OOOSHINEY go crazy, well and once again, when Veronica, OOOSHINEY gets crazy, hang on Dick Weed..

He holds her, moving her slowly in his hand, finding the meaty flesh of her ample full round breast.. The softness, instantly arouses him.. He applies a passionate kiss to her mouth, tonguing her, probing her, slowly, moving downwards along her neck and onto her nipple.. Erotic, insatiable, pneumatic, he lowers his other hand to her groin, her centre, her button, as she squeals.. He's tonguing her nipple, then on to the other.. Her clothes scattered, mussed, as if torn from her.. He unzips, unclasps, Veronica tenses with the sensation, then relaxes with anticipation of the attack.. No, she whispers, what if someone comes? No one is coming Veronica, just you, no one is going to save you..

Veronica and Drisk had a great time in B.C., loving the island.. There were some good times and some great times, for sure.. There were some bad times and some worse times and sometimes when the whole world went crazy, it was still just her and him.. Drisko took his time on the little island, showing her around, after all he'd been here before, in another life, another life time.. They took it as a vacation, play time, discovering the place, enjoying the island, before heading off to another assignment.. He did a few small contracts to occupy his time.. Did a small reno for the owner of the property there, in Qualicum Beach.. He bought an old 78 Chevy short box pick-up, 327, auto, in rough condition and was fixing her up, booting her all over the island.. Getting her tits tweaked, as he'd call it, getting her primed, ready for paint..

Then it happened one night, right out of the blue.. One minute he was looking up into the blue sky.. The next he was staring at the awesome force of that moon.. He watched it, as it took it's place in the darkened skies, there in front of his eyes.. He watched it settle there, as he looked right at it, in awe, the song playing.. The biggest moon he had ever seen, *"Pick up the phone I'm always home, call me anytime."*, there in front of him, hurtling at over a hundred thousand miles per hour, or thirty thousand kilometres per second.. He watched, as it approached, *"I lead a life of crime."* and he watched..

She was angry, agitated, no real reason, just mad all the time, at everything.. His little Veronica, he couldn't understand her anger, why was she so mad at him? What could he have done to deserve such an outburst and attack on his person, *"Dirty deeds done dirt cheap. Dirty deeds done dirt cheap."*, he questioned her sanity, who talks like this? Her standing at the door of the country property, screaming, about orbs and fairy dust, things he just couldn't understand.. She grabs her coat, *"Dirty deeds and they're done dirt cheap,"* and dashes out of the door, quickly, she's gone.. Drisko's flabbergasted, what, what does it all mean? He heads out back to the glass topped shed, tinkering there with his tools, pondering, her words, her actions.. He looks up into the moonlit night as it penetrates through the glass and into him, there, that moon, why, why are you here.

Drisko picked up a large reno job in Port Alberni, his landlord loved Drisk and liked the work he had done for her.. She asked if he would do her parents place out there.. They were retiring, wanted to sell the property but she was well worn, old and in need of repair.. Drisko put his creative eye on the property.. This is what we're gonna do, then gave them a killer price, hopped in the old Chevy and went to work.. The hour drive across and then back, plus the eight ten hour work days kept him busy.. First he needed to repair all the cracked stucco on the outer face of the home, all four sides, by hand.. Then paint the pink home, harvest green, dark, rich..

Then all the windows, doors, the soffit and fascia all trimmed nicely in black, contrasting the colours.. Then the natural wood trim, shellac, clear, above the garage and the pillars that held the porch.. Then the back, refaced, board and batten, colour coordinated to the front.. Then he re-tarred the driveway and blacktop sealed it.. The old folks rejoiced, Drisk had saved them thousands and the place was outstanding, beautiful, they all said to him, you can't even recognize it.. He would come home feeling great and then he'd feel the wrath of Veronica, her, always angry, always complaining, mad..

Veronica was still working, just part time, evenings.. Waiting staff at the Rocking Horse Saloon, a very cool little pub, down in Parksville, in Nanoose Bay, near the resort.. A beautiful spot, a ranch turned into a pub, a hundred years ago or so.. Great menu, real crowd pleasing specials everyday, great atmosphere and live music, nightly, a great little hang out spot, off the beaten track.. Drisk would go visit her sometimes.. Till it happened, he notice her a little too flirty with some of the locals, as he'd question in his mind.. Her arguing at the slightest mention of it, as if he were crazy, jealous.. He was aware of her past, her PTSD, her problems and her mental state.. At some point, he almost understood some of it.. But now, the eyes, seeing, all, his fly eyes, questioning it all.. The eyes he so relied on, him, his heart, the Viking Child..

The days, the weeks with Veronica went by, the on and off frustrations continued, her anger.. Then that sunny crisp summer afternoon, the phone rang.. Drisko sat on the back porch, the same spot he sat the night before.. The second night, he had seen that moon, approaching him, watching it hurtling toward him, the spot he sat in now, his mind twisting, questioning.. He listened, he could hear her, giggling, okay, I'll come pick you up.. She gathered her things, Drisko could hear her, moving through the rooms.. He walks toward the door as she's leaving.. Where're you going, he says, she walks away without a reply.. Thought we were going to the trails today, she keeps walking away.. She gets in her car and leaves him staring at her as she pulls out the driveway, he's lost, what is this?

Drisko's lost, he's playing in the yard, doing some gardening, cleaning the area up, hanging in the tool shed, his favourite place.. The afternoon's approaching, the suns high in the sky, he decides to go for a cruise.. He revs the little 327 Chevy short box and heads out the Island Highway, south, *"make a social call. Come right in. Forget about him."*, into Parksville, heading to Nanoose Bay, there he'll hit the backroads for a boot. *"we'll have ourselves a ball."*.. He drives down the ocean front drive of Parksville, in through the quaint little town, *"done dirt cheap. Dirty deeds and they're done,"*, cruising the strip..

Down past the Chink place, out past the grocery store, along the main drag.. Then passing the music emporium and over to, then passing the A&W.. Just as he passes, *"got a woman and you want her gone. But you ain't got the guts."*, he looks right, just for an instant, a second, a moment in time.. There she is in the drive through line up of the A&W, with a guy in her car, top down.. Drisk wheels the rig, hard right, *"Concrete shoes, cyanide, TNT. Done dirt cheap."*, into the adjacent parking lot.. Turning the truck on its wheels as he stops beside her, looking, he revs the beast and then he drives away.. Now he's looking at the Devil herself, her lies, her treason, *"neckties, high voltage, Done dirt cheap."*, now she's done, she's through, let her kiss the Cod as he stares into the rear view mirror..

Drisk had finished his dinner, clearing and cleaning, re-stacking the dishes, neatly back into their place in the kitchen cupboard.. Never let them know you were even here.. Clean up after yourself, he remembers telling his boy's on the job, he lived by it.. Clean as you go he'd say, it's easy.. Then he went out to the deck to enjoy the evening sun, watching it slowly sliding across the sky, soaking, relaxing in the hot tub, puffin on a doob.. Drisko losing himself in thought, watching a jet airliner as it gently glides through the suns rays, heading south, leaving the jet stream.. Somewhere exotic he thought to himself, Cabo, as he dreams.. Sitting there, looking out over the Sea of Cortez, high on his deck, drinking his Fresca, puffing on his doob.. Looking out past the cactus nursery and the giant Mr. Cactus.. Looking out over the golf course, the tiny people chasing their balls..

Out there, to the edge, just before the sea, looking, focused, there.. The grave yard, there, just down a block or two, past the Gun Tower.. Drisko watching from the deck as he sees, seeing, as he watches.. There in front of him, Mr. Graveyard, the stranger, he would never know.. An amazing man, a man of pure dedication, pure insanity.. The seventy six year old man, that sleeps with his mother, on her grave, each and every night.. Him, roaming the streets of the tiny Mexican town, the barrio's, day after day.. Wondering out loud, how she could ever leave him, talking to anyone that would listen.. Talking to her spirit, him bumming food or money for their way and has, since he was six.. Drisko sitting there, watching the jet, jet out of sight.. Value, he though, what value do you put on your life, thinking of the old man, his journey, the tortures he must have faced, everyday? Drisko puffed on his doob, he slides back and relaxes..

He hears the car door slam, it's her.. He hears the steps and then the outer sliding door, as she enters the home.. He's puffin his doob, relaxing in the hot tub, on the deck, watching the jet fly away, not a fuckin care in the world.. Grateful, he's not Mr. Graveyard, but worse, missing him, right there, right now.. Drisko hears the outer gate open and the slow movement of footsteps, approaching.. Listening as they climb the four steps, to the deck, then stops, there on the built-in bench, that circled the forty foot deck..

She sat there and started to cry, I wasn't doing anything, she said.. No problem, Drisk replies, puffin, sipping.. It was just a friend from work, he's a kid, like eighteen.. He called because he got me some really good weed.. No worries Veronica, no worries, Drisk replied, puffin, sipping.. I gots' really good weed to's doe, darlin', puffin, talkin from the Edge.. Veronica, blabbering, crying, just come in, lets talk, talk to me, nothing happened..

Drisko could see, the vision of Mercedes as she stood in front of him that night.. Him swearing to her, begging her to believe him.. Her not, her getting up, taking his kids and leaving the island, for something, he was definitely innocent of.. It had torn through his soul, his blood crueling, she, now standing, here, begging and begging, pleading as she swore her innocence.. I'm telling you the truth Drisko, she swore to him.. Drisko please trust me, she cried, he cried, they cried, then they went to bed and slept, peacefully, as lovers would.. Drisko, the voice said, softly, almost silent, the truth is always right in front of you..

The visions flashing, flashing, the Witch pressing her sizzling lips up to Drisko's, as she speaks to him.. Drisko can see her snake like tongue slithering around her teeth.. He can see the two, very thin, long and lanky, Razer snakes, wrapping her neck like jewellery.. Their horned heads, inches from Drisko's jugular veins, on either side of his throat.. You want the truth, she says sincerely, you want to try and to understand the time that has passed.. You seek too far, you look beyond the distance that is required..

The truth is always close at hand, directly in front of you.. There is no seeking, only seeing of the truth.. The truth comes from the souls of the ancient ones, the truth is always of breed, of what is bred.. Even the caterpillar, with her amazing performance of metamorphosis, must face, the solemn truth, the inevitable.. When one eliminates the probable and removes the impossible, one is left with only one ultimate answer, all that could remain, is, what is to be the truth..

Drisk, rises early, gets his coffee and goes to hang out on the back deck.. The beauty of the morning sun striking him.. He sits and sips away, he drifts into deep thoughts, what should I do? He knows, she could be lying to him, the signs were all there, the Witch.. He brought her with him on this journey, he feels the responsibility of it all.. He feels his love for her, how he cares, how deeply she's been hurt, by every person in her life.. How do you not trust, he said, in his silent voice, how.. Drisko standing there, in the tiny bathroom, staring into the mirror.. The shower, running hot as he prepares to enter, looking as the steam fills his view..

Staring there into the mirror, he rubs at it as he stares, deeper, rubbing, clearing the steam.. It's there, present, he sees it, there as small as it can be, but there.. With his fly eyes, he sees it, clearly, he rubs at it.. A crack, there in the corner, starting, rubbing, tiny, pin size, but present, there in front of him as he stares into the glass.. He rubs at it, briskly, cleaning the surface to get a better look into it.. As he rubs, it moves, opening, tiny, but opening never the less.. Running, too small to notice, but running, cracking, splitting, wide open, possibly, probably, more likely than not.. Drisko knew, once the mirror was cracked, it would just never, ever, look at you the same.. He showered quickly, and then ran the Chevy down into town, once around, then to the hardware store, for fun..

Drisko was enjoying the island life, he loved the corporate work, the boardroom, but the boy also loved getting his hands dirty.. He loved landscaping, Reno's, inside in the winter, out in the summer, he'd say.. A huge garden job out the back side of Qualicum, out in a quaint little property.. Then a Volley Ball court, on the front lawn of the another property, hedge the edges and build the court out of sand, Drisko loved the work.. Then clear cut a property and burn the bush, fun, fun and more fun for Drisko.. Veronica was busy at the Rocking Horse Saloon, it's late September.. The little cell phones ringing, Dave, a guy Drisko worked with from the resort.. Come on into town, Cams here, were just hanging in the yard, pop by for a BBQ.. Drisko dusted off the shoes of the little 327 Chevy pick-up and steered her south, to Nanaimo..

Dave was a good connection, he had good dope, his sister was the main man in the area, so he got Drisk great prices on great shit.. Cam and Dave worked in the sales department at the resort.. Drisk and them would hook up to get high together and chew the fat.. They were sort of friends to Drisko, buddies, so Drisk showed up with a smile as he opened the gate, the song singing, *"you're having trouble with the high school head. She's given' you the blues."*.. Drisko standing there, in the tiny bathroom, the steam filling the room as he rubs into the mirror.. There he sees it, there in front of him, *"You want to graduate but not in her bed. Here's what you gotta do."*, the crack, it's growing, larger and larger as he rubs.. He stares at the clearing, blue eyes crystal clear, ice steel eyes, staring back into, ice steel crystal clear, blue.. Staring as they go black to black as the mirror, gently reflects back..

She would have done us both right there on the rocks.. She wanted to come with us, *"pick up the phone I'm always home, call me anytime,"*, she was bored, you were working in Alberni, I think.. We were just going crabbing, so we brought her.. Drisko, no lie, you're a brother, a good guy, but she came on to us both.. That's the truth man, Cam said, sitting at the table in the yard, sipping his beer, he hung his head, sadly.. Drisko, I'm not bullshitting you, *"deeds done dirt cheap, dirty deeds done dirt cheap,"*, it's the truth.. I know you're not making it up, I got it Dave, I brought her here, I gotta figure some things out, he said.. Drisko rubbing on the mirror, clearing the steam for a clearer, cleaner, view.. Tell him the rest, tell him the other bullshit so he knows, Cam egging Dave on, tell him..

We were at a business diner late one night at the resort, in the Landing, the private room.. Veronica was our server, Mel the G.M. and Kevin the Assistant Sales Manager and the sales staff were all there.. Well, she was putting on quite the show for Mel and especially flirty with Kevin.. I didn't give it much thought at the time Drisk, Dave said sadly, then he went silent.. What, Drisk asked him, probing him, what happened, Dave, waking him, what happened?

Later, I walked by the sales office, the glass window, the fish bowl.. They thought everyone had left I'm sure, he went silent.. Drisk was silent, silence was abound, as Drisk rubbed and rubbed on the mirror to get a clearer, cleaner view, the crack was cracking.. They were kissing each other, **_"Dirty deeds and they're done dirt cheap. Dirty deeds and they're done,"_**, he was feeling her up, she was hugging him back, **_"you got problems in your life of love. You got a broken heart. She's double dealing"_**, they were in a full embrace.. Drisko watched as the mirror cracked.. The glass in the greenhouse, implodes, upward, then everything shatters inside.. The pieces of glass will rip throughout you, slicing and dicing the organs, the muscles.. The dust will scour your lungs, dissolve your teeth and disintegrate your tongue.. Leaving you, totally, breathless, without sight and speechless, without hope or doubt.. The Devil doesn't come to you wearing horns and a tail, she comes dressed, clothed like a friend, with a smile..

Drisko runs the waterfront road home, **_"with your best friend. That's when the tear drops start, fella."_**, taking his time, thinking, pondering, planning, he needs a strategy, he needs to prepare for battle.. This is a year now they've been together.. Almost a year since they were up in the little cottage, working on the water company, up in the Kawartha Lakes.. A year since they got together as a couple.. A trying year, Drisk recalls, questioning everything now.. He decided to let her go, he'd be cool, till he could figure out how to get her out of his life..

It's late now, in October, Drisk hadn't confronted Veronica about the stories from, Cam and Dave.. They were getting along well, like nothing ever happened, but Drisk could feel the distance between them, or maybe it was just him.. Late October, Veronica's birthday, I'm working late tonight, a special function, so I'm going to stay at Silvia's tonight.. Drisk, thinking but not, why would you stay there, we're probably the same distance.. Drisk woke the next morning, Veronica wasn't home.. He went on with his daily business, returned home late, to Veronica.. How was the function, your night, Oh, she goes on with her story.. Drisk paying it no mind at all..

Mid November, the resort is finally closed, completely, everything is closed now, all features of the property, closed.. Drisko is out in town, just booting around in the little Chevy.. He pops into the local coffee shop to grab himself a coffee and mingle with the natives.. Cousty was his name, a Filipino, Cousty.. Drisko always got a kick out of him, they were buddies, from the resort, another salesman.. How you doing Drisko he says, grabbing the seat beside him.. Good, good, Drisko replies quickly, glad to see his friend.. How's it going Coust, he shortens his name.. They banter back and forth, laughing, joking around, catching up on the bastards from the resort, the crooks.. They cost a lot of people their jobs around here.. Drisko feeling his frustrations, his anger with the management, as all felt in the area..

Ya Cousty cries out, they give the fuckin V.P., a couple million and send him on a ski vacation.. Gives Mel his payout for G.M., plus bonus and then fucks everyone else.. Kevin, that useless piece of shit, can't close a door, little lone a deal, gets a free weekend in the resort, from Mel there, Halloween night.. Then he's got some whore up there in the condo, banging her all night.. Fucking the shit out of her, some poor fucks wife and we all get squat, nothing, we all get fucked.. Ya Drisko replies, they had Veronica working there, Halloween, her birthday..

Cousty stares at Drisko, then he opens up, ya, except she got to leave early.. Sheila had to close and take care of it all, herself, she was so pissed.. No, that's not right Drisko said, Veronica worked with her, then she stayed there with her, at Sheila's place.. Ya, no way, Cousty said, Sheila's my wife, well ex-wife, but we talk everyday.. Kevin got Veronica off early, his speech slowing as he chooses his words with caution.. She had something important to do, so Kevin got Sheila to let her go.. Drisko could hear the Witch, shrilling in his tiny ears, the truth is always right in front of you Drisko, you search beyond the distance required..

Drisko returns home, he's going to confront Veronica with the facts.. He's going to pack her things and put her on the first flight out of here.. He gets home, the house is empty and black, the night comes early now, and with the night, comes the darkness.. Drisko sits in the dark, pondering, trust, truth, how, how do you not trust? He starts the fire in the hearth, it glows warm, November, still nice on the island, but the nights cool down nicely.. He putters around the big house, turning on the TV, for background noise, watching the Weather Network.. Big chance of rain, big chance of sleet or hale, no chance of the sun ever shining on you again.. The report said as he listened, no chance for you at all, just dead, dead air and no chance in Hell.. The Devil doesn't come to you wearing horns and a tail, she comes dressed, clothed as a friend..

He hears the car door close, tiny footsteps leading down the outer steps to the patio door as it opens, she enters, smiling, happy.. Drisk lets her go on, chatty about her day, all excited like, talking and talking, jabbering on about nothing.. In through the house and into the shower before he got a word in.. Drisk feeling his frustrations, there in the dark as she returns, then sits herself down, there on the couch beside him.. Drisko just starts, I bumped into Dave and Cam a couple of weeks ago, they had quite the story about you.. Oh ya, those two assholes, she starts.. Ya' those guys, they said you went crabbing with them one day.. Ya' she said, so, well you never mentioned that you were with my friends.. They said you were trying to fuck both of them out there on the rocks.. Ya bullshit, they wish, they were the ones coming on to me, come on we'll have a threesome, it was them trying to fuck me..

They saw you with Kevin, in his office, Dave saw you, bullshit, she replied, he saw me give him a hug.. Why were you hugging him, Drisko questioning her, that late at night in his private office? I dropped the bill off to him, Mel was gone, Kevin had to sign for it, so he put a hundred dollars on it as a tip, *"leave her alone. It's time you made a stand."*, so I gave him a hug.. Then, Drisko continues, I hear that you weren't at Sheila's that night, you didn't stay there on your birthday, Halloween night.. Call her, ask her, she says, ask her, *"for a fee. I'm happy to be, your back door man."*, I was there..

Drisk not divulging how or who gave him the info, just trying to dig for the truth.. Drisko I love you, you're the only man I love, she says to him, kissing him, softly.. Those guys hate you Drisk, ya' they're your friends sort of, but they hate you.. *"Dirty deeds, done dirt cheap."*, You're the one that closed the resort, you're the one that took their jobs, careers away, it was all you.. That's all they did that day, was talk bad about you, that's why I didn't tell you I was with them, *"done dirt cheap"*, because they're assholes and they hate you..

The mild winter with the occasional cool nights, passed gently on the island.. January, February finding Drisko and Veronica, happy and in love.. The trauma, the thoughts and the Witch, was over.. Even the moon, the moon that would never stop rising to show it's wondrous face, didn't show it's face.. Things on the little island were cooking along, settling back in.. Everything looked perfect, like one of those picture perfect postcards, a scene from a Norman Rockwell painting, perfect..

Except, the mirror, Drisko couldn't avoid it, he had no power against it.. It simply was, always present, always there, in front of him, always.. Every turn, every corner, the reflection in the buildings in the glass, always there, every time he entered the tiny bathroom.. He'd rub it, looking, staring into the tiny, teeny, little crack.. There, in front of him and as he rubbed it, to clear it, to get a cleaner, clearer picture, looking, staring, searching for the truth.. There, directly in front of him, he sees it, the crack..

It's March, the sky's above are all blue, the sun is shining on the little island.. The flowers are in full bloom, everywhere, it is simply breathtaking, beautiful and divine.. Drisk is just sitting there on the deck with Veronica, enjoying their morning coffee.. The cell phone rings, it's us, the Newfies eh', weez sunk the BLUE NOSER, the voice said, talkin' from the Edge.. Drisko, goes cold, the voice, the cops, the feds, the RCMP.. Drisko the voice inquires, yes, he said I'm here, what can I do for you? It's us, the Newfies and we've decided to save the entire world.. Our boat's been fucked, so weez needs yous' to fly to Newfoundland, help us out a bit..

We need yous' to design us, an $80,000,000. world class resort, complete with water parks, spas, restaurants, dining rooms, bars, gyms, aquariums and weez gots' an open deep water marina.. Shit like that, he continues, ya's kno's were's we are boye, right ere, jed aboot 250 kilometres nord of St. Johns, eh' boye.. Newfoundland, he's screechin' at Drisko, de Rock.. They go on, we want you to set up the marketing, promotions and sales systems including, the voice went on.. The voice speeding on with the list of requirements.. I'll put the package together, Drisko replied to the caller.. I'll send it out to you in a couple of days.. Drisko, the caller said, no promises that we'll be do anything right away, but it's a damn good time for planning, no's whats I mean.. Yes, Drisko said, it is that, in his Double-0 voice, concealing his Edge..

Drisk put the final touches on the contract, detailing and customizing each step of the program specifically for them to follow.. Ready for their authorization, laid out clear, clean, concise, easy to understand, easy to approve.. He then priority posted it to them as they had requested.. They signed it, returned it, then sent the airline tickets and flight roster.. Then little Miss OOOSHINEY, went bouncing all over the place, once again.. I've travelled a lot, he told her, holding her, still in his arms.. There's little or no chance that we would ever get to Newfoundland in this life time, except through this contract.. Drisko, keeping his self-oath, of his silence, his past, well protected.. They ordered the contract, so let's go, let's go to the Rock, he said.. They hopped on a flight, from the farthest point west, completely across to the other side, the farthest point east, a true leap of faith..

Le Woof, the story of the Cascades, the blue whales, the golden eagle, the black bear, the icebergs, the brown moose and the great Canadian Arctic Wolf.. The resort located on the Cloud Sound Inlet and situated precisely at the edge of Terra Nova National Park.. The breathtaking views, sights and scenery of Newfoundland, deep within the back drops, of Gros Morne National Park.. The beauty of the Appalachian Mountain Range and The Long Range Mountains.. Gently grazing the borders and slightly encroaching into the park.. There laid three of the 18-hole, world class golf course vantage points.. Deep inside its jungles, the river's crest as it splits and sends the rushing crisp mountain waters cascading deep.. Down into the gorges that snake their way in and out, making it almost a complete mirror image of Vancouver Island's, Qualicum Falls..

Slithering through the park and onto the 250 acre resort property, colliding into the shores of the Sound, the resort and the decrepit pier.. The two 20 to 50 foot drops in obligated locations scattered strategically to create the Twin Falls and the namesake of the main golf course.. But the Falls, the Falls were spectacular.. Breathtaking, as Veronica and Drisk explored, there deep in the heart of his Mother.. His words exhaling in vibration of the thunderous roar below the tiny bridge.. Stopping, jerking staring intensely with his fly eyes, nothing escapes them.. Every angle, every shot, explosive, The Cascades, he blurt out to her..

The Cascades, that's what we'll call the new resort.. We'll build the spas right into the Falls.. Using the natural rock and circumventing them with glass tubs making them disappear into the rush of the river, heat them and cover them.. Glass pads, the natural wooden walk ways.. Keep it eco, keep it natural and my Mother approved as he set his plan into motion.. Nothing escaping these eyes, there where the river meets the Atlantic, a 80-slip deep water marina allowing the international sailing class and the big ships to come to our new world class resort..

There at the water's edge we will build the tower ten stories plus four, two-floored penthouse suites.. The Cascades completely surrounded by ocean views, golf course, falls and a National Park.. One hundred units, full service, condo structure, full ownership, partial membership and corporate.. This was it, this was the last frontier where the ocean meets the land, Lands' End.. The farthest point in Canada, the heart of mother nature.. God was here too, right there that day in the Sound.. Drisko could feel him, he was busy, working on another miracle and so was Drisko..

OOOSHINEY had never seen the Bond man when he was in full undercover action.. She started bouncing to the point she was getting a little crazy, and when OOOSHINEY.. Not now Veronica, he dove into Bond mode, losing Veronica in his words.. I'll pick it up, oooooh, fuck boy genius, he's screaming, inside his silent voice, 00 Bond Man, you've gone insane.. Fuck Veronica, he looks her in her eyes, she knows, she knows he's gone insane.. We'll pick it up, she, poor little old OOOSHINEY, her shit, fogging her brain.. How's he going to pick up a National Park and oh yeah Bond Man, then what, put it in your little spy guy briefcase, then what? He see's her tiny head spinning, really, like in the Exorcist.. She's angry, it's blowing her mind, he slowly releases the pressure..

I'll video-feed it, feed it into the foyer of the resort on huge towering screens, a video feed of these amazing falls, Cascading, live feed.. See every moment, movement, see every picture, inset, freeze frames.. The constant live, real, turning from camera location to location, capturing every living moment, winter, spring, summer and fall.. Live animals, the forest, the salmon, the Cascades.. Full sound as if you're walking into the Falls.. Glass encased front desk, for privacy and check-ins.. Dual side video screen, that way the registered guests, the Restaurants, fine dining and pubs can all see the video, live.. A world class resort interactive, that delivers nature, to world class guests..

Then, his brain catches on fire, ooo fuck eh brain, brain, brain, brain pain.. Bond's thinking in overdrive.. The aquarium, we'll aquarium the floor, a live underwater show as you walk through the Cascade's front entrance filled with the aquatic life indigenous to the Sound.. Stretching Bond's brain again, it can connect the restaurants to the outside as the walk in entrance.. Topped with a reflection pool, with lights and water spouts for the show.. Completely visible, with two huge towering fifty-foot, giant Blue Whales adorning the exterior front of the entrance.. Exhausted, they make their way back to the main lodge.. They enter into the original structure, the main area and head for the grand dining room, of the posh resort.. I got plans, big plans and I got to get to work on them..

They stroll down to the Ocean View Restaurant.. Drisko's still new there, so he introduced himself to the staff, her name was Barb.. Veronica eyes were all over her quickly and precise, a Newfy beauty.. You wanna fuck 'er don't ya Bond man, as Barb fetches their drinks.. Veronica's bouncing, he's almost in shock by her words.. As Barb returns, her natural bubbly Newfy hospitality and warmth enthralls OOOSHINNY and she gives in to Barb's warm ways and personality as Drisko leaves her the tip.. Returning his corporate discount and a substantial reasonable additional cap.. I know how hard you girls work, Veronica feeding Barb now, leaning in, kissing Drisko, a sign for beautiful Barb..

The days went by working hard on the designs, the features, the systems, the promotions.. Drisk needed to head out to the Cape the next morning, he invited Veronica to join him.. Leaning into Veronica, handing her the sparkling nectar of the grape, Naked, he said.. Pardon, she asked. Naked, she stares at him, the wine, funny name, Naked Grape.. We'll head up the Bona Vista Highway out to the point to the lighthouse.. I need to do a little PR work up there, go meet the locals, hang with the natives, he said.. We can stop on the way back down through the Outer Cape Highway.. We'll wrap back around into Trinity, giving us a firsthand look at the whole place, the majestic and picturesque Discovery Trail..

They loaded the company truck and headed on up the highway.. Look, she points to it first, what is it, she ask?. Drisko driving, shuffling to look in his seat to see.. A falls, she guessed, he laughs, no, no she says as she squints out at the mass.. He pulls the company truck off to the shoulder, still snickering inside, laughing at her.. They stare at an iceberg, five stories high, a mile long just sitting there, floating in front of them.. I've never seen one in the wild, it was a vision almost like a mirage, she said.. See it Drisk, yes he says, cool as he plays along.. She took pictures, made faces and posed as if they were standing on it..

Sitting back on the deck at the resort, there in the golf club lounge.. Gladys comes by, all nice and bubbly, dropping two Black Horse Ales on the table top.. Veronica's looking a little faint, chatting it up with Gladys.. We saw a slew of them, she cried to the tiny Newf.. I boye, days dos dat a lot, lots a peepols faintin' whens day sees du massive icebergs, is like days seen a freakin' unicorn of sumtin, especially des many, days out in full force, days is I says and she did.. Ow's about a good shot of dat Newfy Screech fer ya dar darlin, she offers Veronica, she'll perk ya up.. Strip du freakin clothes right off ya she will..

Ya two please Drisk orders, not that she was waiting for the answer.. Seventeen in all, in the tiny inlet, she says.. Seventeen massive icebergs, a record this time of year the drunken waitress said, a world freakin' record.. Drisko solves another one, smiling in his silent voice.. Him remembering trucking the little backroads of Bona Vista, watching the icebergs drifting endlessly in the rear view.. He hits the florescent flashing tuner knob, on.. The Newfy Rock station, 104.9 The EDGE.. Veronica was only half visible in the front passenger seat, bouncing to the tunes.. Mr. T's grill, was a-gleaming..

"Wolf Shot on Island at the Border of Newfoundland Labrador", the headlines read.. Plastered right across the front page of the Newfy

Times.. International news once it hit the internet and the world cried.. The experienced outdoors man and naturalist mistakenly fired a fatal shot at what he thought was a coyote and into the heart of the Arctic Wolf, thought to be non-existent on the island.. Ten years earlier they shot another coyote.. They did the DNA on both animals, both Le wolf.. The wolves are returning, they're known as elusive and rarely seen, yet often heard..

The king of the jungle, at least the Canadian jungle, the great white north.. They hunt, they store and they are intelligent.. Their fly eyes are even more intense, complete with true night bright vision.. They store, never taking more than they need, allowing the circle of life to survive.. They know within their territory where every bug, mouse, squirrel, rabbit, deer and antelope play.. It is their store and their floor, there grounds.. She wolf feeds her children and stores the food in her secret burrows.. He wolf hunts and gathers, defends.. The Natives believe in Spirit Wolf, the leader of the forest.. The wolves are coming back, there's a spiritual change in the world, the wolf spirit, Le Woof..

The contract was ending in Newfoundland.. Drisko saved the world again by fluke, for sure.. Winter was settling in.. The two years away from home had taken their toll on Veronica.. She left her teenage son, Kyle safe with his father, her ex, but still not in her arms.. Her son and her had a small falling out just before she left with Drisko for B.C... She spent the last two years on emails and rare phone calls.. The life, the job, the missions, he'd say to her, trying to comfort her.. But she still missed him, deeply, as a mother would, as only her, OOOSHINNY could..

Drisko needed to get her home, before Christmas and he wanted to see his kids too.. The car, was packed and loaded in no time.. Again they decided to take advantage of their free time and drive.. Tour their way home, through Nova Scotia, New Brunny, Quebec and on home to Ontario.. Hauling their belongings, their secret lives, disguised as a tiny U-Haul trailer.. Life changes in a instant, one minute you're there safe and warm in your Newfy home.. There with your safe little Newfy life, the next minute you're some kinda international undercover, crime fighting super hero or a covert 00 secret agent, on a mission.. Sent to fight, by God for truth, for justice and honour, for fame, for the American/Canadian way, for money..

The white van slides in behind him as Drisk notices her, the silky shiny black hair as they board the ferry to the mainland.. OOOSHINNY was hungry and totally unaware they were being tailed.. I saw you looking at the dark haired beauty, she says.. Oh, reminds you of Jacqueline, your precious Jacqueline, your stupid book.. I know what you're thinking Bond man, as she stares him down.. You'd like to fuck her wouldn't you, she sighs at him.. You wouldn't know what to do with it, turning her back to Drisko.. He hands her a bowl of soup, some kind of granola and bean crap.. He churns his face in a scrunch, from the smell, this ought to shut her up, he's thinking.. He scopes the aft of the ship, he sees the reflection in the mirror, there in the mirror, reflecting, it catches him immediately.. Its Dr. J, Jacqueline with her jagged band of 333s, Joey and Nick, the three of them here, now, all in one place..

Why are you here, in his silent voice, why now? He thinks fast like Bond man would, it's a trap.. Without pause, he drops, rolls and pulls the PP47 from his perfectly fitted sparkling white, with matching little Sunfire red bow tie and cummerbund, tuxedo.. He aims and fires three shots, in concession.. All three assassins collapse to the deck of the tiny ship.. Veronica jumps up in perfect timing oooooh.. Oh Bond man, that was perfect, it really hit the spot.. You're good Bond man, you're good.. Can you get me some more, with a slice of whole wheat, grain fibre bread and buttered, lightly..

She hugs him, giving him a sweet, long, lingering kiss and a squeeze.. Feed 'em and fuck 'em, what can I say, Drisko, in his silent voice? We' gots' no time for this, he scolds her.. Grabbing her hand tightly around her slender back, squeezing her tight.. They leap the four-story drop, landing perfectly, onto the orange lifeless sheet, floating alongside the ship.. The blob of orange rubber goo explodes.. As their weight tops it, it bubbles and churns forming itself into a lifesaving Zodiac..

Complete with dual 150 Mercury inboard turbo jet engines.. Q, this one is incredible, he's thinking.. Who, Veronica asks, over hearing Drisko's words? Him Ignoring her request, he hands her some more food and she devours it, thoughtlessly.. He hits the throttle onto full, the tiny craft races across the ocean top, skimming the surface.. He hits the green button, it explodes into nitro and thrusts it like a rocket through the tops of the deep dark blue Atlantic Ocean and into open waters..

He fires the flare gun and it explodes into space, the parachute slowly falling, the cloud-like mist lands perfectly over the Zodiac, covering it, making it completely invisible.. He takes her in his arms, he kisses her perfectly.. They feed on red, green and dark purple grapes, Brie and fresh baked bread from the mini custom kitchen built into the tiny Zodiac.. He ravishes her, making wild animalistic love, as only the Bond man could.. The ship slowly appears out of the surf.. They, 00 Drisk and OOOSHINEY, naked and enthralled in each others arms.. There as he notices, M., standing on the deck of the giant ship, yelling something to him..

Drisko, the BLUE NOSER, the Navy, the beer, he shakes off the daze.. Hooters, Bond, what he questions, Hooters, she's yelling? I know, nice eh, he replies, to M's observation, slightly confused.. Veronica being all naked and such, M's all lustful looking, 3-3-3-sum, he's thinking, she's thinking.. Drisko's eyeing her, watching her as she's checking out Veronica, then Bond.. I knew she was into it, he said, in his silent voice.. Hooters for lunch, my treat, M shouts out to him.. The crew, wasting no time helping Veronica aboard the fully manned, missile guiding, torpedo launching, fucking atomic ship..

Canadian dogs, Drisko is cursing them.. You'd think the girl had no arms or something, her all naked and such.. Oh, he protest, ya M, he hollers, thanks for rescuing me bitch, talk about timing.. Oh, and thank you boys, Veronica replies, smiling.. Hooters, ya' great Veronica says, staring down at M's ample set, cuz I'm still really hungry, she cries, licking her lips.. Bond, she yells, get over here Dick Weed.. Bond's fucked, coming or going.. You know, sometimes you just gotta give it up and go with the flow, find your heart, your passion and just go for it, get on with it, get on with LBC..

Le Woof.. After Drisko killed off all the demons of his past, Veronica and he moved into a cool little country property in North Albert Township.. Just minutes from the water, a creek running through it, surrounded by forest, which is surrounded, by protected wetlands.. Drisk is settled nicely into the country home.. He's still writing Stealing Home, the story about The House On Silver Creek.. He writes the final words, preparing to write the preface and the story is based on, to direct the ending.. He stops, takes a small break, grabs a cup of coffee and rolls a doob.. He walks out the solid blue door of the old country home, steps onto the deck and stares out into the wetlands..

The forest is thick and runs into the waterfront or the other way behind the house to the trail and up toward the highway then out into pure wilderness.. Drisko has heard their howling since the night they've moved in.. Neighbours, although few, claim they're out there, but they're elusive.. He fires up his doob, the dog's acting strange.. He's out there girl, as he calms her, with his touch.. The pup is panting, turning and twisting, sniffing and snorting but she won't leave his side.. He could feel it, the Spirit Wolf was there.. Drisko opened the blue door and puts the pup in..

Directly across from the deck and backing onto the property is a shed matching in colour to the door and the siding of the house.. Beside the shed and piled, leaning on the end of the shed, were six heavy 5x5 windows.. Beside them and leaning into the window were two pair of 255/55R/16 Nordic Goodyear winter tires, the rims painted gold.. On top of the old worn tires, the windows, the shed and the ground, was a perfectly fresh, four inch layer of pure white snow.. Behind the scene was the forest and right there, right then, that very moment.. Everything changes in an instant.. Directly between the forest and the tires, framed by the shed and the trees, where his fly eyes stopped, there looking directly back at him, Le Woof..

He freezes, he can't move or the animal will bolt.. He moves slowly to the door.. Reverse swing it open a crack.. VERONICA, he scream whispers, Veronica com 'er.. Veronica's busy on her blue rubber stinky yoga mat.. He hears her at the blue door and he warns her shhhhhh, he's here, where, she asked, kneeling.. He whispers, above the tires, three feet back as he grabs her shoulder.. He lowers her to the wolf, so she could feed on its beauty.. She looks the animal in the eyes, she gasps.. She holds it in her sight, for a fairly long time.. Le Woof turns, leaps, jolts left, then right and out of sight.. So few people in the world have seen a wolf, let alone looked one in the eyes Veronica.. It's an omen, the natives would say of seeing the Spirit Wolf.. If you see a wolf and ask it to protect you, you will always be touched by the Wolf, the Spirit..

They turned to go back into the house.. The end, Drisko said as he walked toward the door.. That's it, it's all over, that's my ending, to my book, he said to her.. Everything was just the way it should be, everything.. He noticed at the same time as Veronica did, reaching for the door knob, the blue door was closed, shut.. They never noticed it, all the time they've been there in the blue house.. The tiny sign, nailed just under the doors glass window, hanging there, swinging..

"WELCOME" it reads, with two flowers on each end, carved into the tiny wooden thing and painted, same as the words were.. Then hanging, attached by fine wires at each end.. The second sign, white with black letters and two black paws, "LE' WOOF", hanging there.. Drisko turned as he closes the door he peeks back, just one last glance "LE' WOOF".. Then he turns back to her, looking into Veronica, she was bouncing.. OO Drisko, OOOSHINNY, *"Dirty deeds and they're done dirt cheap."*..

CHAPTER TEN

Why Can't This Be Love

The "NINE DOLLAR MURDERER", and his name was Freddy.. The dead man was the simplest of men, a grandfather, father and a friend.. Mark was Drisko's friend from his past.. He opted out of corporate Canada years ago, bought a hammock and moved to Mexico just north of Cancun.. Retired and not dead yet, he works a little at his favourite past time, fishing.. He's L.B.C. and definitely one of Drisko's favourite people, a great friend.. Mark passed his time at a local fishing marina and ended up being one of the tour guides..

With his skills in tracking the elusive barracuda and a steady dose of comedic anecdotes and fish stories he would build up free time on the boats.. He was going to use some of that time up.. Sunday morning, Drisko's day off, Mark's banged on the condo door.. This better be good, Drisko's swearing through the door as he makes his way to open it, Mark barges in.. Come on, we got a cancellation.. I'm off and the boat's free and some piss and vinegar about them standing him up at 5am at the dock.. Him sitting there with his dick in his hand and some other noise he was making, fuckers stood me up, he swore, fuck em'.. Packed and ready they hit the road.. Mark's got the gear and the beer, Drisko's got the doob..

Racing through town into the jungles of Cancun, past the last tourist traps, the last resorts, no hydro, no water, no golf courses here.. Up into the wild life, where the scorpions live, Disk fires

245

up the doob.. Up into the turtles hatchery, the stereo rings out the beats.. The triple timed heart beat pounding on the pig skin.. The unimaginable guitar riff, smashing through the speakers, loud, louder, deafening the passengers, ringing out into the jungle, rocking the place.. Then the roller coaster ride as the guitar cord, gyrates, almost shaking it loose, dropping it down then quick back up, unmistakably Eddie..

Coasting down into where the road turns to sand and the sand turns to sea.. Right there, where the blacktop meets the dirt.. There in the back of it all, out behind the wilderness, back to where the Mayan's and Aztec's fished, a thousand years ago.. Drisk could feel it, see it, he could taste it's vile juices, then he hears the voice, David Lee Roth screaming, *"Oh here it comes. That funny feeling again, winding me up inside."*, it's historic, sacred.. They pull up to the entrance, Mark directed Drisk to jump out and unlatch the chain link fence, the song blaring out in the wild, *"where to begin, cause I never ever, felt so much."*.. Mark drove through as Drisk reattached the chain and ran to catch up, to where the truck had parked.. Killing the truck, killing the song, killing the noise, shattering it back into tranquility..

The dogs approach as Mark greets each one by name, it's sad for Mark, this is where he had Flaco and her pups, she's long since run away.. Mark cared about the important things in life, that's what made him L.B.C. and a friend.. Mark was a very talented, strikingly handsome man, well framed and an artist.. Mark and Drisko made their way up to the hut, up the graded stone walkway.. The shack, no more than 12 by 12, light blue exterior and interior shining out through the two window holes, that had no window glass, a dark blue door and latch, painted.. The dirt floor, typical Mexican.. Inside the walls lined with fishing rods standing upward hung in place along the blue water coloured walls.. Inside the door-less doorway, it opens to a hammock, hanging alone..

The old Mexican laid back, relaxing, his foot dangling, wrapped in white gauze, the band-aid leaching a trace of bloody stain, tilted outward, from the edge of the knotted twinned bed.. Hola Freddy, Mark said, como esta, he goes on.. He introduces Drisk to Freddy, a friend from Canada.. Si Canadiansi, Freddy was inquisitive.. Drisko tried to answer the best he could.. When real Mex speak they speak fast, sharp and with heavy accents.. They left the hut, Mark said Freddy was telling him that the boat wasn't running right, that it's better if we don't take it out today.. They sat there under the shade of the crooked twisted tree.. Smoked a joint and cracked open a couple of beers and enjoyed the afternoon view over the lagoon side of northern Cancun..

What happened to his foot, Drisko asked Mark, referring to Freddy, the night watchman, laying in the hut? He stepped on something in the lagoon and it got infected, tourist Mark declared.. Throwing their bottle caps into the shore line, hooks, shit like that, glass, plastic bottles, their crap.. Mark had a way of flaring up when he spoke about the disrespect shown to his mother nature.. He always showed her the utmost respect and practising it, catch and release.. He would file the barbs down so the hooks could be removed easier, from the creature's mouth..

Drisk asked Mark again about the wound on Freddy's foot if he had medicine for it.. He said Freddy had said his family was going to get him a prescription to fight the infection.. They had a couple more beers, a few more joints and packed their shit back up into the little pickup as Mark fired up the engine up.. Drisko grabbed the gate and they were on their way, heading back to the condo, where Drisko would give his meeting with Freddy no further thought..

The next week came and went, then partway round again.. The same process, up early off to the marina.. Mark had double checked that the boat was ready, available and full of gas.. The weather's sunny and warm.. They're going fishing, Cancun style.. What a beautiful day as they made their way down through the jungle road, *"can't recall any love at all. Baby this blows em' all away"*.. As they approached the last pass to the marina, Emilio's truck was heading toward them, *"it's got what it takes. So tell me why can't this be love.*", one of the guides from the marina.. The two vehicles came driver to driver in a halt, Drisk lowered the stereos roar.. Mark leaned out the window to Emilio as Raff occupied the passenger seat of the old Chevy pick-up.. Emilio passed the joint he was smoking over through the window to Mark..

Where you off to, Mark asked the Mexican fishing duo, then he takes a puff of the joint and passes it to Drisk.. A funeral, Emilio answered sharply.. Who kicked, Mark asked, jokingly? Freddy the night watchman at the marina Emilio answered.. What, what the fuck, Mark said, stunned? What happened to him, he was fine? Then the quick Spanish came out of the passenger, of the pick-up.. The Chevy pulled off first then Mark speeds forward toward the marina.. What was that about, Drisko asked, Freddy died? I thought his family was going to get him medicine, Drisk said..

They couldn't come up with the money for it, he said, almost in tears.. How much was the fuckin' medicine, Drisk asked? Ninety, Mark said, ninety bucks Drisko questioning Mark.. Fuck dude, I would had given them the ninety fuckin' bucks for fuck sakes.. Peso's, Mark said sadly, ninety fuckin' Peso's Drisky.. They were dazed and confused, hit from all sides.. The left hook, both a double cross hook, two K-O's, one shot.. Nine fucking dollars Drisko said, that's unbelievable, what a world.. The words hurt so deeply, scarring Drisko deeply, for life.. Nine fucking dollars, converted to Canadian for a man's life, that's murder and they cried, Freddie's dead..

Drisko sat there on the back porch of the blue house on Wilson Point Road, there in Albert Township, staring out to the wetlands and the forest.. Thinking about Freddy, the simple loss of his life, the value of nine dollars and the value some folks put on life.. Things hadn't always gone well with Veronica, her psychological problems, her anger issues and her down right mean demeanor.. Sometimes it would all just overwhelm Drisko.. He could feel her torture, building up in his brain, her anger at him, at nothing, her constant barrage of insults and innuendos all the time, her jealousy and threats.. Drisko just couldn't figure it out, he loved her, she loved him, what is this?

She'd attack him, his person with flares of anger, you're no good for anything.. You're a useless piece of shit, Drisko had never encountered this and it was definitely getting worse.. She'd scream, with hate, anger, swearing at him at the slightest error, leaving a dish in the sink or a coat over a chair.. Insane reactions, to the point of Drisko thinking, it doesn't matter to her.. If you killed her dog, she would attack you at the same level as she would if you left a coffee ground in the sink.. She had no degree of hate, all of it full force, any of it.. Anything that would allow her to display her power over you, Drisko was getting worried.. OOOSHINEY was loosing her shit and Drisko had no weapons against it, he was defenceless against such an ugly, yet beautiful, sexy foe, the Witch..

She'd scream at him without warning, crying without cause, angry without a word being said, it was crazy when it happened, but rare enough.. It always happened so unexpectedly, out of the blue and more so without real cause.. Drisko questioning it all, is she crazy.. She'd yell, holler out obscenities at him, run around banging all the doors, pots, pans, anything to make noise.. Then as if the tap had been turned off, she'd come and sit beside him, apologizing profusely, declaring her love for him.. Loving him, kissing him, holding, hugging him like nothing at all happened, nothing.. Then, when he'd try to talk to her, she'd start bawling, crying out, screaming out her anger, defusing the conversation, changing the topic.. Ignoring the past, completely, refusing to acknowledge her part, that it ever even happened, any of it.. It was all just way too crazy for ole' Drisk, all of it, constantly, twisting up in his mind, slicing and dicing his little brain..

Drisko returned to work, busy working away in the town just south of him.. He was able to hook up with a heating and air conditioning contractor, who ran a fair size company that was a growing concern.. He was trying to figure out how to leap into the next stage of his business.. How he could take it to the next level.. Drisko liked the man and the plan he had, his enthusiasm about the industry and his willingness to pay for professional guidance.. Just keep her growing Drisko my boy, the man said.. Get us up with the big boys, we're ready, we're there and we can achieve this with you on our side, so Drisko went to work.. The work was simple for Drisk, like a big checker board, move this guy here, that one there and presto, Checkmate, all in the moves.. Now, seems easy enough, like a little checker game, but not everyone knows how to play checkers, Drisko was a master.. The work allowed him lots of time to enjoy his country life on the point.. There with Roxanne the pup and Veronica his love, he was slowly fixing the old place up..

Painting all the interior, colour coordinated.. Rebuild and re-design the kitchen and create, in mud, a white brick effect behind the sink splash guard and stove area.. Re-trimming all the ceilings and baseboards, then redoing the floors.. Then he hung the shower stall wrap around, tub enclosure and new faucets and taps throughout.. Then he redid the deck, the small four by ten deck, that the forest side was closed into.. He opened it up for the summer, spring and fall, leaving the post frames.. Then he built a detachable outer face, that you could easily install for the winter winds and snow block, with an upper glass partition for the views of the forest, the wetlands and Le' Woof..

It was a beautiful crisp summers day, the perfect summers day.. The sun was up and warm in the sky, a slight enough breeze to keep the yard cool and Drisko.. He was just sitting there on the back porch of the blue house on Wilson Point Road, looking out to the forest.. He had just returned from work, sitting there enjoying the warmth of the sun shining down on him, drinking his coffee.. Roxanne, silent there at his foot, the song playing, *"straight from my heart, Oh, tell me why can't this be love. I tell myself, hey only fools rush in"*.. He hears the car door slam, the foot steps shuffling up the stone drive and walkway to the back porch.. She steps up, onto and in, passing Drisk without a word.. Drisko could feel the temperature in the tiny enclosed space, chill to a freeze as she left behind her breeze, slamming the door, *"run to win and I'll be damned if I'll get hung up on the line"*.. Drisko fired up his doob, sipped on his coffee and back to his thoughts of Freddy, his simple life, the value that other people put on it, his murder..

It had been over five years he's been with her.. Five years since the little tree fort, their first place together.. Five years from one coast to the other and still, she is so disrespectful to him.. To everyone, arrogant, ignorant, insane behaviour, crazy stuff, selfish.. Yet when she first meets people, it's like she's their best friend, someone they've known all their lives.. Simply, unbelievably, just the most loving sweet person on the planet.. Such common interest they all have, how they click, how interesting she is to them and she's such a good listener.. They could talk and talk, they'd say, for hours..

He wonders what value he puts on her life, if any, anymore.. What value she puts on his, if any, ever? He wonders, sipping his coffee, sitting on the back porch of the blue house, listening to the song singing into him, *"from the heart, Oh tell my why can't this be love"*.. Watching the sign on the door, swinging, still shaking from the thunder of her slamming it shut in his face. *"I tell myself. Hey, only fools rush in,"*.. The sign, "Welcome" shaking, swinging, "Le' Woof," gyrating, shaking her junk like a punk, swinging..

He's listened to all her stories, sadly, for years now.. The violence, the pain she has suffered.. The violation of her as a child, the abuse she's faced and suffered, from people she trusted.. Watching as her mother drove away on the back of a Harley, the next and best new boy friend.. Abandoned by her mother at eight, left to care for three younger siblings as a mother, feeding, guiding, trying.. While being forced on for wifely duties, abused, mentally, physically, sexually by a man, *"and only time will tell. If we stand the test of time. All I know. You've got to run to win and I'll be damned if, I get"*, she was just left with.. She grew of evil, the witchy one, killing, molesting and eating the young.. Imprisoned, forgotten, a cast away slave, confused, abused and raped day by day.. A child she was, straight out of the crypt.. All things remain dead, here aboard the Grave Ship..

251

Her mother leaving her there, with a man she would grow a need, to call stepdad.. The sadness she must have felt, experiencing it all, trying to overcome it all.. Her tiny brain, the fear in her, trembling, tearing.. Then trying to grow up as a woman, loving, giving and yet the mind, the behaviour and the thoughts of a child.. Fourteen, in her approach to you, in her fears and her anger.. The thoughts constant in her head, not worthy, not wanted, disposed of, left for the bears, dead inside.. Living it day by day, her childhood, her adolescence, high school, boys.. You knowing, you, what you truly are as you look, deep into the mirror.. Her teens, adulthood, her twenties, then out working in the world.. The young woman, out there in the world, brought up with this influence, this image of right and wrong, then set free, to go try..

That was the part that took Drisko to his very soul, the hardest part, the truth.. The part that hooked him, the part that he almost understood.. How child like in her behaviour, like she was never permitted to grow up, the child, long gone.. Yet there, remaining there in her thoughts permanently, her actions and in her defensive, thought mechanisms.. Like the eyes of the giant serpents head, the ugly stick.. Spinning, looking, closing without thought, instantaneous reaction to, any sign of danger.. Veronica would simply react, lash out, as a protection mechanism, a reflex action..

She came busting through the door, onto the deck, the song singing, *"Woo. It's got what it takes. So tell me why"*, Kevin's coming to pick me up.. I'm going to a BBQ at his place, his brother is coming up for the day and my son is going to be there.. His brother's going to take Roxy, he's got a farm and lots of space, her just babbling on now.. What, Drisko reacting, you're going out with Kevin, and you're not giving Roxy away, are you nuts? She gets angry at him, she's my dog, snapping, and I'm only going to see my son.. Kevin, her baby dad, *"straight from the heart."*, the man she talks about all the time.. Now just out of the blue, he questions her for more details, she starts, screaming and acting up right away..

Screaming this about Drisko, than that about him, him trying to defend himself, her extreme anger, no remorse, no care for Drisko's feelings.. Drisko standing on the deck, *"**Got to know why can't this be love**"*, as Kevin drives into the gravel driveway.. Veronica walks past him with Roxy in tow, she's waving at Kevin, then gets in his car.. Drisko standing there, helpless to it all, defeated by it, *"**why can't this be love.**"*, she stares at him, he stares at her as they roll back out the driveway.. Making their way down Wilson Point Road, together and out of Drisko's sight..

She sneaks in quietly, its just after midnight, Drisko was on the back deck sipping his Fresca, watching the moon.. She enters around the corner, seeing him, she says hi, how are you doing.. I'm just running to go pee, then I'll be right out, roll us a doob.. She enters the house, Drisko without words, silent, watching the moon, rolling a doob.. She came out with her wine, taking the chair to his right and starts in on him.. She's sorry, but it was all last minute, her son Kyle called.. He invited her to the BBQ, she said and Kevin's brother wanted the dog.. Drisko could hear the screaming of the ropes holding the Casandra at the pier, he could smell her plume, taste her vile juices, hear her singing as she sung.. He could see Veronica, lashed to the post, knelt there in front of the great King, Drisko..

He could sees himself, giving the order of the Blood Eagle and sees as Dooley slices and dices into her vertebrae, with the precision of a surgeon.. Here, I give to you, the sacrifice of the Kings, the Blood Eagle.. Kicking her tattered and torn, lifeless, yet alive, pulsing body into Parsons Pond.. There at the Arches, there at the Sea of Lost Souls.. Let her kiss the Cod he says, standing as the wings of the Casandra flutter above him, the eyes spinning..

The Wizard, poking his ugly stick into Drisko face as the Witch is screaming into his ears.. The truth is always right in front of you Drisko.. Ya' no problem Veronica, it's all cool, I understand, he says, firing up the doob.. I love you Drisko, more than you'll ever know, you know that, right.. Oh ya' you love me, he repeats the word for her to hear, to ring back.. I know you love me, he says.. They drank, they toked on their doob, he watched the moon, as she carried on with all of her lies..

The summer had come and Veronica had been invited to a pool party, a girlfriend she had recently met.. Her and her husband had a pool and Veronica invited Drisko to go.. The afternoon was going well, there were only about four couples there.. Drisko was enjoying the company, getting to know Veronica's new friend Janice and her husband Cal.. They were having a blast of an afternoon, drinking, toking, hanging in the pool.. Great company, good food, good fun, great music and really nice people.. Drisko makes his way in through the house, the song shattering the silence, *"no I can't recall, any love at all, oh baby"*, as he heads to the bathroom. *"this blows em' all away. It's got"*..

Leaving, he stops at the slider, anyone need a drink he offers, then grabs the orders and makes his way back to the pool.. Looking for Veronica, he can't see her anywhere and she wasn't in the house, so he ask Cal.. Oh, she just took off, he said, she'll be right back she said to tell you.. Where did she go, Drisko asked him, she didn't say, *"want it straight from my heart. Oh, tell why can't this be love."*, she just got up and said tell Drisko I'll be right back, *"I tell myself. Hey, only fools rush in."*, the guitar sounds, shifting, twirling in his brain through the song, *"and only time will tell. If we stand the test of time."* and she left, he said..

The hours went by, Drisko entertaining himself with her friends, but he doesn't know these people.. Yet he was comfortable, till now.. Now they're all questioning him, Veronica and her absence from the party.. Was she hurt, have you heard from her, they asked? Was she lost, kidnapped, or is she just fucking that rude, to do this, they're all thinking? Drisko was feeling a little weird, concerned, embarrassed by her, he was confused by it all.. Why in hell would anyone do this, to anyone, ever, why, just her, her ignorance?

Veronica returns three hours later, everyone had left, other than the owners and Drisko.. What was that, him asking her on the drive home? You fuck off on me, leave me at a party with your friends, fuckin strangers, where did you go.. Her being evasive, why, why she asks, you don't trust me, is that it, you think I was out fucking around on you? I went to a friends, a friends Drisk asked, her being evasive.. To Kevin's, she shouts, okay, he lives at the end of the block, in the condo's at the water.. He called to see if I wanted to come over for a swim, my son was there.. So you fuck off on me, at a pool party to go to a pool party.. Leave me fucking hanging here, with your friends, who by the way think you're a fucking asshole.. You don't answer my text, don't answer my phone calls.. You go see your old boy friend, while I'm in the bathroom for two minutes.. Without a word to me, you sneak out, like I'm nothing to you, you are an asshole, bitch..

The tears start, **"Oh here it comes. That funny feeling again winding me up inside."**, the I'm sorry starts, the I love you and only you starts and the stories and the world, it just keeps on gently rotating, turning and turning, just like you simply didn't matter.. Just like you were simply a tool, **"I don't know. Oh, tell me where to begin,"**, a possession, a prop to be entertained with, by you.. Drisko knew she was twisting the story around, withholding the true story, the details.. The truth was, Drisko knew Kevin didn't like Veronica much.. She left him with her son, ran off to join the circus, sort of to speak and left him and her son behind.. She would come back to them now and then, they'd try again, then she'd leave them, walk out again, gone.. So in Drisko's mind, maybe she was, just trying to reconnect with her son in any way she could..

Drisko recalls her frustration way back in B.C., when she first told Drisko, about the fight with her boy Kyle, the falling out they had.. How she keeps calling him, telling him to do this and that, him short with her, hanging up in arguments.. Drisko, sometimes hearing it all, he eventually stepped in.. Stop it, stop trying to fix it, stop telling him he has to do what you say.. Stop it, all of it or you're going to lose him forever.. She would never tell Drisko what conspired to make the boy so distant from his mother.. But Drisko guessed the worst, control freak, manipulative personality, abuse..

Stop, he said to her, stop, the kids twenty years old, stop, stop telling him what to do.. Ask him, how was your week, be there as a listener, listen to what he's telling you, care.. Then he'll tell you how to win him back, when he's ready..

Kids love their parent, they can't help it, it a natural bond, built right in.. Even if they hate you, they love you.. Stop forcing his love from him, stop it, stop it all.. Let him know you're there for him, if, he ever needs you, you're a friend, that's all.. Your parenting days are over, that mother teaching shit, that's gone, your time has passed.. Tell him you love him, let him tell you what he wants you to know.. Send him Christmas cards, Valentines, all the holidays, just so he knows you're there.. Let him go, let him go become the man he will and you, you can be there as a part of him, not own him..

You want to be there don't you, he asked her, sternly, yes, yes, yes she said, tears filling her eyes.. More than anything in the world Drisko, more than anything I could ever wish for.. Then stop, stop owning him and start sharing his life.. He loves you, he will always need his mother, let him show you.. Just let him know you love him, you support his decision and you're there for him.. He doesn't want you to play the game for him.. He wants you to watch him win.. She would tell that story too, to anyone that would listen, how it changed her life around, forever.. How Drisko saved her relationship with her son, the son she loved and how she loved Drisko for it..

Thanksgiving had come, Drisko went out hunting for the elusive, Thanksgiving Turkey.. Sneaking his way deep into the jungle, sneaking stealthily up past all the old hens at the check out line.. Treading deeply into the frozen tundra of the local grocery store and then safely home again.. Veronica was making dinner and her son Kyle and his girlfriend were coming and everything had to be perfect.. And it was, the night went off without a hitch, the meal was delicious and filling.. Everything right down to the cranberry sauce was superb and the cherry cheese cake and apple pie for desert, everything was perfect.. Veronica was in her glory, happy, cooking in the kitchen, something she rarely, if ever did.. Her, there cleaning up the plates, her, serving up the pies and just being a mom, there in the tiny kitchen.. Drisko could tell how happy she was, he knew this was a huge plateau for her and for Kyle her son..

The evening ended, the kids left for their journey home, to his fathers condo.. Drisko and Veronica retiring to the porch, a glass of wine, a couple doobs, watching the moon in the night sky.. Drisk was happy to have finally met Veronica's son, he said to her, he's a good kid.. I feel like I already knew him, over the last six years Drisko had heard so much about him.. I was glad we got along so well, he's got some good plans for his future.. Drisko was being so open to him, listening, inviting, reassuring the boy.. Just try it, he said, then told his story of JT, his sons hockey stick, just try it.. Veronica being Miss Mom, the perfect combination, the perfect couple.. It must had looked like a prolific scene straight out of a Norman Rockwell painting, picture perfect, a post card, the family dinner, suitable for hanging on your wall..

Drisko came home, only weeks later, I found it he said to her, on the waterfront.. Right there on Cooch, the short name for Lake Couchiching, out off of the Atherley Road, right before the bridge.. Come on lets go check it out.. They drove across town quickly, then back out straight over to the other side of town and down into the property.. It's for rent, I heard through the grapevine.. Veronica gets out looking the property over, it's perfect for us Drisk, the lake, the yard, it's so perfect, lets call on it.. By early November Drisko and Veronica had moved into the little blue lake house.. He started right away on the upgrades, and fixed and rebuilt the pit, the fire pit for the lake front yard..

It wasn't even four days after moving into the home on Atherley Road.. Drisko was sitting at the fire pit, late one night, the tune playing, *"I tell myself. Hey only fools rush in and only time will tell, if we stand the test of time. All I know"*, she came home.. Walking straight up to him, she sits down near the fire and starts bawling.. I'm so sorry, she whimpers out, I've done you so wrong, *"No I can't recall, anything at all. Oh baby this blows them all*

257

a way.", the fire crackling in the pit, sparking out crisp clicks as it sheds the embers.. What is it, Drisko, inquiring, softly, Oh Drisk she cries, I'm so sorry, I've been with another man, Larry.. I've been seeing him for weeks now, he was going to move in here with me, Drisko, his ears, hearing, his mind seeing..

Drisko seeing, him, Larry and her Veronica, loving each other there at the tiny lake house.. Sitting there out by the lake, out by his fire pit, the one he just built, for them.. The two of them there laughing, joking around, touching, having just a wonderful time, there, as the sparks were flying.. He sees them there in the kitchen of the lake house.. Her cooking dinner for him, serving him, touching him, showing him, her deep, deep, deep love for him and for only him.. He sees them there on the couch, watching the Weather Network.. She hated the weather, the clouds, the thunder, the sun and the rain, all weather, she hates it all, all of it.. Snow, sleet and hail, it's warning, of what's approaching them.. The red warning sign flashing on the TV screen, flashing, flashing, there, dangerously red, strobing, flashing throughout the house, splattering the room with blood.. To Drisko though, it was all so inviting to him, kinda, almost like they left the door wide open and the welcome mat out for him, so to speak..

Larry holding her there on the couch, kissing her, his hands all over her body, hers all over his.. Drisko's ghostly figure struts in, silently, up behind the couch, because there are no walls in his vision he's a ghost.. So he can sneak up behind them, easily, magically, without them noticing as they are distracted.. Larry drives his head deep into Veronica's open legs, slopping at her as she squeals with her delight.. Lifting his body above her frame with exertion.. Then planting his shaft deep into Veronica's open, waiting, wet vagina, clean and shaved for him, warm and moist, ready.. Drisko lowers the PP47, to the back of Larry's tiny skull, aiming it perfectly in his sights, with skilled marksmanship.. Directly into and to guarantee the correct placement and penetrate into her, fucking her in her skull, hard, with his lead.. A true double O move, one shot, a double

TKO, both dead, one shot.. One shot, two kills, instantly as he pulls the fuckin trigger on the PP47, then he turns and simply walks away, gone from the lake house, forever..

What, he asks, yes, she says, I was going to leave you weeks ago and move in here with him? Drisko again with disbelief, how, it's my house, he's confused.. I talked to the landlord, before we moved in, he said it was okay with him.. What, Drisko in disbelief, the fuckin landlord knows you were going to fuck me, with another man and he said okay? It was nothing, and nothing happened, *"Oh baby this blows em' all away. Woo. It's got what it takes. So tell me why"*, I was just confused, I didn't think you loved me, what, Drisko asking again? I broke it off, I told him I'm with you, you know that I love you and only you, don't you Drisko?

Ya' no problem Veronica, it's all cool, I understand, he says, firing up the doob.. I love you Drisko, more than you'll ever know, you know that right.. Oh ya', you love me, he repeats the words for her to hear, to ring back.. I know you love me, he says, *"straight from the heart. Oh tell me why"*.. They drank, they toked on their doob, he watched the moon, as she carried on with all of her lies.. Please believe me, nothing happened, you can call him, ask him.. Drisko, his mind disappearing in the fog, his brain, him, sinking, there aboard his Grave Ship, sinking deep into the mighty blue of the Atlantic..

Drisko douses the fire and heads into the house, Veronica calls to him, come to bed as she's heading up the stairs of the four level split home.. Not right now, I'll be along shortly, got a little paper work to do as Veronica heads for bed, takes her pills and sleeps easily.. Drisko makes his way to the dark lower level of the blue lake house, to the rec room, turning on the television for the light, listening to the Weather Network.. The Farmer's Almanac reports a cold hard winter, the announcer starts.. Canada should prepare for above average snow fall and large occurrences of ice storms..

Freezing rain expected and a guarantee of those sinking, drowning feelings eh' Drisk.. Brought on by the low pressures system created from the greenhouse effects, you remember them eh' Drisko, the announcer said, softly.. The greenhouse effect, you know Drisk the ones imploding in on you.. Devouring you, everything, down to your bones Drisko, the announcer announced.. Cold strong winds, heading in off the bay, sleet, heavy fog, rains.. More cold, cold, cold fronts moving in, along the southern tip of your bay Drisko and cold, very, very fuckin cold..

Rain expected all year, everyday, every fuckin day Drisko, believe it.. Every fuckin day Drisk, it's going to rain on you.. The announcer, cheerfully announcing, professionally and accurate.. Drizzle kid, tons and tons of drizzle, just drizzling down, all over you, all around you, everywhere you go.. You can expect temperatures to drop into the single digits, the minuses and deeper, unbearably deep.. With scattered patches of relief if you're lucky, Dick Weed.. All in all, it looks like it's going to be just another beautiful fall day out there for you.. Listening to the report on the Weather Network, the broadcast of the dim news, of the bad condition of things coming and how they are going to get worse.. Dreaded tales of the end of the freakin' world and possibly, the end of him, the end of Drisko, the Viking Child..

Once again an Arctic cold front is about to blanket, anywhere you are.. Expect white out conditions, blinding, painful, throughout all areas of your life Drisko.. But remember this Drisk, if you do fall off the edge, no one will find you, no one will ever try to retrieve your body, no one has ever returned.. You will simply be gone, obliterated from the face of the earth, the abyss.. Turning his voice, into the prize giving TV. game show announcer's voice..

But you do get the free T shirt and the no charge custom embroidered inscription, "Stupid Gringo", that everyone seems to just love so far.. Freezing fuckin rain, expected to completely blanket you overnight.. Expect heavy winds from the east with the wind chill factor, it should freeze ya' up solid in no time Drisko.. Minus fuckin thirty-forty-fifty, your call, what ever it takes Drisko, we're all friends here, what ever you need, were here for you.. We're simply here to provide a profession and rewarding service, just ask and its yours Drisko, anything you fuckin want..

Mind you, my little Viking Child friend there, it is fucking as cold as fuck outside.. So all you good folks make fuckin sure ya' all bundle up, the cheerful, helpful, friendly announcer, announces, smiling.. Drisko's thinking, I don't feel it, what's he fuckin talking about, and to me, and why me? Why the fuck is this fuck stick just talking to me, why? I must be numb to it all, what ever he's talking about anyway, talking about me, I'm numb to it all, he screams at the announcer, in his silent voice, not to wake the dead, screaming..

He sees his reflection in the T.V. screen, speaking to it, you make no sense, I have no feelings, I'm just numb to it all, completely numb.. I just can't feel anymore, I can't feel a fuckin thing anymore, anything, nothing.. It's like I'm dead here, no heartbeat, no brain, no feelings, no thoughts or movement, just dead.. That's it, that's the only logical answer, now that makes perfect sense.. Thank God, finally the answer, the truth, it must be, the truth, I must be dead.. Or no, no, more like a monster, a horror creature thing from the night of the living dead, that's it, "I am Monster".. Ah' fuck that shit eh', that can't be right, is it, is it me.. No, it can't be, is that me that I see, am I, no, besides, I'm not a monster.. I'm a fuckin warrior, I'm not worried about bundling up, keeping warm, any of that shit.. It's fuckin hot as hell in Hell, just ask my friend the Devil, when you meet her..

The lake house was designed with a bathroom off the kitchen.. The placement of the table and the cushioned chair set in front of the fridge, allowed access to the reflection of the bathroom mirror.. Veronica would stand in front of that mirror, staring at herself, for hours.. Playing with her hair, make up and eyes or simply just staring, looking at herself, questioning.. Drisko would sit at the table sometimes just chatting with her, her seeing him, directly in the mirror.. Him sitting drinking his coffee, not talking, but just sitting quietly, thinking.. Their eyes glance, they meet, she's playing with her face, picking at it, scarring it.. He sees her, her reflection, he's looking at her as she screams.. Quit staring at me, she's angry, inflamed, she reaches for and slams the bathroom door..

She comes charging from the bathroom, screaming enraged.. What's the matter with you he says, what's wrong? She's crying covering her face, I can't stop, I can't stop picking at it, there's little dots, skin missing from the spots, a reddish rash, prominent, red.. Why, why are you doing that to yourself, Drisko inquiring, why? I don't know, there're little blotches busting out all over my face, they keep showing up.. Drisko was fully concerned with Veronicas actions, her thoughts, her mental state, her mind.. What could she be possibly be thinking and why? The time slides by in the little lake house, winter has settled in.. Christmas, family time, Drisko's yearning for the day to come, he can go visit his kids, him and Veronica, sharing having fun, here at the lake house..

Drisko has the lights up, the tree all decorated and ready and everything looked great.. The home, warm and welcoming.. Three days before Christmas, Drisko is in the living room, reading, sipping on a Fresca, watching the snow fall, through the picture window.. I need to speak to you, she comes down the stairs, entering the room.. She stops and looks at him, I'm leaving she says.. I'm going to stay at Kevin's till spring, then I'll get my own place.. Why Drisko asked, why are you here, now? Drisko staring into her, seeing only the reflection in her blackened eyes, of that moon..

He turns to look out the picture window, there across the lake.. The biggest moon he had ever seen, there directly in front of him as he stood there, flopping his junk like a punk.. Standing there, screaming as the words turned to song, him screaming.. Singing to the dead, screaming it out, *"Welcome to the jungle we got fun and games"*, as the asteroid once again is hurtling there toward all them poor little fuckin Newfies.. Turning the entire world, once again, upside down.. She grabbed her things, Drisko helped her pack the car without a word and she was gone..

Drisko was enjoying his new found freedom, getting back in the game, making some moves.. The call went out, then the calls came in, you available for the project, she asked.. Well they're looking, she said, just pop in they told me to tell you, they just want to talk to you Drisko, then she hung up.. He took the drive, west into the sunset, he took his time, it had been quite some time since he ran the strip, along the beach of Wasaga, along the back out and into Collingwood, back to the little resort, there near the water, near the foot of those tiny mountains.. As he drove, he remembers the pain he was delivered here, the life he had, the one that they stole.. This time, he was heading to the Brothers resort, the little one at the other end of the property line of the big one..

Drisko couldn't help but wonder what they could be up to.. The world had collapsed back in 08, the entire world, the time has passed, the projects not effective.. But this, this was a call from a friend, just talk with them Drisko, they just want to talk to you.. Nobody, ever wants to just talk to Drisko, he knew that.. This is really different than anything you've ever encountered, they said, leading him into the boardroom.. I highly doubt that, Drisko says with his confidence and a Snidely Whiplash smile.. I believe I've done everything twice, he said, they laughed, you probably have my friend, they acknowledging Drisko's vast experience in the industry, his strong leadership skills and they laugh again.. Then they layout the plan to him, their creative idea, the concept of how to recapture their lost inventory, they wanted to buy it all back..

Well this is an extremely effective approach, he said to them, smiling and yes, I've seen something similar to it in my past experience and it was very effective.. Drisko took the deal without any other negotiation.. They gave him what he asked for and the use of a condo for three weeks, till he could get settled, done deal.. Drisk returned to the lake house and prepared for another adventure, this time back in time, back to where it all started.. Back into the little Blue Mountains and the little lake side community of Collingwood.. Drisko sat there that night deep in thought, out by the fire pit, the song singing, *"here it comes. That funny feeling again"*.. Veronica only steps away from him, down the other side of the lake in the little condo by the water, staying with Kevin..

Drisko sat there, watching the fire pit explode, into pictures.. Him alone and lonely, the memories, the thoughts of her.. Her face eating into his brain, plastered there, permanently.. The fire sparking, the wind breezing up gusts, *"time we touch. Hey I don't know. Oh tell me where to begin"*, the snow lightly falling, fluffing on his shoulders as he sat alone. *"I never ever. Felt so much. And I can't recall any love at all. Baby this blows them all away"*.. Drisko see's himself standing there, at the little condo by the lake.. He watches as he sees, he sees all as he watches.. Them, rubbing into each other, bumping as they manoeuvre through the tiny space of the condo kitchen.. He touches her, she touches him, he leans in, then he kisses her..

Drisk watches as they go for a swim, him standing by the fence watching them.. He undresses, dropping his shorts to the pool deck, hanging, showing it off to her.. It's long, huge, unbelievably huge, gigantic as he dives a perfect jack knife into the pool, as it dangles for her there, in the night.. Her standing by the edge, stripping her clothes off, slowly, to the song for him as he stares up to her, high on the pool deck above him.. She's moving erotically for him, dancing for him, touching herself gently.. Her breasts full round and erect.. Her V, bare, clean, shaven and wet as she rubs it for him, then slaps her own ass hard, assertive.. Then she slowly descends the steps, dancing, slowly, then wading, out, toward him, they embrace..

He watches them there in the little condo, him staring through the back window, peeking over the fence, he watches.. He sees her and him there, sitting on the comfy couch, holding hands.. He watches as they watch together, their favourite show, The Weather Network.. There on the big screen, the biggest and best TV money can buy, wall mounted and he watches the show, with them, as he watches the show.. He sees him, lean in and kiss her, he sees, as he watches her, kiss him back.. A long, long, long, long, very long, the longest kiss anyone in the world had ever given anyone, that long..

He watches, as he stands to remove his pants, he watches her as she removes hers, slowly, stripping them off, erotically.. His huge thing, her massive erect nipples, her enormous huge breasts, heaving, heavily for him..

He watches as he inserts his huge thing into her open mouth, he watches as she sucks the huge thing in, barely getting it in past her first set of teeth.. He watches as he applies pressure to her V, hearing as she screams with her ecstasy, he watches.. Screaming like a thousand eels screaming in a vat of boiling water, shrieking out her ecstasy, her pleasure, releasing her venom on him.. He sees her laid out on the couch, he watches for the movement, but the figures disappear as if, they were merely made of smoke.. So he watches, for any shadow, any trace, anything that would give some truth to the dream, as he watches..

He sees his head, then ass, then head, bobbin up and down over the edge of the darkened couch, hidden by the back.. Then finally, he could see clearly again, them in full vision.. Him the unmistakable figure of the silhouette bobbing, the short hair flinging.. Then he sees as he watches and he sees, the unmistakable, silhouette of her, bobbing below his head as it bobbed.. The hair being tied up into a bun, her little hair stick, sticking out as she sticks it in, holding her hair in place as she bobs.. Bobbing there, to a pornographic dance, bobbing there in the dungeon of doom, as he watches..

He watched as they danced together that night, embarrassed in the dance of the dead, he said, as he watched.. He watched as the key turned in the lock, the door handle turning freely, effortlessly.. He watched as the door then somehow, just mystically, opened as he stood there, he watched.. He watched as he saw, the flames of the fire place light the sex.. The drips on his back, the wet, sleek lustre of it as it glistens into his sight.. He watched as she laid there, beneath him, screaming, in her ecstasy, thrusting back into him, screaming, he watched, he could see, see all as he watched.. Him kissing on her as he's pounding, pumping, thrusting, kissing her, grabbing at her breast.. Kissing them, kissing her neck, throwing his fingers into her mouth as he kisses and sucks on each full round breast, kissing them..

Kissing her mouth, deeply, tonging her sensually as she screams, fuck me harder, fuck me mi Lord.. He watches as he takes the sword from it sheath, shining it toward the sky as the fire reflects the windows pain.. It shimmers in his eyes as he watches.. Aiming the sword, downward, over the two useless bodies, thrusting at each other.. Raising it thirteen times, the sword shining back at him, shimmering in his blackened eyes, shimmering, their reflections.. He watches as he sees the reflection, mirroring back, he sees as he watches.. Then he sees, the sword, striking down, through both bodies at once, sloshing through their core.. Simply slicing and dicing its way, directly through both, easily, with one clean sweep.. The sparks igniting in the firepit.. He watches as he sees and he sees all, as he watches.. He goes into the lake house, it's quiet, strangely quiet, dark, but somehow, now peaceful..

Drisko moved into the little town, famous for their ship building lumber industry, before the sixties and set up house in his free digs, then went house hunting.. Calling, texting, getting the word out, Drisko was connected and one call leads to another.. Ya' Drisk, he's my ex, she said, but he's a great guy and is looking to share his place with someone.. He knows you, you probably know him as she delivered the name.. Can't say it rings a bell, Drisko probing, probing.. You're not trying to pawn your X on me are you, he laughs, no, no she laughs.. He's a real good guy Drisk, you guys will get along great, I promise.. You'll like him, he's a cool guy, plays guitar and he tokes too.. Stop selling, you got me, at guitar, give me his number, and she did, Drisko made the call..

Drisko moved into the ground floor condo, there on the big resort property, in the tiny village near the lake.. The first night the two of them pulled out the guitars and the rest was history.. You stink dude, Drisk said to him, how come you been playing all these years and you still stink, in his silent voice.. Drisko finally asking him, how come you only play half the song, we need some practise..

Get some tunes down, the whole song, you pick ten songs and I'll pick ten and we'll learn twenty new songs together.. Now the rest was history..

Drisko and Mike got along well as a matter of fact and in the strangest coincidence of timing and place.. Mike was a salesman at the resort Drisk was working at.. How do you know Victoria, Mike asked him, knowing the answer but digging for a lie? Then without waiting for the answer he spieled his life history, non-stop, everything on the table, why they fell apart.. Drisko laughing, his vision of Veronica, spilling her life history, ten minutes after he met her.. Plus the Bipolar and slight O.C.D., with manic depression, he goes on.. Plus I lost my licence for D.U.I., now I gotta blow into the box to start my car, hey maybe you can do it for me when I can't..

I could give you the long version of this story, but I won't, the short version will work just fine.. Drisko and Mike became very good friends.. Skiing, fishing hanging with other friends and friends of those friends, then they all had friends.. They had some great times together, just hanging around there on the mountain, there in Collingwood.. Chasing girls, getting laid, getting drunk and high.. Drisk had left Veronica far behind, he was moving on.. He had a lot of friends in the area and the chicks still dug him, so he was off to the races as they say, outta da gate.. Drisko and Mike went on working and sharing the condo for a good year and a half, before Drisko returned to Albert Township or anywhere near the little lake house.. The company closed their doors, the owners running off with all their sales staffs final commissions and closed forever.. But now that's getting back to the long version of this story..

Back to the short of it, Veronica called one day about three months into Drisko's contract, I just wanna talk, she said.. Well actually she didn't call, she got a friend to call, she just wants to talk to you Drisko, she said.. Well actually the friend didn't call, what actually happened, the bitch just came to the house and banged on the fuckin door.. I just want to talk to you Dick Weed, she said.. Dick Weeds heart dropped when he seen her there, standing at the door.. There in front of his eyes, bawling, his heart dropping, his mind stopping, no memories of ugliness, only her sorrow, her pain, her beauty.. The only thing Drisko could see, there in the doorway, his love, crying, crying, crying..

The day went on, he entertained her, there in the condo.. Dick Weed was on full alert though.. Dick Weed was in tune with every word, every movement of her, making him stand at attention.. Dick Weed could hear her sorrow as he stood straight, hard.. Dick Weed, feeling her as she touches his hand, his leg, blabbering, blabbering on into the wind as Dick Weed stood there strong, obedient and tall.. Dick Weed, fell to her as they made love for the first time in three months.. Her passion had overflowed, all over big strong Dick Weed as Dick Weed was overflowing all over her..

I can't, he said to her, I'm here in Collingwood, I'm not moving in with you again.. It was all just a big mistake she goes on, I just wanted to see my son more, she tells him.. I got my own place she's stressing, it's not much but it's mine.. Just a one bedroom, but it's comfortable and I fixed it up nice, you'd be proud of me.. I love you and only you, you know that, can I see you, can we see each other, she asked.. I live here, you've a long way to go but maybe we can catch up on the weekends.. Dick Weed doing all the talking, Drisko just standing there listening to the blabbering, blabbering, blabbering into the wind.. I'll see he say's, you know how busy it is with start up.. I'm jammed for time right now, but we'll see.. She leaves him with a passionate kiss, tearing, crying out the words, I love you Drisko, you know it's only you.. He smiles, ya' I know, you love me, as she walks to her car..

It was only three days later that she called, Drisko, someone's been try to get in my house, she's crying, terrorized.. I heard something a couple of nights ago, but it stopped right away.. Then last night around two in the morning, I heard it.. The door was rattling Drisk, I'm really scared, what "what should I use as a hook Drisko", she asked him, as the word came out of her, what should I do Drisk? The door kept rattling so I slowly crept down the stairs..

I stood there on the third step, I could still hear it Drisk, I was so frightened..

Then it rattled like it was turning, I couldn't remember, I prayed and prayed I did Drisko and thank God, I did.. I locked the door that night or I swear they would have found me cut up dead, in little pieces this morning.. I'm telling you, I didn't get to sleep a wink last night, I've been up all night and now all day and my tits hurt and my ass hurts and this and that hurts and Drisko, are you there, ya' I'm here, wow.. Wow what do you mean wow, she asked.. I mean wow, you haven't shut the fuck up for five minutes straight, I'll be right there? Now that's the real short of that story and you can guess the rest..

He sat there in front of the high priest, there in the church office, there in front of the man dressed all in black.. We want to do a cross promotion, a fund raiser for the Young Men's Christian Association, Drisko the Priest said to him.. Are you Catholic Drisko, the man in black asked him.. Yes father, I am, Drisko said, I've converted from the Church of England, Anglican to Catholic when I married my wife.. My children are all Catholic, but I'm open to allowing a man to pray or worship whatever God gives him peace..

I personally believed and tried to pass on to my friends and children.. That quite simply, God is just a short form for good, and how can good be bad.. And the truth is that, I don't believe I need to be standing in the house of the Lord, to worship him or to believe in his miracles.. Let me ask you a personal question father, Drisko leans into him, about love, about trust and the truth.. You got a minute, because I got a story for you, that's gonna blow your mind.. This is a story, you could write a horror novel on and I think, I may need his help here.. Here father, you might wanna spark this up first..

Standing there at the church steps, saying their good byes.. I wanna thank you for everything father and you have my word we'll do a great job for you.. Oh and thanks for the talk, I got it, good stuff, I know exactly what you mean and I know what I have to do.. Oh and Drisko thanks you for the beautiful prayer candle.. It has a special shine from it, it will always remind me of the gentleness of all your old souls Drisko.. Oh and spark this up, good one, good joke, like the burning bush ah', funny boy, I got it, the candle.. Peace go with you King Drisko as he makes the sign of the cross above Drisko's head and may love find you again and for always my Viking Child..

Thank you again for the great promotion and opportunity, the kids, all will love you.. Oh, oh one more thing, here take this information with you, read it Drisko, it will help you.. Keep it close to you at all times, read it, promise me.. Drisko took the flyer, shoving it in his briefcase, leaving his promise with the man in black, then driving away.. Watching the church in the rear view, the cross glistening back to him.. He could feel the hands of Valhalla lay upon him.. Him listing to the bells chime, four times, ding, ding, ding, ding.. The sound reminding him of something, something distant, something from his past as they rang..

Drisko drove back to Veronicas apartment that night for dinner and a Friday night movie and sex, lots of sex, all kinds, all different, all new moves.. All the same but different, like first time sex or stranger sex or taboo sex or just, dirty lust sex.. Dirt cheap fuck her in the ass sex and send her home to papa sex but so much sex, they were running out of sex, okay, now they're back sex, everywhere you looked there was sex, sex and more sex.. Sex, sex, sex, then the fuck that sex, Drisko finally says, I've had enough of this sex shit.. There has to be more to us than this, wanna fuck she said, then the rabbit was down the hole again sex..

Anyway the point is Drisko was spending more time at Veronica's than at the condo.. Then the place closed, the crooks took off with all the cash.. Everyone got sex and some were even actually just waiting, waiting there in line patiently for them to have sex with them.. We called this one, the them sex, sex, just because it's them that are actually waiting there to get sex.. Them knowing the big dick was about to swing and they would all be fucked in the ass sex and they were..

So that's how Drisko and Veronica ended up back together again, nine years later, go figure.. So nine years and three days later, when they broke up again well, no one was really surprised.. With that it would be equally safe to say, the same be true as when three days after that, they were back together again.. Drisko would just go stay with friends, his sons, drop in on buddies till shit cooled down.. It was getting sad, and sadder yet was, there didn't seem to be an end to it, at all..

Drisk was driving the back out one day, back into Bass Lake.. He pulls down the little lane and parks the truck, rolls a doob and sits back to chill.. He's got his little briefcase there with him and he opens it thinking this and that, poking around.. When that pops into his hand as he pulls that out, it's that, the sheet, that the priest gave him, promise me Drisko, you'll read it.. Drisko pulls it clean from the case, puffs on his doob and reads the head line, out loud, then lowers the stereo for his concentration as the leaflet is read.. As he started reading, it jumped out at him, dramatically, with impact.. Drisko is transfixed into the page..

The Physiology of Human Behavioural Studies: From the *Young Mans Christian Association:*

The Twelve Signs Of Pure Evil..

Every person has their own definition of evil, however a truly pure evil person is sometimes a little more difficult to recognize, especially if you're in an abusive, love hate relationship..

Good people always try to find something good in others and don't treat others poorly, ever..

If you're not sure if you're with someone that is pure evil, watch for these signs..

One could be dangerous, two could be deadly, three, you should run immediately..

Denying of Reality:

These people will often deny the truth no matter how obvious it is, even if you've witnessed it with your own eyes.. Their truth is the complete opposite of the reality and it is an interpretation of their own twisted ideals.. They need you to believe them, even if that requires degrading you as in, you're seeing things, you're hearing things, you're making things up or straight out, will accuse you of lying, reversing the onus on you..

Twisting the Facts:

They will easily twist facts, lie and mislead any information that is not in direct relationship to their motives.. They need to conceal their involvement in any evil acts or devilish ideals.. They have an uncontrollable, overpowering need, to manipulate reality at any cost to achieve their self absorbed, self fulfilling goals..

Withholding Pertinent Information:

If there is something that will compromise their manipulative attempt, goals or ideas, they will keep this a secret.. They believe that withholding information is not lying, however, if their silence succeeds in the manipulation, then yes, it is just that, lying..

Misleading People:

They have a way of making you feel important to them, loved, then totally incompetent, attacked, vulnerable, weak, useless, hated and unloved or not lovable by anyone else except them.. Them being the only one that would ever love you and how they gave you everything.. It is their power over you and you are left simply afraid and feeling unwanted, as they intended..

Lying All The Time:

Lying is the evil's greatest gift or enemy.. Mostly we feel a slight detection, the gut wrench, when we're being mislead or lied to.. But to evil people, it is the only way of expressing themselves.. They always have to add juice to the story, the little extra, leaving you guessing, doubtful, unsure of, to whatever they are talking about.. You could say, if their lips are moving, they're probably lying..

No Remorse:

They will never really feel sorry for hurting people, being unfaithful or giving themselves to others easily.. They don't have the capacity, they don't care about themselves, their own self dignity, therefore they are generally very sleazy people.. Willing to destroy relationships or your ideals of the relationship, belittling it, sometimes just for the pleasure of making you feel the pain.. They will easily destroy personal things, your treasures as their privilege.. Things meaningful to you or others, because they can hurt you that way, deliver pain.. Hurting someone, gives them power, their greatest pleasures, creating havoc and drama, it all feels good to them.. They'll deeply apologize and then try to make up with you, to regain control.. Then so on and on and on it goes, as a self satisfying need.. The only pattern they truly know and are totally comfortable with.. You are and always will be, a simple object to them, a meaningless toy for their self pleasure, however perverse that may be.. You are only there as a prop, as a part of their entertainment..

Avoiding Responsibility:

These people have no morals, they are reptilian, cold blooded.. They would never apologize or take any responsibility for their actions, no matter who or how much harm they do to a person..

Stating things like if you don't like it you can leave.. I don't need you here, all the hate words, all the uncaring things they will deliver to you, so you can feel their hate, the pain they're creating..

Manipulating:

They are masters of manipulation, which they have a plan for in every situation.. Beyond friendly when you first meet.. You'll believe you've just met the nicest person in the world, an angel you'll think, for a moment.. But then, when they're ready and want to make you feel small or stupid, they will at their command, without warning, to test you, then apologize profusely.. Then when they have you, they will show you how they really feel.. How you're not important to them, you're incompetent, useless or stupid, even for the things you did accomplish.. They can't allow you the gratitude you deserve, they'll steal it from you and you won't ever understand why..

Fair Weather Friends:

They are what they are, they will ride the tide when times are looking good and high, success is there at hand.. But with the slightest suggestion of things not so good, they will turn on you, blame you and quickly be gone to the next best person.. Better yet, sometimes, it's only temporary, stating it was nothing, he meant nothing to me, were just friends.. I love you and only you, I only wanted to teach you a lesson, make you jealous, make you angry, desire me more.. Then the offers of sex will pour in, in exchange for your love once again and the performance will be magnificent, because it's that simple for them, and crazy women are crazy in bed.. They are, very needy, for love and affection always, but can't give it and rarely, if ever for them, truly, find any real love..

Stealing Your Time:

They know when you're doing something important or on a deadline.. They will do whatever it takes to make sure they steal that time.. They hate seeing you succeed, happy, they despise any thought of you becoming better than them.. They feel true fear inside them, of you ever finding real success, but will take credit when you do.. They love creating disrepair in the extended family or with friends, the work place, shattering images, degrading reputations, through rumours, innuendos or sexual slants.. They would do anything they could to belittle you in groups for the greatest impact.. You were lucky, if it wasn't for me you'd be no one, kinda thing.. Depleting your credit, taking credit for the good, giving blame readily, easily, for anything they deem not so good..

Leading Double Lives:

They will often literally have double lives, or even more.. Normally very sleazy, seductive lives, multitudes of sexual partners, drug and alcohol related, addictive personalities.. Telling one person or group one story and the other a completely different story personally catered to them.. Sometimes, blending the lies, to confuse the issues and mislead the curious.. Talking about others in a negative way, to enhance their stature and social creed.. Redirecting conversation or ignoring, pretending it's of no interest.. You will never get to know this personality, theirs is never a clear picture, because no one really knows them, including themselves.. They truly start to believe their own lies, living in the dream and will often take on the characters properties..

Control Freaks:

The one distinctive common denominator in all evil people, is manipulative personality disorders.. They all need complete control of situations and relations.. Even if it means being possessive of things and people.. They will shut you down when you're speaking, not allow you to finish important points in conversations.. They will override all subjects to regain full control.. Any possibility of exposing their lies, converted to conceal.. This is usually very obvious, when they can't control a situation, they will lash out and lose control quickly, defensively and there is no hiding it.. There, their true evil feeling towards you and others will come out..

Normal people don't usually lie, the lie is always harder to remember than the truth and most people would stand up for there actions, right or wrong.. As we know we are normal, we all make mistakes and yes, we all tell little white lies, mostly to protect our innocence..

Drisko reading the final paragraph recognizing them all as it goes on with the warning.. Most normal people in our society carry a slight of one or two of these characteristics, everyone loses it once in a while, gets angry.. However, beware, because the truly evil are among us.. You will recognize most, if not all of the characteristics in that person, in the truly evil.. But it will be too late for you to survive, to escape, unscathed, undamaged, un-deranged, unaffected by their evil.. When you finally do, if you ever do, recognize the overlapping triangles of love, hate and multiple personalities.. Run, don't walk, run, as quickly and as far away as you can.. Remove all thought, hope or desire of them completely and forever from your life, save yourself, make the change..

Then in bold, the number, for the help line.. **Suicide Watch; Call: 1 800 FOR HELP**:

Drisko read the sheet, then read it again and again.. Within every ending, there comes with it a new, as it is written in the Viking Oath, as brother for brother, he said to himself.. Within it, you will finally find yourself, there, on the Grave Ship, in the Sea of Lost Souls, right there in that very spot and it will be very frighteningly familiar to you, him speaking to the winds, regurgitating the sermon from the Priest.. But then you will know it Drisko, you'll feel it, you'll smell her wretched plume and you will taste her vile juices as they're soaking through into your pores..

Then and only then, right there at that very spot you will choose, to believe if the demons are real for you or simply an image in the mirror, he's preaching the priests words, back to himself.. He's remembering his confession, their agreement.. But then, and only then and from that point on to forever more, once you've chosen Drisko, Drisk hearing the priests words flowing through him.. You will be free of it all and you will live, a life of the brave and you will be fearless once again..

Then, and only then you will find yourself surrounded by good, healthy minded people.. Drisko sobbing in the darkened confessional, the father preaching to his souls.. Beautiful souls Drisko, like yours, giving, sharing, caring, fun loving happy people, Drisko sobbing, speechless.. They will always be there with you, for you, to protect you, to keep you safe, shelter your mind.. You will feel the love again around you, inside you and then you will know, the truth above all..

That is, that true love can only exist from within you.. It's always brought out, never forced into.. It has been that, since the very beginning of loves time.. It has always been about, what you give, giving, not what you get.. Like the saying goes Drisko, you need to lay it down, before you can pick it up, how simple of a truth that is.. Then again, sometimes love is not equal, what you give, is not always in any way comparable to what you get..

Then that's pretty simple too, that's not love my child, love is always equal, love is just two people, being in love, that's all.. Two minds growing, sharing, caring about each other as one, as equals.. So just be careful, in this new life of yours, as to whom you give your love to.. They're out there, visible, yet concealed there, deep, inside the fish bowl.. So a word of warning, just be aware, a little caution out there, a second look, a trust in the gut, just to make sure they're not pure evil..

Because like the Sirens of the Sea, they don't come to conquer, na', nor to enslave, na'.. They come, through violence, with their hell fire and bleeding tales of woe's.. Flooding our heavenly hearts with love, then shattering, the trusting gates.. As they march on past one body at a time, with one, pure, evil intent.. To steal our souls and devour the good of every, living, thing, in their path.. The Devil doesn't come to you with horns and a tail, she comes dressed, with a smile, clothed, as a friend..

CHAPTER ELEVEN

Animal

The Note:

If you're reading this, I'm gone.. So this is my good bye..

I'm sorry, I was hoping I missed you yesterday, that you were out, it would had been for the best.. I wanted you to feel my pain, the devastation you left and I felt..

I wanted you to remember me exactly the way you saw me that night.. I want you to know that I watched you release your mouth from his cock and raise your head and look at me.. That, would have been, the last picture you're ever going to see of me, is that.. Me, watching you suck his cock.. It is a perfect ending though, as you were the inspiration to "I Am Monster", to the making of me, what I am today.. With all your lies and faults, loves, for all the Kevins, Larries, the Billies, the Bobs, all the Jimmies, Jerries and for all the Johns.. Your faults, loves, now for this one, for Max, this is the making of a perfect ending.. I couldn't have written this or creatively thought this up without you, he said in his note as he wrote..

I don't really know how it all came about, Drisko telling me the story in his confession to me.. Me sitting there patiently taking notes, recording as he bleeds it all out.. Preparing for the ending, to the novel, the Viking Child's life, as he asked me to, as he confessed it all to me that day, showing his soul, praising, then accusing him, himself, God.. Confessing to me, there really wasn't any thinking capability in him by now, he said.. He was the walking dead, him staring into me, through me.. My soul has abandoned my body, he cried out, my mind, no longer capable of deciphering information, tearing..

Everything is a lie, everything, he said.. All that I thought was honest, truthful, just, all that were here to protect me, all of it a game.. Joey, Nick, Jacqueline, now her, Veronica.. The cops, the system, now I'm in, I'm playing, I'm losing and it's their game.. He chose his words carefully as he was hiding his face from his, so he couldn't see him.. He kept changing his mind quickly, so he couldn't read him.. Him try to fool him as to which direction, his assault on his good name would come to, from him.. So he, himself, would be tricked, deceived like he was, his trusted friend, him, outsmarted by him, with his vicious plot.. I listened and I prayed for him, as if the Devil himself was speaking.. It was all I could do, all anyone could do now.. Finally, with perfect pitch, with perfect timing, he looked him straight in his eyes.. Fuck you Lord, fuck you and every fucking thing you stand for, just fuckin' fuck you..

He then turning his head, to look away, not looking back as if to say, you're never, fuckin' ever, ever fuckin' gonna ever fuckin' see me a fuckin' again.. Come, he screamed out, I beg you he cried, right there in the confessional.. Come, hear me now, take me I'm yours, screaming to the Devil himself.. Send me right to Hell, I'll be your most obedient slave forever, help me avenge this injustice.. Give me the keys to purgatory and when they show up.. Me, he said, me, standing right there in front of them at the path, and it's me, "I Am Monster", the fuckin' Devil himself.. Then my Justice on this earth, will be, forever more..

Drisko and I just sat there out on the edge.. I was listening to it all, through his tears, through his confessions, me being the only one he ever told the truth to.. Me knowing the truth was told to me by a liar.. Me knowing, that within that truth, there were lots of lies.. But within the lies, there was a lot of truth.. The Devil doesn't come to you wearing his horns and a tail, he comes with a smile, dressed, clothed as a friend.. He left that evening, hopping in his truck, then driving away, into the sun as it was slowly going down.. I feared for him, thinking this may be the last time anyone, sees him alive.. He went to his friends place and wrote the final chapter the ending to the novel..

It was only days later, before he'd sent it to her, Veronica, in an email, the subject line simply read; the truth.. The ties that once held their hearts together, had now been ripped apart, by her hands, her will, he said, sadly, exactly as she wanted it to be, exactly her way.. Things were good, mostly, Drisk knowingly fooling himself, with his love.. They had gone out to a couple of events together, as usual.. A powwow show, and market thing Veronica wanted to see.. A couple little events, concerts and garage sales, just killing time, hanging together.. Veronica had a great deal of traumatic moments in her little life, Drisko had felt the brunt of them all..

Drisko now more aware, thinking he can handle her ups and downs, her triggers.. Only weeks earlier they sat in the apartment together, talking, joking, watching T.V., enjoying the day.. Then Drisko said something, or did something, or looked the wrong way at the wrong time.. But whatever it was, set Veronica a blazing.. Screaming endlessly of his uselessness, how he's no good for anything and on and on with her over dramatic performance..

Get out, she screamed at him, get the fuck out now, she screams in a rampage of evil.. Veronica he questioned her, then replying in command, I'm not leaving my apartment.. I fuckin live here, settle down, get out she screams again and again.. Charging in and out of the long hallway like a bull, with fiery, charging fists clenched.. Face contorted, words slurring, swearing, screaming.. She picks up the phone, dials, then proceeds with police, then she's trying to explain her call to them..

Condemning Drisk for every possible reason she could conjure up.. She's hollering into the air, he won't fuckin leave, he has a record, he has drugs.. She hangs up the phone and screams viciously, get out

Dick Weed.. She runs into the kitchen, rattling the drawers, shifting the silverware, hunting for steel.. She returns empty handed, fists clenched, screaming, insanely, get out now, shaking.. He stands, tall, walking past her, to the door, with ice shattering blue eyes staring deep into the black..

Drisko leaves, not taking anything, not rushing out, just grabs his smokes and cell phone from the coffee table.. Then shuffles his way down the stairway, to the front porch.. He sits there, waiting, waiting, smoking and waiting.. Then he gets tired of waiting, so he grabs his stash and rolls himself a quick doob.. Sitting there on the front porch, waiting for the cops to come, to bust his ass again.. His deja vu as they're throwing his ass, back in jail, hands cuffed behind his back.. An hour or so goes by and then two, three joints later, Drisko is getting inpatient..

He calls the cops, from the front porch, he wants to explain, she's crazy, you've been here before, she loses it sometimes.. Please don't hurt her he said, she just gets a little crazy sometimes, she can't help it.. He didn't want her to get hurt, he's trying to explain it all, simply to the cops.. He didn't want himself to get hurt, his record.. Like all the times before this, that Veronica's called the cops on him so far, he needed to protect himself.. The cops answer, there's no record of the call they say, but now they want answers to a lot of questions and they're on their way..

Drisko sitting on the edge, there on the front steps waiting, waiting for the cops to come.. Waiting for them to come and take her way, to the skull ranch or take him to jail.. Drisko knew it wasn't his first kick at the cat, for either of them choices, jail or the fish bowl.. The cell lights up, a text, Veronica, come up, lets talk, I didn't call the cops.. He replied, I know, I did, they're on their way, no reply.. The door swung open as she hit the last stair, she sat beside him, crying, sobbing like a child..

They're going to lock me up, put me away, throw a way the key.. Why did you call them she asked as he replied, I needed to protect myself, get my side of the story to them? Then he looked deep into her tears, you need to go, he said to her gently.. You need to go and get some real help, someone, a professional, a real Clinical Psychologist, can give you true help, clear your thinking.. I'll take care of things for us, no worries Veronica, just get the help.. She rose and headed to the doorway, sobbing, sobbing, Drisko waiting, waiting, his heart bleeding, his eyes in tears.. Veronica, opens the door and then heads back up the stairway to apartment six..

Drisko sitting there on the edge, there on the front steps waiting, waiting for the reds, whites and blues, the cops.. The cell phone lights up again, it's Veronica she's calling him.. Come up, come up, it's all good, I called them back, everything is okay, they're not coming, the cops.. He waited and waited for the red and whites, the blue lights, was it a trap, a trick, can he trust her.. Should he trust her, like he trusted Jacqueline, back then.. I would never call the cops on you Drisko, I know you're innocent.. I love you Drisko, he's scared, he's frightened by it all, the thought of it, being thrown into the snake pit, again..

He got up, went up the stairs to her and sat and watch the T.V, like nothing happened.. They had some dinner, take out, I think, Chinese, he paid.. They went to bed together that night, Veronica showing him her love, her way.. She got up, went to the refrigerator, opened the door and poured herself an ice cold glass of water, the same glass she would use, if she was giving him head.. She returned, as he listen to the sounds of oral sex, as she performed for him, does it feel good, she asked him, softly, do you like it.. The sounds of pure agony, rang through the tiny room, bouncing off the walls like a thunder storm..

They were passionate lovers, taking up each and every corner of the bed, rolling, touching, slurping on each other.. Kissing, sucking, torturing each other, touching each hole erotically, penetrating, in unison, driving with force, shaking and moaning.. Drisko on her, loving her, his passion driving deeper and deeper through her, into her.. She feels him, his love for her, his kiss with meaning for her.. He feels her, her love for him, her kiss for him, with passion, with meaning.. Her under him, him on top of her, she looks up to him, their eyes connect, her child like look.. Her silly crooked smile, as they explode together in timing.. She feels it as he fills her tight crevasse, with the warmth, of his flowing juices, from his love for her, from his undying love, for her..

The week went by like any of them would, lightly, no big problems in fact things were on the up swing, everything almost seemed good.. Drisk had a few contracts to take care of, so he had lots of running around to do.. Veronica was busy with work, a couple of late nights, a little stress here and there but for the most, the evenings were fun.. A little dinner, a little TV, a little fun, it just was an easy week.. Then Friday came around and Veronica wanted to go out, get out of the house, have some fun..

They hopped in the truck and cruised over to the Crooked Cue, Billiard Hall to let lose.. Just a fun night out, shooting the shit, breaking some balls, sinking the black off the break now and then.. Veronica filling the Jukebox with her favourite tunes, the song came on, *"A wild ride, over stormy ground. Such a lust for life, the circus comes to town. We are the hungry ones, on a lightning raid. Just like a river runs, like a fire needs flame, oh. I burn for you."*, and then she danced her way around the table as he grabs the menu and another round, just having a great fun night..

Then Saturday rolls around, they're up and out by two, doing this, doing that, doing Veronica shit, running somewhere and late.. The legion's got a Pirate night, she says, as they're racing through town.. It's a dress up, costume thing and it supposed to be a really good live band there, we should go.. We don't need to dress up though and if its really lame, we'll just hit somewhere cool downtown.. She was so excited and happy, he was so in love with her, so they went.. First they returned home to the third floor apartment they shared with two cats, a black one named Max and the white one named Bowie, after David..

They had some dinner, a light snack, watched some TV. got cleaned up, dressed, smoked a couple of doobs and got ready to go out for the night.. She looked beautiful, her simple white dress, the matching roped belt, her white shawl.. They walked the couple of blocks from their home along the lake front boardwalk, to the Legion, in that warm, mid September night air, as Drisko loved her, they walked hand in hand, all the way to the front door..

The place was hopping, not a lot of people, but the band was good for the local venue.. They drank and danced, chatted with the other couples.. Then they danced and drank and danced some more, all the slow ones and most of the fast ones.. They twisted and shuffled and did the jitterbug and the dirty boogey, and all in all had a great time.. Lets go across the street to the patio bar, they have a live band there too, so they went.. Veronica looked beautiful, her red hair shining into Drisko, as she danced for him, *"I gotta feel it in my blood, whoa oh. I need your touch, don't need your love, whoa oh. And I want, and I need,"*.. She was so fucking sexy to him, his eyes, ever, only, for her..

They danced, once again on the patio, to the rhythm of the band, embracing each other, eye to eye.. He held her, he kissed her, he showed her that he loved her, more than any other man ever could.. He held her, as he told her, you're mine and they danced.. Then back to the Legion, then over to that other bar and the other one, till finally, Veronica had her fill of the night and gave up.. Lets go she said, lets go make love again, I need you inside me now Drisko, she said, kissing him.. Then they walked the lake front path home, in love and he never let go of her hand, not once..

Sunday, Veronica woke, the midday sun had lit her room with its rays of warmth, Drisk was already busy with his day.. Usually, Veronica and waking up aren't a good thing, Sundays are worse.. Like the song says, *"every time you walked in the room, could never be sure of a smile, you were never the same way twice, I'm falling in love, oh night after night, It's crazy."*.. But this Sunday, she woke up cheerful.. Drisk could hear her calling him from her bedroom, "Wake Stock", she called out, fundraiser in Innisfil, tonight.. Drisko recognizing the place, forty minutes south of their home.. Outdoor, four live bands, she shouts out, we should go, it's only twenty bucks, she's happy, Drisko loves her, so they go..

The night sky came shining into the apartment they shared.. Drisko, sitting on the couch, the door on the bedroom is missing so the cats could come and go.. Drisko could sit there and watch Veronica, as she dresses for him, or sometimes she'd dance and strip for him as he'd watch.. She liked the door off, it made the room feel bigger, she could lay in her bed and watch TV, as she'd fall asleep, there in her bed, there, under the colourful duvet cover.. He could listen to her as she would fall gently into a deep sleep.. Comfortably, knowing he was there, her protector, her love.. He could listen to her, gently breathing, then her wild snores.. The sign, she was gone, deep into her dreams, the dreams of him and her together, in love forever, her nightmares of times gone by..

Drisko loved Veronica deeply.. They spent many nights there in that bed, but Drisk had his own separate room.. Veronica's snoring for one reason, plus, her thrashing and lashing out as she slept, kicking and wailing the whole night through.. She took heavy sedatives, to help her sleep and she drank a lot of wine and coolers, mostly to numb the feelings.. She slept on her stomach, as a protection instinct, one she adapted from her childhood..

Her way of hopefully protecting herself from the men her mother would bring home, get drunk, have sex with, then her mother would be passed out on the couch.. As Veronica would watch the men and her mother through the tiny crack in the door.. She could hear them as the sounds of oral sex filled her room.. Her mothers drunken whispers, does it feel good, do you like it, the words singing through the walls, singing into hear tiny ears, there in her tiny room.. The words, locked into her brain, ringing through like thunder..

It would have just been unbelievably frightening for her.. She lived her childhood in pure fear.. Without trust, without ever understanding any of it, without life's lessons, guidance or love.. Leaving her totally vulnerable to all the sleazy men that would then come to her room, late in the night and rape her, in her sleep, in her bed.. Just her pure protective instinct, somehow thinking if she laid on her stomach, she wouldn't see it, so then, it wasn't really real..

That she wasn't just left out, to be used, as entertainment, a piece of meat, an object for her mothers many boyfriends to use.. A mother that never protected her from anything.. Including her stepfather, one of moms boyfriends she had soon left with, abandoned.. Someone, anyone, her mother would run to, anyone more important then her, anyone.. The using of her, the converting her, into a nympho child, creating a lust for sex, her accepting, what she knows as totally unacceptable behaviour.. The starting point, of all her mental madness, her breakdowns, but still, Drisko loves her, unconditionally..

Drisko sat there in the living room, watching some seventies show on the tube, laughing at the lighter side.. Veronica naked, darting in and out of the bedroom, living room, bathroom as she attempted to get ready for the big event tonight, Drisko enjoying the show.. Her, beautiful structured ass, dancing as she darted, her large breasts heaving into his sight, his lust for her, driving, deep into his soul.. Veronica darting, darting, she stops in front of the dresser, she grabs her silky paisley coloured blue bra from the dresser drawer.. Fastens it as she stares deep into the dresser mirror, evaluating the fit and look.. Then flinging it across the bed, bra-less, she said.. Drisko watching her, staring into her mirror.. She grabs her flesh coloured see through g-stringed panties from the drawer and secures them fit, between her butt and her V..

She stares deeper into the mirror, there above the dresser, staring, securing, checking and double checking.. The look, the fit, her figure, her approval, staring, lost, lingering in stare, stuck.. Till finally securing her thoughts, she darts out of the room.. Drisko, laughing away at the bit on the tube, grabbing his senses, tickling his thoughts.. She darts, back in front of the dresser mirror.. Drisko's thoughts diverted onto the tube, the skit, he laughs.. The bolt of yellow lightning comes flying into his peripheral vision.. The dress, she's flinging it as she slips it over her head, as it dangles and untangles, to fall gently over her frame, she darts.. She's gone, the skit playing away and playing away, she's gone.. Drisko thinking with some certainty that she's lost in the bathroom, swallowed by the mirror, the skit plays on, he laughs..

Then suddenly, she darts, the big screen now filled with the Veronica show, he laughs.. She twirls and twist, she dances and prances, felling the thrill, the pageant of the beauty queen.. Drisk looks at her, the eyes connect, beautiful he says, you look fuckin great.. She stood there, the yellow dress flowing as she twirled, modelling it, feeling it wrap her body.. The dress was fit to her, forming with her figure completely.. It was low cut across the top, showing her lustful breast, without being revealing.. The skirt hung midway to her knees, shorter in the front and back, deeper to the sides, revealing her legs as sleek and shapely..

She looked beautiful to Drisk as he told her, then she darts.. Past the tube to the window frame, to the long full length mirror Drisk had hung there for her.. She stares, at her shape, the fit, the look.. She again asks for approval, again no words match his approval, she was beautiful, she was everything he knew she was in his eyes, to him, as she stared.. My hair, how's my hair look in this? I should cut it maybe, go straight across the bangs, as she leans her breast into him.. The cleavage now open, as she finger snips her hair line.. Oh, never mind, I'll just let it grow, do you think I should dye it blonde, maybe a mix, lighter red with streaks of blonde, as her breast filled his eye.. Oh forget it, I'll just leave it for now, as she stares in the mirror, then she darts, then she's gone..

Drisko drove the forty minutes down the Four Hundred Highway, south bound to Innisfil Beach Road, then east a couple of clicks into the community centre in Lefroy.. Then into the quiet dark side road and on to the family fundraiser, that she invited him to.. The place was hoping, the bands playing some great cover rock, *"and I want, and I need, and lust, Animal. And I want and I need and I lust, Animal."*, driving the notes into the guitar leads.. The singers, singing, backing up the singer, they sing, off time, *"and I want, and I need, and I lust, Animal"*, the voice strangely different, deep, dark, monstrous.. The words, perfect, lingering as they were now being broken up, *"An-im-al"*..

Drisko paid the twenty dollar entrance fee.. The place was filled, two, three hundred people.. The raffles and the fifty fifty draws, the fundraiser was a pure success.. Drisk quickly found a great spot in view of the stage.. He dropped the cooler and set up the lawn chairs, together side by side.. They sat there, relaxing, enjoying the evening, enjoying each other.. Watching the people, laughing, chatting, drinking, listening to the music.. Come on Drisko, this is our song as she drags him onto the grass centre stage and an empty dance floor.. He loved her, she looked beautiful to him, her yellow dress flowing, her smile, the love in her eyes, so he went and he danced with her..

They danced and danced three, four songs, then they'd break, drink and laugh.. Then they'd dance he said, his tears filling his eyes now.. His memories, of those dances, his love for her, her yellow dress flowing, hugging her frame as she flowed and they danced.. Veronica, the yellow dress, her twirling it making it perform for her, revealing her inner most secrets, her thighs and the trace of her invisible panties.. She danced for him as if she was alone, twirling, gyrating, twisting her hips, smoothly, erotic in motions..

Like the dance of a stripper, sexy, provoking and mesmerizing him, as she bumped and was grinding the moves, then bending and knelling while sliding beneath his crotch.. They'd break, relax into the chairs, enjoying the music.. They drank and joked and they laughed together a lot, then watched, while just enjoying each others company, being there, together.. Drisk recalling, two men arguing behind them as Veronica, fires her hell into them to move on, take their troubles somewhere else.. They took the message to heart and Drisk and Veronica sat there, drinking and laughing, together..

Then it happened, right there and then.. Drisko could see it coming, he could see it blasting it's way in through the northern sky, the song playing behind his vision, *"I gotta feel it in my blood, whoa oh. I need your touch, don't need your love, whoa oh. And I want and I need and I lust"*.. He stared up, upon it, as it was staring back at him.. It's coming he said, in his silent voice, staring outward, up, somewhere out there.. Slicing and dicing it's way in through the Milky Way, in through the Aurora Borealis, ripping into and through the Helix Nebula, shattering the true vision from the Eye of God..

Drisko knew this was not the first time he lost a love.. He knew he had loved before and lost, taking some blame for the past, but never really understanding truly why.. Most people want a future together, they want someone true in their lives.. Someone to share it all with, to be there, to love them, to have in your life as that someone special.. Drisko could see the asteroid clearly, hurtling there into earth, *"Like a movin' heartbeat, in the witching hour. I'm runnin' with the wind, a shadow,"*, he had no doubt the end was near, the moment it all happened..

Drisko had no way of knowing what was about to unfold, as any one would have been totally unaware, completely deceived.. There was no way to predict it, just an act of God, from nowhere, or the Devil, whichever way it was, it was about to be.. He knew it as it did unfold for him, the moment they sat down.. Six men, older, to Drisko's right, Veronica on his left, them setting up their chairs, laughing, having fun about ten feet away.. Veronica, quickly to Drisk lets go smoke a doob, Drisk rolling it in between his lap, as they search the area, for a hide-away.. Then the party to her left, sparks up a doob, so, someone threw a house on it, and the place took to burning as Drisko sparks up theirs..

They sat, they laughed and they drank, they danced and they danced and they twirled in the night, and they kissed as they danced in the moon light as they held each other tight.. Then they rested, then Veronica said hi, to one of them, then to the others.. Friendly like, introducing us, as a couple, then the night went on and on.. Veronica started chatting to the one of the men and in the general direction, to all of them.. Then the night went on, and Veronica was still chatting to the one man, mostly now.. The others standing, drinking, as her and him sat chatting.. Not ignoring Drisko but real chatty to the one man.. She came to tell him she's going to dance with the girls, she leaves to dance, she dances provocatively sexy, flinging the yellow dress as she shook..

He came over and grabbed a chair and sat, introducing himself and chatting with Drisk as his name disappeared from thought.. Friendly chatty, nice guy, this, that, what Drisk was about and then the question, ya Drisko said, we've travelled a lot together.. We've been together for ten years now, actually this month, I love her.. She's a real free spirit, that Veronica he says, how old are you Drisko as he replied to the question.. Good for you man, I wouldn't had guessed that at all, good for you, good work.. He was meaning Veronica and Drisko's out going spirit, but mostly Veronica.. Drisk felt his pride, replying, yes she is beautiful and yes, she's all mine..

The thought made him smile inside.. My friend there, he said to Drisko, in the fedora, he loves to dance, but he's shy, do you think Veronica would dance with him, ask her Drisk said.. She returned from the girls dance, hanging around the group of men, calling Drisko over to join her, holding Drisko close, chatting it up to him.. She asked Drisko to dance and they danced, then back to the group, then asked him again.. The man now reminding Drisk of his friend in the black fedora.. Veronica offered to dance with the friend, a simple thing.. The man, only wanting one dance with any woman, not a handsome man, just a man, so they danced..

Drisko stood there on the grass with the group of strangers, all watching the band perform behind the dance floor, all so unsuspectingly, unaware as it unfolds.. Her, Veronica there on the dance floor, provocative, sexy, dancing with the man, like she was with Drisko, sexy, a stripper.. Bending into him, rubbing, diving to his crotch, *"I need your touch, don't need your love, whoa oh. And I want, and I need, and I lust. Animal. And I want and I need, and I lust,"*, the man unsure, as he's dancing, like an animal, with her..

Veronica, moving into him, driving him, him, unable to control, counters with a thrust.. She's completely receptive, there, in front of all.. They return from the dance, she laughs and giggles and releases the air for all to hear.. I told him, he could eat my pussy, if he'd give me his fedora.. She inhales the air again and release her vile words, louder, giggling with joy.. I told him he could eat my pussy, if he'd gives me his fedora.. Drisko listening to the words as he stood there silent only inches from her slutty mouth, *"in the witching hour, I'm runnin' with the wind, a shadow in the dust. And like the drivin' rain, yeah, like the restless rust. I never sleep. I gotta feel it in my blood, whoa,"*, shocked, embarrassed, alone and truly afraid..

The boys, the one mans friends all gathering around their prey, they know.. The dancer man speaks up, I'll eat your pussy but you can't have the fedora.. His friends all gather to agree, the fedora came from a friend from France in the war.. He couldn't give up the fedora for anyone, his friends gathering to agree.. He'd eat your pussy right here for you honey, but no fedora.. The men all looking at Drisko, without concern.. Drisko, slowly made his way back to the chair, sat there rolling his doob and smoked it alone.. He watched as the asteroid approached, he waited as it hurtled its way to earth.. The night was coming to a close, the end was near.. Veronica was just getting warmed up, she needed to perform her grand finale.. All eyes were now, on her, the yellow dress had served its purpose, to bare her true self..

He sat there as she spent her time talking to the one man, in the silver goatee, the one man.. She'd pop by to Drisko now and again, they're all friends, she said, from the army.. They're all retired but get together now and then, Drisko, nodding.. The band announced the last raffle numbers as her and Drisko sat side by side.. Veronica heading back to dance, she stops in front the group of men, then flashes her panties to them.. As Drisk watches, then to the one man directly, then she darts to the dance floor, dragging mister fedora, and she dances..

The band announced the last set of their songs, with a huge thank you for all the support at this grand event.. Veronica standing in front of the group, swaying, dancing sexy, her back to them, then her front, all watching her, all, each one, less none.. She dances like a stripper, there for them as Drisko looked on, then without warning she grabs her little dress and pulls it over her head, *"I need your touch, don't need your love, whoa oh."*, and off her body to revel herself to them..

Then giving the man on the end of the group a photo opportunity.. She egged him on, as did his friends and he took the picture of her, naked body.. Let's post it on Facebook, the one hollered out, I'm not posting it on mine, the man that took the shot, said.. Send it to me, another hollered out, I'll send it to everyone, I'll post it, and it was sent, then sent, then posted.. Straight through the entire army post, the base at Base Borden, then all points out and gone, completely off the edge..

Drisko, sat there in true disbelief, how, how could she do this, a fundraiser, a family event and I brought a stripper and the hooker to an event.. She dressed herself, and then, see went and danced with him, the one man, dragging him on to the dance floor.. The friends all standing, drinking only feet away from Drisko, drunk.. He's gonna fuck the shit outta that bitch tonight I bet, Drisk heard the words clear, meaning, the one man, the one on the dance floor with her.. She's a fucking pig, a whore for sure, the one said.. We could all bang her I bet, the others offering, the words only feet away from Drisko's ears..

She's a two dollar tramp, like the bitches from Africa I bet, two bucks a throw, who's in, we can all fuck her at once.. Every once in a while one of the men would look back at Drisk, then another, not caring that he was there.. Defeated, unable to stop the truth as he saw it.. While there all passing her naked picture around.. She don't give a fuck about that old fucker, the one said, looking directly at Drisko as the others turned to check.. We can all fuck her, while he watches, the words ring like a thunder storm, the fear, his Viking blood crueling, the truth, that he couldn't help but see for himself.. No fight left in him, not for this, not for their words, not for the truth..

She returns to Drisko as the crowd is now thinning out, standing beside him.. We should get going, she says and grabs another cooler from the cooler.. Leaving the lid off as she walks away from Drisk, to the group of men, the one man and the man that took the picture.. Send me a copy she lets it out, I'm on Facebook and gives her alias to find her and special instruction as to the photo to look for, as her profile pic.. She sat with them there, mostly him, the one man for another twenty minutes.. The others still talking about her, only feet from her ears.. How the one man, their friend she was talking to, was going to fuck her tonight or all of them, letting her hear it, clear.. Drisko stood and walked over to her, I'll meet you at the car, bring the chairs, I got the cooler.. He said a polite good night to the army men, they know he heard them clearly, but clearly didn't care, nor did she, nor did he..

So Drisko, smiled and walked out of the park alone, with his pride as if that whore wasn't really with him.. He then laughed as he waited, for the asteroid, to continue its approach there in the car.. He sat in the cool night air, the engine idling as he lit a doob, *"Cry wolf, given' mouth-to-mouth. Like a movin' heartbeat, in the witching hour. I'm runnin' with the wind, a shadow in the dust."*, he waits another ten, twenty minutes for Veronica to come around the corner of the bushes, at the community centres fundraiser entrance..

He walked her to the car, the one man, the one with the goatee, the one she spent her entire night with.. He put the chairs in the back door for her.. He said good night again to Drisko through the window, he shook his hand.. Standing by the back driver's side door with her, out of Drisko's sight.. Then he hugged Veronica, for a moment too long, then he said I'll talk to you later.. Drisk heard the kiss behind his vision, on the cheek he though, as she replied, ya get a hold of me and she got in the car..

Drisko motors the vehicle down the dirt road, lane way and out into Innisfil Beach Road, mentioning it's nice down here, ya we should move to an area like this Drisk, Veronica says, get a house down here.. Drisko somber, quiet, heading up the road, he looks at her.. She says to him with pride, all these people came up to me after and told me how good of a dancer I am.. The men, those men, of course you fuckin idiot, you showed them your tits and cunt, at a party.. They think you're a slut, they're all gonna try to fuck you, what do you think? Then you give them your fuckin contact info, to everyone in ear shot.. They're all gonna chase you, they're all army buddies, your names gonna be plastered everywhere, for a good time call, fuckin everywhere..

You fuckin embarrassed the shit out of me, you fuckin stripped for those guys at a fuckin family fundraiser that I'm with you at.. Then basically ditch me for some other fuck, he was interesting, she said, he was interested in me.. He knew stuff you never bother learning about me.. All about Reiki, the Tabernanthe iboga healing, the chakras, he studied those thing and he said I was an empath, I could read people, their feelings, he understands me, he gets me..

Of course he fuckin gets you, you fuckin dip shit.. Who didn't fuckin get you, you're acting like a fuckin stripper, a slut, a fuckin two dollar whore? He'll fuckin tell you anything you want him to, if he thinks your gonna suck his dick.. What an asshole you are, that's all you are Drisk said to her, a fuckin asshole, fuckin two dollar whore.. Oh, they're all adults she laces back, don't be a baby, you're so jealous all the time.. There were fuckin families and children, teenagers there, Drisko reminding her sternly, asshole..

All his buddies standing there, betting, that he could fuck you tonight in the back of his car, your car, fuck any car.. Their friends coming over from the other side, to look at you, to get the story about you, you fuck, Drisko blurts on her.. While I had to sit there and listen to the shit about you from them all, exactly what they thought of you, the whore, they all called you a whore.. Oh' Drisko, they all know I'm with you and who's taking me home tonight, that's all that really matters, I'm with you, I love you and only you.. I was just being me, a me Drisko had never seen before, up close anyway, a trace once, but not like this, seeing her..

Quit worrying, I can handle myself, I'm a big girl, they were all good guys.. Drisko wasn't worried about her, as he headed up and onto the entrance ramp for the Four Hundred Highway, north bound.. He knew the asteroid was approaching and he knew a lie when he heard one.. He could feel it in his guts but somehow he was prepared, so he let it go.. I'm quite sure at that point, Drisko, really didn't care about her anymore, anyway.. They made love that night, Veronica's forgiveness, her way, there in that room, in the darkness, there with her ice cold glass of water..

The week went off again without a hitch.. Veronica and Drisko, enjoying dinners together, movies, and talking, having fun.. Veronica moving furniture, watering the plants, playing with the cats, Max and Bowie.. Doing some art work, going to the gym, painting the huge wooden floor, occupying her mind with good thoughts.. Till Friday, she woke all good, they said good morning, she had some things to do today, just running around things.. Drisko had to work, he was finishing up on a job, but they arranged that they would catch up around six and he left..

His day flew buy with a breeze, Friday night, this is a big night for Drisk, supper big, he's been waiting for this for so long now.. They made plans weeks ago to go for a romantic dinner and grab a concert they planed to see as he thinks of his love for Veronica.. The job went easier than he had planned, he got it done quick, so he headed home to the apartment on the third floor.. There with the two cats, Max and Bowie and waited for Veronica to come home.. He fed the cats, made a coffee, rolled a doob, then settled into an original series on the tube..

Then Veronica entered without a hello, she turned and entered the kitchen, banging doors and cupboards, silverware and slamming the fridge door closed.. A sign to Drisko, he silently watches the show.. She's gone, the tub is running and she's gone into the back of the third floor apartment.. She darts into her room, from the outer hallway door, Drisko looking at her, through the living room entrance, her not looking back, searching her things without words.. Then she darts again, Drisko could hear her in the bath, splashing, bathing, washing herself, relaxing.. The music blaring out of the tiny bathroom, the song singing, *"I never sleep. I gotta feel it in my blood, whoa oh. I need your touch, I need your love, whoa oh. And I want"*, singing, something sad..

The draining sound of the water as it rushes out of the tub puts Drisko on edge.. She walks naked down the long lowly hallway and enters her room without words, through the hall door.. She shimmies and shakes the towel to her hair, patting and dabbing at it as she bounced.. She reaches into the dresser drawer, searching, Drisko, unaware, waiting for her to speak, thinking she's just getting changed, ready for the evening.. She pulls her black push up bra from her drawer, without looking at Drisko or speaking a word.. She reaches for her black g-string panties, pulls them into position and darts from the room.. She returns minutes later, darting across the room to her closet..

She comes back into his view, there in the door frame, there in front of the mirror.. She pulls the dress over her body, moving it, into place as Drisko watches her.. The beige coloured, paisley flowered dress, was fit as she stood there in front of the mirror.. You look beautiful he finally said to her, unaware of what is going on, he asked.. What are you up to, looking at her, repeating his words, that really looks great on you? I'm going out, she said, Drisko looked at her, *"And I want and I need and I lust, Animal."*, their eyes locking.. He asked her softly, the fedora or the kiss at the car, the car she said, *"want, and I need, and I lust. Animal"*, never admitting to the kiss.. *"I need, and I lust. Animal.".. "Animal, Animal, Animal, Animal"*, Enjoy, have a wonderful night with him was all he said..

Don't worry, the fedora will be next, he added, they're all gonna want a shot at that whores ass, after all, they've all seen you naked already, so they know what they're fuckin in advance.. Then he turned his eyes from her, watching the violence unfold there in front of him.. Watching this monstrous person, here in this life series as it filled his eyes with tears of fear.. Her stereo blaring in his ears, *"want and I need and I lust. Animal. And I want, and I need and I lust, Animal"*.. He just knew, he pictured the asteroid crashing into earth.. Him feeling it, as he's lost his love for her, here that night and forever, he felt it, as she left.. It crashed, with an incredible impact, he felt it all, crashing into him, at once, the deep shattering voice, *"An-im-al,"* the Devils voice, backwards, the moment she closed the door..

CHAPTER TWELVE

A Killer Queen

Drisko was getting ready to crash, it's late, one thirty.. He's tired and wants to get started early.. He fires up his last joint, watching the end of his show.. The door to the apartment opens, her voice friendly to him, as she says hello, I'm home.. Then the male voice behind her, hello Drisko, it rings out loud like a long lost friend.. Drisko recognizing the one man, there now in front of him now, in the third floor apartment.. That the two of them shared, with the two cats, Max and Bowie.. The man enters in through the hallway, he's big, six four, big glasses, bald head, fat beer belly and gangling, he reminds Drisko of a Gomer Pyle.. Max, Veronica says introducing him, Max, Drisko laughs like your cat, her pussy he thought.. He laughs at the thought of Veronica being attracted to the man, they're friends, he's certain..

Drisko being cordial, polite and unconcerned, he stayed up a while, shooting the shit.. He's thinking the guy was going to be leaving shorty.. Veronica sat on the couch with her friend, joking, playing around, chatting.. Talking about their night together.. How she met him in Barrie, because he was coming from the London area, she thought he was from Innisfil, where they first met, last week.. So she brought him home to crash here for the night, so he doesn't have to drive to Strathroy.. Then, they got into the night they had together, where they went and what they did..

Max telling how she took him to her friend's restaurant for dinner, to introduce him to Holly.. Then Veronica had some concert tickets to see a live band with some friends, at Sticky Fingers.. Drisko listened with hate and anger in his heart.. Him talking like Drisko wasn't even there, like he didn't matter, like she fed him, her lines, her lies.. Drisko said to her, as Max sat there beside her, you took him on our date, to our restaurant, to our concert you and I were going to, he looks, really, he asked her, staring into her eyes.. She didn't even know, when she told him weeks earlier of her plans.. Drisko though it was her way of setting him up, he was ready, the night was their tenth year anniversary, September 8th, he had been with her, ten years that day..

He stared at her, disgustingly, she's playful now to Max, leaning into him.. She stared back, uncaring, without a heart, she has no idea.. The date, this day, it meant nothing to her, she didn't recognize it as important at all.. They laughed at all the texts they had made to each other.. Sixty, Max announced, laughing, at Veronica's happy faces, happy face, happy face reply's.. They laughed together, touching each other.. Oh she says look at you, to Max, all your texts to me, with the little space man reply.. They laughed and compared their notes, in front of Drisko.. Sixty texts to him and she didn't know he was from Strathroy.. Drisk knew she lied to him, but worst in front of Max, the one man.. Drisko, bravely got up, showing no concern for her or care of it at all as he went to bed.. He was hurt deeply, he looked at her and said good night, you two, enjoy your romantic evening together..

He went into his room, he texted a friend, and cried to her, she texted him back as she read to all his pain.. Drisko laid there knowing, she was just trying to hurt him, there's no way she would fuck that guy, so he tried to sleep.. The television, the music network blaring, their laughter overwhelming Drisko.. The noise blaring, his voice loud, blaring obnoxious, blaring in through the whole apartment.. Drisko stopped fighting the noise and got up, it's four in the morning.. He sits watching the music video's, her and Max are in deep conversation..

Drisko, noticing that Veronica was speaking perfectly clear and proper to Max.. Noting, how he, Drisko would always have to ask her what she said, but here, she was with Max and he didn't need to ask her once.. The conversation, the caring she showed him, listening and replying on cue, this facade, Drisko never got to see.. *"She keeps her Moet et Chandon. In her pretty cabinet. Let them eat cake, she says. Just like Marie Antoinette"*..

Her genuine interest, hanging on his words, all fake, a trick, from a phony, a pure illusion.. Drisko sat watching them, looking toward her then and again.. Then back to the boredom of the music video.. The one that she's watched fifty times over and over again, still listening to it, there in front of Drisko, with the one man.. Max, now insulting Veronica, as she snorts out her noise, three, four times, insulting her, you're snorting, you're snorting, he says.. Drisko laughs at her silently, *"an invitation, you can't decline."*, her not even noticing his insults to her.. Her to focused on the facade, the love she's pouring out over him.. Drisko watched her as she watched Drisko, her now touching Max at all his jokes..

Drisko, texting to his buddy's sister, Debbie, the play by play, her acts, the scene.. Drisko says something to her, what's going on, Max pretending not to hear.. Veronica, now angry at Drisko's words, attacking him, how he can't take it, rude things to him.. Degrading him in front of Max, her new best friend, Drisko texting.. Then Veronica takes Max's hand in hers and drags it over her lap.. Then into her crotch, so Max could feel the warmth and moistness of her pussy, *"well versed in etiquette, extraordinarily nice. She's a Killer Queen. Gunpowder, gelatine,"* and Drisko died right there.. His heart just stopped beating, right there at the very spot.. He knew then, as he looked at her, *"well versed in etiquette, extraordinarily nice.",* then with his silent voice, sending the words to her little brain, clearly.. I will never love you again, never care for or about you, ever.. Never be there for you, in anyway, ever again or ever want to look at you in anyway ever again..

He stared his words directly into her, ice blue steel, looking direct into pure shit brown evil and he knew, as they stared at each other, it died.. Max, now looking at Drisko, Veronica at Drisko, Drisko at Veronica, is there a problem.. Max asking Drisko, with assurance, his hand buried deep in his whores cunt and he knows it.. Drisko looking directly into Veronica's blackened eyes, *"a laser beam. Guaranteed to blow,"*, answering Max, everything's just the way it should be, he said.. Still smiling into Veronica, as he turned to the tube and watching, *"recommended at the price. Insatiable an appetite. Wanna to try."*, as the asteroid struck.. He sat there, him facing the TV. it's five in the morning.. Her facing Max, Max side ways to her now, *"again incidentally. If you're that way inclined. Perfume came naturally from Paris."*, her legs spread far apart in her stretchy pants, her cunt, exposed to him and Drisko.. Then as she spoke to Max, Drisko could only heard the words say, this is what you're going to get tonight, as Max stared into the ripe vile juices of her cunt, as Drisko stared into her evil..

The text came in, it's okay Drisk baby, just come here, I should be home by seven this morning.. Debbie, his buddies sister, the nurse.. Just come and stay here, as long as you need, just run now, no man should be forced to watch this.. Just run, leave that bitch behind, get away from that ugly witch now.. You're a good man dude, a great man, run, now.. Drisko could see the bodies piling up.. Don't let her drag you down for one more second, just run, come here.. Drisko got up, politely said good night, you to lovers, have a great evening, good bye, and he went to bed.. Now truthfully, Drisko had it in his mind that nobody would ever try to fuck this guy, in fact Drisk was betting that the guy can't fuck worth the shit, and only a two dollar skank whore would really fuck him..

He was paying two dollar hookers in Africa for sex, and the Goderich army base has twenty five dollar rub and tugs that they all use.. So no, when Drisk went to bed, he knew he was leaving her, but he never ever thought she would fuck this dufus.. So he laid there in his bed, thinking he'd head out in an hour, go crash at his friends, get his head straight, plan his new life.. He figured when he got up in the morning, she'd be in her bed, dufus would be gone or crashed on the couch.. So he laid there, listening to the whispers, the laughter, quietly, the noise lowering, he thought they would crash.. He heard her in the kitchen, him come in behind her, lingering.. He went into the bathroom, then past her, yet stopping for a moment, around her, near her as Drisko listened.. Then he returned to the living room and she went into the bath room and lingered, there in front of the mirror, staring, questioning..

The Ending was never in question for Drisko.. He knew it ended when she put his hand on her crotch.. It was gone for him, it left him just like that, no more love, ever for her.. No more heartaches from her.. He saw the truth, what she was, what he meant to her and he knew.. He laid there in his bed that night, listening through the walls, staring up into the darkened ceiling.. He could hear them shuffling in the living room, playing, playfully and then heard him get up and go into her bedroom.. Then quickly, her upon her bed.. He could hear them playfully playing again, kissing, touching her like her and he would have, and then she stopped and got up, went back to the kitchen, Drisko listening..

She opened the refrigerator door, then poured herself, an ice cold glass of water from the jug.. The same glass she would have poured, if she was giving him head.. He felt his heart collapse from the pressure, he waited, he listened for her to return to the bed.. She laid with him, the one man, touching him, holding him, kissing him, her mouth slurping on him.. Drisko could hear her ask him, does it feel good, is it okay, she said quietly.. He could hear him answer clearly, yes, as it swept through the room like thunder.. He waited as the sounds of oral sex performed in his ears..

He got up, grabbed the door knob hard, shaking it, making it rattle loud.. He walked, heavy footed through the long lonely hallway to the double glass living room windows.. He turned, and looked through the open space of the blackened room they, now occupied, together.. His life flashing there before his eyes, his tiny world had ended right then.. To see it, to hear it, to know the language is lost from the ancient ones, a language not spoken by a new.. He heard the ancient cries, he picked up his grinder and rolling papers off the coffee table.. He stared at her, there in the darkness with him in her bed, she stared back at him.. He looked without words at the darkness, at whom he could see within the black.. Yes I remember she'll say, this will be the very last thing she remembers of me, he said..

Each night when she goes to sleep or when she wakes in the night with her fears.. She'll look off the end of her bed or anyone's bed she's sleeping in.. Then as she stares across that coffee table, into the windows pain and she'll see me watching her, sucking his cock.. Then and only then, will she realize, I'm gone, his love is dead for me, she'll say, he's just a ghost now and forever.. I ripped his heart out, for my pleasure, he's gone now forever.. Every time she looks in a mirror she'll see herself there alone, looking back at her and she'll wonder, how did her life end up this way.. What made her so miserable, how she lost herself, her respect, her true friend and her one real love, Drisko? The one person that loved her unconditionally, cared about her and was always there for her.. The mirror, will look back at her and it will respond, "I Am Monster"..

He turned from her stare, walked back down the hallway to the sun room, hit the stereo.. He used his little pocket grinder thingy on his pot and rolled two joints.. The song lit up the room, *"a man from China. Went down to Geisha Minah. Then again incidentally, if you're that way"*, Drisk lit his doob and stashed one for the road.. Then he stuffed the rest of his dooby into his baggy, then into his pocket.. He went to his room and slowly, with a lot of noise, got dressed, banging, every door, everything.. He grabbed his armour, his combat boots, his weapons, knifes, bows, hand grenades, pepper spray, the PP47, the magnum, the Ak47 and a load of ammo.. Oh and his rocket launcher, gun powder, some Gelatine, Dynamite and oh ya, he couldn't forget his laser beam..

He then proceeded down the darkened hallway.. There at the end of the hall, *"came naturally from Paris, (naturally). For cars she couldn't care less."*, bullets rattling, the one man, there with all his friends there, laughing at Drisko.. They're, there, all their armies, flanking, attacking Drisko, a direct assault.. He sneaks in through the hall way door of her room, sneaking in behind one of them.. He grabs, *"Fastidious and precise."*, slices his throat and throws him to the ground.. Then sneaking past the doorway, where he stood to watched her perform, her acts of oral sex.. There another soldier, they fight, *"She's a Killer Queen. Gunpower, gelatine, Dynamite with a laser beam"*, Drisko beating, beating on him, Sky the wolf and her pack, devouring him, tearing him apart, limb from limb..

Drisko drops, rolls and makes his way deeper into the darkened hallway.. They're firing, tearing the little walls down, bullets flinging past him, barely missing their mark.. They see him, there, at the end of the darkened hallway.. There they open fire on him, *"drop of a hat she's as willing as,"* the three remaining warriors, emptying their weapons, their artillery on him.. Drisko grabs a hand grenade from his stash.. Not releasing the pin, he tosses it down, deep into the hall way, they duck, take cover, scatter.. Drisko dives through the opening of the hallway, *"Playful as a pussy cat. Then momentarily out of action. Temporarily out of gas."* past them all, firing from two feet in the air.. Directing his shots, in perfect marksmanship and timing.. Hitting his mark exactly between the eyes, one shot each, killing all *"drive you wild, wild, she's all out to get you,"*, of the remaining warriors but the one man and her.. He grabs the one man, pounding on him, pounding, pounding, the one man, falling hard to the stupid painted floor, he rises, with some fight still in him..

Drisko, lines him up, the one man, *"Killer Queen. Gunpowder, gelatine, Dynamite with a laser beam."*, the one man, he's tired, struggling to stay up, to continue with the battle.. But this was a battle to the death for Drisko.. You knew I loved her, you knew I cared about her, you knew we've been together for ten years, what kind of man are you, Drisko ask, looking into his eyes? None

Drisko says to him, no man, gone man, not the one man.. Drisko lines him up, runs full out toward him, Max.. Drisk lifts himself off the ground, still moving in a forward motion to the, gone man.. Delivering a perfectly aligned flying drop kick, straight out, his body aligned straight like an arrow.. The foot, twisted up and the bridge of his foot, straight, opened to a solid edge.. He delivers it with thrust, *"Guaranteed to blow your mind, anytime."*, kicking the leg straight out as it impacts the flabby chest, exact on it's mark.. The one man, his body lifted by the force.. He goes flying out through the triple glass, as the window reveals his pain.. Drisko looks out, over the edge, looking, *"insatiable an appetite. Wanna try."*, the blood, the guts splattered there, out front of the third floor apartment, blood, bleeding, down on the ground..

He walks up to her, wrapping his left hand around her neck, lifting her, tip toed off the ground, squeezing so she could feel his power.. That's what you wanted, *"Drop of a hat she's as willing as. Playful as a pussy cat,"*, what you really needed, to see, who King Drisko really is.. You wanted to get to know me, did you, well here I am Drisko the Viking Child, here I am in full fucking colour for you.. Drisko squeezing, watching, watching, Veronica grasping, grasping, fighting, hitting, *"out of action. Temporarily out of gas."*, her searching for air.. Drisko applies his second hand, lifting her, high off the floor.. You wanted to summon the Viking Child did you, meet the Witch, kiss the Wizard sceptre, well here it is.. Squeezing her throat, her grasping, her eyes tearing, bulging from the sockets, spinning, spinning, her kicking..

Her throat collapsed, *"absolutely drive you wild, wild."*, the blood is not reaching to your brain, he says to her.. In moments, you will be nonexistent, obliterated completely, **"She's a Killer Queen. Gunpowder, gelatine, Dynamite with a laser beam. Guaranteed to blow your mind, Anytime."**, removed from the face of the earth, the abyss.. Knowing the last thing she'll ever see of him, is just that, her looking straight into his eyes, as the life flows from her body.. Her watching him, watching her, suck on an other man's cock, the one man, just like the two bit whore she was.. The end, he thought and what a perfect ending it was.. Exactly as it was written, exactly as she wanted it to be, exactly, what she is, dead to him..

He wrote her a note, but didn't email it yet, he saved it to his file.. I don't ever expect to see you or hear from you ever again or in any way want to know you, ever, it said.. You're fucked up baby and now you're fucked for life and that, that's the perfect ending for you.. I believe you're going to live a very lonely life, exactly like your mother, since you are all that and the Killer Queen.. I highly doubt you could walk down the street without hitting someone you fucked.. But none of those men are going to show up at your funeral and I believe, that nobody will want to spend their life with you..

Not to love you, to give you their love as you only take from them.. I was the only fool that kept on giving you love, without it ever coming back to me, in almost ten years.. Yet still I was there for you always.. But never again Veronica, you blew him and every inch of your life away with it and I hope you realize that.. There is nothing anyone could ever say about you and you are right.. You truly are who you are, and maybe, you'll figure that out one day, what you are, as I finally have.. It's all, in them three little words honey, what you are..

You foolishly asked me why I would stay with you, your crazy ways.. The answer was always right there for you Veronica, right in front of your eyes.. You look too far, beyond your reach, beyond what is required, the truth is always right in front of you.. I loved you, truly loved you and I believed in true love.. Giving it all, all your love to the one person you really love.. I always cared about you, I never stopped feeling your pain.. There for you, through it all and never once did I sway and I thought we'd be together till the end.. I always believed that deep inside you, you knew, you cared about us as friends, as a couple, about me as a person, as your man, your one man..

I just thought maybe you did really always love me.. Maybe, maybe it's true and you and your lonely life will suffer the loss of a true love forever.. Now, all we're doing is writing your perfect ending.. Everything about us has died, everything turned upside down, inside out, completely destroyed.. Everything about you and about the life you wanted, everything gone, ripped away from you.. I hope he was worth everything and everything you ever dreamt he would be.. That he was well worthy of such a perfect ending of your life, or at least he made you cum..

Oh by the way, show them your tits and cunt at the party so they know what they're fucking when you get them home.. P.S., what happened to, they know you're taking me home Drisko, eh', oh well, my loss again? Enjoy your shit life and all your new shit cocks that you can gather.. I regret ever letting you in this heart, ever or trying to share a life with you in peace.. Your mirror doesn't hide ugly, "Life Without A Mirror".. Don't think this is an, I want you back letter.. No, never, in fact, it is, just a harsh reminder to you, everyday, to whom you just really fucked, for the rest of her useless, ugly, fucking whoring life.. Then he simply wrote, "The End", then he left..

Now, for you, as you follow the true and tragic tales of Drisko, you crave the need to know.. You wish now that you could ask the Witch the questions of times that have passed, ask, she will tell you if it's true.. You may ask her, how, why, would Drisko ever do this, allow it to take him so far in, so deep in? Why, why would someone, anyone stay with her? Well, the answer is simple, and it is the absolute truth.. When he told me about the Angels, how, when they saw how wounded Veronica was.. The Heavens sent Drisko to her, to love her, to protect her from her own insanity.. To care about her, to save her from herself, to help her get through her ugly world in peace, with pure love and harmony.. For her to have the comfort of a good man by her side, to guide her, understand her, to protect her.. To treat her kindly, to let her feel the joy of pure unconditional love, to have some of it.. To teach her what love is about and how to love again..

But at the same time, the Devil had sent his trusted servant to Drisko.. To taunt him, betray him, deceive and lie to him.. They named her Godiva, the wicked one, the wretched castaway.. She eats her young, but everyone here knew her as Veronica.. Sent to him, to cheat on him, infiltrate him, gain his trust, then rip his heart out, insult him and embarrass him, beyond belief.. All of it designed to drag him down into the deepness of her pure insanity, her evil, into Hell..

But the Devil knew Drisko was the Viking Child, a fearless warrior, a brave, a King.. He knew he could battle each and every foe to protect his love with his life, if needed, prepared, willing and strong.. But the Devil was wrong about ole' Drisko and so was Drisk about himself.. Drisko now knew he had mistakenly, not recognized the true face of evil, the Devil herself.. It was him, him always trying to prove his love to her, to prove himself, his worth.. That was the Devils real hold on him.. He finally realized, he had nothing to prove to anyone.. Least not, to her, or the Devil or to any of her demons ever again.. The people, that truly cared about him, loved and respected him.. He had proven himself to, a long, long time ago.. This wasn't a battle worth fighting any longer for Drisko..

Then he looked closely as he saw her there, piled with the dead before him.. The Witch calling to him from afar, you seek to far, past your reach, the truth is always right in front of you Drisko my beautiful boy.. So, Drisko reached for her, holding her in as he toked on her venom, as she supercharged the toxic smoke deep into his open lungs.. Then she said, in a slithery voice, tell me Drisko, what do you seek, ask me, and I will tell you if it's true? Then he knew, he had reach that place, that sacred place, where if you sail to far, you will simply fall off the edge, the abyss, the end of the world.. Then he saw his truth, clear in front of him, clearly.. The truth that this is a war, that no mortal man, could ever win.. A war against such a sexy and beautifully deranged evil foe, a war against someone he once thought he loved, his love, his self, his worth..

The most beautiful of women, the most enchanting of souls, for each man seeing her exactly as he would see her, ugly, yet beautiful.. A lase, Drisko knew the truth, who she was, what she was and that she was truly, only made up of smoke.. He knew, as he exhaled the Witches brew, that this was just no longer a war, he wanted to wage, nor was it worth the cost of winning.. He revelled in the thought that, any defeat was now, forever, for him a true victory.. Like Marks little Barracuda, his half a fish, but still, a full unbelievable miracle, no matter how you look at it, a true fisherman's tale to live on in time, a tale to tell the grandchildren and great grandchildren..

In his heart of hearts Drisko knew, that no matter how loud he screamed, gyrated or shook his junk like a punk.. The words would still just collide into a meaningless song.. A song that only she, truly, would ever know the real meaning of the words to.. So he closed his eyes and listened to the words as he watched it all perform once again in front of him, there in the theatre of his mind.. Nothing he could ever do to stop the giant hurtling asteroid from coming down from up dar, in outer space and shattering his little fucking world once again, so he left..

He left bravely, proud, not feeling defeated but refreshed, clear, anew.. He pondered, then pondered, then pondered some more as he would.. Who's losing here really, he asked himself, expressively, what is it I lose, he questions as he paces? Yes it is obvious to all that can see clearly, he ponders and questions aloud.. But to all, it is in reality, exactly as it should be, her truth.. How she needs it to be the truth about her.. The way she see's it as her truth.. Simply because of how she's completely incapable, of seeing what the truth is about her and her demons, really.. The tales that she is always so desperate to spin.. Her need for everyone else to believe it is the truth from her, to agree with her, to see her as a proper truthful intelligent woman..

It's easy for her though, because she truly believes it, it is just what it is.. It is her way of making her world beautiful, perfect.. Disguising her horrible life and what it actually is to her, if only for a moment of mental relief.. A story, as truthful as she can make it.. The author, an ingenious, creative, psychotic mind, as if, she had written it into a great romantic novel.. A page creatively rearranged, simply taken from her ugly life, "A Life Without A Mirror".. As she see's herself perfectly there in the mirror, seeing her as this perfectly well balanced person, emphatic, a saint and sane..

The mirror though, incapable of lies or any kind of real deception, will answer her with total honesty, as it always has replied, the same as always and always will to her.. "I Am Monster", and she will smile back to it, to her reflection, with pride.. She'll shake her long sexy red shimmering hair into place.. She'll double check her eyes, staring blankly, then she simply goes on, into another perfect dream of just another perfect day, in her simple perfect life..

Now that wasn't the last time ole Drisk went back to the third floor apartment, no it wasn't.. He texted Veronica the next day, mid afternoon, around five, see Drisko had a plan.. He wanted to get out without any big hassle, simple and he needed to get his stuff, without her freaking out or calling the cops on him again.. Sure Drisko had some feelings for her, but just about her evil deceit and lack of trust, but nothing good, not now, not ever again and in that he was certain.. So the text simply read, I'll be back there around seven.. She replied, I'm home enjoying a quiet night, I'm painting the floors.. Her art work, zig zagging scatters of squared paint on a wooden floor.. Drisko looked at his friend, plan B, plan A was easy, he'd go back there, be cool, if she's out, grab his shit and gone.. If she's there, Plan B., he'll be real cool, not saying a word but friendly, then when she goes out tomorrow shopping or to the gym, he'll grab his shit and dart the fuck outta there..

He was cool, Veronica was there when he came in, she was polite, quiet and calm, sitting painting squares on the floor.. Drisko was cool, hello, how's it going, the floor looks great.. Her sitting there painting the artsy design, he complimented her artistic flair.. He offered to grab dinner, order what you like he said, she phoned the order in, he paid the driver and climbed the stairs to the third floor.. They sat together had dinner and chatted very little, about nothing.. They smoked a couple of doobs together and watched the tube.. Drisko said I'm going to make some calls and get some email shit done for the morning as he sneaks off into the back sun room, hiding, alone, finding his peace.. His strategy is to stay clear of her, but stay close, avoiding suspicion.. He texted his friend, she's here, it read, Hey Debbie I'm cool, I'll wait till she's out tomorrow and make a mad dash for safety.. Thank you, ever so much, you're a true friend and a life saver, love ya, see you tomorrow..

He makes his way back to the living room and sat beside her in the seat that Max, the one man sat in.. Max now invading his lap for affection, Drisko's mind twisting, as he rubs the furry creature.. I'm gonna grab a hot tub soon just gonna relax a bit, you need the washroom, as he had asked her a thousand times before.. He rolled a joint, taking his time, then he got up and went to run the tub.. Returning to her in the living room to share the joint he rolled, his perfect timing.. Then he left her and went and soaked his thoughts away.. He returned, she put on a movie she got from the library, so they watched it, there in the living room, there in the dark in the seat that Max sat..

She leans toward him, she rubs his shoulders, I'm sorry as she cries, rubbing him.. I know how much I hurt you, nothing happened she said, Drisko without feelings.. It's okay, Veronica, you didn't hurt me, it is what it is, you did what you wanted to do, for you.. Nothing happened, she cried, I heard the two of you he said.. I told you before I can hear you breathing in the night.. I heard everything, every movement, it's okay, I know now I don't love you in anyway.. It's okay, he's a better man than me, he's right for you.. You two guys were like true love, a love like I've never ever got from you.. He's right for you and I'm not, he's a man you can love and I'm not.. The text came in from his friend, Debbie, are you staying there, she asked, it confused Drisko, but he let it go..

I will probably never even see him again, she said, her rubbing on Drisko's shoulders, rubbing.. I don't know why you would be saying that to me, Drisko said to her.. You absolutely loved him last night, he was your everything.. I'm sure you fucked him good morning, good afternoon and good night.. All I think about is you pounding your face off his fat beer belly, and you got it, you got it all, he's yours now.. It's not me and it won't be me ever again for you.. I hope he was worth it, nothing happened she cries again.. I'm going to bed Veronica, enjoy your fucking life, she held his arm, come sleep with me tonight, Drisko.. Drisko, knowing he doesn't want to be with her now or ever.. Doesn't want to be with her in anyway, ever again have her in his life, he ignores her..

He knows he can't kiss her ever again, Max's cock has been in her mouth, her head banging, repeatedly on his fat hairy beer belly.. He would never want to touch her again, in any way.. Max touched her, his filth was all over her now.. He could never hold her close to him ever again, ever want to dance with her as he did, or really ever look at her that way, as he did.. Now he could only see her and Max, together in his bed.. He knows, he'd never ever want to take her out anywhere, to a function, she was just embarrassing to him now, ugly.. To Drisk, she was with Max now completely, she was Max's girl, always had been.. Their time disappeared in his mind, like he was a ghost, sitting there on the couch, watching them, haunting them, like he was dead.. Like he was never really ever there, he just never really excised to her, ever.. It was always her, her and Max, in his mind now, always will be, her and her everything she ever wanted in a man, the one man, Max..

The battle was won, she was totally victorious, but she didn't like the win, the prize was not grand enough to satisfy her soul.. She only ended up with everything she wanted, now she wanted everything else, she needed another victory.. She was ugly to him that night, the night he saw her there on the couch.. The night she put another mans hand in her crotch to feel her cunt.. The night he heard her ask him, the one man, if it feels good, was it okay, him answering clearly, as it rang into Drisko's ears, him, saying it out loud "yes".. She was then in that moment, that ugly of a person to him, as he remembers her now, laying beside the one man, there, in the bed naked..

Now at this very moment in time for Drisko, she was still that ugly as he looked in her eyes, he knew, she will be that to him, forever more.. His mind set, she's a whore and she belongs to another man now, he is hers now, it's now up to him to care for her, about her and to love her.. She is his, he said to himself in his silent voice, with his tears, his whore now, anyone 's, but mine.. The thought made him sick, the thought of her asking him to sleep with her there, after sleeping with another man in that same bed, she repulsed him.. Every doubt he ever had of her, became a reality that moment.. He left and went to his room, sickened by her.. She came knocking on his door.. Come in he replied politely, with caution, the door opened, she stepped inside, walking up to him, touching him.. Come sleep with me, in my room, it's cold in here, come sleep with me, I'll keep you warm.. The Witch had no back, she only faced you..

Drisko could feel her love, her treachery, her manipulation, he was blank, dead inside.. I can't he said to her, looking away, sadly but firmly.. I just can't and he couldn't, even if he wanted to, he just couldn't ever again.. She was dead to him, he had seen her there piled with the dead.. He had seen her there sacrificed with the Blood Eagle, her treason, as he had led her there to kiss the Cod.. She was dead to him now and forever, nevermore to be.. I can't Veronica, he said to her, as politely as he could.. She gently closed the door as she left the room..

He shut out the lights and prayed for morning to come swiftly.. He knew she was there in the bed beside him, beyond the tiny wall.. He could hear her, he could feel her tears dropping on him, on his lips as he looked up into the darkened ceiling deep into the universe as he remembers.. He, could taste her vile juices, smell her wretched plume, he could feel her, her hatred for him, for herself, her actions.. He listened sadly, as he heard, as she cried.. The sound of a thunder storm, raging in his ears.. He cried, knowing, he still loves her, so very deeply, but she was evil to him now, so he cried..

The question, so deeply insulting, yet has been asked by every man, woman and child, since the beginning of time.. The question straight forward is to be an insult, to every man, woman, son and or daughter, to all, each one, less none.. The answer, similar throughout all, each one, less none, since the beginning of time.. The question has always been, aggressively answered, with anger, replied to as, No.. Sometimes replying with force, brute strength, shoving, hitting.. The question although is non-thought provoking and the answer to each, is instantaneous, without thought..

Science, men of medicine, Psychiatrist, Physiologist, clergymen, teachers, lawyers, judges and the police officers.. Huge corporations with power, will and prestige, like the military.. Freud was quoted as saying humans, man, only uses ten present of his potential brain power.. When the brain is confronted with complex issues, that could damage your normal way of deciphering information.. The brain, would dissolve the question, dilute it slowly from your thoughts, to prevent you from over thinking and creating a mental melt down.. Whereas you could go, completely insane..

Yet still the question remains unanswered, although theorized and scrutinized by all, it's really not the question.. Although the answer to that question by all, each one, less none, is and will always be, No.. But then what if, what if you could study the question, by telling people that it is a scientific study on brain manipulation? Then you told them the answer to the question is always, No, but then you informed them that, that answer is not important to this study.. Although we have to ask it, to personalize your temperament, as a violent personality disorder..

The study was primarily to see if a mentally dysfunctional brain, could actually, understand one simple question, knowing the answer to it is No.. But then we want to ask you a second question, the science minds tell them.. While revealing the question as to, how do you know? That, being the real answer they're looking for.. Again this is only a scientific study, none of this is really factual or in any way can stop a psycho killer from killing.. The science minds all agreed, this never really happened and not, as factual..

So they prepared them all, the whole group, then started the experiment on the innocent crazy people they had caged.. They warned them again, harshly, reminding them that the answer to the question has always been, No.. To all, each one, less none, to all alive, living spirits, ancient gods, warriors and kings, all.. Then they were warned of the consequences of answering the question incorrectly.. Then, they asked the simplest question ever asked.. A question asked more than any other question to man alive, to any society.. They asked to the group, through a microphone, behind the protective glass of the fish bowl.. They all answered the question the same, but without anger or any confusion..

Well the science minds were all, of course excited about this.. The experiment of getting them all to answer a question that science had pondered for over a thousand years, they all together couldn't think of anything more exciting.. Now, here in this very spot, giving the group, the answer to the question in advance that they all answered correctly.. Well it just truly was, the greatest of days, a day to remember, a day to mark in history, the day of celebration, but not quite yet.. Not so fast, the science minds preparing themselves for the worst.. They knew the question wasn't the question.. They all knew that they needed the truth, the true answer, to the real question, the deeper one, at any cost..

The first question only being a decoy question, a set up, an auto suggestion, a psychological trick to throw the group off the track, a mind manipulation you might call it, but truly effective.. So, the one man, the one with the goatee, he stepped up bravely and he kindly asked them all, through the silver microphone, the second question, blurting it out loudly.. Then they all, each one in unison, thought, and then thought and then thought some more, stretching to the farthest points of their thought capacity, then it struck.. They all, each one, less none, all at the same time, precisely on cue, they all just went completely insane, there, inside the fish bowl..

Again the science minds exploding, conjuring, knowing, this is cause for great celebration.. The group, their minds definitely twisted, the brains literally bursting, banging, banging, inside the tiny skulls, bleeding, pulsing the blood through the brain.. The question, how, why, how were we so deceived by this, this viscous monster? Now their tiny brains pounding out the rhythm, banging out the beat.. How was it so capable of slicing the tiny brains, into shattered pieces of grey matter, how? The first question, we've all answered it with anger, the same, No..

The first question, the very first question their young minds would, for obvious reasoning, remember.. The constant banging of that question into their ears.. The question shoved down their throats, again and again.. The question they've been asked all their lives.. The question, pounding in their tiny brains as they were inquisitively beginning to form, growing, learning to crawl, walk and talk, forming their words, sentences.. The question, following them through their young childhood.. The force of it's constant reminder, of the power they wielded with that question.. The question they would had carried with them, through their whole adolescence..

The question always there for them, reminding them of who and what they really are to this world.. The question, they would had been asked as preteen, all through puberty and then on into their teens, their adulthood and their early twenties.. Always there, always present, always the same fucking question.. Then constantly answering of it, with the same force, an instant defence mechanism, like those reptilian eyes made for protection.. The answer, simply, protecting, instinctively, assertively, No.. The question, aggressively asked always the same, the question was simple, "are you stupid?"..

The science, the minds all ticking together, rejoicing at the replies.. The question still remains, unanswered though, the true question, the one concealed, the one most important, the question that will blow your mind if you think about it too deeply.. The question, so simple, them four little words, that could change everything we've ever studied about human behavioural science and the physically or mentally abused minds.. The question, the one man, stepping up to the microphone behind the secure glass, bellowed out, loudly, through the fish bowl.. The science prepared for the chaos that was about to erupt.. He questioned them, simply, the one man.. Using only four very small powerful words, preparing the other scientist, them all knowing the outcome to the question, as he asked it, "how do you know"? then they waited?

Are you stupid, the simplest little question revealing all the answers at once, the answer forever, No?. It's easier for the mind to accept the lie than to decipher it.. The mind as programmed can't relate, the answer quickly replied to as, No, because we truly believe that.. But add to that the factor of fifty percent of the world adult population has within it potential mental problems, and so on.. "How do you know", just a question? Well the true answer would had been yes, since we only use ten percent of our brain capacity, so yes, we are stupid.. Now the interesting part of this whole thing is that clearly, everybody could actually know everything.. Because of new information transfer and language barriers disabled, allowing us to communicate knowledge, freely throughout the world and instantly..

But no single person knows everything, we all have specialized information.. Therefore we are always communicating and gathering specialized knowledge.. Grouping us, into useful communities, with commerce, ingenuity, finance, education and development.. Simple supply and demand, growth, and the consumption and gathering of knowledge.. But what if your knowledge was tainted with corruption, hate, pure evil? Guidance of non-caring, hateful, dysfunctional families.. Mostly already lacking simple social skills and or love in any form.. Science has proven that there are circumstances that prevent one from developing fully.. Real deformed brains, abnormality, genetics and deformities inside the brain stem, true mental handicaps..

Research has shown that you could take a drug addicted infant child, cure the addiction, nurture the child with real love and show them true examples of good morals and manners and that child would flourish in his environment.. The same is true if you took a good seeded child and grew him into a monster.. Filling the child's mind with abusive slurs, their minds filled with low self-esteem, prejudiced thought, degrading innuendos and poor judgments.. Not shown love, caring or feelings of true affection, no holding or real touching, hugging, a comforting kiss.. Their life filled with physical, mental and sexual abuse.. The child would flourish and would grow angry, vengeful, hate thirsty, as in evil.. The scientific minds will all tell you the exact same thing, as I quote, "as the branch is bent, so does groweth the tree"..

Drisko woke to the warmth of the morning sun.. He rose knowing he was still there in the apartment.. It felt strangely haunting to him, like he was in prison or some other mans home.. The feelings, the place, remembering, she belongs to Max now.. Drisko feeds the cats, and the little blue fish, there inside the fish bowl.. He heats up the little copper kettle, there on the burner, watching it steam.. He pours his coffee, goes into the sun room and reads his note.. The hours pass through Drisko's mind, the repeating and repeating of her love for Max.. Her, in his mind, in the theatre of his mind, repeating itself, Max's hand in her crotch, repeating, repeating it, over and over.. There in that apartment, no reprieve for Drisko, no reprieve from him, for her, ever..

He was leaving today, he wouldn't look back, he was waiting, he was cool, he was patiently waiting for her to leave the third floor apartment.. For her to go out for her day, the gym, shopping, fuck some guy, whatever she was going to do, he had no love or care for her, and he didn't.. He just needed her to go, to leave the apartment, give him the time to gather his things and dart.. He needed this, he needed her to return to the empty, dark, lonely apartment.. For her to feel his pain, knowing it's all gone, everything about them.. The plan was set, he was through with her, she will be alone now and without him forever, her new man, her better man, her Max.. He felt his joy, his victory and he gently fell back into his thoughts as he read his note over and over again..

The alarm bells were ringing, the call to alert was sounding, signalling the tiny village is burning, set to blaze and the flames were flying ferociously.. He could hear the sounds of bodies being tortured, burning to death, screaming, screaming the screech of the Blood Eagle.. He hears the thunder approaching, he hears the wind howling, the torturous sounds following the thunder, as it inferno's it's way down the long, lonely hallway and then bursting in through the kitchen of the third floor apartment, screeching at him, breathing fire, like a two headed dragon..

You're leaving me, you're taking off on me, she screams at him, holding her cell phone up to his eyes, what is that, her shaking too hard for him to read? Yes he quickly replies, for fuckin sure, how, he looks at her.. You sent this fucking message to me you freak, who the fuck's Debbie? She holds the cell phone to her to read it out to Drisko, then she cries.. Drisko replies I was waiting for you to leave so I wasn't in your way.. You don't have to go, she pleads, yes I do, I have to, it's over, forever.. Just go to the gym like you were going to, I'll be gone when you get back, no problem..

She flips, screaming no, get out now, I mean it, she cried.. She runs heavy footed into the living room, pulling all of Drisko's things out of the glass shelving.. Then into the bedroom, emptying all of the drawers, and packing all of his stuff into bags and boxes, helpfully, but with anger.. Drisko simply grabbed the boxes and bags and moved them down the stairs, level by level, thinking with every step, it's finally over.. Flying up and down the flights of stairs, grabbing and moving as quickly as she packed.. Loading the lower level with his junk, then running it to the truck.. Filling it, with junk, possessions, meaningless to him, only memories of her..

He fires up the truck, revving the little engine as he stares up into the third floor apartment window.. Max, he thinks, looking up to the windows where he saw his pain, reflecting the night before, the night he saw her with him, together in bed.. Max, the cat and Bowie, he thought, he could never set foot in that place again.. He, the one man, will always be there, always a reminder to her as to why he left her that day, why their world ended? He threw the shifter into D, hit the gas and never looked back.. He knew she was there, behind the windows, watching him, as she cried, without real care, cried because that's what she would always do, cry..

320

He drove the long dark lonely highway, down the 400, to Innisfil Beach Road.. Almost the same place they drove the night she met Max, the last night Drisko took her dancing.. He hung the left early, just before the turn to the Community Centre, then he raced deep into the beach, down to the lake shore.. Deep down the road into Debbie's and safe with friends.. Safe into her open arms, her comfort, her care and her love for others, for him, this broken man.. You're safe here baby boy she said, holding him close in her bosom, no worries Drisko, it's her fuck up boy, she's fucked.. Drisko spent the day with Debbie, lunch then dinner, together, talking it out.. Drisko went into the room she let him have.. He sat on the computer and finished the note he wrote to Veronica..

He entitled it, The End, and then literally wrote the ending of the novel, the story, for me.. He re-titled it, The Note.. He then sent it to her, all the gory details of his pain, what he had felt, what he saw and what he knows he heard.. He then sent it to me, as I read the ending I realized he was right.. No mad man, no con artist, no evil villain and no, not even the crazy could had created this ending.. There was no way anybody could had predicted this, no one could had giving him this, handing him the ending, only her, as she unravelled everything in front of his face.. "I Am Monster," he then wrote those solemn two words, with meaning, The End..

He entered the high rise through the double set of reflective, gold tinted glass doors, as they automatically slid open, to his stride.. He stepped into the glass elevator, watching as the roof tops appear, lifting him up in through the night sky.. The lights glistening as he stares out into the moon light as it's dancing above the Sea of Cortez.. He enters the penthouse condo through the huge custom carved oak doors.. There she stood, beautiful, poised, yakking at him in her Mexican tongue.. Dancing, prancing, gyrating her junk like a punk, jumping, rolling, twirling with joy.. The song played, *"She keeps her Moet et Chandon. In her pretty cabinet. "Let them eat cake", she says. Just like Marie Antoinette. A built-in remedy. For Kruschev and Kennedy."*, her lips moist, wet as she drooled at his sight.. He slammed the door briskly, with silence, as the air pocket muffles the sound.. He walked straight up to her, knelt down to her size, looking, deeply into her succulent eyes.. Her white fur coat, her darken set eyes, the way she growled at him with her wet shout, her tiny white fangs.. Her tiny tail wiggling off her ass in total fear, her bouncing off the floor on all fours..

He grabs the shiny poodle by the scuff of her neck, shakes her, lifts her with ease, *"well versed in etiquette. Extraordinarily nice."*, staring deep into her eyes.. His ice cold steel blue, staring deep into shit filled brown trembling fear.. He walks further down the long dark hallway, into the back of the condo, Veronica and him, her Spanish lover, there in Drisko's bed.. She's on holidays with Drisk, there in bed, *"Perfume came naturally from Paris (naturally). For cars she couldn't care less,"*, with another man.. They jump up, what are you doing here, she screams at him? Her lover running toward Drisko in attack mode.. Drisko slashes him quickly, with one shot to the jugular, using the blood stained paring knife.. The one from the wooden block holder, *"Queen. Gunpowder, gelatine. Dynamite."*, there from the little kitchens centre aisle.. The thin pliable, tapered stainless steel blade, double sided, serrated edge, used to pop the eyes from the tomatoes.. Shiny steel, yellow plastic handle.. The man drops bleeding, spitting out the blood from his throat, as Veronica screams in terror..

Drisko grabbing Veronica by the throat, lifting her high off the ground, holding her there, as he slices and dices her body, *"with a laser beam. Guaranteed to blow your mind. Anytime."*, at the foot of the bed, with the down filled, paisley comforter.. Her blood spewing out of her.. He turns her, lashed to the post, there in front of the great King Drisko.. This is for all your treason to the King, as Dooley steps forward to take the great Kings place.. Drisko announcing to the crowd of cheering bystanders, blood, they cheer as he screams out the words, blood.. Let her kiss the Cod, and not in the good way.. Let her perish here in the Sea of Lost souls, perish forever.. You have been sentenced for treason to your King.. The order was given, the sacrifice of the Blood Eagle..

Dooley takes out his blade, shining it, his hand tight on the grip, as he prepares to drive it into Veronica's ribs.. Drisko giving his final judgment to Veronica, death, death by Blood Eagle.. Drisko cries it out loudly, echoing his voice, they all cheer, blood, blood, let em kiss the Cod.. Drisko raises the sword the thirteenth and final time, holding it up for it to shimmer into the crowd.. He's glaring straight up, eyes locking onto the Helix Nebula, the eye of God, winking down upon him, in through the opening of the cavern above.. The coal reflecting the solar system, the Milky Way and beyond.. Dancing, bouncing off the bottom of the giant asteroid sitting protective, secure up top.. Drisko gives the order of blood, the Blood Eagle..

Dooley, simply grabs Veronica by her long scraggly red bleeding hair and drives the blade into her side.. Far enough below the first rib of her lower left side.. He gently carves the meat open across the lower rib cage, with his skill and caution, he's extremely careful not to kill Veronica, not yet.. Veronica breathes out her words in pain, straining her voice through her beaten lips.. Dooley leans in, smiles and screams into Veronica's dangling bloody ear, that's from my brother, for your lies, torture and deception.. Yanking on Veronica's scalp, Go eh', you traitor.. Dooley's hair slapping across Veronica's face, sticking there, Go eh' as Dooley pulls away, Go eh' traitor..

Then Dooley slowly pics away at each of Veronica's vertebrae, slowly picking, and carving, and picking along the spine.. Meticulously as he smiles away, carving with the skills of a surgeon, carving, picking and slicing his pleasure upward.. Till finally, Veronica is completely artistically sculptured, pornographically displayed.. I give you, The Blood Eagle, Drisko announces, like it was a side show creature from a circus.. The crowd cheers wildly, with lavish praise, to the Kings, to the Gods, blood, blood, blood they all cry, as Veronica bleeds them her blood, the song, sings, *"as willing as. As playful as a pussy cat. Then momentarily out of action."..*

Drisko, looking out over the Sea of Cortez, watching the moon there, the biggest, brightest moon he had ever witnessed in his life, *"Temporarily out of gas"*, shining there in front of him.. Hurtling directly towards him at over one hundred thousand miles per hour or over, thirty thousand kilometres per second, hurtling, there, from outer space.. He believes he can just step out, walk straight off the edge, and step right on to that flying moon.. Standing there, watching the moon, smoking a fatty, *"absolutely drive you wild, wild."*, sipping on his Fresca.. So he does, he steps out, completely off the edge.. There, finally, he can walk on the moon, finally, his life has finally ended, his hand, and so he does, he steps off, out and onto the moon and that was that..

Drisko standing there, hi in the sky, looking down, *"She's a Killer Queen. Gunpowder, gelatine, Dynamite with a laser beam."*, staring into the streets below, a thousand, no two, no three thousand feet above the ground looking straight down.. Then, just then, he wakes, he realizes his error.. Drisko my man, you can't fly boy! Shit' he says, looking into the ground from above, shit'.. What the fuck, what the fuck should I do here now, what the fuck would the Bond man do? Eh' Bond, what the fuck, what should I do here, he asked? Pull the little button on your tux Drisko, he hears through the ear piece two way radio transmitter.. It's a parachute, it's built right into the tux for you Dick Weed.. Drisko, falling, failing dropping like a Boeing 747, failing, falling, from the sky, completely off the edge..

Drisk pulls the cord and the shroud quickly opens, he lands gently on the sandy shoreline.. Striping his tux as he walks away, stripping his shoes and socks, stripping his pants and clothing, stripping down to his custom swim shorts, complete, with a martini bar and pussy radar built right in.. It gyrates the warning, into his shorts.. He walks along the beach a few strides, up to her, she's beautiful.. Can I offer you a martini, *"Insatiable an appetite. Wanna try. You wanna try."*, shaken', not stirred.. Bond, he offers his name, smiling, Drisko Bond.. Oh, Bond man, you got any food in there, sausage, foot-long, anything will do, I'm starving

Dick Weed.. CREAMEY BUMMY, DOUBLE O CREAMEY BUMMY, she says, but my friends call me Veronica.. Oooh Bond.. OOODOUBLE O CREAMEY..

Trying to recall it all, she was a while ago now, but I'm thinking, yep I believe, the last time, I really ever saw ole Drisko my boy, actually alive.. Well he was drifting far out off the edge der, deep into the mighty blue Atlantic.. He was covered head to toe in blood, riding on a silver ice burg he was, just a floating away.. Them shiny ice shattering, ice blue steel eyes of his just a smiling clear back at me, whilst he was chasing this giant Polar bear dar eh', naked.. With only his sword and his spire as he would, yas no'.. Wailing out his words to me, flagging at me, smiling as he's screaming them off the ice, waving ats' me as he ran, chasing the bear der..

The secrets of dat der mirror eh' my friend, and's dat is, some folks just really never gets her', and she is a simple one at dat.. Once you've broken dat der mirror der eh', wells den yous knows.. It just ain't never gonna be able to looks at yous the same way ever again eh', word.. It is the truth and it's just about the truth, my friends.. It's about protecting the ones you love most, keepin dem safe, protecting de tings dats are precious to yous' and yes, it's about trust, cuz dats' all der is to true love..

So when you silently lose yourself, der, in front of dat der precious mirror of yours.. All alone, as you will be, and yous need to ask it, that one question, you know that one question, you've been dying to ask.. Is this me, who I am, am I, "I Am Monster"? Yous will truly knows den, what you really are to this world.. To us, to the normal and how we sees you.. This world made up by and so imperfectly unbalanced for dose exactly like you, de ones that dwell within it.. Pure evil living ere' among us, around us, related to, connecting to, infiltrating the hive.. Sitting, staring, conjuring up potions and secret spells.. Alls' de while, days' be reflecting only upon de image of demselves.. Staring, staring, deep, into dat der glass thingy.. From deep, within the total security, of de fish bowl, den even deeper, ans den deeper, till yous are dar, in side it all.. "A Life Without a Mirror"..

So der's we was, standing der, just him and me's.. Looking out off de Edge dat day, sunny day she was.. Us looking deeps' into da hollows of dat der blue horizon.. Staring out, through de glass, out to der, to wheres ifn's yous' sails your ship too far, yous' would most certainly fall off the edge.. So weez watched, just meez and him, and weez watched some more.. Den weez watched and den weez watched some more, den some mores, watching, standing der, looking out.. Just the two of us, oh ya and some oder peep'os', oder folks, I's guessin', I's thinks days was der..

Boss, yous ain'na gonna believes her if'n's you saws er' with your own eyes, I'm telling you doc.. So's der's we was doe, der, when suddenly all this jibber jabber come ringing through all that silence.. Then alls' a suddens, him, standing, looking in, looking in he was, from out there.. The shiny furry white coat, shinin' into our eyes as it bounced, gyrated with excitement.. Looking in from the other side of the glass.. From where's if, you sailed your ship too far, you certainly would never return from, the abyss. the end of the freakin world, him, now, he was looking in at us from out there.. How the minds thought, how, how could he look in? How, why couldn't we had stopped that question, that one crazy question they'd all been asked a thousand times before? The same fucking stupid question, asked of them all their lives, over and over again and again.. The question, simple, yet so powerful, "are you stupid?".. How, how, how, then the other question, the real question, the one they all wanted to know, "how, how do you know?"..

Then he approach me as I stood there stupid, in awe of him, staring out at him, like he was a God or something powerful.. From there, all the way across the Sea of Lost Souls.. Clear out over to the other side of the tiny room.. I stood there, just silent, stupid.. Shocked I was, I tells ya, fuckin in shock I was, by george, shocked, fuckin electrified.. He spoke, as I watched him speak, speaking, but not to me, no sir, no, but to someone else, someone else Is' tellin yas'.. Drisko, or the Viking Child maybe, or Bond, the Bond man guy, Double O Drisk guy or maybes', I's can't rightly recall it all just now, but not to me directly, never, it wasn't me I swear.. My minds, honestly, my minds is in total shock here doc, no lie.. Still bent up from the trauma of it and all, ya,s' knows.. P.T. fuckin S.D. and shit, I swears to ya.. Just that one thing, ya, know it's totally fucked me up doc, truly fucked, one ting, fucked me up for life..

Hey, by de by, Is' gots this super phenomenal creative idea for ya doe doc, ya eh' a huge plan.. I'm positive she'll work just perfect for ya, Jim Dandy doc, ask anyone, everyone knows me, Go eh'.. So you's go ask the writer guy der eh', eh', or de producer guy eh', de director or even one of dem der other actor guys, or Veronica eh', OOOSHINNY.. Wait, wait there a minute doc, here one itty bitty second there though.. Go to the source, fuck that other shit I was jabbering away at, the writer guy, all dat, forget it.. This will do it, here, dis is what you gots ta do, just ask the Priest.. Every one heres, always confessing all their lies to the fuckin Priest guy, all der bull shit eh'.. Now, Father Oobbew, ya, ask him, he gots the sweet and low on every ting goin on up in ere, by george.. Up ere, in de Gros Morne, up on de Edge, up on Cripple Creek Pass, by george.. Still don't know why anyone would ever venture up ere to de Edge, nobody comes ere, nobody, lesssin der comin ere to die, cuz its dead up ere' by lordy lord, just dead, everything, is dead here..

Then the man stood at the door, looking in through the two foot by two foot, doubled meshed, highly secure glass, staring in.. Good evening the man says, waiting patiently for all the rantings to settle down.. The man is an expert, he wants to properly introduce himself.. To whom, do I have the pleasure tonight, the man asking, politely.. Preparing, good evening Drisko, he replies, gently.. How are you this evening, the man is an expert, the man is published.. He starts, Doctor Hans Knutson from the National Institute of Psychiatric Studies, he goes into the introductions of himself.. Me standing there in shock, all of us each one, less none, in pure shock still, lingering, hanging on us hard.. Un also I may add, un de, Research and Development of Multiple Personality Disorders including un de Psychiatric Disorders Counsel of Denmark, Switzerland..

Drisko, hating every word the doc just spoke, all of them, the accent irking them.. Drisko envisions the doc saluting the Third Reich.. Swastikas filling his head, the hours, months, the wet, cold, terrifying hours.. Dug deep into your own fuckin snake pit, deep in the darkness of the Grave Ship.. The radio blaring of Oompah bands, the constant, fuckin, irritating buzz.. Death, To All, filling his mind.. Drisko knows he could and truly wants to easily, gracefully, strangle the good doctor to death, tonight, right here and now.. Break through the glass cells, open the door and then simply, slowly, easily, strike without warning.. Pounding on him and then simply watch him bleed out, he smiles at the friendly doc, the doc is an expert.. I am here for you Drisko, thank you for reaching out to me, the doc is published.. This is a very serious situation here you have got yourself into Drisko.. Is there anything I can do to help you, please, tell me, how may I be of assistance to you today.. Is there anything pressing, you may have on your mind today..

I'm here for you Drisko, Drisko repeating the docs voice, I'm here for you, in perfect tone reflection, thank you for reaching out to me.. This is a very serious situation here you have yourself in Doc.. Is there anything I can do for you, please, tell me, how may I be of assistance to you today, the doc now frightened.. Is there anything pressing, you may have on your mind right now Doc, like today, Doc.. The docs eyes lighting up, Drisko smiles, the doc smiles back.. Drisko frowns, the cell door squeaks out, open, away from Drisko, slowly, squeaking, eerie sounds filling the hallway as it's blocking the doc, behind it.. He's pinned, helpless, trapped there between the steel door and the double, secure, glass wall of the fish bowl.. How zee fuck man, the doc looking Drisko, face to face now, eye to eye the doc, is an expert? How zee fuck did zee open zee door? The doc cries out his words as the hand silences them, with a gulp, as he whispers, I am de Millouster.. The words filling the docs ears, his eyes filled with DEATH, as Drisko cocks his left arm, the doc gulps, then he chokes out the word, how?

Well, you wanted to get all nice and close, didn't cha, doc, well here the fuck I am, Millouster.. Now what was dat you was saying, it's in de songs? Well doc, eers' a little ditty, cut close to my heart.. I wrotes er' alls by myselfs' for yous' doc, all special like eh'.. Yous' just gonna love it, I calls it, "I AM MONSTER", oh ya doc she's all me, copy-rited the whole shabang.. Me and Freddie here doc, weez gonna wail out the beats for ya, doc, Go eh'.. While I take care of all the pretty cuts.. Drisko releases all his fury, the song sings, flinging rock after rock out, as it beats, as he sings it *"You can't decline. Caviar and cigarettes. Well versed in etiquette. Extraordinarily nice"*.. He hammers the doc with his right, TO ALL, the song singing, *"a Killer Queen. Gunpowder, gelatine. Dynamite with a laser beam. Guaranteed to blow your mind. Anytime"*..

So there yous' go eh', yous got the whole story now eh', the whole sweet n' low.. The truth, right from the horses mouth as dayd says.. The truth about ole' Drisk Oobbew, the Clan, the Viking Child.. I's tellin ya, nottin but the truth, I swear it to yas eh'.. But den again, who knows what the truth really is, an illusion or some crazy pre'mon'a'tion thingy, a gut reaction maybe or a dream or a nightmare even, what is "the truth" really? Peep'os been telling all kinds a wild tails, up der eh'.. Their crazy mad stories about Vikings, and the Grave Ship.. Demons of the night, sea creatures, snake pits, torture, the Witch, the ugly stick, the Casandra and the Wizard, the fuckin brewmeister.. Puppy dogs, wild wolves, giant fish, dragons and two headed monsters.. The stories of the Screech, kissing the horses ass, the wild orgies, massive sex parties and the sacrifices of the Blood Eagle..

Can ya's imagine it, der's ya are, getting all sliced and diced up all nice and neat like.. Like some piece of living artwork, sculptured, displayed for all to see.. Den's ya's ass is tossed into the Sea of Lost Soul, under some giant astoria, a Black Pearl.. Yes sir, lots and lots of tails, comin outta der, some even true too.. So you just never know's', what in the high heavens, really goin on up der in dat der Gros Morne' eh'? Now most folks, not from the Edge, could come up ere and mistaken it for the end of the world, the abyss.. Dats cuz, most folks aren't from the Edge.. Folks from the Edge, know it's where it all began.. This is it, the beginning, the place they landed, the birthplace of where it all erupted, the beginning of all Civilization in North America..

So who'd know, I's guessin' it all dependin on how's' ya's' lookin at it all eh', Go eh'? So if'n's, I's was yous doe', I'd be gettin my sorry tail up dar to dat Rock.. Go Eh', take the visit to de Edge, stop in der, at the big resort property out der on the Cliffs.. Go gives a hi, howdie hello to ole' Drisko, oh he'd be so glad to see yaz all come by he will, he will, Is' swears to ya' on dat.. But I's be warnin yas' all, and heed me here, cuzin by the by, she's gonna happen, sooner or later.. Dat is, you best be gettin your sorry ass up der, beforn's another one of dem der dang asteroid tingies, come wailing down, from out dar in space eh'.. And days turns the whole dang place up side down again.. You's don no's' the trouble all dem ole Newfies had turnin dat fuck'n rock, ass back up right last time eh', by george.. Dats twice now eh', fuckin twice, crazy shit, one big too doo eh', huge kerfuffle up der on de Edge eh'.. Up der in da Cripple Creek Pass eh', up in de Gros Morne, huge kerfuffle, huge I's tellin ya, gih-gantic, just huge, Murder..

The Song Remains The Same..

There within all of us, there have been moments, some good, some sad, some not so good and for sure some bad.. It's been my experience that with every jar to my emotional soul, there's been an equal and totally spiritual alignment in rhyme, as in rhythm, as in the blues.. Another word with every moment of true importance there's been a song.. The song remains the same, consent, always that song equal to that moment, the true marker of the event, the simple truth.. Don't think of a pink elephant.. Now remember a happy or sad time, a frightening or joyful time, a moment in your life and you'll be swept away by the song..

They, the gifted ones, the ones that were always part of me, moving me, controlling, forming, guiding and teaching.. All those that through their drive, their talents, that they submerged themselves unwillingly into my life.. Thank you and with that, I have dedicated my life to them, they will always bring me pleasure.. To all that have had a part in my life and to all those that together helped in their own small way to help bring the Angels to my room that night, to propel me to become.. To all that shared their power with me, in tears, you are my Angels..

With special thanks and dedication to those mentioned and to the so many more and far too many to include, with that again, I thank you, you must know who you are..

j. j. Bond

THE SONGS

1. More Than A Feeling – Boston
2. Travelin' Man – Bob Seger
3. Immigrant Song – Led Zeppelin
4. Fame – David Bowie
5. Funeral For A Friend – Elton John
6. The Cold November Rain – Guns N' Roses
7. Psycho Killer – Talking Heads
8. No More Mr. Nice Guy – Alice Cooper
9. Dirty Deeds – ACDC
10. Why Can' This Be Love – Van Halen
11. Animal – Def Leppard
12. Killer Queen – Queen

Printed in the United States
By Bookmasters